THE VACATIONER:

Journey into Darkness

By Pat Adams

COPYRIGHT

Book Cover design by Mac Dimaguila

ISBN Hardcover: 978-1-952472-03-9

ISBN Paperback: 978-0-9988416-9-4

ISBN e-book: 978-1-952472-02-2

Dedicated to my extended family and their never-ending support. Thank you Mom, Dad, Jen, Daniel, Jonathan, Holly, Rhythm, Lyric, May, Joey, Fred Jr, Jasmine, Mac, Jem and Joana.

PART 1:

DARKENING

Chapter 1

There was no fog or haze to be seen at the Cliffs of Moher. One of the most gorgeous scenes in the west coast of Ireland, and TJ Carlson and Jim Keller had hit the picture taking jackpot. Jim had to bring along his bulky tripod, as he fancied himself as a professional photographer, and was fumbling around getting that set up. This amused TJ, but the results for Jim were usually worth the effort. Jim had positioned the tripod at an angle that would capture the waves crashing into the Cliffs in such a way that he planned to create a centerpiece framed picture for his living room featuring this amazing view. As he snapped picture after picture, TJ walked over to the ledge, leaned on it and took in the scene.

TJ Carlson lived for these moments. An avid lover of traveling to new places and seeing the world, it was these moments that he could point to as giving him something tangible that he could take with him for the rest of his life. He only wished he could capture the feeling in a bottle and experience it at any time. But this was a special feeling, and he knew it was to be appreciated and not to be taken for granted. He had experienced this many times, but seemed to be appreciating it more as he grew older. He couldn't help but compare these Cliffs to seeing the Colosseum in Rome or being on a mountain peak in Switzerland or visiting the Little Mermaid in Copenhagen or visiting castles in England. The more he experienced this feeling, the greater the desire to keep doing it. It was his passion. It was his version of a drug. He knew it deep down in his soul. If he could make a career out of it, he would. That's one of the reasons he was here.

"Have you got the shots you were hoping for?" TJ asked Jim as he suddenly noticed that Jim had stopped taking pictures.

"Yup – I have some seriously good potential masterpieces here. We really lucked out today, man." We knew it was a risk to plan a visit to these Cliffs in February, TJ thought, as there was about a 75% chance we would have no view at all. He was extremely concerned the entire drive here and even fretted the night before about it to no end.

TJ smiled. "The travel Gods smiled down on us today. I hope you are enjoying this."

Jim Keller was always a bit of a homebody. The fact that he was even on this trip with TJ was nothing short of a miracle of persuasion on TJ's part. Jim had traveled with TJ before, to the only place in the world outside of the United States that he would even consider going to – Rome, Italy. A certified history buff, Jim couldn't pass up the opportunity for the historical, and not to mention picture-taking, bonanza that Rome offered. The fun of being in Rome was sandwiched in between a thorough disdain for the travel process of getting to and from anywhere that involved an airplane. But TJ talked him in to going to Ireland and really was enjoying his company.

Jim had recently married for the first time and had trepidations about leaving his wife, even for a few days. But she was very encouraging to Jim and she too knew that he may be creating new artwork for their home. TJ was the opposite – married 14 years already with 2 children, he enjoyed getting away with his best friend and actually thought the time apart would be healthy for his marriage. Although, in recent years, the marriage seemed to have settled into a routine that was growing increasingly unsatisfying. But for TJ, there were no other options. He wanted to be a good father for his kids and wanted to share this travel experience with them one day. More than experiencing these things with Jim, he dreamed of seeing the world with his family. Unfortunately, his wife did not share that same desire.

"You know, I love moments like this" TJ said to Jim to try to hook him into a broader discussion of traveling. "Where else in the world would you go to if you had the chance?"

"I really don't know – maybe Japan. Lots of history there. Maybe Germany. But honestly, after Rome, I'm happy."

TJ gave Jim a look – "Rome, Germany, Japan? Were you secretly rooting for the Axis Powers to win World War 2?? What the fuck?"

Jim defiantly responded. "I want to go to all the countries where America kicked ass! I'm a patriot, you bastard!"

"Japan sounds really cool. I'll start working on that" said TJ, hoping to get Jim to actually agree and give TJ his next project to work on.

"Uhm…..that takes money, something I'm blowing completely on this trip. I don't have an executive job and 10 weeks off a year like you seem to have."

TJ laughed and said, somewhat motivationally to Jim – "Listen, I make this happen because I want it. I have a passion for it. There's so much to see and experience in this world and you only have one opportunity to do it"

Jim looked seriously at TJ. "It may be your passion, but my passion is being with my new wife, starting a family and taking her on a road trip or two. Honestly, I hate airplanes and am dreading this flight home. I'll enjoy it while we are here, but please don't count on me to be your travel buddy."

"I understand" said TJ, although not really understanding. "I love this so much, I'd travel alone. If I won the lottery, I'd pack up the family and we'd tour the world."

"What about your family? Is Paige okay with you taking these trips with me? Or with the idea of you traveling alone? Wouldn't she be suspicious as to why you want to do that?"

TJ started to get defensive. "Paige is okay with this. Believe me, she'd be here with me if I could convince her to try and enjoy life a little more. I'd prefer she be here, because then the opportunity to enjoy these things would be enhanced by the ability to have sex as well."

Jim looked seductively at TJ – "Well, you still have that chance if you play your cards right, you sexy beast."

"Shut the fuck up! Only if I'm reeeeeally desperate. And then I'm sure I could find some guy a hell of a lot more attractive than you!"

Jim nuzzled up to TJ, looking offended. They both laughed and took in the view a little more. TJ took some pictures and then Jim and TJ took turns taking pictures of each other with the Cliffs of Moher in the background. Rain clouds were on the horizon, a sure sign that the unencumbered view that they had enjoyed this morning would soon be gone.

"What's next?' asked Jim as he started to pack up his tripod.

"We are on a drive to the Ring of Kerry and a national park. Should be a lot of opportunities for pictures. We're going to stop for lunch in some small town along the way. We'll have to ask the driver."

TJ had originally planned that he and Jim would drive around Ireland themselves, but TJ couldn't pass up the chance to not only not have to learn to drive on the other side of the road with a right-side steering wheel, but also deal with roundabouts and interpreting signs in Gaelic. He hired a driver at a really good rate who would take them from place to place and providing a lot of colorful facts and commentary along the way. Money well spent in TJ's mind.

Paul Smith was an Irish native in his early 40's who looked every bit his years. Thinning hair with a graying goatee and a penchant for chain-smoking, he nonetheless was a charming guy and an encyclopedia of Ireland facts as they drove along the road from County Clare to the Ring of Kerry. The Ring of Kerry was a route along a peninsula in southwestern Ireland that featured a scenic drive, beaches, quaint small Irish towns and is one attraction that tourists typically eat up. In February though, the scenery was a bit grimmer and less green and lush. And the towns that thrive on visiting tourists weren't exactly going to open up and roll out the red carpet because our Toyota Camry was pulling in, TJ thought. Finding open restaurants was going to be a bit more of a challenge, warned Paul, but he would find one for us.

Jim enjoyed talking to Paul. He had questions everywhere along the path to Kerry, and was even quizzing Paul on how much he knew about American history.

A typical exchange:

Jim: "Name one state involved in the Louisiana purchase".

Paul: "New York!"

Jim – "You are correct, sir!"

Jim was enjoying this sarcastic back and forth with Paul and looked like these two could develop a really solid friendship.

TJ decided to enter the fray with revealing a bit of his family genealogy. "I have relatives on my father's side who lived in the northern part of Ireland and made their way to Philadelphia." Paul seemed unfazed. "Well what's the other part of ya then?".

"I'm a mutt I think." Said TJ. "Irish, German and French on my mother's side and a grandmother on my father's side who is pure British".

"At least ya got Irish in ya" said Paul. What about you Jimbo?"

Jim thought for a moment – "I'm pretty sure it's all British. Must explain why I love the queen. She's by all appearances and actions a wonderful woman."

Paul glanced back at Jim with a look of death on his face. "You love the queen? You love the fucking Queen? The Queen of Bloody England?? Shit, do you realize how many of my fellow countrymen the damn Brits have killed? That they occupied my country? That they stole Northern Ireland and still refuse to let us reunite to this day? Let me give you a history lesson, my friend."

TJ and Jim sat silently and listened as Paul catalogued what seemed like every British atrocity on the Irish ever committed. TJ was enjoying the fact that Paul bitch slapped Jim solely at a mention of his admiration for the Queen of England. He wished he could have recorded the entire exchange. Another priceless moment in a foreign country. For his part, Jim listened diligently and almost seemed to be taking notes in his head.

TJ couldn't help but give Jim expert advice. "Jim – please, for the love of God, do not praise the Queen of England in front of any more of these fine people in Ireland."

Jim ignored TJ and focused solely on Paul. "Wow – I never realized all the horrible shit the Brits did to the Irish. I'm sorry, man. Please accept an apology from me on behalf of my barbaric ancestors."

TJ couldn't tell whether Jim was joking or was actually attempting to apologize to Ireland on behalf of anyone and everyone British. Paul just laughed and the situation seemed defused for now.

"You're alright, friend. I'm just yanking yer chain." Jim continued – "No, all that crap was awful. I've been edu-ma-cated on this drive today."

TJ looked at Jim. "You ass-kisser." Jim replied – "He's behind the wheel here and in control of where we are going. If he hates the Brits, then while I'm in this car, I hate the Brits too. Even if I am one mostly. I hate myself."

Paul indicated they were about to start their drive on the Ring of Kerry. At that statement, things got very quiet in the car. Jim got his camera out to try and grab shots along the way, while TJ sat looking outside with his head pressed against the window, suddenly lost in thought.

TJ's thoughts turned to home. He married Paige 14 years ago after they finished college. They met there in their final year and were inseparable. They were a good match at the time. TJ was a handsome guy – light brown hair with a goatee that complimented his face. Paige was Swedish and French, and had below the shoulder length blonde hair. She was very physically well put together, as TJ liked to refer to it. At first, their sex life was amazing and they couldn't ever get enough of each other. That physical attraction masked something that was also very evident right from the beginning. TJ and Paige did not have a lot of mutual interests. And a vastly different sense of humor. Opposites attract, TJ would always say. Their first child, Steven, was born a year and a half after they were married. Now 12 and on the cusp of both puberty and teenage-hood, he was growing into a young man before TJ's eyes. He was a good, responsible kid and very smart. School was a breeze and making friends was easy for him. He was always thinking of ways he could make money by mowing lawns or babysitting. He was very independent from TJ and Paige and did them a favor by checking in every once in a while, or when food was being prepared. Their second child, Elizabeth, was born 3 years later and was the apple of TJ's eye. There is something to that father-daughter bond, TJ thought. Elizabeth inherited Paige's blonde hair and face and was a complete spitting image of her mother. A creative child, she loved to draw and tell stories. A future writer, pegged TJ. Or actress. She tended to be very dramatic at times. Kind of like her mother.

So, what has happened to that spark? TJ missed it. The spark they felt when the first met. In this way, TJ admired Jim. He was just starting out and he saw in him the same passion and excitement he once had.

TJ was never going to give up on Paige. He always figured they could re-capture the magic. Travel was one way he figured he could make that happen. Take her somewhere romantic. Maybe Paris, enjoying a drink overlooking the Eiffel Tower. Find somewhere where they could be themselves again and make love for days without a worry in the world. The problem, TJ thought, was that Paige wasn't giving that notion a chance. Nothing will ever change unless they change up the routine. Paige seemed content to be miserable and this was something TJ would not allow himself to be. TJ could look past their incompatibilities, but he really wanted Paige to share something like this with him.

As the scenery passed by on the Ring of Kerry, TJ assured himself that everything would be just fine. 14 years is a long time, and most couples probably go through this exact same rut. But Jim's words haunted him a bit. Was Paige really okay with this? Him traveling while she was at home taking care of the kids. TJ really wondered what Paige was thinking at this moment. Surely, she couldn't think he was out messing around with other women. Paige didn't really know Jim well enough to know that he was a good influence for TJ and would keep him out of trouble.

TJ re-focused as Paul announced they would be pulling in to a small pub for lunch. Extremely chilly outside, Paul also warned TJ and Jim not to expect a lot, especially heat or smiling faces. Or good food.   "Eat up, grab some Guinness and enjoy it lads!" Paul said excitedly as he opted not to join us.

TJ turned to Jim – "Not a good sign that he's not joining us here, is it?"

"Nope", Jim said. "But how bad can it be. I've never heard anything bad about Irish food."

"Unless it's potatoes, I'm not really sure what's involved with Irish cuisine" said TJ, all of a sudden not feeling really hungry.

They entered the pub and were the only customers there. An elderly, rather large lady emerged from another room, came over and plopped menus down in front on TJ and Jim. It was freezing in the restaurant. Paul was right. TJ and Jim quickly finished the worst lunch they've ever had and found a smiling Paul waiting for them at the car.

"Come on lads, let's move. Sorry about that, but they were probably our best option. It's February. Lower your expectations a bit. Hahaha!"

Paul kept TJ and Jim entertained for the rest of the day. Even with the bad lunch, it was still an experience that TJ knew he and Jim could commiserate on for a long time to come. Along with Jim's ridiculous antagonizing of the Irish with praise of the Brits.

"Alright Jim – brace yourself. Another stop today of something historic. You get to kiss the Blarney Stone!" TJ said to Jim with over-exaggerated excitement.

Jim looked at TJ puzzled. "What the hell is the Blarney Stone exactly?"

TJ realized he had no idea what it was or even the story behind it. He felt kinda dumb that the only knowledge he had of the Blarney Stone was that he had to kiss it. And that supposedly kissing it would give you the gift of gab. At that moment, Jim gave TJ an irresistible opening.

"What supposedly happens after you kiss the Blarney Stone" Jim asked.

TJ smiled. "First, for guys it will supposedly make their cocks get at least a half an inch bigger. And increase sexual stamina by at least 30 minutes. Oh, and it will make the wrinkles in their balls clear up. Did I mention increased semen production? And the ability to…….."

Jim cut TJ off. "Bullshit!"

TJ laughed. "Actually, it's something about the gift of gab".

"What the fuck good is that? Why are we here?" Jim said suddenly making TJ justify this plan to go kiss the stone.

"Just do it, jackass. We are here at Blarney Castle, for Christ's sake. We're going to kiss the damn Blarney Stone!"

Blarney Castle in February again was not exactly a bustling tourist attraction. So far, the positives at each tourist site has been zero waiting time. The negatives have been cold and rainy weather and an entirely unhappy Irish workforce at these places entertaining ridiculous tourists who show up in February.

It was not immediately clear where the Blarney Stone was as they entered the castle. They made a plan to ensure they took each other's picture kissing the Blarney Stone and will make sure it's a really good shot. Apparently, the top of the castle is where they will find the stone. TJ and Jim both marveled that this was a place where people lived. Jim wondered – "how did they live here in the winter? This is miserable."

Finally reaching the top of the castle, TJ and Jim were shocked to see two elderly, but burly, gentlemen standing on the other side of the castle.

"I think we can guess where the stone is now" TJ informed Jim, who nodded his head. "You get the feeling we are about to get shaken down by these two guys?"

"They must be Blarney Stone security or something" said Jim, jokingly.

The two men waved TJ and Jim over. As TJ and Jim approached, one of the men introduced himself. "Mornin lads! I'm Ian and this is Seamus. I'm assumin' ya want a picture of the Blarney Stone."

"Hi Ian" said Jim. "Where's the stone? We'll just take pictures of each other if that's cool."

Jim was right. Where's the stone. It wasn't that obvious. Ian told a quick story of the Blarney Stone, which TJ half listened to. The stone was actually at the bottom of a series of stones that would require a contortionist to kiss.

"Not okay actually lads. Yer gonna need our help if yer gonna kiss the stone. To hold ya in place", Ian explained. "Seamus here will capture your picture".

"Can you take it with our cameras?' asked Jim. As Seamus pulled out his camera, it became evident what the shakedown was.

Before Ian could answer, TJ asked "How much for the picture?" "20 euros!" said Ian as if it was the biggest bargain you could negotiate. TJ wasn't about to let 20 Euros spoil a picture he knew damn well he wanted. Jim on the other hand refused. "I'll pass. You do it. I think they are going to need more than one person to hold you in place so you don't fall to your death."

With that, TJ was ready. TJ noticed Jim and Seamus talking and laughing, while looking his way. Suddenly suspicious, TJ asked Jim what they were talking about. "Nothing" said Jim. "Cameras". Ian instructed TJ to lay on his back. Ian straddled TJ in a way that was uncomfortable and a bit homoerotic. Ian laughed and asked "Ya comfy, lad?" "Not at all", said TJ. "But let's do this".

Ian instructed TJ to tilt his head back and reach to kiss the darker colored stone. TJ did just that, hoping that Seamus was somehow getting a great picture of this but not imagining how as he was sure his face couldn't be seen. As his lips met the stone, TJ was introduced to a taste that can barely be described. Salty beyond imagination, it is a taste that would not leave his lips. He was afraid to wet his lips with his tongue for fear of getting this taste in his mouth and then it spreading. It was rancid!

Jim was noticeably happy as they walked away, bidding farewell to a smiling Ian and Seamus. The picture was predictably bad, capturing beautifully the straddling Ian and the missing face of TJ kissing the Blarney Stone.

"Dude", Jim said, "that was fucking hilarious."

"I can't begin to explain that taste" said TJ, still wiping his lips with his jacket sleeve.

"I can" said Jim. "Turns out in addition to tourists kissing the Blarney Stone, locals love to urinate on it!" Jim busted out with laughter as TJ stared at him. Then TJ smiled and said, "that would explain that."

"Hey, you wouldn't get off my case about the Queen. At least I didn't kiss a urine coated stone".

"Touché" said TJ. Kissing the Blarney Stone. Another experience that did not disappoint.

Paige Carlson looked frazzled. Elizabeth Carlson was having a meltdown as 9-year olds are prone to do sometimes. Kylie Kendricks, Paige's best friend, sat and watched, feeling sorry for Paige. TJ was a calming force to his daughter in these situations, but he was off gallivanting around Ireland with his friend.

Kylie had known Paige since high school, where they bonded over their mutual disgust towards the same guy. Unknown to them, he was dating them both. Paige and Kylie found out, and then concocted a plan to confront him and "dump his ass." After that, they were inseparable.

Kylie was the maid of honor at Paige's wedding, and initially quite liked TJ. As the years passed, TJ grew to find Kylie a bit annoying and was often cold with her when she was around. Kylie had a diva quality to her and was often talking bad about her husband. TJ often wondered if Paige would reciprocate and put him down.

"I'd never let my husband do what you are letting yours do", said Kylie. "I trust him, but I know men. You give them freedom and distance and who knows what they are capable of". Kylie was sitting on the couch with Paige.

"I know, but it's different with us. I feel like he needs this more and more. I want to do it with him, but we have too much to take care of here."

"Then why let him go?" said Kylie. "It's like giving him permission to shirk his duties as a father. Why should and you get left here to pick up the pieces and take care of everything while he's out having his jollies?"

"I trust him" Paige argued. "But if I ever catch wind that he's screwing around, we're done".

"As it should be" smiled Kylie. "Maybe you should go with him. It's probably something that would help you both."

At that moment, Elizabeth was carrying milk into the living room and Steven suddenly backed up his chair into Elizabeth, knocking her over and her milk all over the place. A now screaming Elizabeth and angry Steven added to the level of stress for Paige.

"Dammit!!" yelled Paige. "Will the two of you be more careful, please? It's just me here and I have to take care of everything. Steven, you help clean that up." Steven looked irritated. "That was not my fault" he exclaimed.

"It doesn't matter" said Paige exhaustedly. "Just clean it up. Are you okay, Elizabeth?" Elizabeth, still crying, did not answer. Kylie tended to Elizabeth, who absolutely loved Kylie. She was like a fun Aunt to her.

Things settled down and Kylie poured her and Paige a class of wine. Paige asked Kylie if she felt like any spark had been lost in her marriage. Kylie had only been married for 5 years, but also seemed unhappy.

"Honestly", Kylie said, "He was a safe option. He's more of a life partner than a husband. He doesn't really rock my world, but he's a good man. We have a lot in common and enjoy doing things together."

"That's one area where we are lacking. We don't like the same music, TV shows, movies, you name it. We are very different." Paige looked off in the distance. "I should travel with him. I'll talk to him about it when he gets back."

Later in the evening after Kylie went home, Paige composed a message to TJ:

TJ – I hope you are enjoying Ireland with Jim. Today was rough. The kids were a pain. They miss you. Looking forward to you coming home. Stay out of trouble. I love you and miss you.   – Paige

TJ and Jim spent a second night in Cork in the southern part of Ireland. An area, along with Cobh, famous for being a gateway to Ellis Island for Irish immigrants. They had spent the day traveling to Cobh and were back in Cork walking down a street looking for a decent place to eat.

"I got a message from Paige" said TJ. "Sounds like she's having a difficult time with the kids. Either that, or she's being overly dramatic."

"Which do you think it is?" asked Jim

"Maybe a little bit of both. She can be that way sometimes if she wants to make me feel guilty."

"Do you feel guilty?" said Jim, whose attention was temporarily diverted by an oddly placed adult book and movie store. "Should we?" asked Jim with a devious look on his face.

"No way" said TJ. "Who knows who is in there. Seems like an out of place store in this nice area. Might be run by the mafia."

"Good" said James approvingly. "Paige would be pleased."

TJ looked annoyed. "Did she ask you to test me with crap like that? Are you a double agent?? Are you wired? Strip down right here!"

"You'd like that, wouldn't you?" hissed Jim, touching and making circles around his nipples.

"Good lord" said TJ. "Is she also asking you to test me to make sure I'm not gay?"

Jim laughed. "I think you are making a bigger deal out of this thing with you and Paige than it is. It's all in your head. You'll drift apart if you allow it to happen. What are YOU doing to make it work? That's what you can control. Start including her in these travel plans. Carrie and I are making a lot of plans for the future, and to me nothing is more exciting than that. I waited a long time for a girl like Carrie, and I'm in it to win it."

TJ once again admired Jim for his enthusiasm and excitement over his new marriage. He had a philosophy of someone who hasn't had time for that philosophy to be tested. Maybe he was making a bigger deal than he should have been about perceived issues with Paige, but he lived it every day and Jim did not. Jim was not in a position to offer grounded analysis on his situation.

"I wish nothing but the best for you and Carrie. She's great and she's great for you." TJ said while looking down. "I hope that 14 years from now you have that same excitement and energy."

"Trust me, we will" said Jim confidently.

"I thought the same thing" said TJ.

"Don't project or wish your problems on me" said Jim with a flash of anger. "People like you want other people to be miserable, just like them. Fuck that. Carrie and I can be different than you and Paige."

Sensing that this wasn't going anywhere good, TJ stopped himself. Jim was right, he shouldn't make him feel like he's doomed to failure as a couple. And perhaps TJ was overthinking his issues with Paige. He was determined to right things as soon as he returned home.

Back in the hotel room that night, TJ composed a message to Paige:

Looking forward to coming home. I miss you and the kids. Sorry things have been rough, but relief is on the way. Thank you for indulging me with this. I'll meet with the hotel rep in Dublin about our business idea and let you know what happens. Talk to you soon. Love you.

As much as TJ loved travel, he wished he could make it a career. He had been working as an Analyst in a health care company for the last few years, a job not the least bit exciting to him. Although he was making great money, he had no passion for his work. One thing he and Paige agreed on was that if he could find a way to make a move to travel, he should. TJ thought up a business idea of becoming a liaison to companies or non-profit organizations looking to hold major conferences globally. This, TJ thought, would combine two things that he loved: working in travel and being able to travel. He had set up a meeting with a prime spot in Dublin to test the waters. It was a hotel in the heart of the city, close to tourist attractions, and best of all, the Guinness Brewery.

His appointment today was with Miranda. He sat in the lobby waiting for Miranda, going over what he would say, hoping that there would be something to his idea. He had two avenues to take – talking to the hotels and then talking to the companies, hoping to be able to earn money on both sides.

Finally, about 15 minutes late, a statuesque redhead appeared and approached TJ. "Hi there, you must be TJ. Miranda. Lovely to meet you."

"Thank you. Lovely to meet you as well. Thanks for taking the time to talk to me, Miranda."

"What can I help you with?" said Miranda, a bit hurriedly.

TJ explained his idea to Miranda. TJ had contacts from a previous job now involved in planning a major conference in Europe. He wanted to link the two up. Miranda listened attentively, but TJ could tell by her facial reactions that the next words out of her mouth would not be positive ones.

"I think your idea has merit, and we'd love to send a proposal to your friends. But we will deal and negotiate directly with them and any contracts we sign will be with them."

TJ had heard of a Finder's Fee that could potentially be negotiated. "I'm bringing you what could amount to tens of thousands of Euros profit for your hotel. I think it would be fair for me to be compensated for that in the form of a Finder's Fee. Would your hotel be willing to negotiate that?"

Miranda thought for a moment. "I'm not sure, but it's possible. I wouldn't expect it to be an extraordinary amount."

TJ was getting curious, as she didn't expect her to even indicate it was possible. "What's a fair amount do you think?" TJ had thought $2000 per signed contract from the hotel was fair. He would negotiate separately with the companies. Both parties were benefitting financially from the arrangements, why shouldn't he benefit from both parties.

Miranda again looked lost in thought. "I'll have to check. Maybe 500 Euros." Not exactly what TJ was expecting to hear but it was a start.

Miranda looked as if she was ready to go. TJ picked up on the signs. This was a test for TJ, and it had worked. He let her off the hook. "Thank you for meeting with me, Miranda. I'll talk with my friends about the hotel here and hopefully we can work something out."

"Enjoy your stay in Ireland, TJ. Look forward to hearing from your friends."

TJ met Jim back at the hotel. "How'd it go?" asked Jim. TJ calmly said, "it went as I had hoped. Looks like a viable business idea, but not sure I can quit my day job right away."

It was the last night in Ireland for TJ and Jim. They agreed to do the one thing they hadn't done yet. Go to an authentic Irish Pub in Dublin and get kinda drunk. After what they both agreed was a fun and entertaining trip, it was time to celebrate.

Close to their hotel was The Black Sheep, a decent looking pub that would surely serve the purpose. Oddly, despite being in Ireland for nearly a week, they had not tried Guinness. For TJ, he didn't particularly think the beer sounded appetizing. Black and foamy at the top, with little particles floating in it. At least, that's how it had been described to him, albeit with a bit of embellishment.

"What are you going to drink?" TJ asked Jim.

"No idea. I'm not really a fan of beer. Do they serve Mead?"

Mead was a great tasting honey whiskey that they had tried at one of their stops on this trip. But they were in a pub. They were in Ireland. They had to try Guinness!

"Let's each get one Guinness" TJ dared Jim.

"No thanks."

"Come on, man! Just one pint. It's the last thing we need to experience here."

Jim looked amused. "What are you talking about? There's no way you can finish a pint of Guinness!"

TJ accepted the challenge, recalling his college days where he could chug beer by the gallon. He had never tried Guinness, however, and looking at the pints of it on other tables, it looked unappetizing to say the least. "I bet you I can. Let's have a contest to see who can down a pint first. Let's put money on it."

Jim declined. "No way. But I have an undisclosed amount of money in mind I will give you if you can down one."

"Fine, you lightweight." TJ called for the waiter and ordered a Guinness.

It was almost as described by his friend. Jim smiled and said "Go for it."

TJ had a strategy. Big gulps. Not stopping to fully taste it. Gulp number one went down rough. This did not taste good. A bit vile, TJ thought. But he carried on, determined to win the bet. The second and third gulps went down a bit easier. Hmmm…..maybe an acquired taste, TJ thought. He quickly downed the rest of it, slammed the glass down, looked at Jim and said "Pay up, loser!"

Jim pulled out a Euro coin and gave it to TJ. "Here you go. You earned it. And, you'll get to taste it all over again when you throw it up later."

"One Euro, you cheap bastard?" TJ scoffed. "I should have known. It actually wasn't that bad after the first few sips."

"That's because it killed your taste buds. That's its secret."

TJ felt strangely proud of winning this Guinness Euro challenge.

The day had arrived where it was time to go. TJ always hated the end of vacations. He had particularly enjoyed this one. He really wished Jim would change his mind and go somewhere with him again. Japan sounded like an amazing idea. But Jim had made it known several times on the trip that it would likely be his last.

Jim looked uneasy. TJ knew why. "Don't worry, man. It's only a 6-hour flight.

"That's 6 hours too long. I just want to get this shit over with." Jim really did not enjoy this process. TJ couldn't understand it. He loved airports and even loved flying. But he didn't push the issue.

After a bit of a silence, TJ looked at Jim and said, "So……. about Japan…."

"How long does it take to fly to Japan?"

"About 12 hours, give or take layovers." Said TJ, expecting a wildly negative response.

"When they invent *Star Trek* style transporters, I'll go to Japan. Until then, I'm out."

The flight went very well. There were few passengers on the plane and TJ and Jim each claimed a row of seats. Jim slept the whole time after quickly downing two drinks. TJ watched a movie and braced himself for his return home. He was excited to see the kids. He was anxious to see Paige again, hoping he could begin to turn things around and recapture the spark.

Chapter 2

TJ and his family live in Fayetteville, North Carolina. A military town, and a decent place to raise a family with anything and everything you could need close by. A 15-minute drive will get you to any important place you'd need to go for food, medicine, shopping, entertainment or repairs. The Carlson home was a modest, one story, 3-bedroom home that looked pristine on the outside but had all the signs of two kids living in it on the inside. Toys in the living room courtesy of Elizabeth, a room she usually fought for space with and won with TJ and Steven. Schoolwork spread on 3 different surfaces courtesy of Steven, and the day's dirty socks usually on the floor nearby, always to be collected by TJ or Paige. On this night, the dishes remained on the table and counter, which was unusual for 8pm. Paige or TJ usually hopped right on that after dinner, attempting to train Steven to do that as well, to little avail.

TJ walked in the door, not really expecting a hero's welcome, but at least an acknowledgement from all that he was missed. He did get a hero's welcome from Elizabeth, who rushed up to him as soon as he walked in the door and latched on a bearhug. There's nothing quite like a bearhug from his precious 9-year-old daughter to welcome TJ home. Daddy's little princess, he thought and smiled and lightly bearhugged her back. TJ gave Elizabeth a kiss on the forehead.

"I know what you want" said TJ to an eager Elizabeth.

"Gifts! Gifts! Gifts!" said Elizabeth excitedly.

"Gotta be patient, sweetie. Let Daddy unpack."

"I'm glad you're home Daddy. I missed you a lot. By the way, Steven made me spill milk."

"It wasn't my fault!" exclaimed Steven, suddenly tuned in to the conversation. "It was an accident."

TJ laughed. "So that explains Paige's rough day, then." Steven was very nonchalant about TJ's return, but TJ didn't think too much of it. He was mastering the art of playing it cool, like many boys about to become a teenager.

Conspicuous so far by her absence was Paige. He knew exactly where she was. In the family room. But not sure what she was doing or why she hadn't even acknowledged him. It was strange, thought TJ, that she hadn't said a word to him. She had to know he was home. If she was irritated with him, he couldn't understand why. He didn't want games the instant he got home, but an immediate silent treatment upon his return home would elicit a similar response. TJ decided to simply take his bags to the bedroom and unpack. Elizabeth had already settled back in to watching TV.

A few minutes after going to the bedroom, TJ heard Paige's voice. "Steven, where's your father?"

"In the bedroom, I think."

TJ waited for Paige to join him, but she never did. She went right back to the Family Room, where she had been all along. TJ got increasingly annoyed as he unpacked and threw his dirty clothes in the hamper.

Wow, not even a Hi, TJ thought. They might be worse off than he thought. TJ wasn't giving in. Paige would say something to him first. He wasn't even worth a Hi, much less a hug or a kiss. TJ shook his head. At that moment, Paige caught TJ by surprise. "I don't even get a hello??" Paige said, with attitude in her voice.

"That's the least I deserve after holding down the fort last week while you were out having fun."

"Sorry", said TJ, not really meaning it. "I thought you must have been busy with something."

"It's okay," said Paige. "Tell me about the business discussion."

"Later," said TJ. "It went fine, we have a chance with it."

"You know, TJ, I don't think I'm going to care for you being away like this. Too many marriages end when they start doing things apart like this."

"I really wish you would go with me, Paige. I've asked you several times. You don't seem the least bit interested. I love the travel part of it. I just wish you did too."

Paige looked annoyed. "We have responsibilities here. Who are we going to leave the kids with?"

"I've told you a hundred times, my parents would be overjoyed to watch them," TJ embellished.

"I don't want to just drop them there and leave," said Paige, not giving in.

"Fine," said TJ. "Then I'll continue to travel without you. Even though you can join me, and we have someone who can watch the kids, I just don't think you want to join me. It would be good for us, you know."

"It's not that, TJ. Never mind, this is going nowhere."

Paige walked out of the bedroom. Great, thought TJ. Off to a great start on re-building this with Paige. Was I wrong, he thought? TJ finished unpacking and went to the living room to watch TV. Feeling uneasy and irritated.

Elizabeth finished brushing her teeth. She was always prompt about getting ready for bed. The complete opposite of Steven. She would brush her teeth, wash her face and even take a shower without being asked. Steven could barely be bribed into doing any of those. Two completely different kids.

"Daddy? Can you read me a bedtime story tonight?" Elizabeth yelled from the bathroom.

"Sure thing, sweetie" said TJ.

Bedtime stories were always much more than just reading the book. Elizabeth insisted that she and TJ become the characters in the book. Sometimes even acting out the scenes. They had their favorite books to do that with.

Elizabeth climbed into bed and said, "Okay, I'm ready. Tonight, you be the Lion and I'll be the Giraffe."

TJ and Elizabeth worked through the story like actors practicing a script for a play. One night, TJ thought, I will record this. Just to remind me of when Elizabeth was still Daddy's Little Girl and we shared these moments.

TJ kissed Elizabeth and said "Goodnight, sweetie."

"Good night, Daddy. I love you."

"I love you too, sweetie."

"TJ is on his way over," said Ann Carlson, TJ's mother. "I'm sure he will fill us in on Ireland."

"OK", grunted Harold Carlson. Harold, TJ's father, was in his mid-60's, and a bit of a curmudgeon with very defined world views. Having worked in many places all over the world, he was happy to finally be able to stay in one place. "He'll get tired of all that traveling one day," said Harold confidently. "Lord knows I did."

TJ walked in the door, hugged his mother and shook his father's hand. TJ got a cup of coffee and relayed stories of he and Jim in Ireland. TJ's parents got a belly laugh out of the story about the Queen and Paul, the Brit-hating Irish bus driver.

"Where to next, son?" asked Ann. "Will you be able to take Paige?"

"Honestly, mom, Paige doesn't seem interested."

"She knows we'll take the kids, right?"

"Yeah, I told her that. I really want to go to the South Pacific. One of those island locations that could pass for paradise."

Harold suddenly interjected – "Go to Bora Bora. That's my bucket list place right there. When it's time for me to pass away, I want to be there surrounded by gorgeous Polynesian ladies with a beer in one hand and the other hand on one of their beautiful behinds."

"Your father's dream," laughed Ann.

But TJ was curious. He and his father had something in common. TJ had heard of Bora Bora but didn't know a lot about it.

"Let me show you something, son" said Harold.

TJ followed his dad to his computer and he pulled up a file called 'Dreams of Bora Bora'.

What followed was about 10 minutes of an uninterrupted slideshow featuring topless Polynesian girls, along with several very lovely pictures of the girls showing their attractive asses.

"No wonder you dream of going there and dying with one of those in your hand" laughed TJ. "If I go, you wanna go?"

"I'm too old to make that trip, son. But you do it, put together another slideshow for me that will put that one to shame."

"Will do, pop" said TJ. "By the way, can you email me that file?"

It was unusual for TJ to have the house to himself. It had been 3 unspectacular weeks since his return from Ireland. Things with Paige were status quo. They just did not seem to be operating on the same wavelength. There were moments where they could connect but they both said or did things that prevented the connection from taking hold.

TJ was thinking a lot about not only his business opportunity, but about what his next trip would be. Focused now on Sydney, Australia, he hoped to find some hotels there to talk with, as that should be a popular location for global conferences. Not far from Sydney was French Polynesia, where Bora Bora was part of a group of islands there called the Society Islands.

TJ began working up a travel plan that could take him to both places. How awesome would that be, he thought to himself. Almost as fun as going on these trips was conceiving and planning them. Admittedly, the Bora Bora slideshow was playing in his head. Paige won't like this at all, he thought. How can I possibly convince her to let me do this? It would take some serious charm, something not really guaranteed to work on her these days.

TJ pulled out a notebook and started mocking up an itinerary and began calculating prices. At the very least, thought TJ, I'll be ready if this becomes a go. And it would give me something to shoot for, he rationalized. Sydney for the business. And Bora Bora for me and dear old dad.

"Steven, are you done your homework?" said Paige as she was preparing dinner in the kitchen. Steven had this way of hearing what TJ and Paige would say to him, but not really hearing it. "Steven!" yelled Paige, now stopping and focusing directly on Steven.

"What?? Yes, I did that hours ago," said Steven defiantly. Steven then made the mistake of not acknowledging a suddenly increasingly angry Paige.

"Steven, dammit, will you look at me when I'm talking to you. Every day, you plug up your ears, tuning us out. You're old enough to be helping us around the house, but you just sit there and play those stupid computer games. You're lucky we've tolerated that to this point. But if you continue to ignore me like that, you're going to find that computer gone. I'm sick and tired of being the only one who does a damn thing around here."

At that, TJ felt like he had no other option but to interject, both to save Steven, who didn't deserve it and Paige, who needed to be calmed down.

"Babe, ease up on him," said TJ, watching closely for eggshells. "He's a good kid. Trust me, we could be dealing with a lot worse than having a kid who likes computer games. You know our neighbors 13-year-old just got suspended from school for bringing alcohol. Dumbass." Sometimes TJ tried to defuse these situations through deferral and humor, hoping to steer the out of control car back on to the road.

Steven was quiet and now focused on the looming response from his mother. Paige was staring at TJ coldly. It was a look he had rarely seen from her. There was something going on. TJ was determined to keep Steven and Elizabeth out of this, whatever 'this' was that had eaten into Paige tonight.

"You know, I really do feel underappreciated here," said Paige. "My son treats me like I don't exist and you always take the kids side any time I share any frustrations about it."

"He treats me the same way, Paige. He's a 12-year-old boy. This is nothing new."

"I would like to see him doing stuff around the house. Here's the deal – I cook the dinner, and you guys take care of the dishes. Fair?" asked Paige.

The problem with Paige's argument was that it was usually TJ who took care of cleaning things up in the evening. This must have been a residual from TJ's recent absence.

"That's fine," said TJ, committing he and Steven to a verbal contract to do household work. TJ knew there was more to this and he would need to find out later.

Steven went back to playing his game and TJ started going through how he was going to start a conversation with Paige later about her outburst. That outburst, TJ rationed, was a call for something. He knew her well enough by now.

"What happened earlier?" TJ asked Paige as they got ready for bed.

"Nothing. I was frustrated."

"About what," asked TJ, anxiously waiting to hear this response.

"It's me, TJ. Don't worry about it. I'm sorry I yelled at him. I'll try not to do that again."

"Hey, it's okay," said TJ, sensing he could fully end this episode. "Don't be afraid to tell me when you are frustrated about things. I'll do anything I can to make your life easier. The last thing I want is for you to be frustrated with us."

Paige nodded and laid down. She leaned over to kiss TJ. TJ reached his arm over and placed his hand on Paige's breast, which he had easy access to as she laid on her back. He would do that on occasion to initiate sex. As TJ began massaging her breast, Paige gave no response. She laid there motionless.

"I know a few ways I can make you feel a lot better," said TJ as he started to move his hand from her breast gently down her stomach. But before he could get to where he was heading, Paige turned over on her side away from TJ, rebuffing the advances of his hand and giving him confirmation this wasn't going to happen.

Now it was TJ who was frustrated.

While home life was giving TJ the occasional frustrations, work was another story. TJ had a good paying job, but the politics of the office he had little time for. He wanted to keep moving up the ladder, but simply lacked the passion to give his full effort at Advent Health Care, where he had worked the last 7 years. He had several good friends there, and they would take turns getting each other through the day.

Karen Coleman was TJ's best friend at the office. They would keep each other entertained throughout the day commenting on everything going on around them like sports reporters analyzing a play. Karen was a pretty girl in her early 30's with black hair and a dark complexion. She was married, but the only thing TJ could ascertain about Karen's husband was that he was a complete doofus. Karen's stories about him always hammered that point home. TJ didn't talk a lot about Paige. He certainly never painted her in a bad light. Jewel Sanchez was another good friend, and one that seemed to follow TJ from department to department. Jewel was in the midst of a relationship with another guy at the office. She was never shy about sharing hilariously embarrassing stories about him with TJ and Karen. Jewel also was very pretty, with naturally black hair highlighted with some brown. Another feature Jewel had that was another consistent topic of conversation was a pair of rather large breasts. A topic Jewel would never shy away from, and something she was actually quite proud of.

"This team meeting we had this morning was ridiculous," said Karen. Not the first time she has opened a conversation that way. "If management wants to always change the rules on us, I wish they would at least give us good reasons for it. I have a really hard time explaining these things to staff."

Jewel chimed in. "If the big boss wants it done, our bosses have no choice but force it on us. We are their ever-present minions."

This was definitely one of TJ's frustrations at his job. He knew exactly what they were talking about, and very cult of personality like culture surrounding 'the Big Boss'. The big boss was actually a grizzled lady in her late 50's who was extremely old school and had a hard time progressing into the future with the rest of us. She sprung to the action of change only at the risk of getting a violation, which was becoming more frequent.

"I think what she needs," said Karen thoughtfully, "is to get laid. Seriously. Get her a young stud for the weekend and loosen her up a bit. Or Jewel…. loan her Matt for the weekend!"

"No friggin way," said Jewel. "I would never touch him again after that."

"Just have him do to her what he occasionally does to you. The thing with his tongue," laughed Karen.

"Yuuuck!" screamed Jewel. "Thanks for putting that mental picture in my head!"

TJ and Karen laughed as they all three now had that mental image of Jewel's guy being a gigolo for the Big Boss for a weekend.

"Maybe I'll lend her Dave for a night," said Karen. "Maybe he'll learn a few things."

"I have a better idea," said Jewel, now looking at TJ.

"Stop right there, "said TJ. "Never in a million years. I just finished my lunch. Keep going with that thought if you'd like to see my lunch again."

"How are things with you and Paige?" asked Karen, suddenly being serious.

TJ shared the story of the Ireland trip and the last few weeks at home, which was an unusual thing for him to do. TJ was interested in what his female friends thought here. They may have some insight into what's going on in Paige's mind right now.

"You two need to have a serious talk. But you're going to have to give in a little, TJ. I know what it's like to feel that way, and all my guy would need to do is something extra special to make that coldness go away. Do something romantic. Make her feel appreciated and desirable, and she's all yours." Karen continued on with a story of how Dave once 'redeemed' himself by cooking dinner for her one night, making her favorite dish, and then planning out a series of activities that he may not have enjoyed, but she did. "If you ever wonder why I stay with that lunkhead, that's why."

TJ appreciated the advice, and thought that might be something that would work. "I'll give that a shot and let you know what happens," said TJ to his good friends.

"Perfect!" said Jewel. "Now I think the big boss wants to meet you know. She'd like to go over you. I mean…. go over a few things with you. Hahaha!"

"I'll send Matt in my place," said TJ as he got up.

"Poor Matt," said Jewel. "Oh well, it was fun while it lasted."

TJ had a different boss than Karen and Jewel. Nora Martin was a lady who had gotten off to a promising start at Advent, but had slacked in recent years. Once the head of one of the most important departments, she had been moved to managing a team of analysts that included TJ. A huge demotion in her mind.

Nora's boss, Curtis Blanchard, was a no-nonsense guy who had been purposely assigned to manage Nora. Curtis was well respected by the big boss, mainly for his ability to understand her old school way of thinking and to present new ideas to her as if they were her own.

On this afternoon, Nora was in Curtis's office for their weekly meeting. Curtis knew the analyst team played a big supporting role for the needs of data by all of the production teams. Dismayed that a few requests were lagging, Nora was hearing feedback from Curtis she did not like at all.

"Nora, exactly how long should it take your team to finish these requests? I'm certain we had an agreement to get these things to our production teams within a set timeframe. Can you give me a logical reason why they aren't able to take the request, analyze it, act on it, and get it back to them in the agreed timeframes?"

Nora was struggling for words. "Let me go back and talk to TJ Carlson. I'll find out what the holdup is."

"TJ isn't the manager of that area," said Curtis. "But if he can explain it, I'd love to hear it."

"TJ used to manage that area until a few weeks ago," said Nora. "He can tell me if there is something happening with these requests and what's been communicated to the team."

"Tell me again what TJ does now," said Curtis, now suddenly wondering why TJ was becoming a focal point of this conversation.

"I moved him over to focus on analysis work for projects. We desperately needed a dedicated resource there."

"You must have thought a lot of him to move him there, right?"

Nora paused. "Yes, he's a good employee. But obviously there's an issue with the team he left behind that has your attention. I'll get to the bottom of it."

"Fine," said Curtis. "Let me know what you find out."

"TJ, Curtis is really upset about the delays in the analyst team getting things over to the production groups. He knows you used to manage that team and wants an explanation from you as to why requests are taking longer than they should." Nora looked down as she said these words to TJ, as if she was studying notes as she said it.

"I don't understand," said TJ. "I don't manage this team anymore, and we were always on time when I did. Why am I the one giving this explanation? Frank should be in here."

"This all started while you were still there. Listen, just your insight as to why there are sudden delays."

Still unable to not feel like he was being blamed, TJ catalogued reasons why requests could get delayed. System issues, unclear requests, complex requests that require more careful research, etc. "Frank really needs to be in here to explain these latest ones."

"TJ, this isn't about Frank. He's still learning the job. I'm looking to you to explain these reasons to Curtis, who isn't going to be happy with most, or any of them."

TJ was getting irritated. Why was this his job to explain? This not only wasn't his team anymore, but Nora was the one Curtis met with. TJ had very little interaction with Curtis. What could TJ say by way of an explanation that didn't bury either Frank or Nora, or make himself look like an idiot who couldn't do his job? "Nora, I'll do my best here, but honestly, I don't feel like I'm the right person to explain the current situation."

"I'm disappointed in you, TJ. I put you in that new role knowing you would not only take that on, but ensure a smooth transition for Frank and make sure I stayed in the loop. Now, I have to be caught off guard by my boss and suddenly explain why requests are falling behind. You could have given me warning. Surely you are talking to Frank each day. I hate surprises TJ, especially the kinds that make us all look bad."

TJ officially felt like dirt, and Nora truly blamed him for this. Frank hadn't said a word to him other than "Things are going great!" since the transition. But now TJ had been talked into thinking that this was now all his fault. Nicely done, Nora, thought TJ. That's what it must take to get to upper management. The ability to bury others along the way.

TJ left Nora's office seething with anger. He would need to spend the next few hours researching everything that has gone wrong with his former team since he left, then explain it to a boss who wouldn't get it and then explain it to his boss's boss, who wouldn't care that he had nothing to do with it.

Fun times, thought TJ. It isn't worth it. Screw this. At this point, he could not have cared less about his current job.

TJ spent all of dinner expressing his frustrations about the day. For once, he did most of the talking. Paige listened, not offering much feedback, but just giving TJ her attention. For Paige, it was rare to see TJ so animated. She was used to his calm, and usually seemingly stress-free nature. But tonight, TJ was stressed.

After dinner, TJ sat at his computer and pulled up the Bora Bora slideshow. It made him smile. It was a reminder that there was a happy place for him somewhere in this world. Paige noticed him smiling and got curious.

"What are you looking at?"

Paige was not a prude. She would enjoy watching this slideshow knowing that the source was a dirty old man, TJ's father. "Sit down, I'll show you," said TJ.

Paige joined him on the couch and watched the slideshow. She leaned her head on his shoulder as they watched. "Those girls are beautiful. I wish I had their complexion. But I don't tan, I burn. And those asses, I'm jealous!" TJ enjoyed the fact that Paige was enjoying this.

"Dad wanted to go there. It's on his bucket list. But now he says he's too old." TJ sought an opening to see if Paige would be open to going there. "Would you ever want to go?"

"And be there next to those girls? Ha! I'll look like a ghost." With that Paige got up and walked into the family room. Not sure what that meant, thought TJ. The stress of his day and then looking at this slide show had TJ longing for the beaches of Bora Bora.

Later that evening, in bed, TJ continued with a discussion of work. "I am seriously thinking of leaving that job."

"TJ, don't overreact. You've been there for a long time and you make good money. Don't put this family at risk by making a career change at this point."

"Paige, I feel like I'm worthless there. That's not a good feeling to deal with every day. Trust me, if I go work somewhere else, it will be for more money than I'm making now."

"Okay, just didn't want you to let one bad day or one incompetent boss ruin your job." Paige wasn't really hearing his frustrations, thought TJ.

"It isn't just one day Paige. I feel like shit every day there. There are many other places I can go. I don't like the fact that I'm bringing this stress home. I also don't like the fact that you don't seem to care. Good night."

TJ rolled over much like Paige did the other night and tried to force himself to sleep. Paige looked at him, concerned. Not like him, thought Paige, to be the emotional one. There must be something to it. Rather than saying something comforting, as TJ was really waiting for as he faked sleep, Paige simply stayed quiet, shut off the lights, and went to sleep herself.

Another nice way to end an evening. TJ needed to get away again. He needed something to divert his stress and get his mind off his troubles. Make this new business work, he thought. I need to go to Sydney.

It took TJ about an hour to fall asleep. He was disappointed with Paige. She was the one person who could make him feel better, but she chose not to. Should I plan on cooking her dinner, as Karen suggested? TJ thought that might be a good idea, and maybe he can work in that he wants to go to Sydney. It's worth a shot.

TJ's meeting with Curtis went as expected. TJ made the decision to take some ownership of the situation, but to be sure that both Nora and Frank were part of the equation. Nora would surely be pissed off at TJ afterwards. Curtis was reasonable, TJ determined. He was about the bottom line. "Thanks for articulating some of the recent issues," said Curtis. "I look forward to hearing how we can remove those obstacles and get things back on track."

Nora afterwards shot TJ a look that TJ knew didn't bode well for him. TJ found himself not caring, really, as he had all but made the decision to leave Advent. Fortunately, he could go out the right way by using his vacation time first. TJ had decided he was going to go on his trip to Bora Bora and Sydney. He would just tell Paige. She didn't seem interested, and he really wanted it. For the business, he thought.

TJ had been researching the best way to make this trip to the South Pacific. Tahiti first, then visit some friends in New Zealand and then stop in Sydney. A two-week getaway that would do wonders for him. All he had to do now was book it. After telling Paige about it. A harder task than paying for it, thought TJ.

"How was your meeting with Curtis?" asked Paige.

"It was fine. He seems very reasonable. He doesn't care about placing blame, he just wants the problem solved."

"Paige," continued TJ, "I really want to give our business idea a go. The more stress and frustrations I have at work, the more determined it makes me. I need to get out and talk to some more potential groups and hotels."

"Where did you have in mind?"

"Sydney," said TJ, happy that she didn't immediately torpedo the thought. "There are several hotels around the Opera House that would be perfect destinations. Sydney hosts conferences consistently throughout the year."

Paige didn't show any expression. "When are you planning on talking to them?"

"I wanted to finish up a plan to go in a few months. I can talk to my friends here and gauge their interest." TJ waited for a response, but did not get one. "While I'm there, I'd like to visit Bora Bora and Tahiti also. Just to see it. It's fascinated my dad for most of his life. Don't worry, I'll be good and not aiming to put together a similar slideshow."

"How long would you be gone again with all this?" asked Paige.

"Two weeks."

"Do we have the money for this? I'm sure we do, but just wanted to be sure."

TJ tried his best now to get Paige to join him. Not really sure he wanted her to join him, but he thought this could be something that could bring them back together. "Please go with me, Paige. We need this. It will be a lonely trip without you."

Paige remained expressionless. "TJ, I can't stop you from doing this if you really want to do it. So, just go. I trust you'll do what's needed to further your business idea and won't do anything to wreck our marriage."

"Paige, are you sure? Why don't you want to join me? Do you not want to spend time with me?" TJ wasn't hurt that she didn't want to go, but was hurt that she didn't really even consider it.

"TJ, I'm telling you that you can go. I'm fine. I think you need to get away. Again. Our kids will miss you. But better you do this if you need to so you can get it out of your system."

TJ was annoyed. "Okay Paige. If that's the way you feel.... that I just need to get it out of my system. Whatever. I would rather you go with me. It's not about me."

"Yes, it is, TJ. You don't have to do this. You are choosing to. Just don't ever lose sight of what's important."

TJ realized he and Paige were at a complete impasse on this topic. But she was okay with him going. He had achieved his main objective, but at what cost. He really began to be bothered by what was going on with he and Paige. For the first time, he wondered if they were going down a path they would not be able to return from.

TJ finalized his plans to go to the South Pacific. In the coming weeks, he would not talk to Paige about it. She certainly was not bringing it up. Things remained status quo at work, as TJ decided to do this trip before seriously beginning his hunt for a new job. He called his dad. "Pop, I will get to work on that slideshow as soon as I get to Bora Bora," laughed TJ. "Make me proud, son," said Harold. Steven and Elizabeth were getting used to TJ traveling. TJ spent time with Elizabeth relating where in the world he'd be going through using a globe and promising pictures of Koalas and Kangaroos.

That feeling that TJ has, similar to what he felt at the Cliffs, was starting to reappear. But there was something a little off this time. The damage it might do to his relationship with Paige. But hey, thought TJ, I begged her to go. She chose not to. That's on her.

Chapter 3

Markus checked his watch. A little late, he thought. His American guest, arriving from San Francisco, would get to experience the hospitality not only of staying at his hotel but a personal escort to it from the owner of the hotel. Markus was a Swiss expat who settled in Tahiti to open his hotel, a dream come true. He was curious to find out what plans Mr. Carlson had on arrival in Tahiti. Unusual that he's traveling alone. Or maybe he's meeting someone here. Oh well, no matter, thought Markus. He's happy that TJ picked his hotel over the others on the island of Tahiti and couldn't wait to meet him.

As the flight touched down in Tahiti, TJ, who had been unable to sleep for most of the flights there, woke himself back up. Already noticing the green, mountainous landscape, he realized that he is entering his self-appointed image of paradise. Complementing the lush green landscape was the captivating crystal blue water. The scenery made TJ feel happy and peaceful as the plane pulled up to the gate. TJ grabbed his things, took a deep cleansing breath, and prepared to enter paradise.

It didn't take long for TJ to notice one other feature of Tahiti as he walked in to the airport. Greeted by gorgeous Polynesian girls wearing a traditional dancing outfit of a grass skirt and a coconut bra, TJ enjoyed the view and fought off the urge to pull out his camera and immediately start taking pictures. He was very attracted to these girls visually. He could not stop looking. The polar opposites of Paige in looks, they had an exotic look to them that TJ really found sexy and sensual.

TJ found Markus outside standing next to his black sedan. A very small car, thought TJ, now worried he'd be unable to fit his luggage in it. It may have been small, but had a deceptive amount of space in the trunk. "Welcome to Tahiti, my friend," said Markus, with a noticeably German accent. This piqued TJ's interest. "It's awesome to be here. Where are you from?"

"Relocated here from Switzerland 3 years ago and opened the hotel we are going to."

TJ was really interested. He'd only been here for a few minutes, and would mentally file away how someone could relocate themselves here and open up a business. "How did you manage to do that? Is it easy for foreigners to open up a business here?"

"Not really," said Markus. "The French govern the region and don't make it easy. For me, as a Swiss citizen, it would be easier than let's say a US citizen."

TJ made small talk with Markus on the way to the hotel and learned about his life in Tahiti. Markus seemed like a guy without a care in the world. Married to a Tahitian woman with two young boys, Markus really had something that TJ was fascinated by. Not envious, as TJ loved his family and especially his kids, but saw in Markus someone who followed through on a dream and leads an amazingly happy life. Happiness is something that has eluded TJ, for one reason or another. He would remember Markus, he vowed.

The Swiss-Haus Tahiti was a quaint little hotel with about 30 rooms, a swimming pool and a view overlooking Papeete. Not quite as paradise-like as TJ may have imagined, but pleasant nonetheless. TJ was only staying there for the night, as he was set to board a cruise around the islands the next day. He desperately needed a comfortable bed and some hours of uninterrupted sleep. TJ couldn't believe he was here. A sense of freedom overcame him at this moment. As much as he would have liked Paige to be there, he was also looking forward to some time to himself, a rare commodity in his life.

Before going to sleep, TJ called home to let Paige and the kids know he made it okay. Paige was unusually sweet and told TJ to be careful and stay out of danger. It was reassuring to TJ that Paige seemed to be okay with this trip now and even asked TJ to get her some local gifts, much like he saw the girls wearing at the airport. TJ settled in and fell asleep.

He woke up a few hours later to notice he had a few guests in his room with him. A couple of lizards crawling on the wall. Carefully, TJ took out his camera and got pictures of them. An early gift for Elizabeth, who loves animals. Even lizards. TJ took a stroll from the hotel down to a local market to grab a few snacks. He felt good on this day. He didn't see any other tourists like himself there, just locals. The Swiss-Haus was a bit off the beaten path and not close to the other with the fancier hotels. No worries, thought TJ. This experience is much better.

A low-key evening, with dinner outside cooked by Markus's wife. Markus joined TJ for a few minutes and asked him his plans for his stay here.

"Cruise around the islands, starting tomorrow," said TJ. "I am really looking forward to Bora Bora."

"Bora Bora is beautiful," said Markus. "A favorite spot for celebrities. Go visit a place called Bloody Mary's. It's a restaurant that loves to keep track of its celebrity visitors. For me, after Tahiti, I prefer Moorea. Some of the most breathtaking views in all of the world."

"I can't wait to see it all," said TJ. "Looking forward to my time in paradise."

Markus took a liking to TJ and they continued their conversation over a bottle of French wine. TJ shared his business idea with Markus, who dually noted that TJ would probably enjoy doing any work that would have him see the world. No arguments there, thought TJ. Markus's youngest son brought TJ a gift. A white flower. Markus informed TJ to give that flower to a pretty girl, and it will bring that girl luck.

"Trust me," said Markus. "You will meet a lot of beautiful girls while you are here. You'll never forget them."

TJ settled back in his room for the night, excited to see the islands and happy to have met Markus, a guy after his own heart. He placed the flower in a safe place. Tomorrow, vowed TJ, that flower will have a home.

TJ boarded the cruise ship that next morning. A ship about half the size of conventional cruise ships, TJ immediately found it more comfortable and less of a hassle to make his way around. It had the usual amenities such as a dining room, workout room and several bars. His room was small, but quaint, and had one thing TJ immediately liked: pictures of topless Polynesian women. An excellent touch, thought TJ, as he stood there and stared at them. TJ had to shake himself out of where his mind was going, and get out there and see what fun was to be had on his new home for the next seven days.

On board the ship, TJ could not help but notice all of the other couples. In fact, it's quite possible that he was the only one there that wasn't with someone. Why didn't Paige agree to this, he wondered. She has no idea what she is missing out on. TJ couldn't help but feel a bit alone. My only option, he assumed, is to befriend other couples. And then explain why his own spouse opted not to join him. Ugh.

The welcome party on the ship was highly recommended as he got on board. Don't miss the Vahines! At least, that's what the excited lady collecting his cruise ticket warned him. Of course, he wouldn't miss it. TJ looked up the word 'vahines' to discover that it meant 'women'. I'm there, assured TJ in his mind.

TJ sat at a table alone and watched a performance by 12 Vahines. A wonderfully orchestrated dance and song that was both melodic to listen to and sexy to watch. 12 beautiful Polynesian girls, thought TJ, that will hopefully be performing quite a bit on this cruise. They performed a few other songs, and TJ was entranced by their style of dance, which involved a lot of hip movement. Making sure he captured this on video, he set up his camera on his table so he could enjoy the performance again later.

TJ was enjoying his third glass of wine as the performance ended. The Vahines left the stage, but went to mingle a little with the crowd. One passed by TJ, and looked over at him and smiled. She stopped as if she was going to come over and talk to TJ, but instead walked over and talked to a few other of the Vahines, who looked over at TJ a few times. I wonder what's going on there, thought TJ. I hope they don't think I'm a creepy guy sitting here by himself, to be avoided by them at all costs. This cruise would suck in that case! He laughed to himself......maybe they are talking about how handsome I am. They are blown away by it. The first one noticed and then had to tell the others. TJ stopped worrying about it until he noticed all 3 Vahines heading his way. Uh oh....... time to get charming, thought TJ as he sat up straight and smiled.

The Vahines joined TJ at his table. "Are you here by yourself?" One of them asked. "Yes," said TJ. "That was an amazing performance. I loved every second of it."

"Thank you. My name is Erita," said the first Vahine. "I am Miri," said the second. "And I am Orama," said the third.

"Wow, Erita, Miri and Orama. Those are beautiful names. My name is Thomas Jacob Carlson, but everyone calls me TJ," said TJ, pouring on the charm.

"It's unusual for us to have single travelers, especially those that are younger," said Erita. TJ had noticed that most of the passengers on the ship were close to retirement age. That, and honeymoon couples, were making up the demographic. "Are you married?"

"Yes," said TJ, instantly regretting that he had said that for no good reason. "But she had no interest in joining me here, sadly."

"How could she not want to visit a place so beautiful and romantic?" asked Orama. "That's very sad for you."

"Tell me more about yourselves," said TJ, moving the topic off his marriage and back to the girls.

"We will, TJ," said Miri. "We will make sure that you have a wonderful time on the ship and are never alone."

That comment was music to TJ's ears. He was looking forward even more to the rest of his time there. Beautiful views in the form of both landscape and women. His father would be both envious and proud. TJ was wondering how the girls would keep him entertained. He was hoping to get to really know them and know more about their lives and culture. He was suppressing any romantic thoughts. Not what I'm here for, he reminded himself.

Miri and Orama got up. "Erita will stay here with you for a while longer while we go visit with other guests," said Miri. "Have a good time, you two, and we will see you again tomorrow."

TJ and Erita made small talk for a few minutes, and then Erita started to make plans for them for the next day. "TJ, tomorrow are you on an excursion?"

"Yes, the island tour," said TJ.

"Okay, good. I will join you," she smiled. "I'll meet you here at 8am for coffee and breakfast and then we will join the others."

"Erita?" asked TJ, with a smile.

"Yes?"

"Thank you. You have already made this a memorable trip for me and we aren't even done the first day. I look forward to getting to know you."

"Same for me, TJ. I'll see you in the morning." Erita got up and headed to a door, but looked back at TJ and smiled. TJ was feeling what he thought may be butterflies. It had been a long time since he had felt that. TJ headed back to his room, looking forward to seeing Erita the next morning.

TJ was up very early that next morning. Pulling in to the port at Raiatea, he did not want to miss this view and was eagerly awaiting his breakfast date with Erita, the lovely Vahine he met the night before. Enjoying a cup of coffee out on the deck and watching as the island of Raiatea came closer, TJ almost wished he had a tripod and professional camera to capture the beautiful lush green mountainous landscape that lay ahead. Amazing, thought TJ. There are such horrible places in this world, but then there are such beautiful places like this. TJ noticed a few locals pushing their boats out into the water, surely to be catching a day's worth of fish. What a stress-free life this must be, thought TJ. He sipped his coffee and soaked it all in.

TJ got a little nervous as 8:00am approached. He would be spending the day with this Polynesian girl. What would they talk about? He already had a few prepared questions, like which island she is from and what is life like aboard the ship. He saw

Erita emerging from the stairwell leading up to the area where TJ was sitting and he waved. Erita smiled and headed his way. She was wearing a Pareo, a traditional Tahitian skirt that was red and adorned with pictures of flowers. She looked absolutely stunning. And, for the first time, TJ noticed a tattoo on Erita's right arm. It looked like a tribal design. Another topic of conversation, thought TJ,

Erita sat down and reached over and kissed TJ on the cheek. "While I give you a kiss on the cheek, you give me one also," instructed Erita. "That is a traditional greeting for us." TJ was enjoying this already. It looks like the Vahines are serious about making sure he has a good time and isn't alone. She did not eat anything at all. TJ also did not eat much, as he felt a bit shy eating in front of her now.

"Will you be able to join me on all of my excursions," asked TJ.

"Not all of them. In Moorea, I can, but we will be busy while we are in Bora Bora preparing for a big performance. If you are free, you can watch us practice."

TJ was excited. "I would love that! I was blown away by your performance last night."

"Are you going to eat anything, Erita?" asked TJ, curiously.

"No, I'm fine. I eat as soon as I wake up. I just wanted to be here for you to keep you company."

"Thanks again. I think I might be the envy of some other guys on this boat……getting to spend time with a beautiful Vahine."

Oh my God, thought TJ. He was flirting with Erita. And enjoying it. It was harmless though. He rarely had the chance to pour on the charm with a girl in any setting, much less one like this that barely seemed real. And nothing was going to happen with this.

She was being exceedingly nice and friendly, but that's part of her job. I'll enjoy it while I can, thought TJ.

The island tour of Raiatea was a lot of fun. Erita was one of three Vahines that went on the tour with the group. The other two had escorted two elderly couples who needed a little extra assistance. Wow, thought TJ, I hope that's not why they assigned Erita to me! Did they think I needed extra assistance?? Erita became a focal point of the others on the tour, but TJ always stayed close by. More than one couple commented on what a cute couple TJ and Erita made. Erita blushed each time, and TJ had fun with it.

"We both are really good looking," was TJ's standard response. Erita would laugh every time he said it, which would make TJ happy. God, I'm like a schoolboy, thought TJ.

They returned to the ship and Erita said goodbye to TJ for the day. "Can you join me for dinner?" asked TJ.

"That takes special permission. You will have to ask the cruise entertainment director, and she will arrange that. You have a good night, TJ." Erita hugged TJ and they mutually kissed on the cheek. TJ took note of how to request a dinner date, and definitely wanted to do that one night to thank Erita for keeping him company.

"Good night, Erita. I'll miss you tonight." TJ gagged at how lame and pathetic that must have sounded the second it left his mouth. He tried to recover. "Today was a lot of fun. Look forward to seeing you again tomorrow." That didn't sound much better, thought TJ. He gave up, waiting for Erita's next words.

"Hey, you're a great guy TJ. Today was fun for me too. Tomorrow is beach day in Motu Mahana and I'll see you then." She started to walk away, and said one more "good night".

TJ went back to his room to get ready for dinner. He could not get his mind off Erita now. So many years since a girl other than Paige dominated his thoughts. Unsure of his plans for the night, he just decided to wing it and try to get to know some of the other passengers on the ship.

This was the day. TJ's father would be so envious. TJ sent a message to his father:

Dad – today I arrive in Bora Bora. We are here for two days. I have my camera ready to go, ready to put that slideshow to shame. Haha! Glad one of us could finally make it here. A few excursions today then a free day tomorrow. Talk soon. TJ

It was early in the morning and the sun wasn't even up. TJ was recovering from a brilliant beach day in Motu Mahana, where he and Erita laid on the beach together and she involved TJ in several activities led by the Vahines, such as all the uses for a coconut, learning how to do Polynesian dances and singing some Polynesian songs. TJ and Erita were becoming known to many of the passengers as inseparable, and they were growing very close. Erita seemed comfortable with him and enjoying her assignment. While in Bora Bora though, it's a different story. Erita is not available to join him. He will get to watch her rehearse later, so at least TJ had that to look forward to after his day. TJ decided to go up on the deck and enjoy the arrival in Bora Bora.

It was quiet on the deck as not many people had gone up there. TJ realized he was about to capture something beautiful. Bora Bora on the horizon during sunrise. He got comfortable, made a cup of coffee and took it all in.

TJ's first day in Bora Bora was going to include a fun excursion underwater and an island tour. Although missing Erita, he enjoyed the island tour immensely. The beautiful beaches and the friendly locals who provided food and pareos for sale at designated stops. The tour guide mentioned something early on that caught TJ's attention. The road around Bora Bora was 18 kilometers. Many visitors would rent bikes or mopeds to travel around the island. What a great idea, thought TJ. I haven't ridden a bike since I was a kid. What an experience that would be. He mentally filed that away in his list of potential things to do on his free day in Bora Bora.

The bus tour finished up at a restaurant called Bloody Mary's. Famous for celebrity visitors, to the extent of having two large boards in front of the restaurant with the names of celebrities dating back to the 1960's who have visited the place. TJ instantly liked it. It was campy, he thought, as he looked at the sand floor, log chairs and large tiki statue towards the back. Another brilliant idea was the "wall of money" inside the restaurant where tourists would pin up their local currency on the wall. TJ and the rest of the tour participants enjoyed a drink and then prepared to head back to the starting point, where TJ would be off on his second activity – an underwater walk that was not far off the shore of one of the larger resorts on Bora Bora. A boat would take a group out to a set location and give them a chance to go underwater and see fish, stingrays and who knows what else up close.

TJ arrived at the boat set to take the tour participants to the underwater walk. Once again filled with couples, with one noticeable exception. An attractive blonde girl wearing a bikini, sitting by herself, who TJ knew for certain was not part of the cruise he was on. TJ went and sat next to her.

"Hi", said the girl as soon as TJ sat down. "Guten Tag."

"Hi," said TJ.

"American," said the girl. "Am I right?"

"Yup," said TJ as he smiled at her. "My name is TJ. I'm from North Carolina in the US."

"I'm Sophie. Switzerland. Zurich." TJ couldn't help but note he was getting lucky on meeting people from Switzerland on this trip.

"What brings you here Sophie?" asked TJ. "All of us are on the cruise, but I don't think you are."

"I'm on a sabbatical from work and traveling around the South Pacific and Asia. After this, I'm going to Brunei, Indonesia and Nepal. Maybe Vietnam."

Amazing, thought TJ. That I would meet this girl who is on this amazing journey of her own similar to what I've started.

TJ and Sophie talked about the different places in the world they've been and where they'd like to go. They instantly bonded over their travel stories. Sophie hinted to TJ to stay close to her while she was underwater. No problem, thought TJ. This girl was beautiful. TJ could not help but check out her body, as she was in excellent shape and her bikini flaunted those assets.

"What kind of work do you do, TJ?" asked Sophie.

"I work at a thankless job at a healthcare company. Seriously, I'm looking for something new. What about you?"

"In between work. I do business consulting work. I will start my own business when I go back."

The instructor asked everyone on the boat to 'buddy up'. Sophie latched her arm around TJ's arm and smiled at him. At this point, between Erita and Sophie, TJ was experiencing a boost to his ego that was off the charts where women were concerned. And he was enjoying this excursion immensely already.

They completed the underwater walk, and TJ took several pictures of Sophie. TJ thought, hey, this will give me a reason to stay in touch by sending these pictures. TJ and Sophie also made sure to take pictures of Ed and Joanne, and American couple on the excursion and a Japanese couple who didn't speak good English but knew well enough how to write down their email address.

"Hey, thanks Buddy," said Ed the American. "I can't wait to get those pictures!"

"Not a problem," said TJ. Ed looked at TJ and Sophie and asked – "What do the two of you plan to do here tomorrow?" TJ looked over at Sophie realizing that in all of their conversations, he never found out exactly what Sophie was doing here if she's not on the cruise.

"Not sure yet," said TJ, "but thinking of taking a bike ride around the island."

"Sounds fun, if I were in better shape," laughed Ed.

TJ returned his attention to Sophie. "Where are you staying? Here in Bora Bora?"

"Yes. At one of the resorts in an overwater bungalow. I'm here until tomorrow, then heading back to Tahiti and then on my way to Indonesia."

"The bungalows…. those looked amazing. I would love to see one of those." TJ unknowingly had set a plan in motion for the next day.

"Why don't you stop by my resort on your bike ride tomorrow. I'll show you the bungalow I'm staying at." Sophie pulled a piece of paper out of her purse and wrote the name of the resort, bungalow name and her email address. "Just email me with what time you start, and when you get to the resort, have the front desk call me."

"Definitely, Sophie. Thank God you were on this excursion. I feel really lucky and that I met a kindred travel spirit." TJ was at a loss for words for what transpired today. Now, in addition to hanging out with a lovely Vahine, he was going to go visit a bungalow belonging to a beautiful Swiss girl that he just happened to meet by random chance on an excursion in Bora Bora. As much as the scenery, the women TJ was meeting on this journey were making it unforgettable.

"See you tomorrow, TJ. We'll grab some drinks when, and IF, you can make it to my resort on the bicycle ride. It's near Bloody Mary's, so you'll have to go almost ¾'s of the way on your trip. Don't die!" Sophie laughed and so did TJ.

Sophie gave TJ a hug and headed back to her ride to her resort and TJ headed back to the ship. On his way to see Erita and the Vahines prepare for the big performance. Life is good, thought TJ, reaching a state of stress free and relaxed he hadn't been in years, if ever. He was falling in love with French Polynesia.

"He likes you, Erita," said Miri, as they prepared for their morning practice. "We all saw the way he was focused on you while he watched us practice."

"He's a super nice guy. Very funny. But he is married, so I would not entertain anything more than just being friends."

Miri continued – "Maybe his marriage is not that strong. Why else would he be here on his own? What kind of wife will turn down the chance to come here? See what he does. I'm sure he will ask you to dinner."

"We'll see what happens," said Erita, wanting to get Miri off this topic. Erita knew that she liked TJ, and this was a different experience for her as she had never had a situation where she was entertaining such a relatively young and attractive guy on these cruises. She wasn't sure what TJ would say or do next, which was both terrifying and exciting. Erita didn't know whether she would give in if TJ suddenly made a move on her. If he asks me to dinner, thought Erita, I think he might want to be more than friends.

"His name is TJ Carlson, and he should be stopping by here later today asking for me." Sophie Kiebler was preparing the front desk at the Shangri-La Bora Bora Resort front desk for TJ's arrival. "He may be in bad shape. He's attempting to ride a bike around the island. Have some water ready for him, just in case." Sophie was excited to talk to TJ again. She too saw him as a kindred spirit when it came to travel, although one who had limitations, unlike herself. Sophie had ended a bad relationship a year ago, one that affected not only her personal life, but her work. Life became unbearable for Sophie, and she took refuge in various sites around the world. Something she was still doing. She did not have any romantic feelings for TJ, as the thought of another relationship made her sick to her stomach. But in him, she saw a guy who she could develop a deep friendship with and someone who had a global view of the world, just like her.

"Is Mr. Carlson going to be spending the night in your bungalow?" asked the man at the front desk. "If so, there will be a fee for an additional person."

"Not a chance," said Sophie, laughing. "I just met him yesterday. He'll have to work harder than that!"

"Okay, Ms. Sophie. We'll call you when he arrives. And I'll prepare Gatorade for him."

TJ stood at the bike rental counter near the pier in Bora Bora. "How much to rent a bike for the day?" asked TJ.

"We rent per hour, sir. How many hours do you think you'll need?"

TJ started calculating in his head. He needed to bake in time to visit with Sophie and make it around the island.

"Let's go with 12 hours," said TJ.

"12 hours? It takes most people only 4 to 6 hours to get around the island. Are you sure you don't want a moped?"

"No, I definitely want the bike. The 12 hours is because I know it will take me longer than the average guy who is probably in shape, but I also will stop at a resort to see a friend."

"Is it a girl?" asked the lady, smiling.

"Yes, from Switzerland. I met her yesterday."

"Okay. Enjoy today, sir. It is beautiful outside. Please remember to drink water, because it is going to be very hot."

TJ went outside to get his bike. To describe this bike as old and rickety would be an insult to truly old and rickety things. A bigger challenge here, thought TJ. But it wasn't about the bike, he'll make that work. He was excited to get going.

Precisely one kilometer into the 18-kilometer ride, TJ pulled off the road and guzzled water. Already out of breath, he collapsed near a palm tree. Oh my God, thought TJ. I should have gotten the moped. Damn. Sophie was right......I might die before I get there. Suddenly dismayed at how bad a shape he was in, TJ realized he was woefully unprepared for his 'Bora Bora Bike Ride', as he had named it. As TJ was figuring out his plan of action, a pleasant surprise happened. The same tour bus that squired TJ and group around the island stopped at the place that TJ had pulled off, and TJ saw many familiar faces.

"Are you riding that bike around the island? The bus driver told us about that." The question came from a lady that TJ recognized but could not quite remember her name.

"Yes," said TJ. "And already regretting it!"

"Well good luck! Join us for dinner and let us know how it went." With that, the group took lots of pictures, a few of which TJ was asked to pose with the bike for. TJ was amused. He was now completely determined to pull this off and prepared himself to get started back on his route.

The next few kilometers went by in a haze of starting, stopping, walking with the bike and guzzling water, which he was already almost out of. It was about 95 degrees outside. TJ would need to find a store and reload with water, or else he was doomed. Dehydration, sunstroke, you name it and TJ would have it before he was done.

At kilometer number 7, TJ came upon a local store. Thank God, he thought. The store owner must not have been surprised to see a Westerner pull in. Makes sense, as other idiots like TJ had probably attempted to ride a bike around the island. TJ loaded up on water and chocolate. TJ ate the chocolate hoping for a serious sugar rush, as the store owner watched in amusement. "Good luck, handsome," said the store owner, a classy looking Polynesian lady who was probably in her 60's.

"Thank you, and thank God you had this store in this location," said TJ smiling as he prepared to get back on the road.

TJ reached the halfway point, which happened to be a prime spot to get pictures of Mount Otemanu, the ever-present centerpiece on the island of Bora Bora. This spot offered a view unhindered by trees or other obstructions. TJ took several pictures, while awkwardly trying to include himself in the shot. Now, thought TJ, would be a perfect time to have someone with me. To get these damn pictures.

At Kilometer 15, he knew that was roughly where Sophie was. He was going to make it, he thought. TJ felt like he was getting a second wind. Either that, or he had completely blocked the pain. The only pain, thought TJ, is coming from my ass thanks to this bicycle seat. I am going to seriously feel that tomorrow. He earmarked kilometer 12, for a beach area where he could grab lunch, and kilometer 17, for another stop at Bloody Mary's, which he was hoping to talk Sophie into joining him for.

As he got back on the bike after the halfway stop, he began passing by many locals on the streets, many of which were kids. They all waved or smiled at TJ, and in some cases said Hello. TJ was loving this now, as he knew what he was doing today would be something he would remember for life. His thoughts turned to Paige and the kids. TJ wondered what she was doing right now. He missed everyone, but he didn't miss the all too frequent tension that seemed to pop up recently. Am I the problem, he wondered? Maybe an experience like this will bring things into perspective and impact him in a positive way.

Kilometer 12 could not have arrived soon enough. Now starting to experience some worrying pain in his stomach, TJ figured it was a great time to stop and get some lunch. Already turning red from the sunburn, he wondered what sort of shape he'd be in tonight as he watched the Vahine performance on the ship. No way I'm missing that, he thought. TJ stopped at an air-conditioned restaurant, ordered some pasta and got some well needed rest. 3 kilometers to Sophie, TJ reminded himself.

The next 3 kilometers were excruciating, and TJ was now walking more than riding. The pain in his stomach was duller, but the pain in his ass from the seat was more extreme. As he pulled up to the Shangri-La, he prepared himself to be laughed at by Sophie for the shape he was in. Turning red, and walking very gingerly, how was he going to fake playing it cool to Sophie, making it look like it was nothing at all. At least I'm not dead, thought TJ.

The guy at the front desk greeted TJ as if he was expecting him. "A bottle of Gatorade, courtesy of Ms. Sophie. She thought you might need it."

"Haha," said TJ. "She probably thought I'd be near death."

"Yes, she did," said the guy very matter-of-factly. TJ laughed to himself. "Ms. Sophie, your friend is here. I'll send him your way."

TJ made his way to Sophie's bungalow. What a beautiful place, thought TJ. I am really lucky to have met her, he thought. Even just the chance to get to see one of these.

"I'm impressed, TJ," said Sophie after giving TJ a big hug. "You've almost made it. But you look like hell," she laughed.

"I feel like hell," said TJ. "And that hell is concentrated mainly on my ass."

Sophie laughed heartily. "Have a seat, TJ, on that nice comfortable chair and I'll get us some wine."

TJ and Sophie talked for the next 2 hours over a few glasses of wine. Sophie was easy to talk to, as she talked to TJ as if she was fascinated with every word he said and was excited with what she was saying to him. TJ invited Sophie to join him at Bloody Mary's.

"I'm sorry, TJ, but I'll be leaving very early tomorrow and wanted to rest tonight and sleep early. But just know, I'm rooting for you to finish this journey you're on today, and on in life. I hope we can see each other again someday."

TJ was disappointed, but he did have a task to complete today, and a performance to watch tonight. TJ got up and asked Sophie to join him for some pictures. Sophie agreed and also went to get her camera for pictures.

"Sure," she said. "Be sure you send these to me, okay?"

"Absolutely," said TJ. With that, Sophie walked over and gave TJ a huge hug. Then, by total surprise, kissed him on the lips.

"Go get'em, tiger," she said encouragingly. "Keep in touch. Promise me."

"I will," said TJ. "I've never met anyone like you, and I'll certainly never forget this."

TJ left the bungalow, and knew it was only two kilometers to Bloody Mary's, his last stop. He was able to surprisingly ride the whole way and pull in to the restaurant with a full head of steam. One drink, he thought, then I'll complete this journey. TJ ordered his drink and ran into a couple from the ship there with their kids. TJ told them the story of his amazing day, and they told TJ how they admired him for doing such a challenging thing. "Sounds like you had a very memorable day," said the wife.

"Could you both do me a favor?" asked TJ. "I've been on this trip by myself most of the day, and I'm not featured in hardly any of my own pictures. Can you take a few pictures of me with my bike and Mount Otemanu in the background?"

"Absolutely. And if you could get pictures of our whole family with that same setting, minus the bike, I think we have a deal."

"Fantastic," said TJ. They each took the pictures, and then TJ prepared for his last kilometer.

TJ had this incredible feeling of accomplishment on that last kilometer. I did it, he thought. I pulled this off. I can't believe it.

This may hurt for days, but this experience will last a lifetime. Time with the locals and solidifying a friendship with Sophie while completing a physical challenge like this, it was one of TJ Carlson's best days of his life.

Paige received her fifth email regarding TJ and his adventures in the South Pacific from some of their mutual friends on Facebook. Apparently, these friends were seeing and hearing more than Paige was, as she rarely ever bothered with social media, and she did not know how to field these questions. She shut off her computer and decided to leave them unanswered. So tiring, thought Paige. He's having the time of his life and probably not giving me a second thought. Paige called Kylie. "Can you please come over tonight? I need to vent, and I need some drinks."

TJ sat, entranced, as he watched the Vahine's full performance that night. He loved watching them all, but he kept his eyes trained on Erita the whole time. She too caught him in the audience, and TJ could swear that she smiled at him. After the performance, TJ decided he was going to finally arrange that dinner date with Erita. He approached her director and asked her:

"I'd like to request a dinner date with Erita. What would I need to do?"

The director looked blankly at TJ. "Please write down your name and room number. We will call you with confirmation of your dinner date with a Vahine. If Erita is unavailable, we will send someone in her place."

TJ was caught off guard at this cold and unfeeling way of getting this set up. Maybe this lady thought I am a pervert or something.

TJ wrote his information down. "I'd really prefer Erita. She's the one who has been spending time with me, and I'd like to show her my appreciation and say a special thank you to her before the cruise ends."

"Show up in the dining hall at 8pm tomorrow if we call you with confirmation of your dinner with a Vahine," said the director, again coldly. "And I'll try to make sure it's Erita," she said with a smile. TJ felt a bit better.

TJ received the confirmation he wanted and was told to be there promptly at 8pm and to dress nicely. Of course, he thought. TJ was looking at this as a date, and he wanted to look his best. He was imagining the rest of the Vahine's preparing Erita for her big date, doing her hair and makeup and helping to pick out her outfit. TJ went to the refrigerator and pulled out the hibiscus flower given to him by the Swiss hotel owner. Erita was going to get that flower, and hopefully the good fortune that comes with it.

Erita showed up for dinner in a gorgeous Polynesian style outfit, looking amazingly stunning. TJ and Erita were getting a lot of looks by the other guests at dinner. People maybe thought that this was a romance that was blooming.

"You look beautiful, Erita," said TJ. "I'm so glad we could do this. I wanted to thank you for everything. The cruise is almost over, and I'll actually be sad when it is. I'm not sure if I'll ever see you again."

"Thank you, TJ, you look very handsome," said Erita, shyly. "And if we are meant to see each other again, we will, don't worry."

"Well, let's make the most of the rest of the cruise, starting with tonight. I hope you'll eat something this time," laughed TJ.

"Oh, I will. I didn't eat lunch so I could be very hungry for our dinner. You'll be surprised at how much I can eat."

TJ learned about Erita's life as a Vahine, including some fun, behind the scenes drama that he never would have guessed. I suppose some things are universal, he thought.

Then, awkwardly, Erita popped an uncomfortable question. "Tell me about your wife, TJ." TJ had no plans to bring up Paige at this dinner. He wasn't sure why. He just didn't feel comfortable talking to Erita, someone he was now very attracted to, about Paige.

TJ answered her question, not revealing much. Emphasizing that they were two people with very different sets of interests, sometimes he wondered if they would last. It was now with Erita that TJ was admitting an uncomfortable truth he had in his mind. That he and Paige may not work out. The dinner got quiet and awkward. The dinner ended after an hour, which Erita said was the time limit given by her director. "They want to be sure that our contact with the passengers stays safe and controlled, especially when seen by the other passengers in a setting like this," she said. TJ felt that the good relationship they had built had unraveled somewhat at this dinner. It's my fault, he thought. I shouldn't have come on strong since I am married. What the hell was I doing here?

Feeling a bit disappointed, he told Erita he understood. "Come on, TJ, walk me to the elevator," she said.

"I'll visit you once more to say goodbye." Erita hugged TJ and gave him a soft kiss on the cheek. "Thank you for tonight, and for treating me with such kindness. I will miss you. I hope you can go on this cruise again."

"Maybe one day you can come to the US," said TJ. He watched her get in the elevator and the door close. She gave a small wave as the doors closed. TJ felt sad, but wasn't sure why. He went back to his room and called it a night.

TJ's last day on the cruise was unspectacular. No sign of Erita all day. He was hoping he could join her on his final excursion in Moorea, the beautiful island favored by Markus. But she did not. It was kind of a lonely day for TJ, as he was growing mentally tired. The spectacular highs of this trip were being replaced by unsatisfying lows. He had a stop in New Zealand and Australia to look forward to, but he did not like how this was ending.

At about 8:30pm, there was a knock on TJ's door. It was Erita.

"Hi TJ, I've come to say goodbye and wish you the best on the rest of your trip."

"Thanks, Erita," said TJ.

"You look sad," said Erita, "Are you okay?"

"Can I ask you something," said TJ. Erita nodded.

"What happened these last few days? I feel like you either got scared of me or maybe were told to stop hanging out with me. I really missed you on the excursion today."

Erita was silent for a few seconds and looked down. "Honestly, TJ, I liked you a lot. If you were single, I would have been open to continuing to get to know you better and maybe continuing our relationship after the cruise. But I don't want to be the other woman in a relationship. I'm not comfortable with that."

TJ finally understood. "I get it. Thank you for being honest. And thank you for allowing me to feel like I had something to offer another woman. You've meant more to me than you can know. And maybe in another reality, we could have been an amazing couple."

"Goodbye TJ, and God bless. I hope to see you again." Erita kissed TJ on the cheek and TJ did the same.

TJ felt better, like he had a little closure on this trip. He felt like he'd been or become a different person, something truer to himself.

After a brief layover in Auckland, New Zealand, where he wandered the airport for hours, TJ was beat by the time his turbulence filled flight landed in Sydney. Feeling a little weak and nauseous, TJ bagged any plans he had for the day to get some rest in his hotel room. He would spend the day out in Sydney tomorrow and make his appointment. Tonight, however, some wine and music and TV in his room overlooking the Sydney Opera House and a complete shutdown of his mind.

TJ called Paige to let her know he had arrived in the hotel.

"Thank God, TJ. I'm glad you're there safe. Sounds like you've had quite a trip."

"It's been very tiring, but a great experience. I'm going to rest today and then spend the day out tomorrow."

"I hope those girls in Tahiti were able to keep their hands off you," said Paige, laughing. "A big, handsome American guy there by himself. They probably wondered what crazy wife would let you travel by yourself."

If she only knew, he thought.

"TJ, we have a lot to talk about when you get home," continued Paige.

"Like what?" asked TJ curiously.

"Things that have been happening recently. We'll talk when you get home."

TJ was now feeling even less motivated after Paige dropped that line and wouldn't elaborate. He liked being in control of things, but maybe he was losing a little bit of grip on that control. It certainly wasn't going to make for a fun last day on this trip wondering what was on her mind.

TJ toured around Sydney and arrived for his business meeting, only to be informed it was canceled. No big deal, thought TJ, who didn't feel mentally ready for it. What TJ was now desiring worried him a little. He had gotten used to being around new girls and getting close to them. With Erita and Sophie, he had something he had not felt in a long time. Though nothing sexual, TJ is not sure what he would have done if the situation had arisen. Would he have said no to either Sophie or Erita if they had wanted sex? He really wasn't sure, and that made him feel guilty.

He got off on a stop near the Chinatown section of Sydney. TJ saw a massage parlor. A massage would be nice, thought TJ. He wanted to make sure the place was reputable though, to ensure he was safe and not going to get ripped off. He pulled up the place online and came to find out this was one of those massage parlors that offered "additional services." In other words, sexually gratifying the client after the massage.

He stared at the place, now deciding whether or not to try this. It would cross a line, he thought. But it was extremely tempting. He stood there, somewhat frozen, trying to decide whether or not to go through with it. He was lured by the potential sexual gratification, but was assured he'd leave there feeling worse about himself and would then have something very bad to feel guilty about in front of Paige when he got home.

TJ turned and walked away, deciding against it. Angry at himself for denying what could have been yet another memorable moment on this trip, but deep down knowing it was the right thing to do. He returned to the hotel, ending his day early. Getting a bottle of wine, he opted to finish out this trip by getting slightly tipsy and getting a long night's sleep.

Boarding the flight back home, TJ was in a bad frame of mind. Sad that this trip was done and going home to uncertainty, his mind was in a dark place. Preparing for the worst from Paige, he steeled his resolve and practiced different ways he could react based on what she had to say. Did she want to end it? Did she want TJ to stop traveling? Did she meet someone else? Shit, it could be anything, thought TJ.

It was an uncomfortable flight. TJ couldn't shake his mood and was feeling a little sick. The passenger next to him was a large gentleman who fell asleep instantly, rudely occupying part of TJ's seat with his elbow. He closed his eyes and thought of the time in French Polynesia, where he felt on top of the world. A magical place, thought TJ. I'll never forget it. And one day, I'll go back.

Chapter 4

It had been seven months since TJ's return from the South Pacific. Paige could not hide her disgust that TJ was in Sydney and had that meeting canceled. That business meeting was the centerpiece of your trip, she would argue. Maybe for Paige it was, but it wasn't for TJ. In reality, TJ knew the idea would not work. Not feasible to consistently make the money they would need.

"Paige, I think I'm going to call it quits on this idea. It won't work."

"TJ," Paige said angrily, "you aren't giving it a chance. Why are you quitting on it? It's your dream. Remember?"

"I'm just being realistic, dear," continued TJ. "We'll need a large network of hotel relationships, requiring face time and requiring money that we don't have."

"So, you're going to continue on with this job you hate and consistently complain about?"

"No, I've decided it's time to start looking for something new."

"I wish you had talked more with me about this before you made up your own mind. I thought we were a team here." Paige got up and started pacing around. "Are you going to try something different with travel?"

"I've thought about it," said TJ. "But nothing concrete comes to mind yet."

"You seem to have lost some motivation. What's going on, TJ? You seem to be different since you came back from that last trip."

"Nothing, Paige. If we had unlimited money, it would be easier to take some risks."

The conversation ended there, and TJ became lost in thought. He regularly communicated with Sophie, following her as she visited Indonesia, Brunei, Nepal and Vietnam. He envied her. He wished he could be going on that adventure with her.

Life with Paige was a series of ups and downs in the last seven months. She seemed fine when TJ returned, and the conversation that TJ was dreading never happened. Maybe she was just having a bad day that day, or just missing me, he thought. The downs were significant though, as they both seemed to be getting extra sensitive to each other and get annoyed with each other easier. Paige seemed very annoyed at TJ for not giving this business idea of his more of a chance. While Elizabeth was not noticing any tension, it seemed that Steven was. During some exchanges, Steven would flash TJ a look that told TJ he was aware of what was going on.

"TJ, maybe you can modify the business idea into something different. Don't give up on your dream."

TJ signed. "Okay, I'll give it some more thought." He decided he would, to be fair to himself. He didn't like that he was losing his passion for something he should have been passionate about.

"Okay, good. I'm going to bed. Good night, TJ," said Paige. TJ was going to try for sex that night, a rarity since his return. Scratch that idea, he thought. Frustrated again.

Kate Ambrose was a close friend of TJ's. Kate was a childhood friend who he had lost touch with for many years but had regained contact a few years earlier. Kate was a free spirit, and often just went where her whims took her. Not married with no children, she was free to do things she desired. They both sometimes longed for what the other had. Kate would sometimes lament not having a family of her own, while TJ could only imagine doing whatever he wanted with nothing tying him down. They would sometimes vicariously live through each other. Kate could usually be counted on to tell it like it is. TJ would check in with Kate on serious topics to get an unfiltered opinion.

"Dude, are you two even still married?" asked Kate.

"Of course," said TJ. "Why?"

"TJ, my perception is that you two seem to be leading completely separate existences. You never talk about her. What's going on with you two?"

"I don't know. We have our moments, but just don't seem to have a lot of the same interests or even thoughts and opinions these days."

Kate sounded concerned. "Not good, TJ. What about sex? Are you still doing it?"

"Rarely," said TJ. "Maybe once every few weeks. Certainly not enough for me."

"Are you getting it from anywhere else?"

TJ was shocked. "Am I cheating on Paige?? Of course not. It's frustrating, but I won't go that far."

"Even if she denies you completely? You're a man, TJ. You can't go without."

TJ thought for a minute. "I suppose there are some situations where I'd have to consider it. If she cuts me off completely, I may have no choice. But honestly, if that happens, the marriage is pretty much over."

"Keep me updated, TJ. I'm worried about you. I know you, but I don't know her. Watch out for yourself, and watch out for your kids."

Kate gave one more piece of advice: "Just make sure the kids aren't feeling it."

TJ sat in bed waiting for Paige. She had hinted earlier she may be in the mood tonight. Some playful talk and innuendo. TJ wasn't about to miss this opportunity. They had to re-connect somehow. TJ had some ideas in mind of some things he wanted to try on Paige tonight that she would really like. Make her want it a little more regularly.

Paige walked in to the bedroom and closed the door and locked it. A sure sign that some lovin' was about to go down. TJ began to remove the remainder of what clothes he had on.

"Period started," said Paige, ruining the moment with those two words. "But I guess I'll give you something if you want it." Paige yawned.

"Don't look and sound so excited about it," said TJ, now no longer in the mood himself. "Jesus, Paige, this is frustrating. Earlier, you were giving hints that you were in the mood." TJ was getting angrier the more he talked.

"Dammit, TJ, I'm not here on this Earth to service you. Why don't you go on some more trips? That's what you seem to love. Even more than you love me."

"Are you kidding me?" yelled TJ, stunned that this was the turn of events tonight.

"What exactly are you doing on these trips? Are you meeting other women? Who have you been messaging here recently? What's her name? Don't think I haven't noticed."

"What, I can't have friends?" TJ was furious, but didn't want this to escalate.

"Why haven't you ever shown me the pictures from Tahiti? Surely you took some. Or New Zealand? Or Australia?" Paige was standing there by the bed with her hands on her hips. She was not herself right now. Something was seriously wrong.

"You haven't asked to see them. You didn't care. You barely even asked me about the trip. Do you even care what I do anymore? Would you believe if I told you I haven't cheated on you? Is that what this is all about?"

"Did you?" Ah hah, thought TJ. We're getting to it.

"I did not cheat on you. I never have. Not all men are scumbags, Paige. You'd think you'd know me by now."

"I don't know you, TJ. I don't know the you that vanishes and goes all over the world, barely even calling home to see how we are. That, plus the messaging, the distance, you're always arguing with me. What should I think?"

"Think what you want Paige. If you don't trust me, what the hell is the point, here?" TJ was done with this argument. Nearly shaking from anger, he got up and stormed out of the room, slamming the door.

TJ dropped down on the couch, praying that Paige wouldn't follow him and continue this. She didn't. TJ poured a glass of wine, sat there and stewed on it. Unsure that he still loved Paige. Trying not to let the anger consume him. TJ grabbed his iPod, put the earphones on, and tuned out the world. He laid down on the couch and fell asleep.

After a few days of silence, Paige finally started a conversation with TJ.

"Did you decide anything about the business?" asked Paige, seemingly trying to break the ice and the tension.

TJ glared at Paige. Still hurting from the argument two nights ago, he had no desire to even talk to her. About anything. Paige noticed TJ's cold stare.

"I'm sorry about the other night, TJ. It was hormones, I think. I wish I could take it all back."

"That's fine, Paige. Apology accepted. I hope we don't ever have that argument again." TJ felt a little lighter now that she had apologized.

TJ continued – "I'm not going to go forward with the business Paige. It's not going to happen right now. I want to focus on getting a new job."

Paige looked disgusted. "I never pegged you for being a quitter, TJ."

"Go to hell, Paige," TJ said and got up and walked away.

"Hey, I didn't mean it like that. What happened to you? This was what you wanted!" Paige realized she once again triggered rare anger from TJ.

TJ turned around and walked back towards Paige. "I need to pay the bills in this house and make sure our kids are fed. I need a reliable job. I can't take the risk. Please understand that. I'm not being a quitter. I'm being pragmatic."

"Okay, TJ. I'm sorry. Again." Paige looked really troubled at this latest exchange. "Can we have a truce, TJ? I don't like this feeling."

TJ composed himself. He had to take this opening. "Yes. Truce. I don't like the feeling either."

TJ sat on the couch, and Paige joined him there. She leaned her head on his shoulder.

"TJ……. tell me about French Polynesia. Was it beautiful?" Paige grabbed TJ's hand and put it on her leg.

TJ relayed the story of his bike ride around Bora Bora to Paige. Omitting all of the details about Sophie Kiebler. Even though there was nothing to be guilty about, it was best not to open up that can of worms now that a truce had been negotiated.

A few weeks later, and things with Paige were going much better. And TJ accomplished a goal he had set for himself. He would be able to say goodbye to Advent Health Care. His job search had finally landed him a much better job at one of the largest financial consulting firms in Fayetteville. As a lead business systems analyst, TJ would be making a lot more money, and had developed an instant connection with his soon-to-be boss.

"You suck," said Karen to TJ upon hearing the news. "I don't believe it. Can you take us with you?"

"Yeah, surely they have a few more openings there for a couple of beautiful friends of yours," chimed Jewel. "I'll make sure I wear a shirt to my interview that shows off my two biggest talents."

"Way to set the women's movement back a few centuries, Jewel," said Karen.

"I'm kidding. TJ's good word should be enough. And he'd better give a good word."

"Are you two serious," asked TJ. "I would love it if you joined me there."

"Go see what it's like. If it's anything like here, don't bother recruiting us. You go do some recon work first and let us know." Karen looked and sounded serious.

"Will do. I'll miss you two the most."

"Duh," said Jewel. "You'd better not replace us with two hotter girls there. We will be a gigantic level of pissed off."

"Of course not," laughed TJ. "Not possible."

The general announcement was made and TJ spent the day receiving a series of questions and congratulations. Nora was less than enthused and wasn't saying a word to TJ or anyone else. TJ would gladly give feedback on his less than competent boss on his way out.

Tonight was the big night. TJ's farewell party at Advent. Always an event that Advent does well, tonight was no exception. Curtis and even the Big Boss attended and made sure to come say their good byes to TJ. Nora Martin was also there. She wasn't one to miss an event where she could make a showing and impress her bosses.

TJ hung back with Karen and Jewel, who almost served as a first level of protection for those wanting to talk to TJ. TJ loved these girls. Two of my best friends, thought TJ. I really will miss them every day. They made this job tolerable.

Curtis called for TJ to address the room, another Advent tradition. TJ had thought of a few words he might say if called on. He didn't necessarily like public speaking but he had braced himself for this.

"First and foremost, I want to say a special Thank You to all of you for coming here tonight to see me off. It was a tough decision, but one I made with my family and future in mind. I had a lot of good times here and got to work with a lot of great people. Two that I especially want to call out, because I truly and dearly love them, are Karen Coleman and Jewel Sanchez. They made every day entertaining and fun, and I will cherish their friendship always. I wish all of you the best of luck and know I will see many of you again. Thank you."

TJ returned to his buddies. Karen faked wiping away a tear from her eye. Jewel smiled at TJ. "Thanks for the shout out, buddy." Jewel hugged TJ and as she pulled back, was legitimately crying. TJ was touched. He really could have cared less about most everyone else in the room. He was really going to miss these two.

TJ made it a point to work the room and force himself to say goodbye to all of the others who had either worked with him over the years or might be a good resume reference. When he got to Curtis, he got a few words of advice.

"Good luck, TJ," Curtis started, "and never forget where you came from. I don't blame you for wanting more money. You have a beautiful family and they should always be foremost on your mind."

"Thanks Curtis," said TJ, gritting hi teeth a little. "I'll miss everyone here," he lied.

"You are always welcome back," said Curtis, as he excused himself when the Big Boss walked by.

Typical, thought TJ. He made his way back to Karen and Jewel and enjoyed the rest of the party with them. After Karen and Jewel left, first chance TJ got, he slipped out and left as well.

"How was the party?" asked Paige.

"It was fun. I mostly hung out with Karen and Jewel. Never said a word to Nora. I was surprised at how lively and talkative Curtis was. He gave me some encouraging words at the end, before he got distracted. Too bad I didn't work directly for him. I may have been in a much better spot there."

"Well, I'm glad you're off to a new chapter of your career. Good that they sent you off the right way."

Paige was fairly low-key tonight. Again, it seemed like something was bothering her.

"You okay?"

"Oh yeah, I'm fine," said Paige. "I'll have your final farewell party present for you a bit later." Paige smiled at TJ and went back to the family room.

TJ got comfortable on the couch and talked with Elizabeth, telling her all about the party.

"Was it like a birthday party, daddy?" she asked.

"Kind of," said TJ. "Except they were wishing me good luck in my new job."

"Did you get presents?" asked Elizabeth.

"No, sweetie. Not all parties have presents."

TJ got the two kids off to bed and took a shower. This was one of those nights he wanted make special, as Paige definitely seemed to be in the mood. He finished the shower, remained naked and climbed into bed. He waited there for what seemed to be 30 minutes and was surprised that Paige had not come up yet. Another 15 minutes passed, and it was already 11pm. Paige was usually up in bed by now.

TJ put shorts on and went downstairs, only to find Paige curled up on the reclining chair in the family room. Instantly irritated, TJ woke Paige up and told her to come on up to bed.

"You still have a gift to give me. You promised," said TJ, trying to make sure this was still going to happen.

"I'm really tired, TJ."

"Fuck," said TJ. "I was really looking forward to this tonight, babe. You can't keep hinting to me it's gonna happen and then it doesn't."

"TJ, can we please do it tomorrow?" TJ took that question in and instantly fell out of the mood on this night. Again, frustrated and angry at Paige, TJ was at a loss for words.

"You'll just have another excuse tomorrow. If you don't want to have sex with me anymore, just fucking tell me."

"Why are you so angry TJ? It's just sex. We can have it any time we want."

"We don't have it, Paige. And any time you hint that it will happen, you come up with stupid excuses for it not to. I'm getting sick and tired of it. And you wonder why some husbands cheat on their wives."

TJ had crossed a line back to that argument from weeks ago that was one of their nastiest.

"What, so if I don't fuck you on demand, you're going to find some skanky woman who will?" Paige wasn't backing down.

"Maybe I will. What do you think of that? Is that what you want me to say? You're treading in dangerous territory here, Paige."

"Is that a threat, TJ? Go ahead. The instant you do, we are done."

"Screw you Paige. I will not be a prisoner in my own marriage. Couples who love each should express it and not use sex as a tool to injure their partner by purposely withholding it."

"I'm just not in the mood tonight, TJ. I don't see what the big deal is. You're making it sound like I'm committing a crime or something. Calm down."

TJ was furious. Paige was doing this on purpose for some reason. His rage at these failed nights of sex was growing in enormity and doing significant damage. But TJ was sure that Paige didn't get how bad it was.

"Go to bed, Paige. I'll see you in the morning." TJ grabbed his pillow and headed to the couch.

"Jesus Christ, TJ. Fine. Come back here and we'll do it. If it's that important. Do what you have to do if that will end this ridiculous argument."

TJ did not respond to Paige and headed for the couch. A few minutes later, he heard the door slam.

TJ Carlson was a man who liked for things to be under control. On this night, he sat on the couch with the lights out, unable to sleep. His relationship with Paige was in serious trouble. The fights were growing in intensity. He was losing control of this part of his life. He was starting a new job, where there was uncertainty.

He sat there; his mind busy. He didn't want to see Paige the next morning. He had nothing to say to her. He wasn't sure he even liked her anymore, much less loved her. It was excruciating. He felt the need to get away again. Not to travel for himself, but to get away. To break free from the stress and tension. To recapture the good feelings that have eluded him in recent months. To be himself again.

TJ was feeling depressed. What am I gonna do, he thought? TJ poured himself a glass of wine and continued sitting there. Drinking the wine and thinking. After his third glass, he finally dozed off.

Chapter 5

Another sleepless night for TJ Carlson. On the couch again. This was becoming a joke, he thought. Couples fight, but this is ridiculous. In the last week alone, he and Paige had gotten into three major arguments. What is happening, he thought.

TJ re-lived the arguments in his mind.

Argument #1 – The Housework

Paige was slamming the plates and silverware on the counter. Very obviously designed to get TJ's attention.

"Now what?" TJ asked Paige.

"You don't do a damn thing in this house anymore. You just sit there, watching TV. Why am I up here doing these dishes?"

"I told you I would do them. Not my fault if you don't have the patience to wait for me to do them." TJ was already fearing where this was heading.

"If I vanished, this place would fall apart in days," said Paige indignantly.

"Well, go ahead and vanish then. You'll be shocked when you come back how in order this place is. You take me for granted, Paige."

"I take you for granted??" Paige was nearly screaming. "You don't appreciate a goddamn thing I do around here. I do everything!!"

"I have a fucking job Paige. I have to make money so we don't have to live on the streets. Do you give a shit about that at all?

Haven't I earned a little rest time in the evenings before I do chores and get the kids ready for bed?"

"Excuses, TJ. On your days off, you do nothing. I feel like a maid."

"Okay, Paige, you're right. I'm a useless piece of shit. I purposely do nothing by design so that you have to do it all. My plan is working perfectly. I'm an evil genius." TJ actually amused by his well-placed use of sarcasm in this argument. "Tell you what, I'll kill myself later so you don't have to deal with my presence any longer. And you can find a guy with your approved level of household chores skill."

"Sarcasm, TJ? Is that the best you can do? I would love to know if you even care about me anymore."

"You started this one, Paige. Yes, I care, but I'm not going to indulge you in a baseless argument. If you don't think I do anything, I can't do anything to change your mind. Even if I got up and did the dishes now, nothing would change. You'd complain about something else again tomorrow. I don't want to waste my time."

"You're a bastard, TJ. "Paige left the rest of the dishes and walked away crying. TJ felt strangely unaffected by this argument. He got up, finished off the dishes, and sat back down. What just happened, he thought.

TJ looked down. "You and me again my friend," said TJ to his couch.

Argument #2 – Other Women

TJ was laughing at a message from Jewel. Nora Martin had been fired by Curtis. She didn't show up for work one day, and then showed up the next without an explanation of the previous day.

Jewel had many theories about what Nora did on her day off that could have gotten her fired.

Paige walked in to the room.

"What are you laughing at, TJ?" she said curiously.

"A message from Jewel. They canned Nora. Finally."

"I'm sorry I never got to meet Jewel. She sounds funny." Paige stared at TJ. "Who is Sophie?"

TJ was shocked at the question. He hadn't mentioned Sophie in any conversation and was wondering how she knew about her.

"She's a friend I met on the trip. We were on an excursion together in Bora Bora. She loved to travel, and we spent some time talking about the places we had been."

"What did you do in her bungalow, TJ?" asked Paige calmly.

"We had a few drinks and talked." This was sounding bad, TJ thought. She doesn't know the truth, that nothing happened. Guilty until proven innocent apparently. "She is a great person Paige. She's from Switzerland. She's a friend. Nothing happened."

"I don't believe you, TJ. She emailed you pictures of the two of you in her bungalow. You gave her our email address? What did you think I would think if this strange woman messaged you and I saw it? Especially with the two of you alone in her bungalow. Put yourself in my shoes, TJ. What would you be thinking?"

Paige had a point. This looked bad. He never thought Sophie would email him. They had other ways of keeping in touch.

"Paige, I swear on my life that nothing happened in that bungalow. I'll take a lie detector test, swear in front of priest, whatever it takes." TJ was really trying hard to sound sincere. Paige wasn't buying it.

"TJ, knowing that this is the type of thing you do on your trips, I don't think I'm okay with you traveling alone anymore." Paige looked sad.

"Fine, Paige. It looks bad. It's probably a cliché for me to sit here and deny everything. But nothing happened. Sophie knew about you. She knew that was a joint email address. Why would she send something like that if we had done more than just talked?"

"Why didn't you tell me about her? Honestly, if you had explained that up front, I'd have been okay with it. You have so many female friends TJ. I'm used to it. It's when you start to hide things from me that I get concerned. Do you understand?"

"Yes, I do," TJ said in a low, defeated voice. "Sorry. You've been sensitive about a lot of things recently. I just decided not to talk about her so you wouldn't wonder about her."

"So, it's better that I found out this way?" asked Paige angrily.

"Okay, I get your point. I'm sorry." TJ was uncomfortable.

"Any other secrets you'd like to share?" asked Paige.

TJ thought for a split second whether or not to bring up Erita. He decided against it. No good can come from it. Plus, there was no evidence left there. They did not exchange email addresses and weren't keeping in touch.

"No, Paige."

"Okay. I'll take your word for it. I won't be as understanding next time." Paige left for the bedroom.

Shit, thought TJ. I feel like I've been caught cheating when I haven't cheated. TJ also figured this wasn't the last he would hear about it. He sent a message to Sophie asking her not to use that email address anymore.

You and me again, couch, thought TJ. TJ was considering investing in a sofa bed for as much time as he was spending on that couch.

Argument #3 – The Sex Life

TJ was getting used to sex becoming a rare commodity between he and Paige. She actually didn't seem to want it anymore. If TJ didn't get upset about it, they would rarely discuss it. But it was becoming a lot for TJ to have to accept in this dynamic. He was determined to understand why.

"Paige," asked TJ as he walked into the family room and sat down on the chair, "can we talk about something?"

"Sure," said Paige. What's up?"

"Do you find me desirable anymore?"

"What kind of question is that?" asked Paige with a laugh.

"A serious one," said TJ sternly.

"Why do you ask?"

"Paige, we rarely have sex any more. You don't seem interested at all or even want it. I need it. I need us to have a fun and exciting sex life. It's gotten really frustrating."

Paige was quiet for a minute as she thought about how to answer this.

"TJ, I'm sorry. I'm just not in the mood that much these days. Apparently, you are always in the mood. Sorry I can't keep up."

TJ didn't like this response. "You didn't answer my question, Paige. And what do you mean I'm always in the mood? You say that like it's a defect that I have."

"You're too sensitive about this. Just because I'm not in the mood doesn't mean I don't love you. We've had a lot of sex in the past. Just, after the kids, I think that desire has left me somewhat."

"Can't you see how this is frustrating me? Every night of failed attempts at sex? I get angry, Paige. This is something that is important to me. I want you to understand that. I don't think you do." TJ was hoping he could achieve a breakthrough on this topic. It had been festering for too long.

"I can see that, and it bothers me that you get so upset. You treat sex like it's the most important thing we have between the two of us. Like if we don't have that, we have nothing."

"It's something, Paige. It's part of our life together. You realize that's the one thing that we both mutually enjoyed? Honestly, we don't have many other common interests. I can't get you excited about travel, we spend each evening in separate rooms, and you don't care for any of my friends or my family. If not for sex and the kids, what else do we have keeping us together at this point?"

Paige was on the verge of tears. "Sounds like you regret marrying me, TJ. I'm sorry I can't live up to your standards anymore."

"Dammit, Paige, you've turned this around on me again. That's not fair. My question to you was about our sex life. If you're done with sex, just tell me so I can plan ahead."

"Plan ahead," asked Paige. "What does that mean? Plan ahead. Plan for what?"

"Whatever I need to," said TJ. "I have needs. If you will refuse to take care of those needs, I'll do what I need to."

"You already have ways of taking care of those needs."

"That's not what I'm talking about. It's the closeness, the intimacy, the lovemaking. That's what I miss and that's what I need."

"Do you still love me, TJ?" Paige looked seriously at TJ, waiting for this answer.

TJ paused for a minute. This pause may as well have taken a year. It was all Paige needed to see.

"Very well, TJ. You can't give me an immediate answer on that question, that tells me what I need to know." Paige pulled out a bag and started packing some clothes. "I'm going to Kylie's. Good luck on finding someone who can give you what I can't. Why don't you message one of your bimbos or fly Sophie in from Switzerland?"

TJ didn't say another word. He watched Paige pack and didn't give her the satisfaction of a response to that. This would blow over, thought TJ. But the incremental damage of these arguments was piling up.

So, there he was, on the couch again. Thinking that Paige may come home tonight, he just defaulted back to the couch. Another sleepless night. Re-living these three arguments didn't really give TJ any additional insight as to why they are happening. He just knew that he wished they could stop. He didn't see things ending well with he and Paige. Tonight's argument about sex opened up some deeper sentiments and differences between the two that may prove to be irreconcilable.

TJ poured a glass of wine. Wine and my couch, thought TJ. Two friends I can count on.

"Good morning, TJ," said Lynne Thompson, one of TJ's new co-workers. "Mary and I wanted to have a quick chat with you."

"Sure," said TJ. Lynne Thompson and Mary Fernandez were two of the people at his new company in charge of systems. Always looking for better and more efficient ways to do things, TJ enjoyed interacting with them. They usually were talking about a new idea or a new product they wanted to check out. This meant meeting new vendors and networking. Mary and Lynne were always traveling. Secretly, TJ was hoping they would pull him in to their world and give him a chance to work with them.

"TJ, we need to know if you're open to do a little traveling," started Lynne. "Mary and I can't be in three places at once, and from what we hear, you're open to do a little bit of traveling."

"Was it my non-stop stories about these places I've been? Sorry, I should have been subtler," laughed TJ.

"Will you be available to go to Las Vegas and Miami in the next few weeks? One week at each place. We are looking at two vendors to replace one of our mortgage software systems. It's right up your alley."

"I'm in," said TJ excitedly.

"Great!" said Mary. "There's also a potential for a site visit to India in Delhi. Interested?"

TJ couldn't say yes quickly enough. India was one of those exotic locations he has dreamed about going to. The Taj Mahal was on his list of must-see's in his lifetime.

"You've made my day, ladies!" said TJ.

TJ was happy to know that he'd get to go back on the road again. Once again, thoughts immediately turned to how Paige would react. Not well, he assumed. But at this point, who cares. This was for work, not pleasure. And if she didn't like it, too bad. TJ's feelings for Paige were at an all-time low. Not sure how to deal with her anymore, they basically stayed out of each other's way now. These trips would be a welcome relief.

It had been awhile since TJ and Jim Keller had spoken. Jim and Carrie Keller were a cute couple. The kind that still held hands when they sat together. The kind of couple that looked still in love, and that still had a strong connection. TJ was sitting in Jim's living room. The purpose of his visit wasn't really to hang out. TJ needed a friend to talk to about his recent troubles with his marriage.

Carrie Keller's previous marriage was a disaster. Married to a scumbag who ended up beating her, she had to have her trust earned. Fortunately, Jim wouldn't hurt a fly, much less ever consider hitting a woman. Carrie and Paige talked. Carrie knew full well that TJ and Paige were having issues. But she was hearing Paige's version only. TJ would have a hard time gaining sympathy from Carrie, he figured. But he wasn't there to get sympathy from Carrie.

Jim Keller was TJ's best friend. But he too seemed none too eager to hear TJ out at the onset. This was the same guy, thought TJ, who in Ireland asked him what *he* could do to make it right.

TJ decided to get right to the point with Jim.

"I'm here to talk to you, as my best friend. I'm not sure what to do anymore. Paige doesn't seem interested in the marriage or in me."

Carrie chimed in. "TJ, she's saying the exact same things about you. Except she's not the one meeting other people in different parts of the world and keeping secrets."

"Carrie, it's okay," said Jim. "Let's hear him out."

"Wait a minute," said TJ defensively. "Hear me out? Do you both think I'm the one to blame in all this?"

"It looks bad, TJ. You going away. The whole issue with Sophie. From our vantage point, it kinda looks like you're the problem." Jim put his arm around Carrie. "We consider both of you friends. And I'm friends with you to the point where I can tell you if I think you're wrong. And in this case, I......we, think you are wrong."

"You know Jim......I didn't come to your house to be judged by both of you. I came here to talk to you as a friend. As *my* friend. One that has been your best friend for years. I need to confide in someone. There's my side to this story as well. Except you don't seem to want to hear it."

"I don't think we need to hear it," said Jim. "She is struggling with you gone all the time, and you seem to live it up when you're gone. I know it…. I've been with you twice."

"Me traveling is not the issue here. Is that what she's saying? This started long before that." TJ dug in for this unexpected argument with his friends. "What would you do one day if Carrie decided she no longer wanted sex? Or you fought about every stupid thing? And neither of you were willing to give in?"

"She's saying that you have become cold, argumentative and distant," said Carrie.

"So, you're taking that as the truth of the situation. Listen guys, if you are firmly entrenched on her side of this and not willing to hear me out, then I'm just going to leave. I just needed someone to talk to."

"TJ, come on, you need to give a little here," said Jim. "It takes two to Tango, and sometimes you have to swallow your pride and give in. You're not going to win a fight with her. If you choose to fight, you lose. Anyone, not just us, looking at your situation will look at you as the one who has to make this right."

"I'm going to go," said TJ. "Thanks for wasting my time. Friends."

TJ walked to his car and Jim followed him out. In TJ's mind, this friendship just ended and he was devastated. He couldn't believe it had come to this. His relationship with Paige crumbling and now his friendship with Jim on the rocks.

"TJ," yelled Jim. "Hang out for a bit longer. Let's just change topics."

"Forget it," said TJ dismissively. "You both proved what kind of friends you are. I would never have done that to you, Jim. If you had come to me with a similar problem, I'm on your side, no matter what. I wouldn't judge and I wouldn't lecture. You two so thoroughly offended me today by not even offering a willingness to LISTEN. That's all I wanted. Take care, Jim. You and Carrie have a great life. I'll no longer be a part of it."

Jim watched as TJ drove away from his driveway. A few minutes later, TJ's phone showed a text from Jim.

Sorry you felt that way. Hope everything works out.

That's the best he could do, thought TJ. TJ deleted the message. A lump formed in TJ's throat as he drove. Is it me, he thought, starting to question his now short temper and disintegrating relationships? Am I causing this? I just want to be happy. And no one seems to care.

"You have everything?" asked Paige.

"Yup. Only there for 5 days, so shouldn't need much more than this. Kids, anything special you want from Las Vegas?"

"Money!" yelled Steven

"A white tiger!" said Elizabeth sweetly, but excitedly.

"Money, a white tiger……. what about you Paige?

"Just come back in one piece," said Paige.

TJ got in his car and drove to the airport. The feeling coming back to him when he's about to fly away to somewhere fun and exciting. This was mostly business, but Mary told him to block off a couple evenings to do Las Vegas right. He'd have a 'guide'…. a girl named Nikki. Nikki had messaged TJ about potential shows he might want to see or hotels he wanted to see. TJ didn't commit. He let Nikki know to just tell him about them when he got there.

Nikki Nester phoned in to Mary Fernandez's office. Nikki was a cute, bubbly 22-year-old contact of Mary's at the vendor site who everyone liked dealing with. Mary asked Nikki to make sure TJ Carlson had a great time in Las Vegas. Let him tell you what he wants to do and then help him make it happen, she was told.

"Oh my God," said Nikki, "what if he wants to marry me while he's here at one of those chapels?"

"Then make it happen," laughed Mary. "Just make sure he has fun."

"Oh, I will," said Nikki, smiling. Nikki knew Las Vegas like the back of her hand. Mary knew she could trust her to make sure TJ enjoyed himself.

The first three days of his stay were all business. Time in the evenings were put aside to mingle with management at that vendor site and talk over dinner and drinks. Day four, however, TJ was going to cut short and head to the strip with Nikki.

"TJ, hi it's Nikki," went the voice message. "Let me know what you want to see tomorrow. Call me at the number I just called you from."

TJ thought about it. Suddenly, an idea came to him that reminded him of his time in Sydney. He wanted to have a little adult fun. He called Nikki.

"Hi Nikki, it's TJ."

"TJ! Nice to finally talk to you. What are we doing tonight?"

"What do you recommend? And keep in mind, I'm open to anything. Help me experience Las Vegas the right way."

"Then you need to see naked girls," said Nikki, matter of factly. "I'll get us tickets for two of the more famous nudey shows here. This will be fun!"

TJ was excited. This will be fun, he thought. And he was glad he ended up with a guide like Nikki, who wasn't the least bit shy about offering it. I'm sure she's making some guy happy, thought TJ.

TJ and Nikki had a blast at the two shows. The shows were tastefully done, but featured a lot of gratuitous nudity. Nikki dropped TJ off at the hotel.

"TJ, I'm not sure what else you want to experience here, but I'll make sure you can do what you want. But if you want to do anything more adult than that, I can let you know how to do it and I'll leave you alone tomorrow night."

TJ thought seriously about it. Not interested in prostitutes, he thought. He was repulsed at the thought of even touching one, considering how many other men probably had before. Assuming that's what she meant, he declined. "I would love to go see a comedy show, Nikki."

"Oh okay. That will be fun. I thought you might be interested in the strip clubs or brothels. All legal here."

TJ was suddenly interested. But once again fought the urge. "Nah, comedy will be fine."

"Okay, TJ, have a good sleep. See you tomorrow." Nikki drove away and TJ headed back to his room.

You know, thought TJ, it's good to have options. I'm not giving up on Paige, but if she continues to deny me, I will not deny myself this kind of fun any longer. Having rationalized the decision he made to his satisfaction, TJ went to sleep.

"Did you go to the Strip?" asked Paige. "My friends and I went there once. Saw Thunder from Down Under. A bunch of naked dancing Australian guys."

"Yes, my guide, Nikki took me there last night. She insisted I see a few shows with naked girls in it. This company really knows how to entertain a guest."

"Hmmm….," said Paige. "A 22-year-old female guide and a bunch of naked girls. Sounds like I had nothing to worry about on this trip." Paige laughed. She seemed in a good mood. "See you tomorrow, TJ. The kids are excited about their gifts." TJ had gotten fake money and a stuffed white tiger. It's what they wanted, he thought to himself and smiled.

"How many more trips like this, TJ?" asked Paige, as TJ packed to go to Miami on his visit to the other site vendor.

"What's wrong? You seemed perfectly fine when I was in Las Vegas a few weeks ago."

"I'm just tired of it. There are times when I don't feel like you live here anymore."

TJ assured Paige – "I have this one, and then a potential to India, and that's it."

"India?? Good lord. Here we go again." Paige walked out of the room as TJ finished packing.

Not gonna engage, thought TJ. Not worth it. Let it just calm down and fade away.

TJ finished packing and got himself ready to go. He said goodbye to Steven and Elizabeth. He then yelled goodbye to Paige. Paige did not respond. He knew she could hear him. He said goodbye again louder, knowing full well she could hear him. No response. TJ walked out the door and drove to the airport.

Miami proved to be a little more business oriented than Las Vegas. No guide, like Nikki, to maximize his time. TJ had to look for his own fun in the evenings. He was content to stay at the hotel the first few nights. But he got bored. On a whim, he looked up massage parlors in the area. He denied himself the massage in Sydney, but thought one might be what the doctor ordered. Plus, he knows the type of "additional service" provided by the one in Sydney was illegal here in the states. Just a good relaxing massage, thought TJ.

He found one called Sunshine Spa, and made an appointment. He arrived to a place that didn't quite look like a professional establishment, more like a makeshift place with "Sunshine Spa" taped to the front of the building. TJ walked in, unsure what he was getting himself into.

He was met by an older lady, who escorted him to a room. "Get undressed and lie face down on the table."

TJ did as instructed. This was his first massage, and he didn't quite know what to expect. A young and very attractive girl walked in the door. TJ had not removed his underwear, assuming that he had to leave those on.

"You can remove those, sir. I'll use a towel." She left the room and TJ got naked and laid back down on the table.

She returned a few minutes later. "My name is Annabelle," she said, making small talk.

"I'm TJ."

"TJ, do you like it hard, medium or soft?" asked Annabelle.

TJ laughed to himself. What exactly did she mean, here? Ah, right, the massage. "Medium," said TJ.

Annabelle gave TJ a wonderful massage for the next 40 minutes on his back, legs, and to his surprise, his ass cheeks. TJ wasn't expecting that, and it got him somewhat excited. In an obvious way. Annabelle ignored that, and TJ became less concerned about it. Although now, he was secretly hoping this might end with "additional services."

Annabelle asked TJ to turn over. Still sporting a highly noticeable erection, Annabelle covered him over with a towel and massaged his chest, stomach and legs, deftly avoiding TJ's erect penis. Annabelle smiled at him as she massaged. They got to talking. TJ found himself talking about Paige and his sexual frustrations with her. Not realizing the irony of talking about his sex life problems while getting his body rubbed by a young girl while having a hard cock.

"Sir, one day she will realize what she misses and will want you again. You look very good. She is lucky."

"Thanks Annabelle," said TJ. TJ was about to bust. He really wanted Annabelle to relieve him now. The massage had turned him on in a big way.

"Annabelle," continued TJ, "Is there any chance you can………" TJ stopped as he glanced down at his erect penis.

"Not allowed, sir. I'll get in trouble. I'm sorry." With that, Annabelle informed TJ the massage was done.

"It's okay. I've never had one before, so I wasn't sure. This was great. Thank you."

"Thank you, sir," said Annabelle. "I hope to see you again."

Back at the hotel room that night, TJ laid in bed wondering about the experience. He really liked it, but was embarrassed by his behavior with Annabelle. She probably deals with many creeps, and hears that question a lot. TJ knew he wanted to experience that again. Could be a good alternative to dealing with his frustrations with Paige, he rationalized. It's not cheating…. just a massage.

TJ still had friends he could talk to. The episode with Jim and Carrie notwithstanding, he needed to talk it out with someone. He called Vera.

"Things gotten any better?" asked Vera.

"Not really," said TJ. "It's pretty bad, actually."

"It's noticeable. Paige sent me a message a few days ago. Asking me something about a piece of furniture she saw in one of my pictures. She didn't mention anything about you. I asked her how everything was going."

"What did she say?" asked TJ, curiously.

"She said everything was great with her. She talked about the kids. Didn't mention anything about you. I thought it was strange."

"I'm not surprised. It's as if none of this is any big deal to her. Maybe she thinks I'll just stop fighting."

"You need to do something soon, TJ. Either talk this out with her or end it. Do what's best for you. You can't go on like this. It's not healthy."

Vera was right. TJ was leaving Miami the next day and heading home. The time was coming for TJ and Paige to talk it out or fight it out.

TJ walked in the door after arriving home and could sense the vibe was not good.   Elizabeth was on the couch, looking sad.

"What's wrong, sweetie?" asked TJ.

"Mommy yelled at me," said Elizabeth. "Because I didn't eat all my dinner."

Steven was in his room. Again, unusual, as he is normally on the computer.

"Paige?" yelled TJ. "I'm home."

"Can you come to the family room, TJ?" yelled Paige back.

TJ walked in to the family room. "What's going on?"

"The entire time you were in Miami, you called me one time. When you go away, I have no idea what you do but it's obvious we are not your top priority here anymore."

"Where is this coming from? Here we go again, another argument. I'm getting sick of this. I'm not doing it." TJ was irritated but calm. "You are always my top priority. Making sure you and the kids are secure and taken care of. You don't seem to appreciate me for that at all."

"Whatever, TJ. We can't seem to appreciate each other anymore. Maybe you'd be happy if I just vanished and you never saw me again."

"That's it, Paige. This argument, this stupid argument, is over. I'm not indulging you on this. It's as if you're provoking me into something here and I'm not taking the bait. You can wait another day to see me."

TJ grabbed his suitcase and started walking out the door.

"Where the hell are you going?" yelled Paige.

"Out!" screamed TJ. "Don't worry about me. Sit here and wallow in your self-pity. I hope you enjoy it."

TJ walked out the door and to his car. Absolutely furious with Paige, again, he wanted to cool off. He headed to a local hotel to stay the night. He would try again the next day. Maybe whatever was possessing Paige would be gone by then.

Chapter 6

"You ready for India?" asked Leanne Davidson, TJ's new boss.

"Without a doubt!" said TJ.

TJ had been waiting for confirmation that he'd be taking this trip to Delhi, India, and now he had it. A week in India, a dream come true. So much to do, he thought. Visa application, shots, figuring out how he would get to Taj Mahal and learning what to do and what not to do. Especially what to eat and what not to eat.

He wanted this trip badly. He needed it. To give himself that ever elusive happiness that this kind of travel gives him.

TJ never knew what to expect any more with Paige. There were good days and bad. TJ had gone to a tactic of non-engagement in arguments. It seemed to work in preventing huge blowups, but he always sensed that was a temporary delay. The big one would come, he thought. Probably soon. Maybe even tonight.......as he will break the official news to Paige about his trip to India.

"It's official.... I'm going to India," said TJ to Paige.

"OK," she replied. "Please don't get sick when you're there. Just about everyone I know who's gone there has gotten seriously sick."

"They will give me some medication for that ahead of time. You okay with me being gone, again?"

"It is what it is, TJ. Just be careful."

It was an emotionless conversation. No matter what Paige thought, he was still going. He was happy that there wasn't any drama involved.

TJ arrived in India after midnight. A harrowing adventure at his connecting flight in London nearly had him still sitting in London waiting for the next day's flight to Delhi. Good fortune stepped in and got him there safely and on time. The fog was dense in Delhi on this morning, leaving the drive to his hotel devoid of any view other than fog. The Indian driver did not speak English well, so the drive was quiet and somewhat boring. TJ was happy anyway. He was in India and was not only going to get a chance to see the Taj Mahal, but would also be entertained each day by the team in Delhi through city tours.

TJ didn't sleep much after getting to the hotel. For once, TJ slept like a baby on the flight from London to Delhi. Business class seats, a few glasses of wine and escaping the chaos that was London Heathrow contributed to TJ finally getting some rest. Channel surfing, he couldn't help but enjoy some of the local programming, even though he didn't understand a word. He had a free day the next day before going to the site. He was to be met by two people named Neha Ganesh and Raj Patel. They would take him out to a famous Hindu temple, some sites in the city and then to dinner.

Remembering advice from others who had been, TJ was very careful where it concerned the water. Even when taking a shower, but especially when brushing his teeth. TJ was determined not to become another victim of "Delhi Belly" and get explosive diarrhea or whatever comes along with that. Unsure of what Indian food he would like, he also packed a number of snacks that could end up serving as dinner if needed.

Neha and Raj showed up that next day at 10:00am. Raj was a young guy in his late 20's. He enthusiastically grabbed TJ's hand and shook it, welcoming him to India. He seemed to be sporting a non-stop smile. He was a handsome guy, nicely dressed, but wearing an unmistakably large amount of cologne. Neha was dressed in a Sari, and was strikingly beautiful with an amazing smile. She was tall and thin, and her eyes were a caramel color. She caught TJ off guard a little, and TJ felt a bit of an attraction already without her saying a word. She extended her hand to TJ and offered a welcome.

Raj laid out the plans for the day. Delhi had many attractions, so they would hit a few each day. Today, the main attraction was the Akshardham Temple, a large and ornate structure built in honor of Lord Swaminarayan. TJ was looking forward to learning the history of this temple, and based on the pictures he was looking at, seeing something that impressive. After the temple, would be lunch and then a few more stops, including the Parliament building and the Red Fort.

Raj was doing most of the talking while Neha was quiet. "My friend, what do you think of India so far," asked Raj.

"I've noticed that there's been constant fog it seems here," said TJ.

Raj laughed. "That's not fog, my friend! That's smog. Pollution. Delhi has a problem with that."

Wow, thought TJ. Nasty. Hopefully it wouldn't be like that every day.

"Some people wear a mask over their mouth and nose. Especially visitors from Japan and China," said Neha softly.

"Well, regardless of the fog, or smog, I'm glad to be here. That temple looks beautiful."

The three of them visited and spent a few hours at Akshardham Temple. TJ was dismayed that he was not allowed to take pictures. What a bonanza that would have been, he thought. During that time, TJ noticed the dynamic between Neha and Raj.

Any time Neha would start talking, Raj would chime in and finish the conversation. May be a cultural thing, thought TJ. But he wanted to talk to Neha. She seemed very sweet. He would look for that opportunity at some point in the day.

He got that opportunity at a late lunch. Raj was pulled onto a business call and stepped away.

"Neha, your outfit is very beautiful," said TJ.

"Thank you. I have many outfits like this. I like wearing them. They are very comfortable."

"I can't thank you both enough for taking me around today. I feel like an honored guest."

"I'm sorry about Raj," said Neha. "He's very anxious to make a good impression on you. Maybe too anxious."

"It's okay. You both have made an excellent impression on me already. Tell him he doesn't have to try so hard, and maybe tone it down a little on the cologne." TJ laughed as Neha did an imitation of Raj interrupting her.

They finished the day and dropped TJ off at his hotel.

"We'll be taking you to Taj Mahal on Saturday, TJ," said Raj. "We'll leave early in the morning so we can get back that afternoon. I have something fun planned for us in Delhi. Just for the boys." Neha rolled her eyes, while Raj flashed that mischievous smile.

"Sounds great, guys! I'll see you at the office tomorrow."

The week of work in the bag, today was Taj Mahal day. Neha and Raj would be there in about an hour. TJ had tried on this trip to stay in better touch with Paige. She was actually excited for him that he was getting to see Taj Mahal. TJ cleaned up, ate breakfast and went to the lobby to wait for his two friends. During the week, he had a standing lunch date with Neha and was getting to know her. He had a standing afternoon tea break with Raj, and he had grown on TJ as well. More global friends, thought TJ.

His friendship with Neha was becoming special to him. Neha was single, and while searching for a boyfriend, was not searching very hard. "I'm very picky" she would always say. She wants an Indian man who is free to choose his own bride. "I've had men I've liked, but their marriages are prearranged already." He was sharing his frustrations about his own relationship with Neha, but not Raj. TJ felt very comfortable talking to her.

The drive to Taj Mahal took about 2 hours. The tour of the site was helped immensely by a guide who spoke both English and Hindi. TJ was really impressed at the site of the Taj Mahal. I have seen this in pictures, thought TJ, but it is so immaculate in person. The Taj Mahal dominated the view once they made their way through some initial structures. The guide was a young, eager-to-please fellow with remarkably good English. Very adept at taking pictures, he ensured there was no angle of the Taj Mahal not being captured for TJ, Neha and Raj. The closer they got to the Taj Mahal, the bigger the bounty of beautiful shots and angles they were getting of this magnificent structure. Priceless day, thought TJ. Another one for the record books.

On the way out of Taj Mahal, they approached a large crowd of people. Neha grabbed TJ's hand and held it as they waded through the people. She smiled at TJ. "Keeping you safe, TJ." TJ appreciated that.

They stopped for an early dinner at a restaurant close by. TJ noticed a man sitting next to a building on the corner with a large snake. "You want a picture with that snake?" asked Raj.

"Hell yeah," said TJ. "It's not going to kill me, is it?"

"No way," said Raj. "It's either drugged, drunk or half dead. You're fine."

The three approached the man who smiled big and had TJ sit next to him. The man put the snake around TJ's neck, and then put a hat on TJ's head. Raj and Neha were laughing as they took picture after picture. TJ was sure this was looking really cool. TJ thanked the man and gave him a nice donation.

"I have to see these pictures," TJ said to Neha.

"Sure," she said handing TJ the camera.

TJ looked at the pictures and suddenly noticed something sticking out of the hat. No way, he thought. Another snake. A cobra. TJ was shocked.

"Is that a fucking cobra on my head??" asked TJ incredulously.

"Hahaha – yes, my friend. You didn't know it. It makes the pictures look better. You didn't seem scared at all." Raj was getting a good laugh out of it. Neha smiled sweetly at TJ. "You're funny, TJ," she said. "Those are great pictures you can show all your friends."

They arrived back in Delhi and Raj dropped Neha off at her house. "Okay, boy's time," Neha said with a laugh. "Keep him out of trouble, Raj, please. He's our guest."

Raj started driving again, but wasn't hinting where they were going.

"So, what's the plan, Raj?"

"My friend, I'm taking you to a Spa. Beautiful Indian girls there. You will get a special treat."

TJ was instantly intrigued by what lay ahead. He didn't ask Raj for any details. Let it be a surprise, he thought. They arrived at the

Spa and Raj talked to what TJ assumed was a good friend. "See you in a few hours, my friend."

With that, Raj's friend introduced two gorgeous Indian girls to TJ and Raj, who were escorted to separate rooms. Once in the room, the masseuse asked TJ to remove his clothes. She never left the room. TJ stripped naked and laid down on the table.

The masseuse gave him a really sensual, slow massage that was turning TJ on quite a bit. This time it was different than his experience in Miami. The lady would occasionally reach under TJ's stomach and grab on to his cock, stroking it a few times. She asked TJ to turn over. TJ, fully erect, laid there and watched as she climbed on top of him and straddled his legs. She drizzled oil on to his cock, and then stroked it until TJ came. She cleaned TJ up and then gave him a foot massage. Only an hour had passed. What for the next hour, he thought?

The masseuse continued to massage TJ's legs. She stopped and removed her top, revealing perfect breasts. She went behind TJ's head and began to massage TJ's chest down to his stomach, ensuring her breasts pressed into TJ's face. After 40 more minutes, she sat next to TJ, put TJ's hand on her breast and gave TJ another hand job. TJ was exhausted afterwards. This was an experience beyond what he could have imagined. "Your friend treated you and asked that I take good care of you. Are you satisfied?"

"Oh my God, yes," said TJ. "That was incredible. I've never experienced anything like it. Thank you. You were wonderful."

Raj met TJ in the front lobby area. "What did you think, my friend?" He gave a big laugh. "A memorable day in India for you."

"To say the least," said TJ.

"Tomorrow, Neha will accompany you. Enjoy the day with her.
I'll be busy, which is why I wanted to take you out tonight."

"Great, thanks man. Awesome day."

"See you again my friend," said Raj as he dropped TJ off at his
hotel.

TJ was extremely relaxed after the massage and the busy day. He
fell asleep nearly instantly. He did not have any pangs of guilt
about what had just transpired.

The phone rang in TJ's room. "Miss Neha here for you, sir."

"Oh, good God……. can you send her up to my room?"

TJ had overslept. Neha knocked on the door and TJ let her in.
"I'm so sorry, Neha. I slept in apparently. Let me get cleaned up
and we can head out."

TJ and Neha took a long walk from the hotel to a park. Neha did
not have a car, so they were going to stay close by to the hotel. TJ
relayed the experience of the previous night, omitting some
details.

"Oh, Raj loves going to that place. He really likes the girls there. I
think they do sexual things to him." Neha looked a bit repulsed at
the thought.

"Yep," said TJ, "I have to admit that's what he arranged for me."

"Did you like it," asked Neha. "I'm sure you did…. you're a guy."

"I did. Mostly for the reasons I told you. I'm not getting that from
my wife."

"That's a shame," said Neha. "A wife should not withhold that
from her husband."

"It's very frustrating," said TJ.

TJ learned about Neha's family and friends, about her childhood growing up outside of Delhi and her love of animals. He definitely felt a strong bond with Neha.

"I hope we can keep in touch after I leave, Neha," said TJ.

"I'll message you often, TJ. I think we'll be great friends."

At the end of the day, Neha walked TJ back to his hotel. "Goodbye, TJ. Please visit India again. And tell me how everything works out with Paige. She doesn't know what she has in you." Neha gave TJ a hug and walked away to grab a taxi.

TJ's visit to India had been quite an experience. And two new lifelong friends, thought TJ.

With India now behind him, TJ was back in the office. All was not going well. While he was in India, TJ had been assigned a new boss. A lady named Jan Carver. TJ did not know her and had never met her. She worked at a different office. One week into being back, and TJ had not heard a word from her. TJ's mindset was not a good one either. This job was not all he had hoped. He spent a good portion of his day bored and with no work. He had a new Karen and Jewel tandem in Anna and Becky, two co-workers he befriended not long after he got there.

Anna and Becky noticed a change in TJ over the last week. He seemed distant, aloof. His mind wasn't fully there. On some days, he simply left the office early without telling anyone. Strange, they thought. And not like him at all.

"Do you think something happened to him in India?" asked Anna.

"Not sure. It's strange. Should we talk to him about it?" responded Becky.

"I don't think so. I don't want to pry. But if others start talking about him, he needs to know."

TJ not only did not have any passion for this job if it didn't involve getting shipped off to foreign lands, he honestly stopped caring about what happened to him there. If they fire me, he thought, I hope there's a severance that comes along with it. Stress was beginning to show on TJ. He felt like his world was "out there." Not stuck here in another thankless job, toiling day in and day out to please higher ups who didn't deserve it. Between home, friends and work, it was a toxic brew that he was swallowing. He couldn't control anything about his life anymore, he felt. Experiencing what he could only imagine was depression, his thoughts were growing increasingly negative. The only positivity he could pull off involved his kids. Keeping it together for Steven and Elizabeth was of paramount importance. Thankfully, he still had the good sense to not project it on to them.

The next day, Anna and Becky watched TJ closely. He seemed completely out of it and not plugged in to what was going on.

"Let's go talk to him," said Anna.

The two girls walked over to TJ, who perked up.

"Are you okay?" asked Becky.

"You've seemed really distracted recently," added Anna. "I hope everything's okay. We are worried about you."

"Let me ask you guys something……does Jan ever talk to you?" TJ looked squarely at the two girls. "Because I have yet to hear from her. I literally have nothing to do. I've handed my other stuff off."

"She does," answered Becky. "But it may take some time to get to know her."

"Well, until she reaches out to me, I'm honestly clueless about what I should be doing. I've called her. No response. I've emailed her. No response. Who is this woman?"

"She'll be visiting this site next week. You'll surely get to meet her then," said Anna.

"Good," said TJ. "It will be about time. Between work and home, I think I'm losing it."

"Can we ask what's going on at home?" asked Anna.

"It's a long story," started TJ, "and one I can summarize in one sentence. Wife and I aren't getting along."

"Sorry to hear that, TJ."

"Nobody's problem but my own. I feel completely defeated. She tries to start arguments, and I don't even fight for myself anymore. All just to avoid having to deal with the fight. Makes me feel weak."

"Everyone deserves to be happy, TJ," said Becky. "Go out and find your happiness. Even if it's not with her. You only live once. Don't bury yourself too early."

Becky's words resonated with TJ. He wasn't happy. He was only happy when he traveled. He was two completely different people. A self-confident man who had no problems making friends whenever he traveled, and a depressed shell of a man at home and work.

"Thanks Becky. I'll be fine. Just need to work through it." TJ got up. "I need to head home. Not feeling well."

TJ left and walked out the door. "Not good," said Becky to Anna.

Jan Carver finally showed up at the site and introduced herself to TJ. TJ was unimpressed with this woman. She didn't seem to have a decent clue. TJ had already formed first opinions considering she hadn't even bothered to talk to him at all. She asked TJ about his background. TJ gave a halfhearted response and glossed over a lot of details.

Jan kept the meeting short. She left the meeting still leaving TJ not quite sure what he was supposed to be working on. As Jan left, TJ was going to ask Jan what she'd like him to be doing. But he stopped himself. He wasn't sure why. The old TJ would have tried to impress a new boss by at least appearing motivated. This new TJ didn't seem to care. The non-relationship between he and Jan wasn't so bad after all, thought TJ. It's like they are paying me for nothing here.

"Did you meet her finally? What did you think?" asked Anna.

"Honestly, I'm not impressed at all. I can't fathom why I was moved under her. I was doing fine with Leanne. This sucks big time,"

"Yeah, but what are you going to do?" asked Becky.

"I don't know," said TJ. "This is unbearable."

"I'm guessing you aren't gonna hang around here much longer, are you?" asked Anna.

TJ agreed. He really thought the answer to his work problems was to leave his last job to take this one. But he felt even more alone and useless at this job. I'm not in a good place, thought TJ. And I don't seem to have the ability to pull myself out of this funk. Very worrisome. For the very first time, TJ wondered if he should seek out help. He didn't like this loss of control in his life.

A byproduct of the timing of the switch to Jan was that it was close to review time. Jan would be giving TJ his review. This should be interesting, he thought. She barely knows me; how can she give me a review.

Jan arrived at the site that day and was sitting in the office waiting for TJ.

"Come on in, TJ. Have a seat," said Jan. "This will be quick. I've gathered feedback from the other managers and peers, and all would agree that your performance has been sub-standard to this point."

"Seriously?" asked TJ, stunned by that opening comment. "Leanne gave me rave reviews when she did my exit interview. In fairness, you haven't been able to witness my work to form a good judgment."

"TJ, your work lately is what's driving this. People are saying you aren't really doing anything."

"You haven't assigned me anything," said TJ, feeling his anger grow. Watch yourself, he thought.

"You're a senior manager, TJ. I shouldn't have to assign you anything. You should be seeking out work."

"Okay, fine. My fault then. Sub-standard it is."

"TJ, is everything okay? You really seem to be disturbed about something. I know the signs. I've been around long enough."

"Nothing I want to talk about, Jan. I'm sorry, I think we've gotten off on the wrong footing." TJ was trying to turn this around.

"TJ, you are on Performance Monitoring. If after 3 months, there's no improvement, we will have no choice but to terminate you." Jan indicated that was the end of the review.

TJ got up and walked out of the office and sat back down at his desk. Unable to focus and very angry at the review, he stared blankly ahead. My fault, he thought. I didn't ask for work. Of course, they will notice that. Anna and Becky looked at TJ, but chose to leave him alone. TJ got lost in thought. I hope something gets better soon, or I don't know what I'll do, he thought.

"My review was awful," said TJ to Paige as he poured his third glass of wine.

"Drowning your sorrows?" asked Paige.

"Kinda," said TJ.

"This is the second straight job that you're having these issues with. I hope our issues aren't affecting your work too."

TJ was surprised at that comment. "Of course, they are impacting my work. Why wouldn't they."

"I'm sorry, TJ. That it's impacting your work. I hope you don't end up losing this job."

"You're only sorry that it's impacting my work?" TJ asked.

"Yes, TJ. We can make this right. I'm ready to. It's all up to you."

"How so, Paige? What have you done here recently to make this right? Nothing has changed. Is this all on me in your mind to fix this?"

"It always has been, TJ. You've been the one getting upset."

"Wrong. Maybe I start some fights, usually about sex, but you initiate all the others. Have you noticed I've held back here recently? I've passed by 20 opportunities at least to engage, and turned them down. And it's killing me inside. Don't act like you are completely right where all of our issues are concerned."

"Even your friends are telling you it's on you to fix us."

"My friends?" yelled TJ. "Jim and Carrie? Fuck them both. They aren't my friends any longer."

"Again, your fault, TJ. I heard about that visit. Jim was just trying to talk some sense in to you."

"Jim was my friend, Paige. You poisoned that."

"Poisoned? My God, TJ, what are you thinking about me? That I'm trying to ruin your life?"

"Not trying, Paige. Succeeding." TJ got up and left the conversation. He walked out of the room, out of the house, to his car, and started to drive. With no destination in mind. And no timeframe for coming back.

Chapter 7

TJ's recent behavior with Paige torpedoed any chance of sex. It had now been well over two months. TJ's last sexual experience happened in India with the massage. TJ was resenting Paige quite a bit for it. TJ had stopped asking. He had hit that zone. The one that existed when sex seemed like no longer an option with he and Paige. He was getting the urge to look for it elsewhere.

He wanted to give it one more shot with Paige. Once he crossed that line and had sex with another woman, it really was over. He didn't want this to get there. I can regain some control, he thought.

He recalled some advice he received from Karen Coleman, his previous co-worker. Make her dinner and then figure out other ways to surprise her. TJ bought a dozen roses, food to make for dinner, dessert and a plan to apologize for everything. He wanted the bad feelings to end. His job, he could drop at any time without looking back. Losing his wife would make him an emotional wreck.

TJ made dinner and waited for Paige to return home. He set everything up nicely, put the dessert in the fridge, placed the roses in the middle of the table and rehearsed the best ways to apologize.

He heard Paige's car pull up. But he heard two doors slam. Paige walked in the door with Kylie laughing. TJ was deflated. He just stood there waiting.

Paige and Kylie walked into the kitchen and saw what TJ had prepared. "Oh my God," said Kylie, "looks like someone's trying to apologize for something." Paige laughed, looked at TJ, and then laughed again.

TJ stared coldly at Paige. "Paige, can she leave? I wanted us to have some alone time tonight."

"I drove her here, TJ. Where can she go? I have to drive her home later. What is all this?"

"Never mind," said TJ. "It's nothing."

TJ went in to the living room and sat on the couch.

"Someone's pouting," said Kylie. TJ sat quietly, not responding. Paige must have realized this was embarrassing TJ.

"I'm sorry, dear. If I had known you were doing this, I would have altered my plans today. This was very sweet."

"Why don't you two eat it then? I'm not hungry." TJ gave up on this night.

"Ooh, he got us dessert too!" said Kylie. "The roses are beautiful, TJ."

TJ didn't respond. He gave this a shot. He couldn't duplicate it the next night or even a week later.

Later that night in bed, Paige tried to cozy up to TJ. "I am so sorry about tonight. Can I make it up to you?"

"I guess so. In what way?"

"I will make you a special dinner tomorrow. Like you did tonight."

"Fine," said TJ, disappointed. And then he rolled over and went to sleep.

TJ had had enough. It was clear that Paige's reluctance or downright refusal to have sex wasn't anything that was going to end anytime soon. A decision was being made in his mind to seek it out elsewhere. Up to and including forming a relationship with another woman. A relationship that had intimacy, closeness and those things that TJ desired and wasn't getting from Paige.

TJ kept his eyes open at the office, even considering a coworker. He would find himself scouting out girls walking around at the mall. He even went as far as checking his contacts to see if any of the girls there might be potentially available. It was a sad thing, he thought. And this was difficult. TJ wasn't comfortable with "chase" mode. He and Paige had been together for a long time. This is useless, he thought. What girl is going to want a guy like me?

TJ would find himself lost in thought about his situation. The thought of opening himself up again to the dating world was frightening. And the fact was, he was a married guy. Girls weren't exactly going to jump at the chance to be with him. Was he really left here without decent options? Why couldn't Paige get interested in sex again? TJ was convinced that this was at the root of their problem. If they were intimate again, TJ's anger would subside, and maybe they could fall in love with each other again.

But that wasn't the reality of the situation. He was even hesitant to ask Paige anymore for fear of how angry he would get at being rejected.

TJ frequently reflected on his time in India. He had developed a nice bond with both Raj and Neha, which continued on since his return home. He was aimlessly searching things up on the internet when a message from Raj appeared. Raj's message to TJ brought a smile to his face. That night at the Spa in Delhi was memorable and something TJ was thinking about quite a bit.

Raj: How's life there, my friend? We miss you in Delhi and the girls at the Spa ask about you. Haha!

TJ: Raj – good to hear from you. Things aren't going too well here. New boss at my job is making life difficult and things with the wife aren't improving. Tell the girls I said hi ☺

TJ got into a chat conversation with Raj about how he and his friends always go to the Spa and their wives know about it. Raj encouraged TJ to find the same sort of outlet for his frustrations with Paige.

Raj: My friend, you don't have to have sex with the girls. But they can help relieve your stress and frustrations. Ur wife loves you, I'm sure of it. But as guys, we usually want it more than they do. My wife knows some of the girls there. She is ok with them. They aren't nasty. She just controls my budget on how much I can spend there. Hahahahaha!

So, Raj had convinced TJ that massages were the way to go. In a way, it made sense to TJ. He did enjoy his recent experiences and it did help relieve some tension and frustration. But that was expensive, to say the least.

TJ also began considering meeting someone through a personal ad. Not for a relationship, he thought. Just for some casual hook ups without strings attached. In his mind, he had tried hard to get things right with Paige, and nothing seemed to work. He didn't like having to consider these options, but he felt like he really had no other choice.

The bad review still in his mind, TJ had begun applying for jobs again. He expanded his search this time to areas outside

Fayetteville, one of the first times he had considered doing that. His efforts landed him a job interview with a sporting good company in Miami, Florida. Having been there recently, TJ was excited about going back. This would be a short trip, but he was always happy to get away, even for a few days.

His job interview was standard fare. It was nice of them to fly him down there, but the interview only lasted for about 30 minutes and they did not seem to ask a lot of detailed questions. Wow, thought TJ. My resume must have been very impressive. Not leaving Miami until the next morning, and it being only 10:30am, TJ had a day to enjoy. A little beach time maybe, a few drinks and some relaxation. Perfect day to look into a massage too, he thought.

TJ spent a little time on the beach and then looked up some massage parlors close by. He found one that looked nice and had good reviews, so he called and set an appointment.

His arrival at Perfect Touch Massage had TJ looking forward to the stress relief. It may not be like the one in India, with the sexual gratification at the end, but he will enjoy it regardless. This place was a lot friendlier than the previous one he went to in Miami. A young girl led him back to his room where he met Mia, who enthusiastically introduced herself and immediately complimented TJ.

"Wow, you look good! I'll enjoy this too," said Mia, smiling.

TJ laughed and said – "Does that mean you'll give me a tip afterwards, too?"

Mia laughed. She told TJ to get undressed. "Do you want me to leave the room?" asked Mia.

TJ thought about it for a second. "No, I guess not." TJ got naked and got onto the table, Mia watching and smiling the whole time.

Mia was very friendly and talked to TJ throughout the massage. Unlike the others, she was actually connecting with him on a personal level. TJ told Mia about his personal issues with Paige and some of the things he had been recently considering. He wasn't sure why he was telling this complete stranger everything in such detail, but it was cathartic. And Mia was a willing listener.

Mia finished massaging TJ's back, butt and legs and paused for a minute. She leaned close to TJ's ear and said "you will like this" in a whisper. With the tips of her fingers, Mia gently moved them on TJ's lower back, his butt and inner thighs. This gave TJ goose bumps and was very stimulating. Mia continued this for a few minutes until it was very evident that TJ was hard.

"Please turn over TJ," said Mia.

TJ turned over and Mia did not cover him with a towel. "Very impressive, TJ," laughed Mia. "You get comfortable…….and you take your time. It's okay." TJ wondered what was about to happen. He knew it wasn't legal here, and wondered what Mia had planned.

Sure enough, Mia poured some oil on TJ's cock and began slowly massaging it. She also grabbed TJ's hand and put it on her ass. "It's okay," she said. "You can feel me."

TJ began massaging Mia's ass and his hand found its way between Mia's legs, testing the waters a little. Mia opened her legs more to give TJ better access. Her shorts were loose, so he started to move his hand inside her shorts up her inner thigh. His hand now rubbing her pussy over her panties, he could feel she was very wet. The more TJ rubbed; the faster Mia would stroke TJ's cock.

"Is it okay to put a finger in?" asked TJ, now completely lost in this experience.

"Yes, TJ. Please," said Mia in a breathy voice.

TJ moved her panties aside and began fingering her wet pussy. Mia positioned herself to give TJ the best angle. TJ began fingering her fast and Mia reciprocated in stroking TJ's cock. TJ could not hold back anymore. He came hard, experiencing a full body orgasm he had rarely felt in the past.

"Wow, that was a lot," said Mia. "You got some on me." She laughed and said, "lay still, I'll clean you up." TJ was laying there, exhausted, but happy. He couldn't have hoped for a better experience. And Mia was so nice and friendly. It seemed as if she genuinely liked him.

Mia cleaned TJ up and they talked more while she finished the massage.

"I don't usually do that for my clients, I want you to know," said Mia. "Our little secret, okay? I don't want you to get the wrong impression and think I do that with every guy that walks in here. Usually, they don't treat me nicely and get offended it I don't do it."

"Thank you, Mia. Definitely our little secret. Why did you do it for me?"

"Because you are a gentleman, TJ. And I liked you instantly. And you definitely needed it. I got the sense that you were here because you did not want to have an affair, that this might be the only way to get a sexual release. I really felt for you."

TJ couldn't believe his luck. Mia understood him better than maybe he understood himself.

"How much longer will you be here?" asked Mia.

"I have to leave tomorrow," said TJ, sadly.

"Come back here later tonight, TJ. I'll be here until 10pm. I'll discount you on that one and give you an even better massage.

Especially on my friend there," said Mia, putting her hand back on TJ's cock.

TJ knew for sure he would come back. Mia, for the first time in a long time, gave him a feeling of closeness and intimacy he had been missing. Sad, TJ thought, that it had to be a stranger in a massage parlor. TJ wasn't sure he bought Mia's explanation that she didn't do this with every male client she had, but he didn't care. He wanted that feeling again. What he just experienced. He was just sad Mia didn't live in Fayetteville.

That night, TJ returned to Perfect Touch and Mia was waiting for him. She brought him back to her room and shut the door.

"Thank you for coming back, TJ. It means a lot to me," said Mia.

"I would not have missed this," said TJ, already feeling himself get hard.

Mia hugged TJ and playfully grabbed his ass. TJ laughed and did the same to Mia.

"Okay, let's get started," she said. "You get naked. I have a special surprise for you this time."

"What is it?" asked TJ.

"You'll see. Lay face down on the table and close your eyes."

TJ got undressed, laid down on the table and closed his eyes. I hope this doesn't involve my ass, he laughed to himself.

"Okay, open!" said Mia.

TJ looked over at Mia and saw that she too had removed all of her clothes except her panties. "To give you something to look at too, TJ. Do you want the full massage, or just for your special friend? No time limit, TJ."

"We can skip the other stuff, even though some of that was a huge turn on," said TJ. "What am I allowed to do to you?"

"I won't have sex. I can't do that. And I don't think you actually want that. Do you?"

"I don't know," said TJ. "Probably not a good idea."

"Let's see where it takes us," said Mia, as she began to gently rub TJ's chest.

TJ reached his hand to Mia's breast. As he began to massage her breast, she moved her breast to within reach of TJ's mouth. TJ began sucking and licking Mia's nipple and reached his hand to start rubbing her ass. Mia's hand reached over to TJ's cock and she gently started stroking it. TJ wasn't expecting this to start or happen so fast, but he let the moment happen. He had missed this badly.

TJ again made a move to Mia's pussy to stick his finger in. Mia removed her panties, and TJ began fingering Mia again. Mia moved into a position where she would be able to give TJ oral sex while he fingered her.

"Is it okay?" asked Mia.

"Yes," said TJ.

Mia began licking the tip of TJ's cock while she still stroked it and soon began taking it into her mouth, sucking down on it to the cadence of her strokes. TJ was in heaven. He felt the buildup and gave Mia warning it was about to happen.

"Mia, I'm about to cum."

Mia stroked harder as she pulled away and TJ came hard for the second time with Mia that day. Equally as intense as before, he was again exhausted afterwards.

"Did you like that?" asked Mia. "I also enjoyed. You made me cum earlier too. Could you tell?"

"Not really," laughed TJ. "I was too busy focusing on what you were doing to me."

Mia cleaned TJ up again, got dressed and sat down next to TJ.

"TJ, I really hope the best for you. And I really want you to come back to Miami. Honestly, and this may sound stupid, but I'd love to see where this could go."

"You mean, outside of the massage parlor?" asked TJ.

"Yeah. Like maybe seeing each other and exploring, you know, if we could be something."

"This is a deep conversation for our first day of knowing each other," said TJ, smiling. "But I know what you mean. Part of me wishes I wasn't leaving. But I have issues to solve."

"I know. I really wish you the best. Don't ever doubt that you have something to offer. And I'm always here. I want you to keep in touch and think of me if things don't work out." Mia leaned over and kissed TJ. "And take care of my special friend, okay? Promise?" said Mia as she playfully reached towards TJ's cock again.

Mia hugged TJ and said goodbye. They exchanged phone numbers and TJ promised to keep in touch. And also promised to return to Miami whenever he was able to. "I really hope you get this job," she said.

TJ left and went back to the hotel. Mia had become yet another girl TJ formed a quick, albeit this time very sexual, relationship with, only to say goodbye and return to the chaos that was his marriage to Paige and personal and professional life in Fayetteville in general.

TJ returned from his trip to Miami and found he wasn't trying hard to engage too much with Paige. They didn't have any arguments, but there was a coldness and distance that was palpable. TJ found it cathartic to talk to his friends about everything happening with him. But there were few friends he would confide in with some of the more recent things he had been doing, both in India and Miami.

Neha Ganesh was one of those friends. She knew full well what TJ and Raj had done that night, but she did not judge at all. TJ talked with her quite a bit, and she would offer nothing but encouragement. I just want to see you happy; she would say.

TJ had emailed Kate Ambrose a few days earlier and talked about Paige and what he had experienced in his recent getaways. With her growing knowledge of their troubles, Kate responded back to him, being supportive, yet blunt.

Dude, it doesn't sound to me like either one of you is really trying to make this work. That's a problem. And you've already opened your world up to other women. Ones you have to pay for at least, you loser (love you!). If neither one of you are happy, you need to end it. It's best for you both. No one should have to go through life being miserable.

I'm here for you, anytime. Need someone to talk to, a place to stay, just call. You take care. Work it out so it's best for you.

KA

TJ had been receiving a lot of advice recently telling him he needed to end things with Paige. But he couldn't bring himself to do it. He was miserable, yet couldn't extract the tooth making him miserable.

Paige had had enough. TJ had ignored her now for the better part of the last few weeks. She didn't want this marriage to end. She had been thinking quite a bit about how to start to piece things back together. She just hoped they weren't too far gone. She had been starting to want sex again. Figuring she would surprise TJ one night with it, and give him things that would rock his world and make him shake.

TJ was on the couch watching TV. Paige would get the kids off to bed and then invite TJ to the room. She really hoped it would melt him. He had been so cold recently. But so had she.

Paige finished reading Elizabeth a bedtime story and went to the room. She put a skimpy bra and thong panties on and yelled for TJ to come to the room.

"Later," TJ yelled back.

"I need you in here right now. I think there is something wrong with the shower." Paige yelled back.

"Shit! Be there in a minute." Paige heard TJ cussing to himself before he walked towards the room. Paige was now wondering if her plan would work. She wasn't sure if she should even try.

"What is it? What's wrong?" asked TJ tensely.

Paige stared at TJ for a minute. She had put a robe on, hoping to reveal. "It was leaking a minute ago, but now it stopped."

"So...there's no problem, then?" asked TJ.

"No, I guess not," said Paige. Her hand was on the knot on her robe. She wanted to drop her robe. But TJ was looking at her coldly, without feeling or emotion.

"Are you okay, baby?" asked Paige.

"Fine," said TJ. "Why?"

"Nothing," said Paige, giving up. "Go on back and watch TV. I'm going to bed."

"Okay," said TJ, and then he left the room.

Paige started weeping as soon as TJ walked out. Feeling to blame for this in her own way, she pulled out a piece of paper and began writing a note to TJ. Paige was considering going to visit her mother. And perhaps making a decision to make that visit permanent. She began writing things to TJ, with the first words being 'I'm sorry it has come to this.'

Paige did not finish the letter. Or even get past the first sentence. I can't give up, she thought. I'll try again another day, but one where he can get into a good mood first.

TJ was taking Steven to a party at his friend's house that night. TJ made small talk with Steven on the way, teasing him about how many girls would be at the party. Steven would immediately always deny anything where it related to interest in girls. But at 12 years old, hell, TJ remembered what he was like as a kid.

They arrived at his friend's house. Steven got out of the car. "Are you going to wait for me here?"

"For 2 hours, Steven?"

"Well, I figured you'd rather be here than at the house." Steven laughed and then walked away.

What an interesting comment, thought TJ. Without a doubt, Steven was noticing and being impacted by the tension in the house. TJ sat there in the driveway for a little while, thinking about his kids. If they were starting to feel this impact, that is not good. I don't want them to grow up resenting us as parents.

"I need to do something," said TJ to himself. TJ drove to the store and got Paige some of her favorite chocolates and bought her a bracelet at the jewelry store. Tonight, things are going to change.

Sensing the opportunity, Paige reacted with excitement to the chocolates and the bracelet. "That is so sweet, TJ! Thank you!"

"You're welcome, dear. I'm sorry I've been so distant recently." TJ walked over and kissed Paige.

"Eeewwww!" screamed Elizabeth. "Stop kissing in front of me!"

Paige whispered into TJ's ear. "I'll have something for you tonight. And it will be good."

Finally, thought TJ. He was really hoping she was talking about sex. He laughed. What else could this be, he thought.

The kids now in bed, Paige put the outfit from the other night back on. TJ was in the shower, so she took that opportunity to prepare.

TJ stepped out of the shower, dried off and opened the bathroom door. He saw Paige there in her robe. As TJ smiled, Paige dropped the robe, revealing nothing but the thong panties. TJ took his towel and simply tossed it back in the bathroom.

For the first time in months, TJ and Paige made love. For a night, everything seemed normal again to TJ. It was one of their best. And why not, it had been such a long time. They were almost new to each other.

Afterwards, Paige lay next to TJ and then rested her head on his shoulder.

"Elizabeth was asking me if we were mad at each other," said Paige.

"Steven made comments to the same effect," responded TJ. "We can't let the kids be affected. It's not their fault we have had some problems. They should not suffer for it."

"I agree," said Paige. "Let's work on us, for the sake of them." Paige kissed TJ and said goodnight.

TJ lay awake thinking for a while. Did everything just resolve itself, he wondered. It can't be that easy. Months and month of tension, nullified by one night of good vibes and good sex. Let's see what happens tomorrow, he thought.

Chapter 8

It had been three weeks since the night the coldness went away and the ice thawed. A thaw that lasted for precisely one day. Attempts at sex that next night by TJ were fruitless as Paige had gone out with Kylie and gotten drunk. TJ was immediately dismayed, but tried to stay patient. He tried to be playful with Paige after that day, but she acted annoyed at what she called "childish" behavior.

TJ was getting depressed again. False alarm, he thought, about that night.

Paige was on the phone with Carrie Keller and TJ couldn't help but listen in to the conversation. Paige was apparently apologizing to Carrie for TJ's past behavior. "I don't know what's been wrong with him." TJ was stunned. Why would she do that, he thought?

The rage was back. Like a pest of a friend who keeps saying, "I told you so." He waited for the call to end and then walked in to the family room.

"Why do you feel the need to apologize to my ex-friends for my behavior?" asked TJ calmly.

"Carrie said Jim is really mad at you. Said you changed."

"I don't give a FUCK what they think, Paige!" yelled TJ. "And how dare you try to pacify those idiots by making it seem like I'm the problem."

"Calm down, TJ. You're scaring me," said Paige.

"I really thought we were back on the right track. I was looking forward to getting to know you again. But then, one night later, you say the hell with me and go hang out with your friend. The same friend who made fun of me for attempting to prepare a dinner and a nice evening for you. What a bitch she was that night."

"Don't call Kylie a bitch! She is my best friend."

"Maybe I should start calling Kylie and confide things in her, like you do with Jim and Carrie, make her see my side of things."

"She wouldn't listen to you, TJ. She's been telling me to leave you. She's convinced you're cheating on me." Paige look angrily at TJ. "I can't believe you are getting so angry about this. I think you have some anger issues."

"Paige……. I'm done. I can't do this anymore. Go hang out with Kylie and talk about me to your heart's content. Go hang out with Jim and Carrie and have a field day about what a douchebag I am. Do whatever you want. "

"Where are you going?" asked Paige.

"Do you really care? Anywhere but here." TJ got up and headed for the door.

"TJ," said Paige. TJ stopped, but didn't turn around.

"If you walk out that door," she continued, "don't come back."

TJ walked out the door. Turned around and kicked the front door, leaving a small dent in the door.

"FUUUUCK YOOOOUUUUU!!!" screamed TJ. He walked to his car and drove away, heading to one place he knew he could calm down.

"I'm at a loss, Mom," said TJ to Ann Carlson. "I feel the rage coming on and can't control it. Only she triggers it, and then she has this way of saying things to fuel it. We had a nasty fight earlier."

"What were you fighting about this time?" asked Ann.

"She paints this picture of everything in the marriage is my fault, even to my own friends. She's very arrogant and doesn't acknowledge her part in this."

"She's protecting herself, son." TJ's mother continued – "She knows there is a big problem, but she doesn't think she's to blame. That's what she wants others to think."

"I want to end it, but I can't bring myself to do it. Because of the kids. I even worry what they are doing right now."

"TJ, you need to go back there. Don't leave it like it is. If you and Paige are going to end, try to do it amicably."

"Mom, honestly, I don't feel like I can control my stress level anymore. I feel like it's physically affecting me now. Might explain why I go into a rage sometimes."

"I'm worried about that too, son. So is your father. You may need to seek medical help."

"I'd hate to go that route," said TJ, now imagining himself in a straightjacket.

"That's better than doing something you will always regret. Just think about it."

"I will. Thanks mom." TJ stayed at his parent's house, had some coffee and let himself finish cooling down. Going back to his house, he thought this this could turn into an all-out battle, and he was bracing for the worst.

TJ's return to the house was met with deafening silence. Not even the kids said a thing to TJ. He sat on the couch. Elizabeth would acknowledge TJ by looking at him and smiling. But Paige truly wasn't making a move towards TJ. Steven glanced over at TJ on the couch with that same look as a few weeks ago at the party. Great, thought TJ. The kids know full well that there is tension, and they are letting me know that they know.

TJ didn't even try to go towards the bedroom that night. He slept on the couch and Paige did not acknowledge him when she would pass by. TJ considered calling a divorce attorney on this day, feeling that this was not going to improve. Silence rules, he thought. Who can live like this?

TJ did not get the job in Miami. Work under Jan Carver had gotten progressively worse. His probationary period extended another two months, which was not a good sign. This effectively ended his chances of getting another job in the company and left him stuck with a job he hated, a boss he hated and with little hope. Things with Paige couldn't be worse. And now the kids seemed afraid to talk to him. He had lost friends, and even former good friends like Karen and Jewel hadn't checked in on him in a long time, knowing full well he had issues.

TJ had little control left in his life. Stress was overtaking him. He was now beginning to understand why people ended their own lives, unable to control things and taking the easy way out.

I'll never do that, he vowed to himself. Nothing could bring me to that point. But he had no solutions to all of the walls crumbling around him. It was devastating him. He was a troubled soul, and no longer knew how to make things right.

The room was very dark. It was a place that TJ was not familiar with. The more he tried to focus on what he was looking at and escape the room, the darker it got. TJ began to panic. I have to get out of here, he thought. But how, I can't even find a door! "Heeeeelp!!" screamed TJ. Then TJ heard a low, disembodied voice.

"There's no way out. It's all a trap." The voice was unfamiliar to TJ. TJ froze.

"Who are you?" asked TJ.

"You want to run but you can't. I'd love to help you, but you don't deserve it."

"Why?" asked TJ. "What did I do?"

"Everything you know is a lie. You are a lie. The world would be better off without you. They would be better off without you." The voice was getting louder, and closer to TJ.

"Who's they? Paige? The kids?" TJ was no longer frightened at the voice. Just curious as to who it was. The room was completely dark now. TJ could not see anything.

TJ fumbled around and found a door and opened it, only to now be perched at the end of a cliff. He looked around but there was no one there. The voice spoke again.

"You can trust me. I won't steer you wrong."

"I don't trust you," said TJ. "Show your face."

"I don't have a face. I'm you. I'm the decisions you've made and the people you are hurting."

"I don't understand," said TJ. "Why are we here?"

All of a sudden, TJ felt hands push him and he tumbled off the cliff into a free fall. TJ screamed for his life, knowing full well he was about to die. Feeling more scared than he ever had, TJ began crying and bracing for the impact and his impending death. I don't want to die alone, thought TJ. Who will remember me? I don't want to leave my kids! Oh God…. someone help me!!

TJ hit the ground, feeling a sharp, numbing pain and then feeling nothing. But he was still aware of his surroundings. Am I dead, he thought? Where am I?

"You're worthless," said the voice. "The sooner you realize that, the better."

"Go to hell," said TJ.

TJ was now back in the dark room. He sat down on the floor and buried his hands in his face, knowing he had no control over what was happening.

"Welcome to your prison," said the voice. A high-pitched shriek started that mortified TJ, who held his ears, crying for it to stop.

TJ woke up in a cold sweat, and was quite possibly screaming as he awoke. TJ never usually had nightmares, but this one was jarring and he could remember it vividly. The voice in the dream was haunting him. The voice now seemed familiar, but it was sinister. TJ put his head in his hands as he sat up on the couch.

TJ sat on the couch staring straight ahead. He couldn't sleep. He couldn't move. He was numb. Everything felt dark. He felt as if he was in that free fall he just experienced in his dream. Paralyzed, alone and afraid, TJ simply stared straight ahead. Into the darkness.

PART 2:

EXODUS

Chapter 9

The day after. The day after one of the worst, if not worst days of TJ Carlson's life. He sat up on the couch drinking coffee. No one else had woken up yet. He had barely slept. Haunted by his nightmare, both real and in the dream world, he was unsettled to say the least. They had fought before. Many times. But this one was different. TJ was feeling hatred for Paige. He could sense the same thing from her. Something in the air was ominous. The vibe was different. TJ actually felt fear at seeing Paige and considered just leaving for work and grabbing a shower there

Elizabeth came out of her room, looking very sleepy and holding on to a blanket.

"Good morning daddy," she said.

"Good morning, sweetie. How are you this morning?"

"I'm okay daddy. Can I have some juice and cereal?"

"Sure thing sweetie."

TJ prepared breakfast for Elizabeth, while Steven also made his way out to the kitchen. Paige was usually up by this point to get the kids ready for school. TJ finished getting the kids ready and got them off to school. No sign of Paige. She was doing this purposely, thought TJ. She must not want to see me either.

TJ had to get ready for work. There were two showers in the house, so he opted to take one in the kid's bathroom. Avoiding Paige for as long as he could. He would eventually have to get clothes for work, and now wishes he had just planned ahead and grabbed them the previous night. TJ went back over the previous day's happenings in his head in the shower and had an inaudible conversation with himself in the shower. He knew this morning wouldn't end without seeing Paige, and now he had to be ready. What if she is normal this morning? Not out of the realm of possibility. What if she wants to immediately pick the fight back up? God help me, thought TJ. He was ready to unload if that was the case. The best he could hope for was complete and utter silence. He was growing comfortable with that.

TJ finished up his shower, feeling quite silly using Elizabeth's shampoo on his hair. At least I smell like a little girl, laughed TJ. The time had come. He needed to go into his bedroom and get his clothes, confronting Paige and whatever mood she may be in. What a ridiculous turn of events, thought TJ. Afraid to go into his own bedroom. He steeled himself, and opened the door.

Paige was in the bathroom. Perfect, thought TJ. Grab my clothes and get the hell out of here. TJ got dressed quickly and headed back out of the room. As he stood in the kitchen, preparing last things to head to the office, Paige quickly came out to the kitchen.

"TJ, about yesterday…….. I've never seen you so angry, uncaring and heartless. I'm amazed you even came back here."

TJ processed the opening line from Paige. Yep, argument it is. Don't hold back, TJ thought to himself. Don't let her win this one. Your pride is on the line. Your sense of worth and being is on the line. She's already looking to strip that from you. Give it right back to her.

"Paige, for the last several months, you have barely been a friend, much less a wife. I can't predict when you're going to be nice, in a decent mood, foul mood, whatever. Every day I hope for the best. You blame all this on me. You don't think you're wrong at all. I disagree. You are wrong. You've treated me like shit. Like you could care less about anything that I say, do or want."

"I really don't know what to say anymore, TJ. We are obviously not solving this or getting anywhere. You seem perfectly comfortable fighting with me or just leaving. That's become your go-to…. walking out of our bedroom or walking out that door. I never know when you're not going to come back. Do you know what that's like?"

"Has it ever dawned on you that I'm doing that so the kids won't have to witness a meltdown between their parents? Have to witness two stupid adults, who can't get their shit together, tearing each other apart. I have been doing my damnedest to make sure that doesn't happen. You want that? You don't seem to hold back. I end every argument. Whether it's by shutting up or walking out, I end it. You should be thanking me for that. I swallow it all for the sake of the greater good. Do you give a shit?"

"Well they aren't here now, so say what's on your mind, TJ. Give it to me. Let's do this once and for all."

The gloves were off, thought TJ. He felt like a boxer who had just completed a round 1 where the two opponents felt each other and threw a few jabs, with neither injured or giving in. TJ could feel the months of frustration building up. He was like a volcano, ready to erupt in a flurry of angry, bile-filled vitriol at this woman he was supposed to love and cherish. Can I hold back, he thought? I'm about to say the most hurtful things I can imagine to one of the people I'm supposed to love the most in this world. The mother of my children. My partner in life. My partner……who was equally ready to machine gun me down.

"I don't think you love me anymore, Paige. You're using me. Using my money to live a comfortable life. You complain about everything, but how bad is your life? Other women would kill for it. Why are you still here? Are you afraid to leave? Afraid the money will dry up? You can't even fake it with me anymore. Why are you withholding sex? You're doing it on purpose, because you know it angers me. Why do that? Do you enjoy seeing me get angry? I can't even begin to tell you the level of frustration I'm dealing with. Struggling with work, watching my friends abandon me…….and you just add to it. Willingly. What other conclusion can I come to that you just no longer love me?"

Paige stared quietly for a second. "First of all, don't flatter yourself by thinking I'm here only because you allow me to have a few dollars every month. And don't treat my life as if I'm living like a princess. I complain because I'm miserable. Mostly because of you. Why should I give you sex? You treat it as if it's my legal obligation. Honestly, it's a power I have over you. The most powerful weapon in my arsenal. You've done nothing to earn it from me. I can't do it unless I'm feeling love or passion for you. You are also treating me like shit, TJ. I have no desire to give you something that should happen between two people who love each other. If I'm making you feel so angry and frustrated every day, why don't you just walk out the door for good?"

Round 2 completed thought TJ. A bit of a small slugfest. But productive in that they were both saying what was on their mind, as hurtful as it may be. Her last line was an escalation. She was hinting that TJ should leave. The first real indication that they should consider ending this.

"Why don't you leave, Paige? Why tell me to leave? I'm paying for this house. Paying for everything in it. I have the right to tell you to get the fuck out."

"Fuck off, you piece of shit. Don't hold money over me." Paige was livid at TJ's last comment and had picked up a glass, ready to throw it at him.

"You gonna get violent? Do it, Paige. Throw the glass at me. THROW THE FUCKING GLASS! Make sure you hit me good. Go for blood."

Paige threw the glass at TJ, ensuring she would miss. The glass hit the wall and shattered. Paige began crying and picked up another glass. TJ had the look of a wild man in his eyes.

"Come on, Paige!! Do it again. Hit me this time." TJ screamed at Paige, trying to incite her. Paige put the glass down and lunged at TJ. TJ caught her and stopped her from connecting with a slap to the face. Paige stopped and pulled back. Staring angrily at TJ. It was a standoff.

Well, round 3 got physical, thought TJ. A development that significantly scared him. That was the first time that had happened. Neither of them saying a word now, just staring at each other, TJ prepared his commencement speech in an effort to end this.

"Paige, you want me to walk out that door and never come back? I'll consider doing just that. In the last several months, you have made me feel like a worthless human being. Someone who has nothing to offer. I honestly love getting away from here, away from you, so I can feel like myself again. I......"

Paige cut TJ off before he could finish that last sentence.

"I'm heading out TJ. I'm done with this. Do whatever you have to do."

Paige grabbed her keys and walked out the door. Wow, thought TJ, this time she's the one who ends the argument. TJ listened for her car to pull away, wondering if what just happened was truly the end. It felt like it. Not sure how either one was going to recover from that. TJ cleaned up the shattered glass on the floor and cleaned up the kitchen as he prepared to head off to work, excited to go there for once.

TJ began considering life beyond Paige. Deep down, he couldn't see staying with her. This happened without the kids there. God help them if they had seen that glass flying or their mother lunging at their father wanting to attack him. Today, thought TJ, I need to start planning ahead.

TJ got into his car, ready to drive to work. He needed to stop for gas on his way. A problem at the pump forced TJ to go inside the gas station to pay. As soon as TJ shut the door of his car, a horrifying realization hit him. Oh fuck, thought TJ, my keys are in the car and the door is locked! This day was shaping up to be the perfect storm of awful.

The only other person to have a key to his car was Paige. He was going to have to call her, wherever she was, and ask her to come open his car door. How the hell would he do this with any dignity remaining? TJ sat for a few minutes on the hood of his car, contemplating his options. Finally, he texted Paige, rather than calling her, and asked if she could bring her keys by the gas station and unlock his car.

15 minutes passed and no response from Paige. Why would she respond after that? He was likely stuck for some time. This wasn't going to look good at work, where he was already on thin ice.

After another 20 minutes, Kylie texted TJ.

Paige is on her way to unlock your car door

TJ should have known that's where Paige would go. He was thankful that at least Kylie gave him a heads up about it. He still did not like her at all. He could only imagine what Paige was telling her. Probably that he was the one who got violent.

10 minutes later, Paige showed up and parked her car. She walked over to TJ, handed him the key, and then walked back to her car and drove away.

Good enough, thought TJ. Feeling like a complete moron, he opened his car and proceeded on to work. Having to call on his wife to bail him out gave him pause about the path they were heading down. But returning home that evening was likely to be another adventure. And the great thing, TJ thought, is that he will have all day to think about this and stew on it. Would it escalate? He hoped not, for the sake of the kids. That, now, was TJ's number one priority. Protecting his kids from seeing what could potentially go down.

During the day at work, TJ sent a message to Mia. He had been thinking a lot about her. Miami would be a place TJ would go back to, if only to see her again.

Hi Mia – been thinking about you. Things with Paige got really bad today. What I wouldn't give to enjoy one of your special massages right now ☺

Mia responded:

HI TJ!! Awww…. I miss you and my special friend. I want you to cum back here – hehe. I'll take care of you like I did last time and you can take care of me some more too. And your special friend will have another "explosive" good time. I miss you.

TJ smiled at her response. He would love to see her again, and that was a very distinctive possibility. Even though he really liked Mia, he couldn't get passed the fact that she might only be doing this for him because he was a paying customer. She may have several guys like that.

TJ finished off the day and headed home. Bracing himself for another potential showdown, TJ was dreading walking through that door. He hadn't heard from Paige all day. He didn't expect to. He just hoped the kids were okay.

As TJ walked in the door, the scene was normal. Paige was making dinner and the kids were in their usual places. TJ went and got changed. When he walked in the door, he had placed his jacket on the door. His phone, still in the jacket, had started to ring. Paige picked up his phone, curious as to who it may be. She did not recognize the number. But out of curiosity, or instinct, Paige pulled up TJ's emails. Nothing unusual. Then she pulled up TJ's text messages.

Paige's horror and disgust after seeing the exchange between TJ and Mia hit her like a ton of bricks. She got her phone and took a picture of the conversation. She put TJ's phone back in the pocket. Her worst fears confirmed, Paige quietly went back to cooking dinner.

TJ came out and sat at the dinner table. Everyone ate dinner quietly. TJ and Paige did not look at each other. Paige's demeanor was calm. Now knowing that she had confirmed her worst fears about TJ, she could proceed ahead. And she had evidence of it. How would she confront him with this later? Paige looked at TJ, smiled and got up.

That was strange, thought TJ. She was calm, as if nothing had happened earlier. The two kept their distance for the rest of the evening and got the kids off to bed.

"TJ, can I talk to you for a minute?" said Paige.

TJ walked into the family room where Paige was sitting.

"You know, you are really bad at this. Hiding things. You can learn lessons from other cheating scumbags." Paige looked coldly at TJ.

"Now what?" said TJ defiantly.

"Can you tell me exactly all the things you did to Mia? I'm assuming she made you cum. She hinted at it twice in her message to you. Explosive…. special friend? Who's her special friend? Your cock? How did she make you cum? Did you fuck her?"

TJ knew he was busted. He also knew that Paige had grabbed his phone while he wasn't looking. Well, if it wasn't the end before, this was the end.

"No, we did not fuck. We fooled around. And yes, she massaged my….um…. special friend. I told you Paige. If you denied me, I was going to have to look elsewhere for it. So, I did. But I drew the line at actual sex. I would not do that."

"How noble of you," said Paige. "You really are a gentleman. Tell me every detail of what happened there. Did she blow you?"

"Yes, briefly," said TJ, wondering why he was admitting this.

"I see," said Paige. "How was it…. was she better than me?"

"I don't know Paige. I can't really remember what it was like with you. It's been that long."

TJ realized that this morning's argument was just the beginning and this was going to get much, much worse. He studied Paige and wondered what her next move was going to be. Paige was quiet for several minutes.

"Are you going to tell me everything that happened there?" asked Paige.

"No," said TJ. "I think I've said enough."

"Yes, you have," agreed Paige.

Paige walked out of the room. TJ could hear that Paige was on her phone but had no idea who she was talking to. No matter, thought TJ. I really need to think about the kids here, who are about to witness the end, I think. TJ sat up in bed and waited for Paige to return to the room.

TJ had nearly dozed off when Paige finally returned to the room. Paige shoved TJ in the head.

"Wake up, TJ. We need to talk," said Paige.

TJ came to and just looked at Paige. Paige did not seem in a rage. Or even overly angry. She waited for TJ to say something, but then realized the look was all she was going to get.

"TJ....... you have hurt me beyond words today. You might not consider what happened in Miami to be cheating, but I do. And I can't trust you anymore. You are the father of our kids and I don't want them to suffer, as you say. But just know, our relationship is very damaged. I want us to seek counseling. We need to hold this together for Steven and Elizabeth. You, however, deserve to pay for what you've done."

"Wait," said TJ. "What do you mean deserve to pay? Is that a threat? What exactly do you plan to do? What happened in Miami is a direct result of your lack of attention and overall frigidness, and I don't apologize for it. I have needs, and you weren't meeting them. I warned you."

"There you go again," said Paige with frustration in her voice. "It's only about sex with you. You may have a sex addiction, TJ. You may want to seek help for that."

"Sex addiction? Anger management issues? Any other maladies I have that you'd like a doctor to check on? Restless Leg Syndrome? Chronic Halitosis? Not everything I do is because I have some horrible infliction. The facts are these – I needed closeness, intimacy and sex with you, my wife, and you gave me none of it. I've explained that several times. You probably will never get it."

"Well get this," said Paige. "I am never having sex with you again. Not a chance. Not when other nasty girls have already touched you. You certainly no longer deserve it. Don't even bother hinting or asking. This store is closed."

Paige got up and left the room. TJ sat there, registering everything that was just said. As he processed Paige's words, he felt a familiar feeling. He tried to control it. It took everything in his powers to keep it contained. He clenched his fists and closed his eyes, breathing in and out slowly. But the rage was building.

This last year had its ups and downs for TJ Carlson. The ups usually took place while traveling. The downs, however, took place at home, and were piercing TJ's soul. Everything he knew and loved, that he had worked long and hard to build – a career, a family, stability……. all had crashed down around him. As he sat there on his bed in a controlled rage, praying that Paige would not walk back in the room, TJ had to decide on his next step.

Being around Paige was no longer an option. One of them had to go. TJ began questioning his own state of mind. The rage was powerful. He was barely containing it. The rest of his body was numb. Was this all my fault, he thought?

No, this is not my fault. I did nothing to Paige to change the way she treated me. I was a loving husband who provided and cared for her for many years. She changed. And my work……. horrible bosses who are destroying my career. A string of bad luck, and now hanging by a thread in my current job. TJ rationalized all the issues in his life, and amazingly, he was the root cause of none. I need to change my situation, he thought. Everyone conspiring to take everything away from me have seized control of my life. Time for me to seize it back.

With that thought in his head, TJ got up and pulled out his suitcase. He locked the bedroom door. Even if she knocks, I'm not letting her in, he vowed. TJ packed as many clothes as he could fit in the bag. He then started pulling other belongings from the bedroom and fitting them into the suitcase. He finished packing, closed the suitcase, and then got back on the bed, sitting up and staring straight ahead.

TJ had made his decision. He's leaving Paige. He's leaving, period. His heart was heavy as he thought of his kids. They need stability, he thought. I'm an emotional wreck. I'll go get myself together, then come back and fight for them. It was late, and both kids were already in bed. TJ wasn't going to leave without saying goodbye, or at least goodbye for now.

TJ quietly opened the door, looked to see if Paige was around, and then went to Steven's room. He knocked on the door. Steven opened it.

"Let me come in for a minute, Steven," said TJ.

"Sure dad, what's up?"

"Steven……," TJ said as he was searching for words, "I'm going to be leaving for a while. I know you are aware that your mother and I have been having issues recently."

"Very aware. Are you coming back?"

TJ felt like he wanted to cry. This was tough. "Yes, of course I'm coming back. I can't live without you guys. I just need to go to give some time and space to this situation. I don't want the two of you exposed to it. I hope you understand. I think you're old enough to be the man of the house for a while, Steven. I'm counting on you."

"Are you going to divorce mom?" asked Steven curiously.

"I don't know, son. But no matter what, nothing changes how much both of us love you and Elizabeth."

"Okay dad." Steven looked worried. TJ rubbed his head and walked out of his room. That was the easy part. Steven is damn near a grown up already. Now comes the tough one.

TJ walked into Elizabeth's room. She was already asleep. TJ stood there and stared at her. This time a tear fell down his eye. He was devastated inside. He had such a deep love for his daughter. A beautiful girl with a beautiful soul that he did not want to tarnish. He would gladly give his life for hers. His love for Elizabeth was the purest love TJ could have for anyone. This was killing him.

He went over and kissed Elizabeth on the forehead and stroked her hair. Tears were falling now as he realized the enormity of what he was about to do. "I will be back, sweetie. I promise." TJ whispered that over and over as he stood over the sleeping Elizabeth. He then turned around and walked out of the room.

TJ grabbed his suitcase and moved it closer to the bedroom door. He sat back down at the edge of the bed. He needed to recover from his emotional goodbyes to his kids. He didn't want Paige to see that. She didn't deserve to see any sign of weakness from TJ. He was to be stone cold as he walked past her and out that door.

One thing TJ hadn't really thought about was where he was going to go. Head south to Miami and be with Mia? Go west to California? Go north to who knows where? To be determined, thought TJ. He took one last look around the room. He saw the pictures on the wall of the family and other reminders of close to 15 years of marriage. All destroyed, he thought.

He grabbed the suitcase and rolled it to the front door. TJ stopped in the kitchen to grab some food that was his to take with him. Paige was in the family room and didn't budge. I wonder what's going on in her mind, TJ thought. What does she think I'm going to do? TJ considered going in and saying goodbye. He thought about it for a few minutes as he gathered his food. Nah, he thought. I've said my goodbyes to the two people in this house who deserve it. She's not one of them.

Paige was sitting in the family room, researching divorce attorneys. She hadn't given much thought to what TJ was doing. Until she noticed the suitcase. The big suitcase. And she heard TJ in the kitchen banging around, opening the closet and opening and closing the refrigerator. Should I go out there, she thought? Paige knew in her heart she had fallen out of love with TJ. Maybe she had known for a long time and simply needed a catalyst like the message from Mia to give her justification to act on her feelings. Her behavior towards TJ wasn't on purpose, in her mind. She just couldn't revive the passion she used to have. Thinking of TJ's behavior over the last year, the realization hit Paige that she was to blame in large part for some of the ways that TJ treated her. So here they are, she thought, a suitcase in front of the door and her husband about to walk out the door. Paige was not going to stop him.

"Are you going somewhere?" asked Paige.

TJ did not answer. Paige didn't ask again. She wasn't really sure why she asked this time. She knew very well that he was.

TJ had finished pulling everything together. The time had come. The time for him to walk out that door into the unknown. No destination in mind. He wanted to simply walk out the door and not acknowledge Paige at all, but the closer the time came to walk out that door, the more his rage dissipated. Something close to feelings started to return.

TJ walked to the family room. "To answer your question, yes, I am."

Paige looked at him sadly. "Where will you go?"

"I don't know," said TJ. "I just know I need to go."

"What about the kids?" asked Paige.

"I said some things to them earlier. None of your business. Personal things."

"If you go to Miami, tell Mia I said Hi." Paige instantly regretted saying it. The look of disgust and hatred on TJ's face reinforced that.

TJ stared coldly at her for almost a minute. Paige steeled herself and gave TJ the exact same look. They stared at each other, devoid of love, of friendship and of any caring. This was a look at mutual dislike. This would be what TJ remembered as he walked out the door. He regretted saying anything to her.

TJ opened the door, grabbed his suitcase and took it to the car. The rage had returned in that last few minutes with Paige. He felt justified in leaving. That moment of feeling that led him to go talk to Paige that last time, gone completely. He was feeling something different now. As he sat in his car, he felt energy. He felt something resembling excitement. A weight being lifted.

TJ started his car. He plugged in his iPod. Music was going to be critically important to him, as it was already late and he was going to need to stay awake. He started to back out of the driveway. This was it. He was really leaving.

As he looked back towards the house one last time, he saw something that shocked him. Paige was looking out the window. Watching him drive away. Wiping her eyes. TJ stopped the car for a second. He wasn't sure if Paige noticed him looking at her, but he didn't want her to. This was her fault. I hope she feels bad about what she's caused, thought TJ.

He continued backing out of the driveway and took one final look at the house. Paige was still looking at him, but now she was far enough away that TJ could not tell what she was doing. TJ drove down his road. His house was no longer in view.

I can always turn back, TJ reassured himself. For now, at least. TJ wasn't sure if the nerve would stay with him to truly leave. He was still close enough that he could go right back and once again try to make this right.

Enough analysis, thought TJ. I am a logical, rational person. I don't make decisions without thinking them through. I wouldn't be doing this if I didn't feel like it was my last and only option. Paige left me no choice. She made life unbearable for me. I would have been dead before I turned 40 if I had continued on like that. This is the right thing to do.

TJ felt the heaviness in his heart start to lighten. He felt good about his goodbye to his kids, and he would call or message them every day until the day he got back. It's not like he would never see them again.

TJ arrived at the exits for the highway. Decision time, thought TJ. Do I go North or do I go South? TJ got on the North exit for the interstate and entered the highway. Driving in the darkness, into the unknown.

Chapter 10

The music in the car was blaring loud, and TJ was wide awake and focused as midnight rolled around. Flying up Interstate 95 North approaching Virginia, TJ realized he still had no destination in mind. His only goal to this point was to get distance. Gain distance from all of the things that had gone so horribly wrong in his life. For that, he was feeling energized and alive. He sang along, badly, with his music and tried not to think too much. While feeling energized, he was also feeling tortured. His kids were going to miss him. This wasn't like one of his trips where they knew he was coming back, usually with gifts. This time around, they would not know. But, thought TJ, I control that. I can go home tomorrow and be with them.

Paige Carlson knew TJ would not be coming home tonight, and wasn't sure when she'd see or hear from him. Closing in on 1:00am, and she was on the phone with Kylie. Kylie did her best to comfort Paige, not because TJ left, but because of Paige discovering the type of man that TJ really was.

"Tip of the iceberg," said Kylie. "Who knows what else he's done and who he has been with. Let him go. If he comes back, make him beg for your forgiveness."

Kylie was being harsher on him than Paige was really even feeling about the situation. The reality was setting in for her that they may have crossed a line too far. But Paige was thankful to have Kylie on her side. She was one hundred percent supporting Paige and saying anything to help her feel better.

"I'll be there tomorrow. I'll bring some wine. I'll stay the night there if you want." Paige accepted Kylie's offer and tried extremely hard to go to sleep. Wondering if TJ headed north or south. If it was south, she knew for sure TJ was heading to Mia. And that, Paige thought, would absolutely kill me. How could I lose him to a bitch who works in a massage parlor, jacking men off for money?

Paige finally dozed off, partly sad and partly angry. And very curious as to the path TJ was choosing.

As 3:00am arrived, TJ was not far away from Washington DC. Still no destination in mind, but no urge to stop. The adrenaline was carrying him through this night, along with the music.

TJ was getting tired. On the road for many hours already, he was starting to lose focus and the music was not helping any longer. He shut off the music, and then his mind went to work filling the void. In the past, TJ carefully thought his actions through. While being impulsive on this night was giving him an adrenaline rush, that rush was going away. And now his left brain was taking over.

TJ began thinking more and more about the consequences of what he was doing. He had given Paige fair warning and had said goodbye to his kids, as heart wrenching as that was. But what happens with them now? If I keep going, he thought, I'll give Paige loads of ammunition to take to divorce court and in all likelihood, lose time with my kids.

And my friends…. what will they think of me? TJ was now going through an entire list of consequences in his head. My good, supportive friends will know why I had to do this and why I had to leave her.

And work? Shit…. minus Anna and Becky, they can all go to hell. TJ thought for a minute about his job. He simply wasn't going to be there the next day. Should I call in sick, he wondered? Or just leave it? Now realizing that that next day was already here, as he noticed dawn breaking as he drove towards Pennsylvania.

TJ stopped thinking. TJ also stopped focusing. Tiredness overcoming him, TJ's eyes started to get very heavy, like he had a weight attached to each one. He was driving in the right lane near the shoulder of the road. He struggled to keep his eyes open. TJ allowed his eyes to close.

The car shook and rattled, shocking TJ into alertness. He was no longer on the road, but past the shoulder on a grassy section that dipped downwards. The car was almost out of control and going 70 miles per hour. Grabbing hard on to the steering wheel to try and regain control, he steered back towards the road, simultaneously slamming on the brakes. He turned the car back towards the road and got the car onto it as he violently turned the steering wheel. The car did a near complete donut on the road as TJ finally got it to stop. His heart pounding, and feeling like he was going to get extremely sick, TJ pulled the car to the side of the road and just sat there. Listening to his heart pound.

TJ stopped for breakfast and got some coffee. Rattled by his brush with near death, he decided to make this an early day and find a hotel somewhere close by. He needed to be somewhere where he could recover. Stress level off the charts, he now feared for his health. He swore he was having a minor heart attack after the near car crash.

He never left the town he had just stopped in. He found a nice hotel with early check in, got to his room and collapsed. Quite possibly asleep before he hit the bed.

"Jim, I'm so sorry to bother you, but TJ left last night and I haven't heard a word from him." Paige had actually assumed TJ would at least check in. When he didn't, she got worried. "I'm just afraid he's going to Miami. Has he reached out to you?"

"No," replied Jim. "What's going on? Why did he leave?"

"He bolted after we had some vicious arguments. He was so furious at me, and I was at him too."

"You mentioned Miami. Why do you think he's going there?"

"He has a girl there. Mia. She works at a massage parlor and apparently had been taking care of TJ, for lack of a better phrase. They were texting each other on the day we had our huge fight."

"Shit. I'm sorry Paige. I wish he would have listened to me when I was trying to get him back talking to you and trying to work this out. I was worried he'd be out somewhere in this world and not be able to resist temptation." Jim Keller was talking calmly to Paige, but inside was livid with TJ. He thought TJ had a better moral code than that.

"Anyway, the point is, he's left me and left the kids, and I have no idea where he is or who he is with. If you hear at all from him, please let me know."

"Sure thing, Paige. Call Carrie and I if you need anything." Jim Keller hung up the phone and immediately broke the news to Carrie.

"So, he left her, huh?" said Carrie, not sounding surprised. "Jim, please try to talk some sense into him. He's wrecking a family with this stupidity."

"I am," said Jim. "He may not want to hear from me, but he's going to." Jim Keller pulled out his phone and began typing a text to TJ.

TJ – I'm not sure where you are or what you are doing right now. A while back, you made a decision to basically end our near 20-

year friendship, all because I was trying to get you to understand that there was more than just your side to the story. But rather than listen, you basically said to hell with our friendship. And now you have left Paige and your kids. What the hell is wrong with you? Get in touch with her as soon as you can and get your ass back home. You are destroying a family. And for what? Some skank in Miami who made you feel good? Look at the big picture here and stop being selfish. Please read my words and don't tune me out. Paige is devastated, and I'm sure your kids are too. As a friend, and I still consider you a friend, I'm asking you to get the fuck home, now.

Jim sent the message to TJ and let Carrie know.

"I'll go get him and drag his ass back if I need to!" said Jim angrily.

TJ woke up in the late afternoon. He felt disoriented and unaware of exactly where he was. He sat up in the bed and focused. In slow motion, the day's events replayed in his head. He allowed himself to collapse right back onto his bed. So, all of that did happen, he thought. Damn. TJ got up, took a shower and brushed his teeth.

TJ picked up his phone and saw that he had several texts and calls. Not ready to read those yet, he thought. He put his phone down.

There was a restaurant and bar in the hotel, and TJ decided he would spend his evening there, eating and drinking this night away. Maybe getting a little drunk would give him some perspective.

TJ sat at the bar, ordered his food and a glass of wine. The bartender, who introduced himself as Bill, struck up a conversation with TJ.

"Hey buddy, what brings you here to Nowheresville, Maryland," asked Bill.

"Bill, this would be a tremendously long story," said TJ laughing.

"I have all night, buddy. Where ya headin' after this?"

TJ still really didn't know where he was heading yet. Just going north. He'd run smack dab into Canada if he didn't stop.

"I don't know, Bill, sadly." TJ was being coy here, realizing that he was simply piquing Bill's curiosity even more with these non-answers.

"Ever been to Niagara Falls? Really beautiful. I went there last year. You're not far from here, just head up through Pennsylvania and New York. You can be there in less than a day."

TJ liked that idea. "That actually sounds like a decent idea there, Bill."

"You'll love it. Now, care to share why a guy like you is sitting here in my bar, drinking, relying on his bartender to give him his destination? I've met all types buddy, but I've never had to steer someone to his next stop. I'm all ears if you want to talk."

TJ laughed. "Okay Bill, why not. Keep the wine flowing."

TJ then spent the next 2 hours detailing his story to Bill, who, in between customers was giving TJ his full attention. Focusing on the differences between he and Paige, his reactions to it and his lost friendship with Jim, he laid out the story as if he was reciting it for a book. TJ started embellishing a bit more with each glass of wine.

After TJ was done, he looked at Bill. "So, what do you think, my friend?"

"Would you believe me if I told you I've heard far worse than that? So much worse. Some stories that damn near tear your heart out. You don't have it so bad, buddy. It's life. People sometimes stop getting along. It's not the end of the world. It's how much you let it dictate your state of mind that counts. You're doing the right thing here. You have extracted yourself from a volatile situation. You made the sacrifice. The fact that she started to get violent tells me that you are the one with the inner strength to make sure your kids don't have to deal with much worse than you being gone for a while."

"Thanks Bill. That really does make me feel better. I've been beating myself up for it since the moment I left. Can you tell me one of the stories that is worse than mine?"

"Sure," said Bill. "I talked to a guy a few weeks ago whose 17-year-old kid just murdered his 16-year-old girlfriend and his wife overdosed on heroin and died. He's here in town for the court proceedings against his son. You don't have it so bad, buddy."

TJ thought about that story for a minute. He thanked Bill, paid his tab, and called it a night. Bill had might quite a difference on him this night. Finally, someone who saw the logic in TJ's actions and decisions and not someone who will instantly judge him.

TJ started researching the route to Niagara Falls. He had actually always wanted to go there, albeit under much different circumstances. Maybe getting to a site like that, something TJ loves to do in other countries, might help put him back in a right frame of mind.

Remembering he had several messages on his phone, TJ decided it was time to see who had been trying to get in touch. Stunningly, no messages or calls at all from Paige, work or his parents. But there was a message from Jim. TJ read his message a few times. Feeling anger rising, he opted not to reply. He was stunned that rather than trying to get in touch with him directly, she called and bitched to one of his former friends and probably asked him to get in touch.

Unbelievable, thought TJ. He deleted the message. He was now more determined than ever to leave that life in North Carolina behind and look forward. And for TJ, forward for now was Niagara Falls.

TJ fell asleep late that night, aided by one final glass of wine delivered to his room. The message from Jim still angering him somewhat. He was awoken by the sound of his phone ringing at 7:00am, and in a groggy state, saw that it was Paige calling him. TJ put the phone back down and ignored it until it stopped ringing. Five minutes later, it rang again. Still irked at Paige for getting Jim involved, TJ decided it was time to break the silence.

"Where the hell are you," demanded Paige.

"None of your business and why do you care?" responded TJ in a still sleepy voice.

"I have a lot of reasons to care."

"Well, loving me isn't one of them, so why are you calling? Do you only care where I am? Want to be sure I'm not heading to Miami. Well, I'll just confirm that I'm not heading to Miami, how's that?"

"You'll excuse me if I don't believe you," said Paige sarcastically.

"Y'know, this is one of the reasons I left. Not even on the phone a minute before we are arguing and you're throwing accusations my way. I'm not doing it anymore." TJ felt his heart rate going up. Feeling even more justified now for leaving.

"I'm just worried about what you're going to do. You are out of control. If you're going to be with Mia, just tell me, so I know. At this point, I just don't want you found dead somewhere."

TJ had had it with this conversation. "Paige, listen to me really good here. I'm going north, not south. I don't give a shit about Mia. I was a paying customer of hers and did that because I needed to feel intimacy again. And it pissed me off to no end getting a holier than thou text from Jim continuing to castigate and judge me for every little thing I do, not even thinking for one minute that you even share an ounce of the blame for this. I don't appreciate you calling him, before you even attempted to call me, and have him do the dirty work. I deleted his message, and he can go get fucked. Him and Carrie both………"

"Okay TJ, I get it," said Paige cutting him off, "you're obviously still full of anger and resentment towards me and towards everyone else. He was worried about you too. Don't you care about anything other than yourself anymore?"

With that question, TJ hung up his phone and shut it off. Fighting over the phone was at least better than fighting in person, with less risk of getting smashed in the face with a glass. But TJ was tired of fighting. He sat for a minute, thinking about his conversation. He allowed himself to dissect Paige's words. In his mind, all she was doing was calling to make sure I wasn't heading to see another woman. No other reason. TJ re-packed his things, ready to check out and move on.

TJ hung around the hotel until after lunch and then got on the road. Still feeling tired, and remembering what happened the last time that was the case, he decided he'll stop driving earlier today. He was in no rush to get to Niagara Falls and could afford to take his time. The drive through Pennsylvania was extremely boring for TJ, and he found the tiredness hung around the entire time.

Across the New York border, he decided to call it quits and pulled in to another hotel.

This hotel also had a bar, and TJ decided he'd try to replicate the one moment on this journey so far that had actually made him feel good. His conversation with Bill, the bartender from Maryland. Maybe all bartenders are wise folk, thought TJ. He got checked in, took a power nap, and then headed down to the bar for dinner.

TJ was disappointed to see that apparently, Vincent, the bartender from New York, could have cared less about TJ's problems and only wanted to be sure whether or not he wanted any more food or drinks. TJ was about to call it a night until a woman sat down a couple seats from him, looked at him and smiled. She appeared to already be a little tipsy as she ordered a chocolate martini from Vincent. TJ decided to move closer and start a conversation. He wasn't attracted to her, as the woman had a bit of a rough look to her and was at least 10-15 years older than TJ, but he was up for good conversation.

"Hi, I'm TJ. Mind if I join you?"

"Sure, but let's go to a table and away from Captain Grumpy over there. I'm Candy, by the way. Nice to meet you TJ." TJ and Candy set up at a table.

"So, what's your drama, TJ?" asked Candy. "Tell me yours and I'll tell you mine."

"It's not so much a drama, as it is a horror movie," said TJ, making Candy chuckle. "Left the wife, lost my friends, missing my kids, all but abandoned my job, and not sure where it is I'm heading."

"Wow, TJ, that sounds all levels of f'd up," said Candy, lighting up a cigarette. "Let's start with the wife. What happened there?"

TJ recounted everything that led to him leaving Paige in the previous days. Candy simply listened, nodded, puffed cigarettes and had her drinks.

"TJ, let me tell you something. You both are right and you both are wrong. You're wrong because neither of you had the courage to solve the problem. It seems like you were happier being angry with each other. But you're both right in that the kids are your top concern. I've been married 3 times and been through the same ringer you have. You seem like a nice guy, though."

"Thanks, Candy. Although I'm a bit confused about how we are both right and wrong. I think neither of us was willing to change the things that the other didn't like."

"Exactly, so you're both wrong. But it's okay, TJ. I'm not lecturing you like your friends. Again, you don't seem like a bad guy to me. But then again, I'm a little drunk already and you might be a complete asshole. I may not be able to tell." Candy laughed and toasted with TJ.

"To both of us getting our shit together. Cheers." TJ and Candy clinked wine and chocolate martini glasses.

"Candy, let me ask you something. You've been married three times. Why do you keep doing it?"

"Because there's no better thing in this world than falling in love. And one of these days, I'll find my soulmate. None of these guys have been it. And it's a sad moment when you realize that, but I'll keep trying. You will also find your soulmate, TJ. Sadly, for you, Paige wasn't it. But don't ever give up. When you find her, surely everything will change and your life will change."

TJ and Candy chatted for a little while longer and then said good night. TJ had met two people on the road already who, just through having a good conversation, and actually listened to him, gave him a lot of food for thought and made him realize he was doing the right thing.

TJ made the rest of the drive to Niagara Falls later that next day and pulled in after dark. Tomorrow, he'd spend the day taking in the views and making plans of what to do from there. He hadn't thought too much about his next destination, but he'd stay there long enough to come up with a solid plan.

TJ was in an amusement park. Except it was empty. The rides were all running, but nobody was running them and nobody was riding them. Creepy, thought TJ. Where the hell am I? Daylight quickly turned to night, almost in an instant. TJ walked around looking for anyone, any sign that someone other than him was here.

"Hello?" shouted TJ loudly. "Is anyone here?"

No response. TJ felt a shove in the back and tumbled over on to the ground. He looked around and saw no one. He got back up only to be hit in the chest this time. This was with the force of a strong punch. TJ gasped for air.

"Who are you? Who is doing this?" yelled TJ. "Show yourself, dammit!"

"You should be getting used to this by now," said the disembodied voice.

"Why would I be getting used to this? Why are you doing this to me?"

"Because you're letting me," said the voice.

"Fine," said TJ. "Then I'll stop letting you."

"Good for you, TJ. But you can't. It's not under your control."

"You have me at a serious disadvantage, whoever you are. If you have something to say or a message to deliver to me, then deliver it face to face."

TJ was hit hard in the back of the head and blacked out. He woke up in a different part of the amusement park, on the ground covered in ants who were biting him. TJ scrambled to get rid of the ants and watched in horror as all of the ants started to grow in size and chased after him. TJ ran, still wiping ants off of him, screaming. I can't make it, TJ thought. I give up. Better to end this than die like this. As TJ ran towards one of the rides, he was determined to jump in front of the ride and let it hit him. That will end this nightmare, he thought.

TJ woke up with his heart pounding and covered in sweat. He looked at his arms and legs to make sure there were no ants on him. Another terrible nightmare, he realized. TJ wondered who this recurring voice was in his dream. This was the second time he had the same person or entity in a dream. Has to mean something, and now he wondered what. The entity in the dream was a bully, mocking TJ and shoving him around. And although defiant in the dream, there's nothing he can do to seemingly get the upper hand.

TJ recovered from that nightmare and fell back asleep.

TJ was at a funeral. There were only a few mourners there, but he couldn't see any of their faces. He also couldn't tell who this funeral was for. He walked a little closer. He was outdoors, and it was raining. There was a man at a podium, reading from a book. TJ could hear the voice. It was him.

"TJ Carlson was a man who disappointed in death as much as he disappointed in life. Meaningless and devoid of purpose, he leaves behind nothing but a sense of relief to those whose lives he destroyed. May he burn in eternal hell."

This funeral was TJ's! A chill was sent through TJ's body. The disembodied voice now had a face. A sinister, twisted face with a smile that was disproportionately big for his face. Small eyes, that seemed black and colorless. The man at the podium looked straight at TJ and smiled. TJ felt horrified. Those handful of people attending the funeral began laughing at TJ. These were no one that TJ knew.

"Come on over and join the fun," said the man. "You're our guest of honor."

"No," said TJ. "But nice to put an ugly face to your awful voice. Who are you supposed to be anyway?"

"I've told you before. I'm you. Don't you recognize yourself? I am the Darkness that you fear. Like this...."

All of a sudden TJ was inside a small, dark enclosed structure. He could hardly breathe. He reached upwards and quickly felt a top to the structure. He could barely move. He banged the top screaming, gasping for air. TJ heard something hitting the top of the structure in intervals. To his horror, he realized where he was. He was in a casket and dirt was being shoveled on to it. He heard Darkness laughing loudly. TJ screamed and flailed, banging the top of the casket until he passed out.

TJ woke up again. Wondering if he was still in the dream or was actually awake, he slowly opened his eyes. He looked around and saw the walls of the hotel room. He reached over and turned on a light. Sitting straight up, he grabbed the remote control and turned his TV on.

He was definitely awake. And thoroughly disturbed at these very realistic and terrifying nightmares he was having. The voice had a face now. And now known as Darkness. Three times he's shown up, and twice on this night. It was 3:30am. TJ Carlson refused to go back to sleep.

Chapter 11

TJ stood overlooking Niagara Falls. He couldn't help but draw a parallel to his experience at the Cliffs of Moher. But his mind was in a different place then. Everything was different. He was laughing and joking around with Jim, thinking about going home to Paige and the kids and had that feeling that he would get when he traveled different places and was taking in something breathtaking.

That feeling wasn't happening here. Too many things on his mind blocking that good feeling out. TJ just watched as he contemplated his next steps. He was going to send a message to his kids, something he had stupidly neglected to do to this point. And what about the job? Not a word from anyone. Did anyone even realize he was gone? Surely, they must have by now. And if not, well, TJ would have actually found that a bit funny.

TJ also thought about letting Paige know where he was. Not for any other reason than to give her a little peace of mind that he hadn't gone where she was assuming he would go. It's amazing, TJ thought, that he was still taking Paige's feelings into account. He wondered if she was doing the same for him.

What a beautiful view, thought TJ, allowing himself to refocus on the falls. He took several pictures with his phone and then took one of himself with the falls behind him. For Paige, he thought. Just in case. For a brief moment, TJ found a little bit of peace and that feeling that he loves so much.

In North Carolina, TJ had lit a fire and walked away. And now, in his absence, worries about him were starting to grow.

Paige was at a loss for what to do. She wished her parents were still alive, as she desperately needed them right now. With a lump in her throat, she dialed the Carlson's.

"He left last week, Mom. He says he went north. Have you heard from him?" Paige's question to TJ's mother, Ann Carlson, floored Ann.

"What do you mean he left, Paige?"

"We had some bad arguments, and he left. I thought he would come back maybe within a day or two, but he hasn't. I've heard from him once and he yelled at me because I tried to get Jim to get in touch with him."

"But you did hear from him?" asked Ann.

"Yes, just once, a few days ago. Mom, I'm really worried about what he's doing. I probably shouldn't say anything, but he has apparently been fooling around with other women."

"That's beside the point, Paige. I know you two were having problems, but regardless, we need to find out where he is. I'll try to get in touch with him."

Ann Carlson was very bothered. Why did it take Paige a week to tell her and why hadn't TJ let his own mother know what was going on? And what about the kids, and who were these other women Paige was referring to. Ann went to find Harold.

"Harold, we have a serious problem. TJ left Paige and has been gone for a week." Ann sounded very frazzled. Harold was immediately pissed off.

"And we had to hear this from her? What the hell is wrong with TJ? Jesus Christ!"

Harold was visibly irritated. "You know, I know that woman was stressing him. But to just take off leaving others to wonder whether he's dead or alive is damned irresponsible."

"I agree, dear. I'll call him right now."

Ann Carlson got TJ's voice mail and left him a message.

"Dear, I don't know where you are right now, but I'm begging you to please come home. We are all worried sick about you. At the very least, call me or message me that you are safe and sound somewhere. You can come here to our house and stay if you need. Call me, please."

Becky Parsons couldn't believe it. TJ had been gone without a trace for a week. She assumed he had been communicating with Jan, but apparently that wasn't the case, based on the email she just received from Jan.

Becky – have you or anyone else in that office heard from TJ Carlson? I understand he hasn't been there at all this week and I haven't heard from him.

Becky immediately grabbed her phone and sent a message to TJ.

Dude? Where are you? Out this whole week and no one has heard from you. Jan just messaged me. I hope you are okay. Pls message me back asap.

Jim Keller knew that TJ probably wouldn't respond to his message. He was having second thoughts about his recent approach to TJ and his issues with Paige. Carrie was set in her mind that TJ was completely wrong and let Jim know about it anytime the subject came up. Carrie definitely influenced Jim in this regard. But Jim was having lingering thoughts about a comment TJ had made to him. All I needed was a friend to listen and not judge, he remembered him saying. I'd have done that for you. That's probably true. TJ would have listened, like he always did, since they were teenagers.

Without Carrie knowing, Jim decided to send another message to TJ. A conciliatory one. Leaving the door open for them to rebuild their friendship one day.

TJ – first let me apologize for not listening when you tried to confide in me about what was going on with you and Paige. I should have listened. I know you would have done that for me. Please take care, wherever you are, and I hope when you return, we can rebuild our friendship. I don't expect you to reply, but please call me if you need anything. – Jim

TJ read the messages from Jim and Becky and listened to the voice message from his mother while sitting in the hotel room after dinner. A bottle of wine by the bedside that was slowly getting drained. The message from Jim was heartening, but the damage was done for the time being. He did not delete this message. He considered how best to respond to Becky. It was probably for the best that he didn't. He had left work behind. He'd confide in Becky once he was officially canned. His mom, now that was a different story. She was probably very hurt that TJ hadn't said a word to her.

TJ crafted a message to his mother. He thought about calling, but didn't want the emotional exchange that was likely to come along with it.

Mom – I'm fine. I'm at Niagara Falls right now, debating on what to do next. The situation became unbearable and I had to go for the sake of my health and so the kids wouldn't witness every meltdown Paige and I were having. I'm sorry I didn't tell you and dad before now. I'll keep in touch, I promise.

TJ polished off his bottle of wine and fell asleep.

TJ spent the next few days building a routine at Niagara Falls. His hotel room was becoming a home. He'd wake up in the morning, have breakfast, watch TV in his room until lunch, go enjoy lunch outside near the falls, take an afternoon nap, have dinner, get a bottle of wine, drink it all while checking messages and then fall asleep. This had been going on for the last 4 days. Messages to him had been zero other than an angry response from his mother urging him strongly to return.

But on this night, TJ would get a phone message that would jar him emotionally. It was from Elizabeth. Elizabeth, at 9 years old, knew how to use a phone and knew TJ's number. TJ returned from dinner with his bottle of wine and had a glass. He pulled out his phone and saw that he had a message from home.

"Hi daddy. Where are you? I haven't seen you for a long time. You didn't even tell me you were going away. When are you coming back? You didn't even say goodbye to me this time. Mommy said you were angry with her and that's why you left. Are you angry with me too, daddy? Don't you love us anymore? Please call me back, daddy, so I can talk to you. Bye."

TJ couldn't stop the tears after hearing her message. He couldn't even listen to the message again. TJ felt absolutely sick and was missing his daughter terribly. He wanted to call her right at that moment. But he couldn't. He knew what would happen. He loved his daughter immensely, but he would be walking right back into a blasting zone with Paige. But he wanted to get a message to her somehow. He was paralyzed on how to do it. He realized he was afraid to talk to anyone in North Carolina. A completely irrational fear, he thought. What psychological damage has been done to me that I can't even call my own daughter who is wondering whether I still love her or not. TJ downed his bottle of wine in quick fashion. With each glass, his ability to call and talk to anyone diminishing. He fell asleep with his phone in his hand and Elizabeth's voice message still ready to play.

The next night didn't go much better. TJ had avoided getting into any angry exchanges with his kids. This night, he actually dreaded looking at or listening to his messages. And sure enough, this time there was a message from Steven. Steven had the ability to send him messages through a computer program.

Dad – Elizabeth has been crying all day today. She left you a message but you never responded. Why didn't you call her? What's going on?

TJ thought of the best ways to respond to this. And he would respond.

(TJ's Message) Steven – I got her message. I wanted to call last night, and thought of other ways to get a message to you both. I hope you are both doing okay. Please let her know that I love her and miss her.

(Steven's Reply) Why don't you tell her that yourself. Why can't you call?

(TJ's reply) I don't want your mother to know. Is she there? The last thing I want is to get into another argument on the phone with her.

(Steven's Reply) I don't get it. Just tell her you want to talk to us.

(TJ's reply) It doesn't always work like that, son. Do me a favor…. next time she's not there, but the two of you are, let me know and I'll call.

(Steven's reply) Fine

(TJ's reply) I'm sorry son. It's not a good situation and I'm doing my best to shield the two of you from it. Remember our talk before I left.

Steven did not reply for several minutes, saddening TJ, who was hoping to get Steven's understanding with the situation. Finally, he responded.

(Steven's reply) Mom's in the family room and Elizabeth is here with me

(TJ's reply) Thank God! Elizabeth, sweetie, I got your message. I love you so much. I did say goodbye to you while you were sleeping that night. I didn't want to wake you.

(Elizabeth's reply) I love you too daddy. Where are you?

(TJ's reply) I'm in New York sweetie. At a big waterfall called Niagara Falls.

(Elizabeth's reply) Okay. When are you coming home?

(TJ's reply) I'm not sure sweetie. But I'll be home, I promise.

(Elizabeth's reply) Okay daddy. Can you call me?

(TJ's reply) Not right now. But I will soon.

(Elizabeth's reply) Okay. Bye daddy.

(Steven's reply) Elizabeth just walked away. I hope that you and mom can solve your problems. Gotta go.

(TJ's reply) Oh okay. I love you both.

TJ's last message went unsent. Apparently, Steven had signed off before TJ had a chance to say his final words. The happiness he was feeling in communicating with his kids had now turned a bit bittersweet, as Steven definitely showed some frustration and anger with him, to the point of simply cutting him off. TJ couldn't fathom losing the love of his kids. Tonight, he felt like that was starting to happen. He sat there on the bed. The lump in his throat reappeared.

TJ thought all day the next day about the exchange with his kids. It was time for him to call home. Even if that meant talking to Paige and arguing. He couldn't let another day go by without talking to his kids. After dinner, he thought, he'll make the call.

He rehearsed in his mind all day what he would say or how he might respond to questions from his kids or from Paige. This could get difficult, he thought. He wasn't ready for the emotions he may experience. This is crazy…. why am I afraid to call my own family? TJ struggled with this the entire day. He was actually scared to make this call. I have to, he thought.

He finished dinner, got his bottle of wine and went to his room to make the call. He sat there on his bed staring at his phone. He was frozen. He couldn't do it. He wasn't ready to face it. He slammed his phone down on the bed in disgust. TJ felt helpless and depressed as he sat there and drank his bottle of wine. This is my new low, he thought. I can't even call my own family. Darkness was right. I am worthless. TJ got drunk and fell asleep.

The next day of the routine followed the same pattern, with one major difference. TJ was hating himself. He felt completely worthless. He had disappointed everyone and anyone who loved him and now was afraid to confront any of them or deal with the situation. It had now been almost two weeks. TJ hadn't shown up at work. Surely, he's already fired. The lifeline in the form of that salary he provided his family was now gone. It wasn't the end of the world, as TJ had funds he could access if needed, and would ensure his family was taken care of. He hadn't responded to any of his friends. He hadn't even heard from his mother in almost a week.

TJ feared the consequences of his actions would lead him to a very lonely place. The relationships he formed were fleeting and always a moment in time. Sophie, Neha, Raj, Mia……. all made TJ feel like a king for a few days. But then it was gone.

As he sat overlooking the falls, he knew it was almost time to move on. Things were going south here. Much like the waterfall plummets downward, TJ could feel that same vibe within himself. He knew it was time again to change the dynamic.

Also worrying TJ was the amount of alcohol he was able to take in every day. Downing a bottle of wine each night can't be good for me, he thought. But that was the least of his concerns. By the 3rd or 4th glass, the pain was numbed. And for that, he was thankful.

TJ needed a friend to talk to. Partially for advice and partially to reassure himself that he wasn't going crazy. Kate Ambrose was his go-to friend in this regard. TJ had a fondness for Kate and her way of knowing how to say the right things. Kate didn't know what had happened with TJ and Paige.

TJ got on the phone with Kate and told her the whole story, up to the point where he was unable to even call his own home.

"Dude, get it together and stop beating yourself up. Don't absorb everyone else's problems and make them your own. You are doing what you need to. Of course, it's fresh in everyone's mind, but that will settle down. Find your new normal."

"My new normal is fucked up, Kate," replied TJ. "I'm drinking a bottle of wine every night and am scared shitless to talk to anyone but you apparently."

"Well, let me take each one of those and break it down for you. One, I'm honored you are able to call and talk to me. Two, a bottle of wine? Slow that train down, dude. Three, why are you scared to talk to them? Are you afraid they'll convince you to come home when you don't want to? That's all on you to make that decision, my friend."

"You're right, on all points. I'm a psychological mess right now."

"TJ, I love you, dude. I'm rooting for you here. If you need a destination, head my way. You can stay with me for as long as you want. Just don't let this spiral downwards any further. Keep your senses about you."

"I'm trying Kate. It's hard. I'm having a difficult time understanding where I'm right and where I'm wrong, what I could have done and should do differently. And it's tearing my mind to pieces every day."

"Shit TJ, I'm really worried about you. Please make it a point to try and at least send me a message every day. No matter what's going on, no matter how good or bad. You can tell me anything, okay. I don't care about anything else, just how you are doing. Okay? Promise me that."

"I'll try Kate. If not every day, I'll be sure to check in as much as I can." TJ appreciated Kate's words and especially her caring about him.

"You'd better. And don't do anything stupid! A bottle of wine a night might start making butt ugly girls look good."

TJ laughed. "Okay, I promise. Talk to you soon."

TJ slept a little better that night. Kate's reassuring words made him feel better. At least for one night.

TJ woke up the next morning in a panic. Something resembling an anxiety attack. He didn't know what was happening to him, but he knew one thing. It was time for him to leave Niagara Falls. It was time for him get away. Far away. The feeling was overwhelming him. It was as if he had been outrunning this feeling and as soon as he stopped, everything crashed into him.

TJ not only wanted to leave Niagara Falls. He wanted to leave the country. Get out of reach of everyone. He packed his things, never shaking the feeling he woke up with. It was really bothering him. He knew that sometimes stress could manifest itself in different ways, but this was unlike anything else he had ever experienced.

The logical and rational part of TJ's brain seemed to be overwhelmed and checked out. He was running on pure idealistic emotion at this time. He tried to compose himself, stop and take deep breaths. He even considered going to get some wine, even at this time of morning, anything to calm his nerves.

TJ started to think about his next steps. If he was going to leave the country, he'd need to determine a place to go. And he'd need to get himself to a bigger city than Buffalo to get himself on his way. TJ checked out, got in his car, and began his trip to his next destination, which would be his hop off point to the rest of the world – New York City.

Chapter 12

New York City was a place that TJ Carlson was very familiar with. So many things to see, do and experience. It's one of the most dynamic places in the world. A fitting stop, thought TJ, as he made his way from Buffalo, to send me out of here the right way. He still didn't know where he wanted to go. Where do you go when the world is your option, he wondered? Where do I even start?

His time in Niagara Falls allowed him time to think. Unfortunately, thinking was a fickle friend and often times did more damage than good. His best times were those where he didn't have to think about anything. The times where he had peace. The times where he could sleep without being tormented in his dreams. Where he didn't have to feel ashamed about his inability to reach out to his own family.

TJ hoped his change of setting would reinvigorate him. Especially as he planned all of his next moves that would take him potentially to places he's only dreamed of going. As exciting a thought as that was for TJ, he also knew he'd have a few constant travel companions: his thoughts and Darkness, his recurring nightmare. He would try to avoid them as best as he can.

TJ arrived in New York City and picked an expensive hotel in Times Square to stay at. I'll only be here a short while, he thought. Why not live it up! He checked in and got himself comfortable. He looked out his window and watched the people bustling around Times Square. He wondered if any of those people were dealing with situations in life like he was. Everyone has their own issues to deal with. I'm just one man, he thought. I can't imagine what some of those people are going through. But no one can tell. And no one looking at me can tell the mental anguish I am going through.

TJ grabbed some dinner and began thinking about what to that evening. His thoughts, however, were encouraging him to do something that he had yet to give in to on his journey so far. He wanted to go and have a little adult fun. Subconsciously planted in his brain, he thought, from when he passed by a strip club on the way to his hotel. TJ tried to re-direct his thoughts on the matter, but he decided to give in. Time to go unwind….and enjoy myself.

The Pussycat Lounge sounded like an innocent enough place to hang out, laughed TJ to himself. After getting shaken down for a $20 cover charge and being allowed to order his one drink minimum, an $8 glass of Coke, he settled down on a couch near the stage. There were three poles and three dancers. Breasts fully exposed, but they were still wearing thong bikini bottoms. They each looked various shades of lifeless. As if life had beaten them down to this point in their existence. TJ was actually feeling a bit sorry for the girls he was watching. One of them had a bruise below her right breast. This was not giving TJ any relief or enjoyment. It was actually making him even sadder.

TJ had never been to a strip club. I wonder if they are all like this, he thought. He looked around at the other people there. This was a motley crew. Obvious foreigners making the most of their stay in New York City, probably showing up with wads of cash. Older, overweight guys who look like life has beaten them consistently over the head with a club, probably escaping to the only place they can to see any action. Then there were big and muscular menacing looking guys, likely employees or bouncers, that TJ did not want to either anger or mess with.

He was about to give up and head back to his hotel, until he was shocked by the sudden appearance of a gorgeous Asian girl in front of him. She had a bikini on, but she was someone TJ immediately wanted to see remove it. She sat in TJ's lap and blew in his ear. Then she whispered to him.

"Take me to the VIP room and I'll give you a private dance," said the stripper.

"How much?" responded TJ.

"Twenty dollars for every five minutes. I'll make it worth every penny."

The stripper smiled at TJ. She was beautiful. For a moment, he again felt sad for this girl and wondered what led her to having to do this for money. But then he remembered the words of Kate Ambrose. Don't make other people's problems your problems.

"Let's go," said TJ. The stripper grabbed his hand and led TJ to an empty room, with one big exception. That big exception being a giant of a man with muscles covering every part of his body.

"Do not touch the girl," the scary giant man said forcefully. "I will be outside the door. If I hear a peep from her, you will regret it."

TJ was already regretting this, but at least he had parameters to work with. His hands would behave, unlike his visits to Mia.

The stripper turned on some music and removed her top. Her breasts were disproportionately big for her size, enhanced surgically beyond a shadow of a doubt, and sporting two nipple rings. She climbed into TJ's lap, rubbing her breasts from his chest and slowly upwards to his face, gyrating her hips to the music. Her arms around TJ, she pulled him in closer and kissed and licked his neck. TJ noticed that the stripper had positioned herself so that she was straddling one of TJ's legs, and she began grinding her pussy on it. TJ was getting uncomfortably hard.

Uncomfortable because he was wearing jeans, and he needed to shift positions. Once he did that, adjusting his cock so it was lying straight and flat, upwards in his pants, the stripper moved up into his lap and sat down right where TJ had positioned his cock. She wrapped her arms around TJ's neck, and grinded her pussy back and forth on TJ's hard cock. At first feeling really good, TJ wondered how this was going to end. He wasn't sure he wanted to walk out of there with either a massive erection or a stain in his pants.

"A hundred dollars and I'll make you finish," said the stripper.

"How?" said TJ.

"I'll keep doing this to you, for as long as it takes."

TJ thought about it, but not for long. Another shakedown, he thought. $20 for every five minutes and then another hundred to cum.

"No, that's okay. I don't have the budget for it," said TJ, frustrated, and now wanting to get out of there.

The stripper immediately stopped. "Okay, that will be $60 for our time and any additional tip for me."

TJ gave her $70. The stripper looked annoyed. "Ten dollars, that's it?"

Again, TJ started feeling a bit sorry for her and gave her another $10. This is how she makes her living. She relies on people like me to be generous.

The stripper gave him a hug. "Come see me again," she said and walked out the door. TJ walked out the door and then quickly walked out of the club. For a brief moment in there, he felt the closeness and intimacy he desired, but deep down he wasn't enjoying it. Physically he was, but his head wasn't in this one. TJ immediately thought of looking for a place to get a massage, or finding a place that would send someone to his room. But, thought TJ, I've already spent enough money on trying to get stimulated tonight. There's always tomorrow.

TJ went back to his hotel room. He couldn't shake the feeling of wanting to be close with another woman. It was dominating his thoughts on this night for some reason. The urge was powerful. TJ masturbated to relieve the urge and get it out of his system. He drank some wine and then fell asleep. His stay in New York City was off to an ominous start.

TJ was sitting in a classroom. He recognized some of the people in the class as people he went to high school with. Strange, he thought, that they still look exactly like they did in high school. He wasn't sure where he was, or what was being taught in this classroom. There was no teacher. On the blackboard was a picture of a man being beaten by a mob. What is this, thought TJ?

Darkness entered the room. It was unmistakably him, the same entity from his previous dream at the funeral. The creepy, too-large-for-his-face smile repulsed TJ. He focused on what Darkness was going to do and say. TJ readied himself for a fight.

"Welcome to my class," said Darkness. "I know you will learn a lot."

TJ heard a loud scream from the back of the classroom and quickly turned around. He was horrified to notice that everyone else in the classroom was now lying face first on their desks with blood dripping out of their faces and off each desk.

"Are they all dead?" asked TJ. "Why?"

"You ask a lot of questions. You're here to listen and learn, not question me." Darkness was focused solely on TJ.

TJ tried to gain some control in this dream, ignoring his dead classmates. "Okay then. What am I here to learn?"

"You're a problem, TJ. A destroyer of lives. You need to be taught a lesson."

"What the hell does that mean?" asked TJ.

"Come up here and look in this mirror. Tell me what you see," said Darkness.

TJ walked up to the front of the room, where there was now a full-length mirror. He stood in front of it and was horrified at what he saw. His face was scarred and disfigured. He was now missing an arm. His skin color had yellowed and blood started to drip from his nose. Scars had covered his body as now the clothes he was wearing were gone.

TJ turned to Darkness, who was smiling. "Fuck you," said TJ.

Darkness screamed the same high-pitched scream he heard in the first dream and shattered the mirror, with all of the shrapnel hitting and embedding itself into TJ. TJ screamed in pain.

TJ jolted himself awake. Not scared this time, but just angry. Another dream. There is no coincidence that with all the stress he has experienced that it was manifesting itself in his subconscious and had somehow created this entity terrorizing him in his dreams, giving him dire warnings of a bleak future. It was 4:00am. TJ decided to not give Darkness another chance at him that night.

TJ still had enough wits about him to realize he couldn't just leave the country and do it without money. He had an IRA that had close to $60,000 dollars in it. It was time, thought TJ, to cash that in and make sure he could facilitate his travels.

TJ went to a Citibank in New York City and set himself up an account. This was to be his source of funds, known only to him. This would be where he would transfer his IRA funds. He thought about what Paige was living on without his salary. They had savings, and she was probably having to dip in to that to pay bills and live. He instructed Citibank to cut a check for $10,000 and send it to Paige as soon as his funds arrived.

TJ had a debit card overnighted to his hotel address in New York City. Perfect, thought TJ. He took care of himself financially while also still taking care of Paige. He felt somewhat noble, even though he knew deep down his actions were self-serving and he was about to put himself out of reach.

TJ visited the Statue of Liberty on this day. He sat in a café outside overlooking the statue and had some lunch. He began composing messages to his mother and to his kids. Steven hadn't messaged him or even been online since the last time they talked. His mother checked in every so often, more than likely concerned about his state of mind. He always responded to her with an "I'm Fine" and didn't go into much detail. He took a picture of himself in front of the Statue of Liberty and sent it to his mother.

Just to let you know where I am. I'll be traveling a bit from here, but please don't worry about me. I'm getting myself together and I'm okay. Can you do me a favor? Please show this to the kids when you see them next. I don't have a way of sending this to them right now.

A short, impersonal message, but at least they could see him. TJ looked at himself in the picture. He was thankful it wasn't the grotesque image of himself he saw in the dream, but he was looking different. His hair was longer. A beard was growing. Some bags under his eyes. He looked like someone who was going through a life crisis. I don't look too bad, he thought. Nothing a little cleaning up and a haircut won't remedy.

TJ knew it was about time to make the call on where he was going to go. He was fortunate that many years ago, he had signed up for an airline miles program and now had enough miles to get himself anywhere he wanted to go. Maybe the airline can help him decide where to go, he laughed to himself.

"Hello, Mr. Carlson. How may I help you today?" said the lady who works with his mileage program.

"I'm about to make your day challenging, in a good way," said TJ. "I want to cash in some miles and go overseas, and I need your help figuring out where to go."

"That would be my pleasure, sweetie. Have you at least narrowed down a continent?" The lady laughed.

"Let's go with Europe," said TJ.

"Okay, that helps. But only a little. Where do you want to go, sweetie?" Her voice was very friendly and soothing, with a definite southern twang to it.

TJ thought about it for a few minutes. "What is your name, by the way?" he asked.

"My name is Rose. Rose Carter."

"Rose, is it okay to ask for you any time I call?" asked TJ.

"Sure, sweetie. Do you plan to call me back today?"

"No, I'll figure out something today, Rose. But I'll be doing more traveling with my miles and just wanted to talk with someone consistent."

TJ pulled up a map of Europe. The first thing that caught his eye was Ireland. It was almost like an entry point into Europe for him.

And he could go back to the scene of one his more memorable visits, to the Cliffs of Moher.

"Rose, I think I know what I want. Can you book a flight for me from New York City to Shannon, Ireland?"

"Is that round trip?" asked Rose.

"No, one way," said TJ. "Leaving the day after tomorrow."

Rose booked the trip for TJ. "Is everything okay, sweetie?"

"Yes, it is. Why?" asked TJ.

"Nothing. Just an odd request. Very sudden and with no return. Just wanted to make sure you were okay. We definitely care about not only getting our clients where they need to go, but also about their well-being."

"I appreciate that, Rose. I'm fine. You'll be hearing from me quite a bit."

"Okay, sweetie, you are all set. I'll email you your e-ticket. Safe travels."

TJ was heading back to Ireland. He felt good that he had a destination, and one that meant something to him. Maybe standing there at the Cliffs of Moher again would trigger something in him and give him some clarity.

Paige Carlson had waited over 3 weeks now and was starting to get it in her mind that she was going to have to live life without TJ. She grew increasingly bitter with him each passing day. She had talked to him once, and that didn't go well. He was really gone.

Kylie had stopped by on this day to check up on Paige. She was worried about her friend. Kylie didn't want Paige blaming herself for anything that was going on. Her support was endless bashing of TJ, and at first Paige lightly defended TJ. Not anymore.

"Paige, seriously, you need to divorce him. He's been gone for nearly a month. What do you think he's doing out there?"

"I have no idea," said Paige. "And I don't care anymore. I need to look out for myself and my kids."

"That is absolutely right. Do what you need to do to take care of your family. Don't let his actions destroy you. And let him know you don't need him."

"I don't need him," said Paige.

"I still can't believe he just abandoned all of you. What a piece of garbage." Kylie was pouring it on. She truly despised TJ. "The sooner you divorce him, the sooner you can find a real man."

"I'm done talking about him. I'll send him a message tonight telling him how I feel."

Later that night, Paige, with a heaviness and anger in her heart, sat down to compose a message to TJ.

TJ – You're out there somewhere. At this point, I don't really care where you are or who you are with. It's clear to me you are gone for good and no longer give a shit about your family. Well, don't worry. We will be fine without you. Go get your jollies wherever you are and continue this selfish indulgence. We could have handled this like adults without you running away like a coward. Maybe you got used to being without us while you traveled and cavorted with who knows how many other women. It doesn't really matter anymore. I still hope you stay safe wherever you are, but I will count on you for nothing. You broke Elizabeth's heart by not even saying goodbye to her. I hope you can live with that.

Paige sent the message and then immediately regretted it and wished she could pull it back. No, she thought, its best that he reads that and knows how I feel. Maybe it will trigger him to change his mind. At this point, despite all their issues, Paige was thinking of their children. They missed their father.

TJ read Paige's message and felt especially bad. He now felt the distance growing between him and the family he knew for 15 years. They were becoming strangers and Paige was now all but writing him off. TJ worried about what potential damage he was doing to the relationship between himself and his kids. TJ turned to the one friend he knew he could always commiserate with - Kate Ambrose.

"She's just lashing out, TJ. If she can give up on you that easily, then she truly didn't love you at all."

"I know her, Kate. I think she was probably feeling like this even before I left."

Kate was adamant. "She's feeling hurt, TJ. Her pride is hurt. You left and gave yourself control over the situation. While you were there, I think she had control. She dictated the mood and the vibe of the house and projected it on you. You took that power away from her. Also, her denying you sex was a power of hers. She said that herself. You took that away also. She's angry, TJ. But not for the reasons she is saying."

"You always know the right things to say, Kate. I hope you're right and it certainly makes sense."

"Do what you need to do and go where you need to go. Go see the world TJ. Do whatever you need to do to fix yourself. Come back with a purpose."

"Thanks Kate. That's my plan. I want to go and reclaim myself. And battle my demons."

"Remember, you promised to stay in touch. Bye, TJ. Please take care of yourself and shoot me a quick message when you land in Ireland. I hope that is the start of something special."

Kate ended the call with TJ. He really enjoyed talking to her. He felt like he was on the same wavelength. TJ had one more message to send. To a friend he had been almost embarrassed to reach out to. But now, TJ did not rule out the possibility of going to India. He sent Neha Ganesh a message.

Neha – how are you? I miss you. Just wanted you to know, I'll be doing some traveling again and would love to make India a stop. I'll be in touch.

This was it. TJ's last day in New York City and the United States for a period of time he couldn't predict. His journey starts tomorrow. He had high hopes that this would be a life-changing undertaking. He had a drink and then fell asleep. Already packed to go to the airport.

The next morning, TJ woke up and readied himself to go. He was feeling many things. It could best be described as a combination of excitement and sadness. Excitement for the adventure he was about to go on but sad for the reason he's doing it. He's leaving because he can't take it anymore. Worried about his state of mind and his physical health. It's driven him to run. Hopefully, he thought, I will find my purpose and slay my demons. I have to, for the sake of my kids, who I desperately want to watch grow up, get married and have families of their own.

He had one other concern. His car. He was about to leave that in an airport parking lot for God knows how long. He considered selling it, but I could be back next week, he thought. Better safe than sorry.

He got in the car and drove to the airport. It was go time.

TJ sat on the plane. This was it, no turning back. The start of something amazing, he hoped. As the plane taxied down the runway and then picked up speed for takeoff, TJ closed his eyes. He allowed himself to feel the ascent of the plane. He tried to let that peace wash over him. He tried to shed the weight of what he was leaving behind. Stress, shame and Darkness – I hope they all stayed there, he thought.

The stewardess passed by when they were finally up in the air and cruising. "Can I get anything for you, sir?"

"Red wine, please."

Chapter 13

It wasn't the same. It just wasn't the same. I remember being here vividly, like it was yesterday, thought TJ Carlson. Now, it feels lonely and looking at this makes me sad. TJ had returned to the Cliffs of Moher in County Clare, Ireland, and was standing at the ledge looking at the waves crashing in to the cliff walls. He remembered his conversation with Jim that day when he was last here. Jim fumbling around with his camera trying to capture the perfect shot. I'm sure he did, thought TJ. It's a picture that has probably been blown up, framed and is hanging on the wall of Jim and Carrie Keller's love nest.

What had happened between then and now? Why had it all fallen apart? At this moment, TJ felt like everything that had happened in between visits to these Cliffs had been a blur. Almost like it wasn't real. Like he had a long daydream while he was standing here in this spot. The weather was almost the exact same as that day. The view was perfect. The only thing that had changed was him.

At this moment, he felt bad for ignoring Jim's last message to him. It was a missed opportunity to right at least one wrong turn that had happened with his life. But what's done is done, and I'm here to get myself back together, he thought.

TJ's return to Ireland was a low-key affair. Going straight from the airport in Shannon to his hotel in Limerick, the beginning of his journey had few frills. The Cliffs were his first and only priority in Ireland, he realized. Now he was here, and the feeling he was hoping to experience wasn't there. Now what, he thought. TJ stood there and stared at the Cliffs for another 30 minutes. Realizing that he wasn't gaining much from the experience, he returned back to the car and driver that had brought him here.

"Back to the hotel, my good man," said TJ to the driver. "Can you recommend any good pubs in Limerick?"

There were a few small pubs close to his hotel and TJ found one that would also serve a decent dinner. Once again, TJ was here in Ireland at a time of year where the weather was a bit cooler and the number of people milling about, especially tourists, were small.

TJ sat in the pub and had ordered a beer. Not brave enough to try Guinness again, he looked around at all the patrons who were drinking that very beverage. Their taste buds must have all evolved to find this drink appetizing, thought TJ. Everyone was quiet and keeping to themselves. The vibe here and in the whole town of Limerick was bleak. It was depressing. Certainly not something that was going to lift or elevate TJ's spirit. As a matter of fact, he thought, this would actually be one place that matches my mood and state of mind. Not good, and not what I want or need.

TJ made the decision that his stay in Ireland was going to be a short one. He considered heading to Dublin, but he had been there before and the thought of treading old ground here wasn't an appealing one. TJ was finishing his second beer when he noticed a couple walk in to the Pub. Both were wearing Chicago Bears sweaters. These have got to be Americans, thought TJ. The couple sat down at a table and ordered some drinks. They were carefully studying some papers and having an animated conversation. Probably an itinerary of some kind. Figuring he had nothing left to lose here, TJ got up and walked over to the couple.

"Are you two from America?" asked TJ.

The couple both looked at him. "Yes," said the man. "Can you guess where from?"

"Green Bay?" responded TJ, knowing this would likely draw a response from the two obvious Bear fans.

"God forbid!" said the woman.

"You are from the good ol USA too I assume," said the man.

"Yup. North Carolina. TJ Carlson. Great to meet you guys. I won't bother you. I figured you both as Americans, so I figured I'd come over and say hi."

"No bother at all. I'm Mark and this is Christine. We are from Chicago. Here in Ireland on a tour. We're heading to see the Cliffs of Moher, Bunratty Castle and some other sites around this area. I have to say, this is a pretty bleak place."

"I was at the Cliffs today," said TJ. "You'll love it, it's gorgeous. Where are you heading after this?"

"Going up to the north," said Christine, "visiting Northern Ireland and then ending in Dublin. We'll head to England and Scotland after this."

"That sounds great," said TJ. "I didn't go to Northern Ireland the last time I was here."

"You want to join us, TJ?" asked Mark. "Grab a seat."

"Sure, I'd love to," said TJ, thankful that this couple had walked in.

"What brings you to Ireland, TJ? You said you'd been here before."

TJ considered telling his whole story, again, to another set of strangers. But on this night, he decided not to. Time to change the dynamic, thought TJ. He didn't want to burden this happy couple with his troubles.

"I just really like it here. I'm single, and traveling is something that I do whenever I have the chance. I'm at the start of a tour around the world."

"Wow," said Mark, "a tour around the world. We're going to do that one day when we pull the money together. Except I think we'd like to do a cruise around the world."

"That sounds amazing," said TJ. "How long is your stay in Ireland?"

"We're here for 7 days," said Christine. "Anything you recommend here or in Dublin for us to see or do?"

"All the usual tourist spots," said TJ. "But let me give you some helpful advice about being here in Ireland. Never, ever, ever and I mean ever, praise anything or anyone British. Especially the

Queen. Except maybe in Northern Ireland, but I would even advise against that."

TJ told the story of the Irish driver and Jim and the beat down Jim received from Paul for his praising of the Queen. This got a belly laugh from the American couple.

"Noted," said Mark. "That is very helpful advice, especially since are headed to the UK after this. Should we insult the Brits while we are here?" asked Mark jokingly.

"Only if the situation calls for it," said TJ. "To get yourself out of a jam here or get people on your side. If that happens, just yell out 'Fuck the Brits!' as loud as you can. Should buy you time."

Christine, Mark and TJ shared a few more drinks, a meal and some laughs. As it turned out, they were staying at the same hotel and opted to walk back together. The streets of Limerick at night on the route to the hotel were not very well lit, so TJ was glad he could walk back in a group. On the way back, a group of 4 young Irish men, apparently coming from a different pub, were heading their way. They started shouting something towards the threesome. Mark and Christine started to look worried. As they approached, all four men were now talking and laughing, looking as if they had plans to engage the three of them with something.

"Haaay!!" shouted one of them. "Yoy……."

"What did he say?" asked Mark.

"I have no clue," said TJ, now worried himself.

The man yelled more inaudible gutterings as they approached.

"FUCK THE BRITS!" yelled Christine, to the shock of both Mark and TJ. They both looked at her simultaneously, wondering why she had done that.

The four men laughed loudly. "Yeeeah haaaaaaah……. fuck the Brits!" The four men then began a chant with those three words and passed by Christine, Mark and TJ, offering high fives as they passed. All three obliged the men and they continued on past them.

"That was great advice, TJ. Thanks!" said Christine with a smile.

"And that took guts," said TJ. I was half kidding with that, but it appears it was pretty sound advice.

They all made it to the hotel and went their separate ways. TJ let them know he'd be on his way again soon and to enjoy their stay in Ireland. A night that started out fairly lame had been redeemed, thanks once again to people who will undoubtedly pass through TJ's life, never to be heard from or seen again. But at least they shared this moment in time.

TJ opted to take a bus to Dublin the next day. He was ready to move on, but wasn't sure where. He was bored, and really had no other plans for Dublin other than to fly out of that airport when ready. The urge hit TJ again. He began to wonder what opportunities in Dublin may exist to meet a girl or go enjoy some adult fun. On this day, he suppressed it. I need to focus on going to the next place, he thought. I'll have other time for that.

"I didn't expect to hear back from you so quickly, Mr. Carlson," said Rose Carter, TJ's friend at the airline miles redemption center.

"I'm ready to move on, Rose," said TJ.

"Have you given it much thought this time," laughed Rose.

"Again, no," said TJ. "But here's two choices, help me pick one. London or Scotland."

"Oh, why don't you do both. Fly to Edinburgh and then take a train to London, and that way you can experience both."

"Rose, that sounds like an excellent plan. Book me a one way from Dublin to Edinburgh."

Rose took a few minutes and then confirmed to TJ that he was all set.

"Thank you, Rose. Talk to you again soon."

"No problem, sweetie," said Rose, "I look forward to hearing from you again."

TJ arranged a ride to the airport at his hotel and settled down for the night. He was pleased that he was able to tame some of the urges he was feeling, especially after the experience in New York City at the strip club. He sincerely hoped that the parts of his personality that were emerging that he was uncomfortable with would hopefully go away on this journey and he could take his steps to being whole again.

TJ pulled out his phone and put an email together to Kate Ambrose, the one person TJ was consistently keeping in touch with. He hadn't reached out to any members of his family since he left. None of them knew where he was. And his job......not a word. No follow up from Becky at all. He simply hadn't shown up, and no one seemed to care enough to even try to message him other than Becky.

TJ dozed off, ready to continue on to Scotland and continue his journey to what had now become a quest for personal redemption.

Chapter 14

TJ was in awe as he took in the scenery in the city of Edinburgh. Edinburgh castle perched on top of a hill, gothic and medieval buildings and an imposing black statue of William Wallace with sharp spires aimed towards the sky. What a scary looking place, thought TJ. It feels haunted. At the same time, he thought it was incredibly cool and couldn't wait to explore. The feeling he would get sometimes in places he would travel came back. TJ was thrilled that maybe he was recovering a bit of himself.

TJ had a lot on his mind as he arrived at his hotel. In his few days in Ireland, he hadn't even checked to see if anyone had tried to get in touch with him. He was feeling completely disengaged now from back home. A feeling he was getting used to and did not like. He missed his kids terribly. But even with that, he knew that this journey so far was doing good things for his mind, body and spirit. He had to continue down this path. But here in Scotland, he vowed, he would start reaching back out to re-connect and finally tie up some loose ends.

His hotel was a quaint place located not far from the hill leading up to the castle. Across the street, TJ stopped for dinner. He ordered a pizza. And then proceeded to eat one of the worst pizzas he'd ever had. Scottish pizza…. off the list, he thought. But that was redeemed by one of the greatest foodstuffs he had ever tried. And one that probably shaved years off of his life the second he finished it. A deep-fried Mars Candy Bar. TJ had never heard of it. He watched its preparation. A candy bar smothered in batter and deep fried. I think I may have just consumed 5000 calories, thought TJ, whose stomach was now getting into an argument with him about his recent activities. "I'll regret that one later," said TJ out loud to himself. TJ was not really an adventurous eater, and there was one Scottish delicacy. No one, no matter how persuasive or beautiful, was going to convince him to try haggis.

"He just left her, Jim. He has barely even reached out to her or his kids. Don't sit there and even remotely defend him." Carrie Keller was on a tirade about TJ Carlson to her husband, Jim. Jim had a lot of concern about TJ and his state of mind. He was trying to convince Carrie that there were two sides to this story and he was trying to reach out to him.

"He's my friend Carrie. I know how you feel, you've made that perfectly clear," Jim responded.

"Then why are you defending him?"

"Like I said……he hinted at problems as far back as our trip to Ireland. That's not all his fault, Carrie. He explained to me what he was feeling back then, but I didn't think much of it. I thought it was minor and they would work it out. I never thought this is what would end up happening."

Carrie looked thoughtfully at Jim for a minute. "I consider Paige a close friend as well. I've been treated the way TJ is treating her. She took care of everything in that house while he was out cheating on her and having fun everywhere he went. I really feel for her. I guess I'm just seeing this happen to another one of my close friends and it makes me sick."

"TJ and I have been friends since we were teenagers. Our friendship wouldn't have lasted that long if he didn't have some good moral character and values. To paint him now as a lecherous womanizer is unfair. He wouldn't have done what he did unless he had no other choice."

"What a male response," said Carrie angrily to Jim. "Justify going out and screwing around because you're not getting enough or getting what you want at home. Sickening."

"What are you getting pissed at me for? I'm just saying, Carrie, that there are two sides to this story. I want to know his. We know Paige's backwards and forwards, but I'm not buying all of it. This is not solely his doing."

Carrie was getting increasingly angry at her husband. "Look at this……even the topic of TJ Carlson is making us fight. He's a cancer, Jim. I despise him and all guys like him. I will not condone or support you continuing to be friends with him. He already wrote you off. Said to hell with your friendship that day when he left here. Why would you even keep trying?"

"Never mind. Let's stop talking about it. I understand how you feel. And I certainly don't want us to go down the same path they did." Jim Keller knew for certain now that he could not bring Carrie into any future efforts to contact or communicate with TJ. But he wouldn't stop trying to reach out to his friend.

It had been almost a month since TJ Carlson had shown up for work. Anna Martin and Becky Parsons would talk for a few minutes each day about "TJ sightings." He was becoming a bit of a legend here at the office.

"I've been watching missing person's reports," said Anna. "Nothing reported. Whatever happened, people know he's still out there. But where?"

"I'm just amazed we haven't heard a word about him being fired or terminated. I checked and I can still send him emails and find him in the company directory. It's so bizarre." Becky showed Anna the last message she sent him. "I know he read this. I can tell, there's an indicator of when my messages have been seen. So, he's out there somewhere, but apparently doesn't want people to know."

"Jan is refusing to talk about him," replied Anna. It's like he's become a top secret in the company. I think they have been having meetings about him."

"I can't imagine they've approved what he's doing. No one seems to know anything. I just hope he's okay." Becky re-read the message she had sent him.

"Can we send him another message?" asked Anna. "From your personal phone."

"What should we say?" replied Becky.

"Just to let him know what's going on and that we hope he's okay." Becky agreed with Anna and they crafted a message to TJ.

Hi TJ – It's Anna and Becky. We both hope you're okay, wherever you are. If you want to communicate with us, it's okay. We won't tell anyone here at the office. You've become the international man of mystery here. We both hope we can hear from you and see you soon. Please take care of yourself. We miss you.

Becky sent the message and really hoped this would elicit a reply from TJ. Or at least an indication, once again, that he at least read it.

Dean Carlson was a man of few words. TJ's older brother was a kind, caring man, but often kept to himself and didn't engage much. He was visiting Ann and Harold Carlson on this day to talk about a subject growing increasingly sad and frustrating for the Carlson family – the whereabouts and the state of mind of TJ Carlson, their son, brother and father of two.

"Did he say what he was doing after New York City?" asked Dean.

"No…. only that he had a plan to do something. We haven't heard a word from him since that day," replied Ann. "I wish he would just send a message every few days that just says that he is still alive."

"Can we ask his bank or credit card company to trace where he's using his accounts? Technically, we could classify him as a missing person here, couldn't we?" Dean was trying to bring logic and order to this chaotic situation. Dean and TJ weren't very close, but they had a good, cordial relationship. Dean was more concerned about the effect TJ was having on his family than what he was actually doing.

"I'm not ready to go that far, son," replied Ann. "Whatever he's doing is something he feels like he needed to do. I just don't like not knowing, especially for the sake of Steven and Elizabeth."

Harold Carlson was listening intently to this conversation, but keeping strangely quiet. Until now. "Our son is a grown man. He's responsible for his own actions and decisions, and the consequences of them. I hope to hell he knows what he's doing. He'll reach out to us when he's ready."

"Shit, do you even care about this, Harold?" asked Ann. "That's our son. I'm worried about his state of mind and what he might be doing out there. I don't want to hear that he's been found dead somewhere and there's something we could have done to prevent that from happening."

"Dammit, Ann, of course I care about him. Am I the only one here who thinks he knows exactly what he's doing? That woman stressed him to no end and he pulled himself out of that situation for the sake of his kids, not to punish them. Let him get this out of his system and see where he lands. Until then, we will do our part to help take care of our grandkids." Harold looked at both

Ann and Dean as if he had just made the final point of the conversation.

"Even if he knows, I won't stop worrying about him," said Ann. "Asking him to check in with me every so often doesn't sound like a lot to ask from him, especially if it will give me, and us, some peace of mind."

"I'm ready to go wherever to get him," interjected Dean. "Just keep that in mind if the situation gets bad."

"Thanks son," said Ann. Ann sat down at her computer and composed a message to TJ.

Son – this is a special request from your mother. Can you please just send me a message every few days and let me know you're okay? That would give me peace of mind. Your father thinks you know exactly what you're doing. I hope so. And I hope you're safe wherever you are. Where are you now? Please respond TJ. We all love you and miss you and want you to come home. –Love, Mom

Paige Carlson had just finished reading Elizabeth her bedtime story. Paige had stepped into that role over the last month to try and keep things as normal as possible for Elizabeth, who was missing her father a lot. Paige even took on the acting roles required to successfully read these stories in the evening. On this night, however, Elizabeth was full of questions.

"Mommy, where's daddy?" asked Elizabeth.

"Daddy is out there somewhere, honey."

"Will he ever call us and talk to us?"

"Yes, I'm sure he will. Daddy wasn't feeling good. He's trying to get better and then he will call us." Paige was getting very uncomfortable at this line of questioning.

"And then he will come home?" asked Elizabeth.

"I hope so, honey. I know he loves you and Steven very much."

"Mommy, I miss Daddy. I like when he would read me stories and made his characters really funny. Is he very sick?" Elizabeth now had a worried look on her face.

"No, honey. He just needed to go get himself better. We will see him again soon, I promise."

"Okay," said Elizabeth. "If he calls, let me know so I can talk to him."

"Of course, I will," said Paige sweetly. "Good night, Elizabeth."

"Good night Mommy. I love you," said Elizabeth, who then rolled over to go to sleep.

Paige felt heavy after that series of questions from her daughter. She had no idea where TJ was, what he was doing or when he would be coming back. She tried not to think about it too much anymore. She tried to get used to her new normal, and was more worried about the financial aspect of the household. She had received a $10,000 check from TJ, but still wasn't sure what had led to that or where it came from. That was the last time she had heard from him. At least he still cares about us, somewhat, thought Paige.

While not harboring any remaining feelings for TJ as a husband, she was worried about him as a person. She hoped he was okay and that someone was watching after him. Even, at this point, if it was another woman. The kids can't lose their father, she thought. I just hope he's safe wherever he is.

TJ settled in for the night at his Edinburgh hotel. He was thinking a lot about home. Tomorrow, he thought, I'll go experience some of the city and then devote the evening to trying to re-connect. He polished off his bottle of wine and a small travel size bottle of Scotch and fell asleep.

TJ finished his visit to Edinburgh castle. The day was a chilly and misty day, almost a perfect setting for this gothic city. He did his best to take in the history of the castle and appreciate being at another very unique place in this world. He really wanted to go back to the William Wallace statue, a structure that he couldn't get out of his mind. One of the fiercest and most imposing structures he'd ever seen. He wanted to get close up and personal to get to know more about it. Within walking distance from the castle, TJ made his way through the Edinburgh mist towards the statue.

On his way there, he witnessed an elderly lady carrying a bag of groceries stumble and fall over. Immediately halting his progress towards the statue, TJ went over to help the lady. She wasn't hurt, thankfully, but it looks like she was going to struggle to get up. TJ approached the lady and offered her help in getting back up.

"Oh, thank God," she said. "I feel so clumsy." Her accent was a thick, Scottish accent, and TJ struggled at first to pick up what she was saying.

TJ helped her back up and collected the few groceries that had fallen out of her bag. "No worries, ma'am. I hope you're okay. Do you need to get to a doctor or anything?"

"Oh no, I'm okay. Just a few bruises to my body and my pride. Where are you from, man without a Scottish accent?" she smiled.

"I'm from the USA. TJ Carlson. Very nice to meet you."

"I'm Dolores," she said, "and I wish we could have met under different circumstances than me being an oaf and tripping over my own feet."

"That's okay, Dolores," laughed TJ. "God wanted us to meet today, so he concocted a funny plan to make it happen."

"Let me buy you a cup of coffee," said Dolores. "Then I'll let you go on your way. To say thank you."

"Sure, Dolores. That would be wonderful." TJ and Dolores went to a coffee shop that actually wasn't too far from the William Wallace statue, something that TJ continually focused on as they got closer to it. He was almost obsessed with this structure.

"Do you have any children, TJ?" asked Dolores.

"Yes, I do," replied TJ. "I have a boy and a girl, Steven and Elizabeth."

"Are they here with you, along with the Mrs.?"

TJ thought about sharing his story again, but once again, opted not to tell another stranger his sad tale. He was becoming increasingly reluctant to re-live the details that led him to this point.

"No, they aren't," replied TJ. "I'm here on business and couldn't bring them." TJ showed Dolores pictures of the two kids.

"Oh, they both have such beautiful blonde hair. Your daughter is a doll. Your wife must be beautiful, because you two made very pretty children."

"Thank you, Dolores. She is very beautiful. Elizabeth looks just like her."

TJ and Dolores finished their coffee and Dolores indicated she would be on her way home.

"You know, TJ, I thank God that I met you today. You are a wonderful man for going out of your way to help me. It's like I was sent a guardian angel from a faraway land to make sure that I wasn't hurt. You should be proud of yourself, and your kids and wife should be proud that they have such a wonderful father and husband. Thank God again for you, TJ. God bless you." Dolores gave TJ a hug and was on her way.

TJ took all of what Dolores said in. He hadn't felt proud of himself much in recent months, until today. Another piece of the redemption puzzle, he thought. This was enough to propel him, with motivation, back to his hotel room to begin re-connecting with the world he left behind.

"Jan Carver, please?" TJ asked the front desk operator. TJ had tried calling Jan's personal phone, but no luck. He was determined to track her down, even have her paged.

"One minute, sir. Who can I tell her is calling?" said the Operator.

"Let her know its TJ Carlson."

"Please hold," she said.

TJ held on the phone for a few minutes. Surely, she would want to talk to him. It had been a month and not a word from me, he thought.

"TJ!! Where in the devil have you been?" Jan Carver screamed into the phone. "It has been four weeks. Are you okay? Where are you?"

"Jan, I'll be honest. I had a bit of a meltdown. I'm no longer in the country right now. But rest assured, I'm okay. I just wanted to get in touch with you, first to see if I'd been fired yet, and if not, to formally resign from my position."

"TJ, we were going to give you another 30 days to get in touch. I'm glad you did now, and I'm glad that you are okay. I'm sorry things got so bad for you."

"Thanks Jan. I'm sorry I did it the way I did. But officially, as of today, I resign. What do you need from me?"

"TJ, just send me something in writing and I'll take care of the rest."

"Okay, will do. Thanks Jan."

"And TJ," she continued, "on a personal note, I just wanted to wish you all the best. I knew you were dealing with some personal issues and I empathized with you greatly. I just had to keep work and those notions separate. Please get yourself better, do what you need to do for you and just know you always have options to return here when you get back."

TJ was floored that he was hearing this from Jan Carver, the same woman who he debated whether she actually knew he existed. She was a caring human being after all. TJ felt relieved to have wrapped up this piece of business responsibly. One fire he left burning that he now had put out.

TJ read the message from his mother and crafted his response.

Mom – I'm really sorry I've been bad about keeping in touch. Right now, I'm in Scotland. This journey is doing a lot of good for me. I'm on the right path. Making myself whole again so I can return and be a better father for my kids. I'll send you a message every few days so you have peace of mind. And don't worry too much about me – dad is right. I know what I'm doing. –TJ

Next up was the message from Becky and Anna. TJ crafted his response.

Hey guys – sorry I've been such a mystery. But I wanted you both to know that I had good reasons and that I finally officially resigned today with Jan. She was surprisingly supportive. You both take care and please keep in touch.

And now, thought TJ, it's time to call home. It was the right time of day. The kids were home from school. TJ was ready to face whatever questions and even braced for an argument with Paige. He dialed his home number. It kept ringing. No answer. Strange, he thought. This is the prime time of day. Everyone should be home. He called again. It again kept ringing. Out of curiosity, he checked whether Steven was online. He was. They were home. TJ began typing a message to Steven but then stopped. It should be registering that this was him calling the house. Why wasn't anyone answering? He tried one more time. No answer.

TJ imagined the scenario that was going on at the house. Someone, maybe Paige, was picking up the phone, seeing that it was TJ, and not answering it. Or maybe Elizabeth had picked it up, seen that it was him, got excited to talk to him, but was then instructed not to answer it. TJ was feeling hurt. The good vibes of the day came crashing down around him, and now all he wanted to do was drink. He went to a store close by, got a bottle of wine, and started to drink.

He sent a message to Steven, who was still online.

Tried calling. No one answered, even though it looks like you guys were home. Tell Elizabeth I love her.

He then immediately shut his phone off and proceeded to down his bottle of wine. He fell asleep with the bottle in his hand, a little spilling on to the bed sheets.

TJ wandered around the streets of Edinburgh the next day, feeling deflated. He checked that morning if there was a response from Steven, but there wasn't. He felt a bit directionless on this day and unsure of what he was going to do next. He felt he had made some progress, but not with the two people who mattered the most, his two kids. He didn't get a chance to talk to them, which he would have traded everything else for.

As he was walking down the street, he heard a sound that he wanted to go research a bit. It was a pleasing sound to his ears. It was the sound of a street bagpipe player. The sound of the bagpipes was mesmerizing to TJ. He'd heard them before, but for some reason it was affecting him on this day. The bagpipe player was in full outfit, kilt and all. He was an older man with impressive facial hair, particularly the moustache. And he was good, no…. great, on the bagpipes. TJ didn't know what songs he was playing until he began playing "Amazing Grace." Beautiful, he thought.

TJ sat down near the bagpipe player and just listened for about 90 minutes. He was entranced with this instrument, the sound it was making, and the skill with which the man was playing it. The man noticed that even though people were stopping and enjoying his playing, he had a permanent audience of one.

The man took a break. "You enjoying the concert, Laddie?"

TJ laughed. "You have no idea how much. I never realized how much I loved the sound of bagpipes. And you are amazing."

"I've been playin it for near 35 years. It's an extension of me, Laddie. Be kind to me when you decide to leave." The man chuckled, obviously referring to TJ leaving behind a bit of money to show how much he liked it.

"You can count on that," said TJ. He listened to the man for another 30 minutes and then decided to go research bagpipe-based songs he could download. He left the bagpipe player a fifty-pound note. The man winked at TJ as he walked away and TJ saluted the man. TJ headed back to the hotel. His day completely derailed by the sounds of bagpipes, but in a good way. It was something that oddly soothed him and he wanted to carry that feeling forward.

Sometimes, being alone with his thoughts wasn't the best place for TJ to be. He had been in Scotland for a few days and was ready to move on. While lying in bed, he re-lived his visits with the Indian masseuses and with Mia in his mind. He was longing for that closeness again with someone, but options appeared to be zero here in Edinburgh. And this apparently was going to be an urge that was hard to fight. The temptation was too strong. He was hoping this wasn't going to be the trend. Be in a place long enough to enjoy the scenery and sights, and then immediately revert to heavier drinking and sexual desire.

He booked a train ticket to London. It was time to leave Edinburgh and re-set once again. He'd be leaving the next day, so he enjoyed his last night in Scotland with a few glasses of Scotch at the restaurant close by and a bottle of wine. Hoping to build on early momentum he had built here, he was excited about moving on.

The train ride from Edinburgh to London made TJ laugh consistently. The train conductor, or whoever was making the announcements, sounded as if he was speaking a different language The first announcement he made, TJ turned to another passenger and asked what language it was. English, he was assured, with a laugh from the passengers.

"Totally incomprehensible," said TJ to himself.

After each announcement, it became a game to TJ to try and guess what the announcer was saying. He continuously failed at this, making him laugh harder each time. I just hope London is an extremely obvious stop, because I'd never know by his announcements, he thought.

As the train ride progressed, TJ began to feel a bit queasy, but he shook it off. I've been through so much stress here recently, must be some nerves or anxiety, he thought.

TJ arrived in London, ready to start anew once again.

Chapter 15

TJ's first day in London was meant to be a fresh start. So why, at the end of his first day, is he passed out drunk in his hotel room, bleeding on the floor and convulsing in his sleep? A look back at his day provides an insight into his current situation and increasingly inconsistent state of mind.

Morning Arrival in London:

TJ's train from Edinburgh pulled into Victoria Station in London during mid-morning. It was a relentlessly gloomy day, the clouds a depressing shade of gray and fully covering the sky. TJ had to go grab another subway train on the Underground to the Kensington area of London. He had brought a bit of Scotland with him in the form of severe stomach cramps which had progressed from the initial queasiness he felt on the train, likely due to the second deep fried Mars Bar and bottle of wine consumed the night before. TJ was feeling very queasy and his walk to catch his next train was becoming increasingly difficult. Overcome with dizziness, TJ had to stop and rest against the wall. If people didn't know better by looking at him, they might think he was a beggar asking for change. TJ couldn't get rid of the feeling in his stomach and knew he was going to get sick.

He became increasingly worried as the pain in his stomach sharpened and his vision began to blur. If he passes out here, everything he has is right there for the taking – his luggage, wallet, even his clothes. He laid down flat on the ground in the fetal position trying to dull the pain. No one walking by was stopping to even see if he was okay. As he lay there, he prayed to God to help him get through this. He feared this happening in some places of the world where maybe the food was more suspect or the water was dirtier, but didn't think it would happen in London. Suddenly, he felt the urge to throw up, and positioned himself facing the wall. For the next 15 minutes, he repeated the process of throwing up and laying back down, waiting for the pain to fully subside. He felt and looked absolutely wretched. And now smelled equally as bad.

He waited long enough for the pain to subside, but now was feeling very dehydrated and needed water. He pulled himself up, gathered his things and started walking again. Still feeling weak, he picked up speed to get to a place where he could rest again. At this point, he would give anything just to be in his hotel bed, but that felt like a world away. He had to travel through hell to get there.

He made it to his next train to Kensington and sat, feeling short of breath and still feeling nauseous. He noticed the stare of others now, likely wondering if what he had was infectious. TJ tried to hold himself together for the duration of the train ride, and barely succeeded. Holding it in for the benefit of these strangers on the train was a Herculean effort that he was amazed he was able to pull off. As soon as he got to his stop, he got off and immediately ran to the bathroom and threw up again. Now, his head resting on the toilet seat, TJ couldn't help but wonder how he had gotten to this point on his journey. Slowly pulling himself together, he got back up and traveled the last leg of his journey to his hotel. The staff there saw he was in bad shape and got him some water and crackers. They got him checked in and to his room. Bed....and comfort, at last. TJ rested there for a few hours, and helplessly felt his stomach pain give way to a massive headache.

Afternoon – 1:00pm

His first day there now shot, TJ woke back up after a short nap. Feeling lousy, and unable to reconcile the fact that no one helped him today, and also that no one at his house, even his kids, picked up his call even though they were home. He was feeling alone and depressed. He pulled up pictures on his phone. He had hundreds, mostly of his kids. As he looked at the pictures of his kids, the realization that he was not there for them right now, couldn't see them, talk to them, play with them or just even watch them play their games they enjoy, really hit him hard. Starting to cry a little more with each passing picture, he missed the normality of his previous life. Where things were simple and predictable, and his kids could rely on him being there for them, posing for these pictures and just being their father.

He couldn't take it anymore. He had to hear from his kids and talk to them. He wanted to assure them he would be home soon and that they could count on him. Come hell or high water, he was going to get in touch with them somehow on this day. London was 6 hours ahead of Fayetteville, so the timing was right to catch everyone at home before school starts. TJ called home and listened as the phone rang again with no answer. He checked online and sure enough, Steven was online again. Irritated, TJ typed a message to Steven.

Steven – I'm trying to call. Can someone pick up the phone there, please.

Steven did not respond, despite having read the message. TJ called again. No response. Getting angry, he typed another message to Steven.

Why is nobody there picking up the phone? I know you read my last message. I'm about to call again. You pick up the phone.

TJ waited until he could see that the message had been read, and then he called again. Steven did not pick up the phone. TJ got extremely angry, picked up a glass and threw it against the wall, shattering the glass all over the floor. He was tempted to do it with his phone, but got a hold of himself before doing that.

Missing his kids was slowly turning to anger at them and Paige for now ignoring him. He hadn't felt this rage in a while. And likely, he thought, Paige is at the root of this. While in a rage, he hadn't noticed that Steven had responded to his last message.

Dad – sorry, Mom was on the phone. I couldn't answer it. I guess she didn't answer it either. Off to school. Will send a message later this afternoon.

TJ felt stupid getting angry at his kids. They didn't deserve it. Paige, however, did. She surely could look at the phone and realize who was calling. She chose not to pick up. She was now fully ignoring him. TJ's only hope to talk to the kids was Steven himself. He responded to Steven's message.

Okay, sorry, didn't mean to get angry. I really wanted to talk to you and Elizabeth. I look forward to your message tonight.

TJ left his room, now feeling extremely hungry. After his experience earlier today, he would not be getting adventurous at all with what he eats. As he made his way out of the hotel, he noticed it was pouring rain. He went to the hotel restaurant instead and got some fish and chips. And a glass of wine.

Evening – 10:00pm

TJ Carlson seemingly couldn't help himself anymore. Enjoying dinner and what was now his fifth glass of wine, he was losing control and abusing his body. He found some more alcohol in the minibar, and opened a small bottle of Jack Daniels. He had never tried it, but he figured, on this night, why not. He waited in anticipation for the message from Steven. He was ready to call on this night, no matter how inadvisable that was. Finally, Steven sent his promised message.

Dad – everything is great here. Elizabeth has a playdate with a friend this weekend. I'll be doing my usual. Talk to you later.

That was it, thought TJ? Everything is great? What the fuck? They couldn't give a shit that I'm not there apparently. TJ threw his phone down and nursed his bottle of Jack Daniels until it was gone. The difficulty he initially had in swallowing it went away. He then opened up a beer from the minibar and started drinking that. He had turned his music up loudly, and was now simply letting the alcohol do its thing. TJ wanted to be numb. No one really cared about him anymore, he thought. Time to shut off the world. He began feeling lightheaded again. He got up to go get a third beer, and got extremely dizzy. His vision blurred and then TJ passed out. As he fell to the floor, his forehead hit a shard of glass from what he had thrown against the wall earlier, opening up a cut that started dripping blood on to the floor. TJ was fully passed out on the floor, face down.

During the night

TJ was up to bat. He was confident he was going to nail this one. Everyone in the outfield had moved up. Losers, thought TJ. They are going to regret it when I send this sailing over their heads. The pitcher's face was obscured by his hat. But once he looked up, TJ knew what he was dealing with. Darkness smiled and held the ball in his hand with a firm grip. He spits on the ground and then looked squarely at TJ. He wound up, threw the pitch, and the ball was heading straight towards TJ's face. TJ dropped to the ground. He got up and was shocked to see blood dripping from his forehead.

"That was a close one," laughed Darkness.

"You still missed," said TJ.

"Did I?" replied Darkness.

TJ's head began to hurt, and as he put his hand up to it, he felt a giant lump and saw that his hand was covered in blood. "Congratulations," said TJ. "Once again, you've proven you can do anything you want to me. What's the point here? Seeing how many ways you can injure or humiliate me? Well go ahead, you son of a bitch, do your worst. I don't give a shit anymore."

"Obviously," said Darkness. "I don't think we understand each other very well. You are doing all these things to yourself. Don't forget, I'm you."

"Bullshit!" said TJ.

"Listen, I'm here to help you. I can be your friend, you know. You are resisting me, and that's why you are getting hurt. Let me into your heart, my friend." Everyone in the field was now gone, leaving just TJ and Darkness. "If you do that, things will change."

"How exactly is that? How will things change? The only option I see here is that it will make things worse. Letting something cold, vicious and evil like you into my life is the action of a mental patient."

"Maybe this will help," said Darkness, "and show you that I'm sincere." TJ and Darkness were now at the Cliffs of Moher ledge, a scene very familiar to TJ.

"This doesn't show me anything," said TJ. "Other than you know that I've been here."

"We've been here," said Darkness forcefully. "Just trust me."

"I don't trust you, and I never will. You are something dark and evil. Something sinister that I can't get rid of, showing up when I am weak and vulnerable. You'll never convince me that you are here to do anything good for me."

"Have it your way. You'll see soon enough. You and I will be good friends once you see my point of view." Darkness then turned away and began walking. TJ was lifted off the edge and thrown into the water below, being pulled by a heavy force to the bottom. Struggling to swim to the top, TJ gave up and let water fill into his lungs. Everything went black.

4:00am

TJ was convulsing in his sleep as he gasped for air when he woke up. He threw up again instantly on the floor multiple times. He noticed a bunch of blood on the floor around the area where he just threw up and feared that was where the blood was from. The thought that he was extremely sick made TJ feel faint again. He laid back down on the floor and felt the sharp pain in his head. When he reached up, he felt a lump and saw that there was blood. For a moment, he thought he was still in a dream and yelled out for Darkness.

TJ pulled himself up and walked to the bathroom. He saw the lump on his head and the shard of glass embedded in it. The glass, thought TJ. Realizing now what had happened, he removed the piece of glass to a massive amount of pain and then began cleaning up the wound. The room was a giant mess and was now beginning to smell very bad. Not sure how I'm going to explain this, he thought. But I definitely need a new room.

TJ was feeling worn out and alone that next day. His self-destructive behavior of the previous day had him really concerned about where he was heading, if left to his own devices. He started reaching back out to his friends, the ones that had stuck with him, with similar messages that sounded unintentionally desperate.

Hope all is well. I'm now in England, but it's been rough the last few days. I'm worried about my stress and my health. I'm reaching out to you, my friends, just to say hi and thank you for not abandoning me like everyone else apparently has. It means a lot to me, and I treasure all of you so much. I'm not sure where this journey is leading me or what kind of shape I'll be in at the end, but I'll keep hoping and trying for the best.

He sent the message to Neha Ganesh, Kate Ambrose and Becky Parsons. It elicited an almost instant reply from Kate.

What is going on there?? You sound like hell. Do what you have to do to get yourself together. And never forget, you have a place to stay here.

TJ realized after re-reading the message that it probably sounded a little worse that his actual situation was. The fact that he was blaming others for abandoning him suddenly felt cruelly ironic. He didn't want to garner sympathy, just thank his friends for being there.

TJ also reached out to his mom, trying to ensure her he was okay and planned to be in London for a while. Ann Carlson wasn't convinced that TJ was okay. She decided to get in touch with some old friends who lived near London, to try and intervene.

A few hours later, Neha caught TJ online. TJ hadn't talked to Neha in quite a while. She was obviously concerned about him.

(Neha's message) TJ, I'm very worried about you. You don't sound well. Either mentally or physically. Please tell me what is going on.

(TJ's reply) Hi Neha – I'm sorry. I was just in a down mood when I sent that. I had a bad day yesterday and it carried over into today.

(Neha's reply) No more bad days, TJ. You need to get better. Are you drinking a lot?

(TJ's reply) Not too much, don't worry. Thanks for being concerned. Honestly, I'm not having much luck talking to my kids. I miss them badly and it seems Paige is preventing me from talking to them.

(Neha's reply) Oh, that's bad. Don't let her do that. You talk to her directly and demand it. These are your children too and they should talk to their father.

(TJ's reply) Yeah, you're right. I've been avoiding a fight with Paige, but I may just have to confront her.

(Neha's reply) TJ, I miss you a lot. Please don't let anything bad happen to you. I will be too sad.

(TJ's reply) Of course, Neha. And don't forget, India may be part of my journey. To see you.

(Neha's reply) I'll be waiting. You're a good person, TJ. Fix your situation.

Neha made a lot of sense to TJ, especially where dealing with Paige was concerned. TJ would have to be more demanding when it came to talking to his kids.

Becky Parsons only replied with a sad face. TJ did not reply to Becky.

Gary and Edna Green were friends of Harold and Ann Carlson from when they were all in their 20's. Once Ann Carlson knew TJ was in London after TJ sent his message, she got in touch with the Greens and gave them TJ's contact information. TJ was to meet the Green's at a small pizza place near Hyde Park. He didn't know them, but he had met them once when he was a kid.

The Greens were a very nice British couple who lived just outside of London. They were aware of his story somewhat thanks to recent messages from Ann. TJ's mom would do whatever it took to ensure her son was safe and sound, and the Greens were now an extension of that.

"Sounds like a bloody mess," said Gary Green, after TJ confirmed a number of the details provided by Ann. "What's your plan here in London?"

"I'm not really sure. I don't have a plan," said TJ. Gary and Edna looked at each other.

"Listen TJ, your parents are very concerned. They are longtime friends of ours, and we'd do anything for'em. If you're going to be here in London for a stretch, we'd like to offer you a place to stay. Just chip in a bit for food and the occasional pint." Gary's offer came as a shock.

"Yes TJ, you're welcome to stay with us. There are buses that will bring you here to London if you wish," said Edna.

"I really appreciate it. I'll take you up on your offer. But I won't stay long, I promise. I'll check out tomorrow. Will you be able to pick me up, or can I catch a bus?"

"No need for the bus," said Gary. "We'll be there at noon to get you."

TJ was thankful that he had a place to stay with family friends, ones that may help keep him out of trouble and give him voices to listen to other than his own thoughts. He went back to his hotel and started getting his things in order. For the first night in a long time, he didn't drink at all. And he figured London might be a place to stay for a stretch.

Chapter 16

TJ was settling in to London. The Greens proving to be hospitable hosts over the last several days, TJ took the time to get himself looking and thinking sharp again. Taking a renewed interest in appearance, he had visited the same London salon twice in recent days, now sporting a short but stylish haircut and a neatly trimmed goatee. He once heard that to look good was to feel good, and anything at this point was worth a shot. The one thing TJ was lacking was a plan. A true and realistic plan forward. His stay in London was like a comfortable rest stop on the highway, and you're not quite sure when you're going to move on. This couldn't be a final stop. He knew that. But would this be the last stop on this journey before he turned it around and decided to head back to North Carolina? In a strange way, that thought comforted TJ, knowing that he could end this self-imposed exile at any moment.

"So, what are your plans today, TJ?" asked Gary, while sitting at the table with some tea and a newspaper.

"People watching!" exclaimed TJ. "There are some characters around here. And the truly interesting whackadoodles seem to converge on Hyde Park."

"Bloody twats," said Gary, dismissively. "They need to go get a fookin' job is what they need to do, rather than blather on about politics and crap."

TJ had definitely pegged Gary Green as a curmudgeon, set in his ways and not really willing to deviate. The Green home was fairly immaculate, and while Gary would do just fine with his tea and newspaper, Edna loved collecting trinkets and spent a lot of time placing and arranging them. Edna also had a talent for ignoring Gary's constant editorial comments about what he was reading in the newspaper.

"Isn't freedom of speech great?" asked TJ, jokingly. Gary just glared at TJ and didn't respond.

"Gary would slap them upside the head. All of them," interjected Edna. "Don't get mixed up in that crowd, TJ. If Gary finds out, he may slap you upside the head when you get back." Edna said that statement with an unsettling mix of sweetness and seriousness.

"No worries, guys," assured TJ. "I just enjoy watching them. When life has kicked you in the arse a bit, sometimes a little mindless entertainment can help." After eliciting a small chuckle from Gary, TJ decided to bolt, get out and enjoy his day. The Green household had grown a little too stuffy for his tastes on this morning.

TJ loved hanging around Hyde Park. There were occasional gatherings of some truly interesting people, voicing their opinions, outrage, support or protestations at the most serious to the silliest range of topics. One group might be protesting the government while the other might be railing against people with handlebar moustaches. People watching was always a treat. Some days, TJ would bring some snacks, find a convenient place to sit and simply watch for a few hours.

On this day, TJ had settled in on a bench to watch a group protesting the London Mayor. The barker, the person standing on an elevated perch and shouting the talking points while whipping the usually small but animated crowd into a frenzy, was shouting loudly a laundry list of all the evil things the mayor had done while in office, apparently taking London back to the stone ages. Joining TJ on his bench was an attractive young woman with her dog, a white schnauzer named Patsy. She looked over at TJ after watching the group for a minute and laughed, acknowledging the lunacy of what they were watching. She introduced herself as Mary. As she went to introduce her dog, TJ indicated he knew the dog's name was Patsy.

"How did you know that?" asked Mary.

TJ laughed. "I could hear you talking to her as you approached. She's adorable. I love dogs. Can I pet her?"

Mary lifted Patsy up on the bench, and Patsy made quick friends with TJ, giving his hand and arm a tongue bath.

"She usually doesn't take to strangers quickly, especially blokes," said Mary. "She must sense you are friendly and like dogs."

"I'm a dog whisperer by trade," said TJ jokingly. "Does Patsy have any behavioral issues you need taken care of?"

"No, she's a wonderful dog," said Mary. "You a pet owner?"

"No, but my family has some dogs. They used to have schnauzers. They were some of the funniest and friendliest dogs."

"So, what do you think of my fellow Londoners?" asked Mary, gesturing over to the crowds.

"This is high value entertainment here, Mary. I love watching this. We don't have anything like this in the US."

"Some of these people are regulars. If you pay attention to some of them over the course of time, you'll notice that they come to the park simply to join in on these. Some bloody tourists even join in, getting a good laugh." Mary had a sweet face and reddish blonde hair. She wore bright red lipstick and a decent amount of makeup. All of it worked though. What made Mary even more attractive was that she seemed to be very friendly.

"Are you here visiting from the US?" asked Mary.

"Yes, I'm visiting some family friends," said TJ. "Staying at their place and just enjoying London."

"Are you married?" asked Mary, while noticeably looking at TJ's ring finger and noticing nothing there. "Any kids?"

"Not married," said TJ, now not even acknowledging Paige. "But I have two kids. A boy and a girl."

"Oh, I see. Divorce?"

"Yeah," said TJ, now lying full on assuming that Mary might be interested. "What about you?"

"Not married……. waiting for Mr. Right still," said Mary.

"It will happen when you least expect it," said TJ.

TJ wanted to ask Mary to join him for lunch, sensing that this could lead somewhere. He was trying to play it cool, but now that an opportunity presented itself in the form of Mary, he started to feel those urges again and wanted to make something happen. Mary wasn't giving any obvious signs that she was interested, but maybe she was waiting for TJ to make the first move. TJ decided to go for it.

"Mary…. would you and Patsy like to join me for lunch?"

"Sure, why not," said Mary. "Let's find an outdoor place so she can sit on the ground next to us."

TJ and Mary went to the same pizza place where TJ had met the Greens, knowing it had an outdoors area. It was chilly, but they couldn't have Patsy inside the place. Small sacrifice to make, thought TJ.

TJ and Mary enjoyed a nice lunch and made small talk about their past relationships and their respective professional lives. Mary worked for British Airways, which interested TJ quite a bit. At one point during the conversation, TJ began to notice Mary getting fidgety, looking as if she wanted to leave. They hadn't talked about anything that should have made her uncomfortable. I wonder what the problem is, thought TJ. He had planned to ask her to meet him for dinner the next night. Mary began pulling out her phone and looking at it with regular intervals. She began talking less as she was doing this, and looked increasingly uncomfortable.

"TJ, I'm gonna need to head on now," said Mary abruptly. Mary began to stand up and gather her things.

"Is everything okay?" asked TJ.

"Yeah, this was nice. Thank you. It was great to meet you. Enjoy your time in London." Mary leaned down to wake up a sleeping Patsy.

"Mary…. would you like to join me for dinner tomorrow? I had a lot of fun talking to you today. I'll take you somewhere nice, wherever you'd like."

Mary stared at TJ for a minute, with almost a pained look on her face, like she was trying to figure out how to deliver bad news. "TJ, I'll pass on that. Thanks for the offer though."

"Can I ask why, Mary? It seemed like we were getting along well and enjoying each other's company."

This question made Mary uncomfortable and TJ could tell. She looked at TJ again and didn't say anything.

TJ was getting annoyed. "Okay, hey….no problem. Sorry to bother you and waste your time today." TJ got up and walked past Mary and Patsy and didn't look back. Mary seemed very nice and classy, and TJ would have loved to try to get to know her better. But why did she suddenly lose interest, he wondered. He thought about their entire conversation as he walked away. He was nothing but polite, didn't say anything offensive to her and treated her very nicely. This was the kind of girl that TJ would have loved to get to know. But there was something about me that turned her off, he thought. What is it? TJ couldn't help but think about this encounter for the remainder of the afternoon. He decided to hang out in London a bit longer and go over to the Thames River area to experience the London Eye at night. But not before finding a nice restaurant and pub to have some dinner and a generous amount of drinks.

TJ ended up at a place called the Slug and Lettuce pub. During his stay with the Greens, TJ had avoided drinking heavily like he had been in the time leading up to London. But tonight, he was in that mood. He felt like getting numb again. TJ sat alone at the bar and nursed a few glasses of wine. He felt his mood getting darker. On a whim, he decided to order some different drinks to try out. He started to feel a buzz kicking in, enjoying the numbness as it took over.

There was an older gentleman sitting a few seats down from TJ, also by himself apparently. TJ decided to start a conversation.

"Can you help me figure out women, my good man? I've given up hope and they've driven me here." TJ laughed as he took a healthy gulp of a rum and coke.

"That's birds for ya," said the guy. "They've probably driven more than half of us here."

"Is that why you are here?" asked TJ.

"Nah…….my bird flew away a long time ago," he laughed. "But don't let it get you down mate. There's plenty of birds out there.

Don't let'em run your life. If they don't fancy ya, fuck'em. Move on to the next. You have billions of options!"

TJ laughed and toasted the bar patron. He was right. Getting flatly rejected by Mary had landed him here at the Slug and Lettuce, moping. And for what? One girl didn't like him. His skin would need to be thicker than that. Feeling somewhat better and emboldened, he said goodbye to the wise, slightly drunk guy at the bar, and set off for the London Eye to get some great views of London. The larger than life Ferris Wheel and its uniquely spacious passenger capsules were on TJ's to-do list for a long time. TJ had been on many Ferris Wheels at small town fairs around North Carolina, and couldn't imagine the seats actually being standing room only enclosed room with windows.

It seemed like everyone waiting at the London Eye was in a group. TJ instantly felt awkward and self-conscious that he was by himself. But the drinks were kicking in now, so his courage was elevated and his worry about that was short lived. TJ quickly noticed a group of girls laughing loudly near him. All three were very pretty and dressed up as if they had been out for an occasion. TJ was feeling bold and wanted to attach himself to a group. He walked over to the girls.

"Pardon me, ladies. I'm here on my own and couldn't help but notice that most everyone else here was in groups. Can I temporarily join your group so it doesn't look so pathetic? No need to talk to me. Just allow me to walk next to you or something." TJ smiled at them and waited for a response.

"What's your name, pathetic stranger?" laughed the Asian girl in the group. TJ quickly took note that the girls in this group seemed a bit drunk as well.

"TJ. Pleasure to meet you all." TJ was trying not to look or sound drunk, unsure if he was succeeding.

"I'm Fay," said the Asian. "This is Sharon and Leah. TJ, that had to be one of the greatest ever first lines. We weren't sure whether to laugh, cry, run away or give you a big hug."

"Laughing and a hug will be fine," said TJ. "Can I be your fourth wheel?"

"Just promise us you aren't a weirdo or a pervert, and that we can ditch you at any moment," said Leah. These girls were obviously from the US, although Leah had a bit of a Canadian accent to her voice. All three had black hair and Leah and Sharon looked like they could have been sisters.

"Done, and done," said TJ. "Thank you. Now instead of people thinking I'm a loser, they'll see me hanging with three hotties and think that I am a total winner."

"But we'll know the truth," laughed Sharon.

Sharon and Leah took turns continuing to banter with TJ about his approach to joining them, but Fay was quiet. She laughed whenever jokes were told, but TJ caught her looking at him a few times and smiling. TJ didn't think much of it. He took his attention slightly off the girls as the London Eye made its rotation around so he could take pictures.

"This view is amazing," said Fay after walking up to TJ. "Want me to take some shots of you?"

TJ agreed and Fay did a pictorial. After about 20 shots, she began including herself in the pics with TJ. They mugged for the camera, and it became less about the scenery as it did about the two of them. Leah and Sharon then walked over and they took turns taking various pictures of each other. The ride came to an end, and they got off. TJ was about to thank the girls and make his way back home to the Green's house, when he got an invitation.

"TJ, we're going to go out drinking. Want to join us?" asked Fay.

"Absolutely!" said TJ. "Lead the way, girls."

"We've extended your membership a few more hours in our club," said Sharon. "For good behavior, and for not hitting on any of us so obviously in the first 2 hours."

TJ laughed. "So, if I had done that……"

"Gonzo," said Leah. "We have no time for drunken morons."

TJ and the girls hit another pub. These girls appeared to be professional drinkers and were ordering tequila and vodka shots. As the night progressed, it became obvious to TJ that Fay seemed to like him, and she would muscle past the other two to stand next to him, and didn't even seem to be engaging with the other two much at all. Just with TJ. In fact, the other two now seemed to be scoping out other prospects, giving Fay exclusive access to TJ.

TJ was full on drunk now. Fay was also very drunk. But they weren't stopping. The two of them left Leah and Sharon behind and went on to another nightclub. On the way, TJ got a glimpse into what Fay was thinking.

"You're really handsome, TJ," said Fay. "Especially the way these lights are hitting you right now."

"Are you sure it's not the alcohol?" laughed TJ. "You are gorgeous. And it didn't take these lights to highlight that. I thought that from the second I saw you."

Fay laughed heartily. "Ha! A pickup line! You're out of the group!"

"I think we're both out of the group. We just ditched the other two."

"They'll be fine," said Fay. "We're staying close by."

"Good," said TJ. "Now that we are our own group, what's the plan?"

"Nightclub, and then getting a little more drunkier," said Fay, stumbling over the word "drunk", uttering several variations of it before settling on the word "drunkier."

"Awesome," said TJ. "Let's high five it."

They high fived and Fay held on to TJ's hand when they met. She pulled it toward her mouth and licked it.

"What the hell was that?" asked TJ, laughing.

"I really don't know," said Fay. "Seemed like the thing to do. But I should be careful, I don't know where the back of your hand has been."

"Don't worry…. nowhere gross," said TJ. "You can lick that as much as you want."

"Another great pickup line," said Fay, laughing at herself now.

They arrived at the club, went in and ordered some more drinks. Although drunk, TJ was fully aware he had something with Fay and it was conceivable this could go somewhere tonight. He didn't want to get too drunk. But Fay was not stopping and TJ kept up.

TJ began feeling a weird sensation coming over him. He didn't like it at all. He felt like he was losing control and slipping away from his surroundings. Fay began to become a blur. All of a sudden, everything was gone. TJ had blacked out.

It was starting to come back in to focus. TJ felt like he weighed a million pounds as he opened his eyes and tried to figure out exactly where he was. He was lying flat on his back and staring up at a ceiling. His right hand, however, was on someone. Someone's stomach, obviously, as his finger could feel a belly button. He moved his hand up a little bit and felt a naked breast. TJ slowly moved his aching head to his right, and Fay came into focus. He moved his hand back down Fay's stomach. No panties either, thought TJ. Fay was naked, and so was he. TJ closed his eyes again, as the light in the room was giving him a splitting headache. He knew one thing for sure, and that was that he somehow ended up in bed, naked, with Fay. But he had no clue how that happened, or anything else that happened after he blacked out.

He rolled over towards Fay and put his hand back on her breast, massaging it until she woke up and took notice of him as well. They caught eyes finally and just stared at each other for a few minutes.

"Fay?" asked TJ.

"Uh huh?" she replied.

"Can you tell me what happened last night? Did we?" asked TJ.

"Yes," said Fay. "We were both in bad shape when we got back here last night. I remember that much. We had sex and then I must have fallen asleep right away. I think you must have been out of it quickly as well."

"Fay…. I don't remember anything beyond the nightclub. I think I blacked out."

"Really? You seemed fine. You were less talkative. And in no shape to go anywhere else, so I brought you here. We were getting very playful at the club and I think we were both getting turned on. I figured you must have wanted it. So did I."

"Dammit! I don't remember any of that! I'd have rather blacked out the rest of the night and been conscious for that." TJ couldn't help but laugh at the irony that he had had sex with this beautiful girl, but didn't remember a second of it.

Fay was finding this funny. "Oh my God, that is hilarious."

"Was I any good?" asked TJ.

"I don't think either of us brought our "A" game," said Fay. "But tell you what, if you make us some coffee to shake off this hangover, we can try it again so we both remember it."

TJ quickly obliged with the coffee, causing Fay to laugh once again. They both lay in bed for a while, downing their coffee and trying to shake off the cobwebs from the night before. Fay put her cup down, leaned over and kissed TJ passionately. TJ's hands explored all of Fay's body as they kissed. Fay climbed on top of TJ and they made love, again, with both of them fully aware and engaged this time.

This was a huge moment for TJ. Even though they apparently had sex the previous night, this was the first time TJ was knowingly and willingly engaging in actual sex with another woman while married to Paige. He had finally crossed that line. His lovemaking with Fay was passionate and gave him such a different feeling than it did with Paige. It had been a long time since he was feeling that his partner was equally enjoying it as much as he was.

Then another realization hit. Fay was going to be another one of those transient people in his life who enters and exits it, leaving TJ with nothing but memories. But these would be incredible memories at least, he thought.

"Fay, when are you and the girls leaving London?" asked TJ.

"This afternoon," said Fay. "We'll need to head to the airport after lunch."

"It figures," laughed TJ. "Where are you from in the US?"

"California. San Diego."

"Other side of the country. Again, it figures." TJ knew he had a few more hours with Fay, but was determined to maximize it. "Can I hang with you until it's time to go?"

"Sure," said Fay. "Hope you have one or two more rounds left in you." She said that with a big smile, and TJ was happy to at least have that time.

They made love two more times, and then TJ saw Fay and the girls off to their car to the airport. He got a long, sweet goodbye kiss from Fay.

"TJ, I'm so happy we met and shared this time together. But I just wanted you to know something. I'm actually married. My husband and my 4-year-old are waiting for me in San Diego when I return. I really, really like you, but just know that this is where it ends. I'm sorry."

TJ laughed. "It's okay, Fay. I'm also married, but just barely. You take care okay? I had an amazing time with you, and you did more for me than you can ever know."

TJ watched as the car drove away. This was an experience he had waited for, but now he felt empty as he watched her drive away. And he felt guilty. He had left everything behind, and was now actively chasing and bedding women. He pushed the guilt aside. No more time for that, he thought. I had the time of my life last night, made love to a beautiful woman and gained a measure of my self-esteem back. I don't need to feel guilty about this experience, he thought. I need to duplicate it. Over and over again.

As he headed back to the Green's house, and despite the hangover, his thoughts appeared to be crystal clear. He wanted to experience more of what he just experienced with Fay. That was a missing piece. No guilt. I've done so much to take care of others, he thought. Time to take care of what I need. For the first time in a while, TJ had a direction. That direction was not abandoning this journey and going home. It was now to continue on and sow as many wild oats as possible.

Chapter 17

"You could have at least called us! We were worried sick about you." Gary Green was highly upset with TJ Carlson. Even though TJ was a grown man, he was still a guest of the Green's, who felt a personal responsibility to Ann and Harold Carlson to make sure their son was safe and sound here in London.

Gary continued – "You are an irresponsible young man. You show back up here still obviously drunk or hung over. You look like hell. Where did you even stay last night?"

"I was safe last night," TJ lied. In reality, TJ could have been killed after he blacked out. Fortunately, he was with Fay, who got him somewhere safe.

"Bollocks!" screamed Gary. "London is not as safe a place as you think. You could have been robbed, beaten or even killed if you were as drunk as it appears you were if you are still feeling the effects."

"Gary, I met a girl last night. I was with her. We both drank, but we watched out for each other. For as late as it was getting, we just decided to stay at her place."

"So, not only drinking, but sleeping around while you still have a wife and kids at home." Gary was furious with TJ, and TJ was getting irritated with him.

"I'm sorry Gary, I should have called. I didn't mean to make you both worry."

Edna chimed in. "TJ, we have been friends of your family for a long time. Ann and Harold are dear to us. They are good people and we'd do anything for them. We live a simple life here. We don't bother anyone and no one bothers us. Last night, you put yourself at risk out there, hooked up with a strange girl and got pissed drunk. If you had come back here, people could have followed you. You would have brought that stupidity to our doorstep."

"We can't have that," Gary interrupted. "Even if you are Ann and Harold's son. You were inconsiderate and took advantage of our good nature."

"Guys, I don't understand. It was one night, and I apologize for that. I thought I've been a model citizen here. I don't understand why you are judging me so harshly now." TJ was indignant about the treatment he was getting from the Greens. This was becoming a highly tense exchange, and it was becoming clear to TJ that he may no longer be welcome there.

"TJ, we're going to have to ask you to leave. Getting drunk and sleeping with strange women, that's not going to fly for us here. We have every right to judge how we please. This is our home and you are a guest. You obviously have some personal demons, and we wish you the very best in exorcising them, but we don't want it happening here." Gary Green had made his point and TJ was done with the conversation.

"Fine," said TJ. "I'll pack my shit and go." TJ walked to his room and Gary followed.

"I'll drop you wherever you want to go in London," said Gary.

"Thanks Gary, but don't bother. Just point me to the bus."

"Don't be a twat," said Gary. "I'm offering you a ride. Just take it."

"You just treated me like I'm a deviant and criminal in there, Gary. Like I'm garbage that can be disposed of. I appreciated your hospitality but I loathe being preached to like I was in there. You made your point. You owe me nothing else."

"I'll be waiting in the car. Pick a spot in London and I will drop you." Gary left the room. TJ angrily threw his things in his suitcase.

TJ debated whether to simply walk past Gary's car and head to the bus. But the truth was, TJ had too much stuff to haul on and off buses. He had no choice but to take Gary up on his offer.

"Bye Edna. Thanks for everything." TJ even debated whether to say goodbye to Edna, but decided to take the high road.

"Take care, TJ. God bless," said Edna, as she once again turned her attention to her trinkets.

Fuck off, thought TJ, as he walked out the door. He got in the car with Gary. "Just drop me at a hotel in Kensington. I don't give a crap which one."

The drive was silent for a while, until Gary finally spoke up. "I understand what you're going through. Just try to make the right decisions."

"No one understands what I'm going through. I did everything I could for everyone, but in the end, I'm disposable. When Paige no longer had use for me, she simply decided to stop loving me. My kids haven't even messaged me in the last few weeks. Haven't heard from my friends. Or even my parents. The only person who I can count on is myself. And that's who I need to look after and take care of now."

"I think your view is jaded, TJ. Think of what others may be thinking of you right now. You're the one who ran and continue to run."

"I had no other choice, Gary. It was either leave and save myself, or stay there, accept my lot in life and die a slow, unhappy death. Honestly, I don't know what to do now other than to keep going. I'll find what I need to. On my own, if necessary." TJ was talking himself into a truly foul mood. He was so pissed at Gary; he wasn't going to allow him to give him any advice he would consider.

"TJ, just promise to look after yourself. Find what you need to. But understand that people do care about you. Right now, they are leaving you alone, as you wish, so that you can work things out. We talked to Ann and Harold a few times while you were there. They care, trust me. They care about you. We told them not to worry, that you were okay. You still have a journey to go on. We won't tell them what happened today, only that you decided to continue on. Get out of London, TJ. Move on. Go find what you need to."

Gary was making sense at last. London wasn't the end of the journey. It was a continuation of the beginning.

"Thanks Gary. Makes sense. I'm sorry it ended like this, but I appreciate you letting me stay there. I'll make plans to leave London soon." TJ swallowed his pride. He wanted this car ride to end. He wanted his time in London now to end. He suddenly felt a strong urge to get out. To run, once again, from a place that was making him uncomfortable.

They arrived at a Hilton hotel in Kensington. TJ got his things from Gary's car. "Bye Gary. Thanks again."

"God bless, TJ," said Gary as he started to pull away.

Fuck off, thought TJ as he watched him drive away.

TJ checked in to the hotel and got settled in his room. Alone again. But he wasn't depressed this time. It was more like a determination to go seek what he needed to find. Only he really wasn't quite sure what that was. The only thing he knew was that he wanted to feel the way he felt with Fay. Now that he had crossed his self-imposed line, the damage was done. He really wanted to explore that wild part of himself that had laid dormant for most of his life. His night and day with Fay were only a taste of that. He wanted more. Time to stop denying myself, he thought.

He got comfortable in his bed and fell asleep, still shaking off the effects of the previous night.

"I'm sorry Ann," said Gary Green. "He needed to move on. He has many things he still needs to work out. I think he's battling a lot of demons."

"What did he do there, Gary? This seems a bit abrupt. Is he okay?" Ann Carlson seemed a bit frantic on the line.

"Don't worry…. he'll be okay. He's just seeking something and won't find it here in London. But Ann, you and Harold should definitely keep reaching out to him. I think he's feeling a bit alone and abandoned."

"Oh, Jesus," said Ann. "That's the last thing he needs. Okay, we'll get back in touch with him."

"Ann……how bad is it with TJ and Paige? He didn't talk much about it, and he surely seemed to have his eye on birds here."

"It was a bad situation, Gary. For both of them, sadly. Okay, thanks again for watching after him and we'll talk again soon."

"Sure thing, Ann. And please let us know how it turns out with him. We may not hear from him again." Gary hung up the phone with Ann and turned to Edna. "I couldn't let them know the truth,

Edna. He's messed up in a big way. I'm pretty worried about it.
On the drive there, he had a fuck all attitude. I'm not sure what
he's capable of at this point."

"You did the right thing, Gary. It's not for us to babysit him. I just
hope he gets himself straight." Edna and Gary put the incident
with TJ behind them, to their relief. But deep down, Gary worried
whether he just catapulted TJ deeper into his own mess.

TJ bought a few bottles of wine and settled in his room for the
evening. Opening up his world to new possibilities was an
exciting thought, and, as usual, he began to plan out what he
wanted to do. He hated that he always felt the need to be
organized, but that's what worked for him to ensure he
accomplished what he needed to. All of his plans seemed focused
on how to go out and find pleasures of the flesh, and the list had
only seen the following added:

- Make love to beautiful women of many races in many
  countries
- Experience a threesome
- Visit sex themed clubs
- Explore more massage experiences

His urges were overwhelming him now. He wanted to jump head
first into this. It was dominating his thoughts. You only live once,
he thought. Why not go out and experience these things.

"Do you really miss him?" asked Kylie. "Do you even know where
he is?"

Paige Carlson hated talking to Kylie now about TJ. Kylie was
relentlessly negative and Paige had softened a bit on the subject.

"Of course, I miss him, and the kids especially miss him. But what can we do? He needs to finish whatever it is he's doing out there. His mom said he was in London staying with family friends. At least I know he's safe somewhere."

"Do you know what he's doing?" asked Kylie.

"It doesn't matter anymore," said Paige with exasperation. "Can we please drop this, Kylie?"

"Okay. I'm just worried about you. I want to see you move on and not held hostage to this."

"I know. You've made your thoughts perfectly clear where TJ is concerned. Enough." Paige hated being dismissive with her best friend, but she didn't want to be hit with constant reminders that TJ had left her.

"Sorry Paige. Okay, I'll talk to you later."

TJ looked at his short list and laughed. He knew exactly where he wanted to go next. The Red-Light District in Amsterdam would be a great place to start for someone looking to open himself up to a whole new world of sexual exploration. He researched information on it and took careful notice of the Do's and Don'ts there.

TJ was definitely feeling different. But he was feeling good. It's as if making this decision again lifted a weight off of him. He was now thinking less of back home and more about what lay ahead. That's what was becoming important. Is this who I really am, he wondered.

TJ decided to head to Paris first, as he was going to take the train to hold on to his airline points and leave his friend, Rose, alone for a while. Paris seemed to be a good spot to kick off the next chapter of his journey. TJ imagined himself sitting at a café overlooking the Eiffel Tower, toasting himself with a glass of wine. He booked his trip through the Chunnel, a tunnel connecting London and Paris under the English Channel, and was heading out the following morning.

Riding through a tunnel never bothered TJ. He had done it many times. But doing it under an entire body of water connecting two countries unnerved TJ a little bit. It was a cool experience though, he thought. He was glad to bid farewell to London. As much as he tried to settle in and fix himself, it seemed it wasn't destined to be the place where that happened. Especially since he really wasn't sure what was broken any more.

Starting to feel a renewed sense of self-confidence, TJ was in a particularly good mood on this train ride. It was peaceful, as he had a section of seats to himself. It didn't bother him at all that his only goal at this point seemed to be a fulfillment of sexual desires. His moral code was taking shots to the body and head and was collapsing. He barely even thought of messaging his family and friends anymore. Even those friends who have supported him the entire time.

TJ began to doze a little, and when he came to, he saw the countryside of France out the train window. Thank God, he thought. No longer underwater. He laughed to himself. He dozed on and off again for the remainder of the trip to Paris.

TJ's arrival at Gare du Nord in Paris started off easily enough. But then it got chaotic. Still feeling good, he watched as a gypsy woman, holding a sign that said she was from Bosnia and affected by the war, walked up to him asking him for money. TJ never usually fell for this, but he had some Euro coins in his pocket and gave her one. This caught the attention of about 25 other "Bosnian" women who suddenly flocked over and mobbed TJ. All of them were now holding out their money collectors and yelling inaudibly at TJ.

TJ began to panic and wanted to get away, realizing he had been victimized, but the only way he could do that was to start pushing his way through these women. He was getting angry at them and started yelling.

"LEAVE ME ALONE!" yelled TJ. "LET ME GO!"

The women continued yelling and all were seemingly getting angrier at TJ. TJ couldn't help but notice some shady looking men standing and watching the whole thing unfold. Even the French guards holding their big guns were just standing there watching.

Finally, TJ started shoving his way through the women and ran once he made it through. He saw a taxi outside the station and flagged it down. The women were following him and so was one of the shady looking guys. He got into the taxi. "Get me out of here, please," said TJ to the cab driver, unsure whether the guy actually understood him.

The cab driver laughed. "Where to, mon ami?"

"Any hotel near the Eiffel Tower," said TJ.

"Mon ami…. did you give one of those girls money?" said the Cab Driver with a thick French accent.

"Oui," said TJ, laughing. "Tres stupide."

"Never do that. It's a business. Those girls work for foreign men who come here from Eastern Europe. None of them are who they say they are."

"Lesson learned," said TJ. "My fists were about to fly."

"That would have gotten you into more trouble. Their bosses would have followed you."

"Great," said TJ. "In Paris for five minutes and a marked man."

"Don't worry……I watched. No one followed us from the station."
The cab driver was a jolly older guy, and apparently a great source
of advice for TJ about Paris. A nice tip was coming his way.

"Merci," said TJ.

"*You parlez Francais, mon ami?*" asked the Driver

"I just used up all the French I know," said TJ. "Except for the
word Merd. Which I was apparently in a pile of at the train
station."

That got a big laugh out of the cab driver. "The areas around the
Eiffel tower and Arc de Triomphe are safe. Just watch your
belongings at all times."

"Once again, thanks," said TJ. "You were a life saver today."

The cab driver dropped TJ off at the Pullman Paris Tour Eiffel, just
less than half a kilometer from the Eiffel Tower. TJ booked a
room that gave him a view of the Tower out of his window. This
is perfect, he thought. Exactly what I wanted and needed. TJ
dropped his things and just stared out the window.

TJ went to the top of the Eiffel Tower the next morning. The
Tower was becoming a beacon for him, a central focused point in
Paris that constantly reminded him that he was here to start
anew. He looked out over Paris. He felt calm, something he
hadn't felt in a long time. This was a high point in his journey, he
felt. He had arrived here with a renewed purpose and was ready
to go. Strangely, since deciding he would go looking for his sexual
thrills, the urges had calmed down. He wasn't even feeling like he
needed to go searching for it here.

He spent the rest of the day touring around Paris. He stopped at the Louvre, and laughed to himself that out of all of the priceless and classic paintings and sculptures there, he made a beeline right to the Mona Lisa. After that, he lost interest. He also made a stop at Notre Dame cathedral. Now, it was time to follow through on a vision he had for himself back in London.

TJ went back to the hotel, to the café, and found himself a seat outside overlooking the Eiffel Tower. It was nighttime, and the Tower was beautifully lit up. He ordered his glass of wine. A glass of wine at a café overlooking the Eiffel Tower, he thought, and now the vision is realized. TJ toasted himself and toasted new beginnings. At that moment, he felt a tinge of guilt. He was celebrating the fact that he had made a decision to throw everything to the side and satisfy his carnal desires. Am I being selfish, he thought? TJ caught himself quickly and shoved all of those guilty thoughts aside.

"No," TJ said quietly to himself under his breath. "I've earned the right to do this. It's my life. I'll live it the way I want. Time to make myself happy for once."

TJ finished his glass of wine and decided to go back up the Tower. Tomorrow, he will leave for Amsterdam. Time to enjoy one more moment here in Paris.

He made it back to the top and was in awe at how breathtaking the view was at night. It was similar to landing in a big city on a plane at night and seeing the entire city lit up. He stood there staring once again. A peaceful feeling overcame him.

"Tomorrow, it's for me," he said to himself. "I begin living my life for me."

PART 3:

DESCENT

Chapter 18

TJ arrived in Amsterdam's Centraal Station, feeling determined but also wondering just how far he would go in the exploration of the new "him". On the train, he began to think whether or not this was an incorrect reaction to everything negative that had gone on, whether he was adopting this new attitude to hide from is demons and responsibilities. But then, as he had become prone to do, he pushed those thoughts aside and prepared to dive in to Amsterdam.

He really wasn't sure how far he would go. His experience with Fay and with the massages were one thing, but TJ had never considered going to find prostitutes, like there were plenty of in Amsterdam and where it was legal. He had checked in to a hotel not far from the train station and not far from the Red-Light District. He would have plenty of time to see Amsterdam, but his thoughts immediately turned to going and satisfying his curiosity about this legendary area, where sex, and even soft drugs, were legal and easy to be had.

TJ considered stopping at a "coffee shop" to try pot brownies. He had always had an aversion to smoking in general, and in particular pot smoking. But what if it was in a delicious brownie? He filed that one away to potentially try later.

TJ made his way to the Red-Light District and was actually quite surprised to see how normal it looked. There were restaurants galore, and a lot of people walking around. It almost seemed like a rather normal place. There were a couple of sex shops, selling toys and movies, and there was a store there called Peep Show.

Okay, maybe I can start light here, he thought. As expected, he had to go into a grungy little room, put coins in and then a little screen moved up so he could see the girl on the spinning bed. The girl looked thoroughly uninspired and went through repetitive motions of touching herself that were decidedly un-erotic. Making TJ laugh even more were that there were tissues in some of the stalls. The experience was much like he thought it would be. He watched in amazement as a group of girls all crowded into a room to watch that same train wreck he just watched. TJ laughed again and then continued on.

He began to see the trademark of the RLD…. the working women advertising themselves in the windows with the red lights. He decided to make a pass around the area to have a look at all of them. He decided that this was where he wanted to start. Easy pickings, thought TJ. Just pick one, agree on a price, then sex was his for the taking. His first tour around the area did not turn up much in the way of anyone tantalizing. As a matter of fact, there were some that were downright scary. On his second pass, there was one that got his attention. She was a very pretty, tall blonde girl who had a really nice body. TJ saw a couple of guys walk in to her room and then walk right back out. He wasn't exactly sure what he was supposed to do here and was shy to walk in to the girl's room with so many people walking around. The girl noticed TJ was looking at her, and she seized on it. She smiled and continued to wave him over. This was a big step, thought TJ, if I go and do this. He stood there for a few minutes and then finally decided to walk into her room.

"How much?" asked TJ.

"50 euros," said the blonde girl.

"What do I get for 50 euros?" asked TJ.

"You can have a suck, or a fuck. Whichever you prefer." The girl had a very Russian sounding accent

"Can I get both for 75?" asked TJ.

"For both, it will be 100 euros," said the blonde. TJ hadn't done enough research on negotiating with these girls to know that he was getting ripped off. Most girls would do both for 50.

"Fine," said TJ. "Let's do both."

"Okay, you get undressed and we'll start with the suck. For another 20, we can add some time and include foreplay. It may help to get you hard." The girl was really trying her hardest to milk TJ out of everything he had. "I think you will need it. You look nervous."

"I won't need it, trust me," said TJ. Even though he wasn't even remotely erect standing there in front of this girl. He was actually nervous.

"Come on, loosen up and have fun," said the blonde, presumably Russian girl. "20 more euros and I know you'll have a good time."

"No," said TJ, drawing the line. "100 is enough."

The girl instructed TJ to lay down on her bed. She rolled a condom down on TJ's not even the least bit hard penis. She proceeded to give a "suck" that looked and felt a bit suspect, in that she really wasn't doing it much. TJ decided not to complain, as at least it was doing the job of getting him prepared to have sex with her. She quickly ended that and then told him it was time for the fuck. She laid down on her stomach and had TJ go in from behind. What was odd was that she continued to hold on to his cock as he put it inside her. At least, he thought it was inside her. He honestly wasn't sure. The hand was throwing him off. She told TJ that he needed to hurry.

TJ knew that he had been had. This girl wasn't doing anything for him and he really didn't want to go on any further. TJ stopped and pulled back.

"What's wrong?" asked the blonde. "I don't think you finished. Let me help you."

"Don't bother," said TJ. "That was not worth 100 euros and I'm very disappointed."

"Whatever you wish," said the girl. "I still think you need to loosen up. You could have made this more enjoyable with a few more euros."

"Of course, I could have," said TJ. "Maybe I was too stingy, but that was my decision. You still had 100 euros of mine, and you could have at least pretended you were into it."

"It's my job," said the blonde. "I need to earn money. It's like most things. The more you pay, the more you will get."

TJ couldn't argue that point. But this experience had turned him off to trying this again. He got dressed and left the room, quickly realizing how many people were watching him walk out of that room. He felt very embarrassed and walked quickly away from there. So far, the RLD was not quite what TJ had built it up to in his mind. There were other ways though to get girls. Time to try those avenues, he thought to himself.

Where are you now, butthead?

The message from Kate Ambrose was a typical opener in better times.

(TJ's reply) In Amsterdam. Checking out the interesting colored lights here.

(Kate's reply) Sweet shit! Amsterdam? What kind of place is that for someone who has gone through what you have?

(TJ's reply) I'm looking to experience u few things I never have.

(Kate's reply) Well, you're certainly in the right place then. Smoke any weed yet? Bang a hooker? My god, what are your plans there?

(TJ's reply) Between you and me, I tried it. Hooker banging. Lame. Complete rip-off. If you don't pay what they want, they rush you and try to get you out of there.

(Kate's reply) Check that one off the bucket list for you, eh? Is that it for your sexual misadventures?

(TJ's reply) Nah – I think I will try a brothel or sex club.

(Kate's reply) Moron. Don't catch any diseases. Seriously though, how are you doing? You okay?

(TJ's reply) Actually, yes, believe it or not. Feeling as good as I have on this journey so far.

(Kate's reply) Not sure I believe you, but okay. Keep in touch and let me know what degenerate things you do there.

TJ ended the conversation with Kate, and prepared to head out to day two of his Amsterdam adventure.

TJ researched brothels in the area and made sure he was prepared. He found one about a kilometer outside the main area and took a tram there. It was a very unassuming place, only identifiable by a small sign on the bottom of the door. TJ ringed the doorbell and was greeted by a woman that apparently worked the front desk.

"Welcome, sir, come on in," said the lady. TJ remembered the night before and was hoping this would be much less of a hassle. So far so good. She handed him a price list. "I assume you're not Dutch, correct?"

"That's correct," said TJ, smiling.

TJ picked the service, which included massage, oral sex and then intercourse. The lady then indicated she would go get the girls. TJ had heard of this kind of set up at brothels, where the girls would line up and introduce themselves, and then you would pick the one you wanted. Except TJ could not believe that he was actually here at one doing that. A very surreal moment indeed.

A group of nine girls lined up. They were all very different and it looks like the variety was intentional. TJ realized at this moment that if he had ever had a type he was curious about, it was his chance to try it right now. There was a very exotic looking girl with dark hair who was smiling big. She was the only one doing that, TJ noticed. It made her stand out. TJ picked her.

"Okay, sir, follow me," said the front desk girl. "Alexis, it will be room two. Sir, go ahead and take your shower and Alexis will be right in."

TJ looked around the room. A large bed and a shower in the room. Everything they probably need, he thought. He started his shower and Alexis entered the room. Once he finished, she helped him dry off and told him to get on the bed and lay on his stomach. Alexis removed her clothes. She drizzled oil on his back, then proceeded to give him a massage using only her breasts. This is awesome, thought TJ. He got relaxed very quickly as he realized this would be much different than his Red-Light District experience.

After about 15 minutes, she had TJ turn over and started doing that to his front. TJ got fully erect quickly, and Alexis seized on it, pulling out a condom and putting it on TJ. She went right into oral sex, but again TJ noticed she wasn't really giving that her all. He chalked it up to the condom. He couldn't imagine what that would taste like, but it couldn't be very pleasant. She only did that for a minute.

"Do you have any position preferences?" asked Alexis.

TJ thought for a second, because this was happening fast. "You can get on top," he replied. Alexis climbed on top and they began having sex. She looked like she was enjoying it, and TJ was definitely enjoying it. It was over after a few minutes. A very satisfying experience this time, thought TJ, but very rushed. He paid for 60 minutes, but really only about 20 had passed. What would happen for the rest of the time?

Alexis began to make small talk as she resumed the massage. She was from Romania. TJ laid there, still very relaxed, and now determined to enjoy the rest of whatever else was going to happen. Alexis was actively trying to get TJ excited again, and then he found out why.

"For second sex, it will be another 60 euros," said Alexis.

I knew it, thought TJ. That's why she rushed me. "No, it's okay. You can massage for a few more minutes and then we can be done."

Alexis finished the massage, and then they both showered.

"Thank you, Mr. TJ," said Alexis.

"No, thank you. That was wonderful," replied TJ.

TJ left the brothel, thoroughly satisfied with his experience. I'll be back here, he thought.

TJ was now getting what he had hoped for and came to Amsterdam for. A chance to really explore his wild side. However, to TJ, wild really was solely focused on sex it seemed. His days became wrapped around it. He went and saw the live sex shows in the Red-Light District, and for the next several days, he was becoming a regular at the brothel. It was a part of his schedule, to be included with breakfast, lunch and dinner. He was picking out a new girl each day and having sex with them. This was like a dream come true.

The more days that passed, the more that the initial fun of Amsterdam was starting to slowly dissipate. TJ had started drinking each day from the moment that he woke up until the moment he went to sleep. He was always in an alcoholic fog, but never quite drunk. After about 6 visits to the brothel in his first week there, he realized two things – his wallet was becoming much lighter and the routine had stopped exciting him. The girls really didn't care about TJ. He was a paying customer. So, while he was getting sex, the closeness and intimacy he loved and desired were not there. He needed that, but that would mean he would have to look around, find someone, establish that emotional connection and then make love. He had neither the will nor the resolve to put the effort into that.

One day, TJ decided to skip the brothel visit and simply walk around Amsterdam. To try to clear his head. Is this really what I wanted, he thought? It seemed like a great idea in Paris. As he wandered through the city, he became lost in thought. The people here seemed happy. They were probably enjoying their lives in this fascinating place. Why can't I bring myself to enjoy this more? TJ knew the answer to that. No matter what he did in any of the places he had been to, the circumstances and the reasons that he was here would not change. A failed marriage and TJ leaving town and running away.

"Fuck it," said TJ to himself. "I think too much."

TJ had been walking for a long time and realized he really didn't know where he was and there weren't a lot of people around. He was shaken back to reality by the fact that he noticed two guys following him. TJ quickly altered course and crossed the street. The men followed him and picked up speed, trying to catch up to

TJ. TJ was frightened now, wondering what these men had planned. He was carrying around a lot of money, thanks to his daily brothel habit, and several credit cards in his wallet. TJ began to run as well and now it was a chase. Other people around didn't seem to notice or care.

TJ was losing steam and the men were catching up. Finally, he gave in. I probably deserve this, he thought. Karma biting me hard in the ass.

One of the men shoved TJ backwards, while the other one yelled at him. "Gimme all your fookin money," said the guy, with an unidentifiable accent. He displayed a knife. For some reason, this didn't scare TJ that much. He was more concerned about it being a gun. "All your money, now, or you're a dead man," said the guy. Again, this threat didn't really seem to bother TJ. He pulled out his wallet, grabbed the euros and threw it at the men. The wind started blowing some of the money away. This was a good move, TJ realized, as the men focused on the money and stopped focusing on him. He took that opportunity to run again. The men did not follow.

TJ got back to his hotel room. His adrenaline rush at having to escape that situation gave way to a deep anger in himself that he let himself get into that situation and get robbed. He punched the wall, seriously hurting his hand. He tried to keep his anger in check, as he realized that he could replace the money, but what if he hadn't thought quickly and threw the money? Then it dawned on him how little he seemed to be bothered by the threats of the men. They could have killed me, he thought, so why wasn't I that scared?

Feeling stupid, and angry at himself, TJ decided to drink himself to a better place that day and stay where it was safe. The next day, he thought, back to the brothels and back to doing what I came here for.

TJ returned to the brothel the next day. He picked out a girl and they went up to their room. The girl was very friendly and talking up a storm to him. TJ felt a bit distracted on this day and not as in to this as he had been when he arrived in Amsterdam. He made small talk with the girl and then removed his clothes.

Something was wrong with TJ on this day. Usually he was ready for action, but today, nothing. His cock wasn't getting hard at all. The girl was doing her best to get TJ excited, but it wasn't working. TJ was getting embarrassed and angry at himself. He tried to concentrate, but nothing changed.   The girl assured him that it was okay, that he was probably just nervous.

"It's not that," said TJ. "I'm not nervous. It's just…. just…. not working today. Dammit!"

"Would you just like a massage?" asked the girl. "Maybe that will help."

TJ agreed and the girl gave him a massage. He was extremely tense. He chalked all of this up to the events of the previous day. Getting robbed was probably still affecting me, he thought. I'll try this again tomorrow. He apologized to the girl and left. He spent the evening on a cruise through the canals of Amsterdam, lost in thought about what happened at the brothel.

He went back the next day. Determined to recapture what he experienced the previous week, he psyched himself up for it. He was spending a lot of money there and he couldn't accept not getting his money's worth.

But it happened again. TJ had to leave once again in frustration. And that frustration was getting palpable. He was afraid to go back and waste more money. The stresses were starting to pile up. Once again, a visit to a city started off great and went south.

TJ decided it was time to leave Amsterdam. This is the way it's gonna be, he thought. Use up a place and wait for all the negativity and demons to overwhelm him and make him run again. He was sad. He was looking forward to this place as his new start. But maybe this wasn't his place after all.

"How are you doing, Paige?" asked Carrie Keller.

"I'm fine," said Paige, "hanging in there."

"Do you need anything?"

"No, I'm making due. Thanks Carrie. How's everything with you?"

"It's good. But Jim has been talking a lot about TJ recently. He's feeling bad about the way things went down with them. He's thinking if he had been a better friend, maybe some of this wouldn't have happened. Do you know where he is now?"

"Sadly Carrie, I don't. He's out there somewhere. I hope he's okay." Paige wondered exactly why Carrie was calling. It was unusual. They weren't close friends and as far as she knew, Carrie despised TJ.

Carrie sighed. "Let us know if you hear anything."

"Carrie, can I ask you something?" asked Paige, quizzically.

"Sure, what is it?"

"What's up? Why are you asking about TJ?"

Carrie paused for a minute. "Honestly, Paige, the topic is causing friction between Jim and I. I loathe him for what he did to you and how he treated Jim. But Jim feels differently, and thinks maybe he can help get TJ back."

"I wish that was the case. Jim caught TJ at the wrong time. I hope everything can get back to normal with those two."

"Do you think you'll reconcile with him?"

"I don't know," said Paige with an audible exhale. "Anything is possible."

TJ packed his things, went to Centraal Station and bought a train ticket to Berlin. He got comfortable on the train and watched as Amsterdam faded in to the distance. Another city TJ burned through, wore out his welcome and left. What's next, he wondered. All of the events in Amsterdam fresh in his mind, TJ pulled out a notebook and wrote down some thoughts. I need to capture these events for posterity, thought TJ, because if someone ever finds me dead, having been robbed, stabbed or shot, because I wasn't paying attention, at least I'll have some words about my last days. Sad as they may be.

AMSTERDAM, NETHERLANDS

Hello Journal – TJ here. Until I can figure out my life, we will become great friends. Amsterdam......Well, that turned out to be a clusterfuck. Am I going crazy? I arrived with a sense of purpose, but like Ireland and London before it, had to get the hell out because I couldn't hack it anymore. Couldn't even get hard there at the end with the girls. And sex was the ONLY thing redeeming about being here. Things just seem to go south on me. It's probably karma. I use up the good will of a city or country, and it spits me out. I know what I'm doing is wrong, but it feels right for me. I miss my kids, but I would be a shell of a man at home right now with Steven and Elizabeth. I don't want them to see me like

*this. I don't want anyone I know to see me like this. On to Berlin.
Wish me luck, Journal.*

Chapter 19

The train ride from Amsterdam to Berlin was very pleasant. TJ found himself enjoying the scenery as it passed by. There was something very calming about watching the Dutch and German countryside pass by, as TJ sat alone in the first-class cabin seat he had purchased. It was very quiet, no one was bothering him and he was alone with his thoughts. He didn't regret his departure from Amsterdam. He knew it was time. He was re-evaluating some of his personal goals of the new "TJ", but the problem was that without those, he really had nothing.

The train pulled in to Hannover, Germany, and much to his dismay, a German gentleman joined TJ in his cabin. A businessman, thought TJ, based on the briefcase. An announcement came over the speaker, in German, that caused a bit of a stir. TJ saw people moving around. Then, to his shock, the German businessman began yelling what TJ was certain were German swear words. The man stared at TJ and began talking loudly in German and pointing his finger. His nervousness beginning to rise, TJ waited for the man to stop his tirade and then asked if he spoke English.

"Ya, Ya, I speak English," said the angry German.

"What is going on here? What was that announcement?"

"The German rail system is very bad," said the German man, "you have to leave this train and go wait an hour on the other platform for the next train to Berlin." The man commenced swearing in German, then looked back at TJ. "I had a business meeting in one of the stops on the way. That other train will not stop there. Scheizen!!"

TJ grabbed his things and left the train, now irritated that his peaceful trip had been disrupted.

Berlin was a city that had always fascinated TJ, much like Rome. It was a place that was full of history. For one of the first times on his journey, he was legitimately interested in seeing every nook and cranny of the place. But he couldn't get the memories of Amsterdam out of his head and what happened there. He arrived at his hotel, unpacked his things and quickly researched some places where he could have some fun. His initial thoughts were to go to a "biergarten", but he was more interested in satisfying his desire for sex than getting drunk.

TJ found a place that was a combination of spa and brothel. You could actually hang out there for hours, swim, drink and then choose a girl when you were ready. That place sounds great, he thought. Surely, I can get relaxed there and then have fun, hopefully without the same issues I dealt with last week. TJ made a plan to go there the next day.

After relaxing for a while, TJ was surprised with a message from an old friend. He hadn't heard from Sophie Kiebler in a long time. The timing was impeccable, as he was on her doorstep. TJ recalled that she lived in Zurich, Switzerland.

Hi TJ – long time since we chatted. How are you? Are you doing any more traveling? I'm planning a getaway in a few months to Nepal. I'm planning my trip now – so excited! Drop me a line when you get a chance and let me know how you're doing.

TJ didn't respond to the message right away, although he had every intention to. Perhaps if it can be arranged, especially since he was just a country away, he could surprise her with a visit. He decided to play coy with where he was at the moment.

TJ traveled to the spa/brothel the next morning. Upon arrival, he was given a key to a locker, a towel and a bathrobe. Immediately, he saw several naked girls walking around. And also saw several men walking around in just their bathrobes. He went and got changed into his bathrobe, and the second he left the changing area, he was accosted by two naked girls asking him to take them "upstairs." TJ wasn't the least bit ready and already felt a bit intimidated. And he wasn't even remotely turned on by the naked girls walking around. Strange, he thought. He found himself avoiding the girls and went to the pool area. A bunch of naked guys swimming in a pool……. this is great, he thought. I'm at a place with naked girls walking around, and I opt to go where the naked guys are. He got comfortable at the pool bar and ordered a drink.

The girl working at the bar had an interesting job. She served guys in bathrobes drinks all day and watched as they swam naked.

"This must be an interesting job," said TJ to the lady at the bar.

"Ya, it is. But I'm used to it. Seen them all, all types. But everyone is very nice. Where are you from?"

"I'm from the US. We certainly don't have places like this there," said TJ, laughing.

"That's too bad. You should be more liberated. We Germans know how to have fun and relax."

TJ sat and people watched for a while, noticing that the girls would sometimes show up at the pool entrance. He would pick his time and moment, and would pick the girl he really wanted. He was determined to make this work. He stayed at the bar nursing his drink for a long time. He finally saw a girl peek through the door that caught his interest. He left his drink and went and chased her down.

"You want to go upstairs, baby?" she asked.

"Not yet," said TJ. "Talk to me for a few minutes."

"Okay, I will do the standard blow and fuck, but we can talk about extras."

"Not that," said TJ, "what's your name and where are you from?"

"I am Marta, and I'm from Germany, but one of my parents is Turkish. We go upstairs now?"

Marta was beautiful and had long blonde hair, perfect breasts and was very appealing. TJ decided to go for it.

"Yes, let's go," said TJ.

They went upstairs and got settled into a room. Marta came on very strong. TJ realized this was actually turning him off. What is wrong with me, he wondered. Marta tried to get things started by giving TJ a blowjob. But once again, TJ was not responding. Not again, he thought. He tried to get into it by being playful with her and feeling her body. Nothing. Marta was getting irritated.

"What is wrong? I'm not turning you on?"

"You are……I don't know what's wrong," said TJ dejectedly.

"Don't worry, you are just nervous. Buy more time with me so you can get comfortable."

TJ was getting angry at himself, but also realizing that this was not him. He didn't belong here. He didn't belong with these girls. He didn't belong in this kind of lifestyle.

TJ gave up. "Marta…. I'm sorry……. this isn't gonna happen. I'll pay you for everything."

"It's okay, TJ. It's not the first time it's happened. Guys like you don't allow yourself to enjoy it. Something is preventing you. It's all in your mind."

TJ paid Marta and then quickly left the spa/brothel, disgusted that he wasted so much money discovering that that easy option no longer worked for him. At the same time, he was glad. Glad to discover that maybe he still had some shred of morality left in him. As he headed to the train station, he carried on this internal monologue in his mind, trying to realize what was holding him back in the pursuit of this new "TJ."

TJ knew the train number he was supposed to be on. But he was paying little attention to the signs showing the train destinations. He got on the train, not realizing that it was a train that was going out of service for the evening. He got a bit nervous when he realized that no one else was on the train, and the train was moving very slowly. The train came to a stop, in the middle of nowhere, and shut down.

TJ assessed the situation. He was in a dark train, stopped in the middle of nowhere in Berlin, and no one else is around. He could still see the spa from where he was in the distance. He pushed the buttons to open the door, but nothing happened. I'm a sitting duck here, he thought. A stupid American who didn't know what the hell he was doing. He started banging on the windows. TJ was starting to panic. He felt his heart racing. He started yelling.

"IS ANYONE OUT THERE? HELP! I GOT ON THE WRONG TRAIN!!"

TJ repeated this over and over. He couldn't help but think he was getting punished somehow for his recent behavior, getting stuck on this dark train in the middle of a foreign land. Easy prey for anyone around. He sat down on one of the seats, dejected, almost accepting this fate as punishment.

Finally, an older man in a hat knocked on the window. TJ was shocked, but thankful. He looked friendly. TJ repeated his problem to the man, who looked at him and smiled, nodding his head. He held up both hands, as if he was showing TJ his palms. What the hell, thought TJ. He gestured for TJ to sit down, and then held up both hands again.

Ten minutes maybe, thought TJ. He sat back down. Alone in this German train, again forced to re-live the disaster that the last few hours had been. "This new TJ is a failure", he said to himself. "I can't do anything right."

Exactly ten minutes later, the train began moving again, back to the same train station. It was going back into service apparently, but TJ would have none of it. He left the train and waited for the next one, paying very close attention now to the signs.

TJ was in a foul mood that night. His excitement of these last few destinations had turned to shit fast and he was once again at a loss for what to do. He sat in the hotel restaurant after eating dinner and found himself ordering glass after glass of wine. His waitress, Kira, was very friendly and continuously just bringing him glasses. TJ enjoyed it as the numbness started to wash over him. After his fourth glass, Kira stopped bringing him glasses.

"Are you okay? Maybe you should go back to your room." Kira said, and then offered to bring the bill.

"Just bill it to my room," said TJ. "I'm fine."

TJ got up, and instead of going to his room, he went outside. The night was cold, but it felt good to TJ, who was numb anyway. He found a pub, walked in, and ordered a beer. He sat there alone. Unlike other places, where he was able to interact with others, that wasn't happening here. He just sat there drinking his beer and looking around. He had a second beer, and then a third.

TJ was now fully drunk, but feeling good. He needed this to put his day behind him. He left this pub and went to another. More drinks. TJ was in bad shape as he left this pub and was now wandering the streets aimlessly. At some point, he lost perspective as to where he was. He had wandered into a dark area. Once again, he had put himself into a dangerous situation. But this time, he didn't care. He didn't have the mental capacity to.

"Go ahead and kill me," said TJ to no one in particular. "I don't give a shit anymore."

He kept walking and found an open area, a small park that had some benches. TJ went and sat down on one of the benches. Everything was spinning, so he laid down flat on the bench. It had started to rain, but TJ didn't care. He closed his eyes and fell asleep on the bench.

TJ woke up, head pounding, sinuses draining and an awful sore throat. He was drenched and severely hung over. He could barely move. He had no idea where he was. He recalled what an awful day he had the previous day, but really couldn't remember how he ended up on a park bench. How could I be so stupid again, he thought. TJ struggled to get up. He looked at the street name and didn't recognize it. He tried to start walking, but began coughing very badly. He was beginning to realize how dire his situation might be. He had slept all night in the rain, was obviously sick and lost in Berlin. He needed to find his hotel.

He found the street called Friedrichstrasse. That was familiar, as his hotel wasn't far from it. He walked up the street, saw the signs for Checkpoint Charlie and walked as fast as he could to get back to his hotel.

He got back in his room, took a hot shower and laid down in his bed. He vowed not to leave the room for days. Every time he left, to his own devices, he was getting closer to getting himself killed. He buried himself under the covers of his bed and fell back asleep.

TJ woke up again in the afternoon. Still feeling sick, but not as bad. Earlier, he was worried about pneumonia setting in. He was also getting increasingly worried about his state of mind. He continuously was putting himself in stupid and dangerous situations. He knew he needed help. But from who? Who would care enough about him anymore to help him? And how could anyone help him if he could no longer help himself.

He pulled up the message from Sophie again and decided to respond.

Hi Sophie. I know it's been a while. I'm going through a bit of a rough time now. I was married, but all of that fell apart. It got so bad I had to leave home, and then had to leave the country. I'm actually close to you. I'm in Berlin. It's been particularly bad here. I really don't know what to do any more.

I'm sorry to be a downer. I hope everything is okay with you. I was actually planning to surprise you by showing up in Zurich, but I'm in no shape now, mentally or physically.

It didn't take long for Sophie to respond.

TJ – I'm sorry to hear all of that. You are in Berlin now? What is your phone number?

TJ sent Sophie his phone number, and was shocked when his phone rang a minute later.

"Hi TJ, it's Sophie."

"I knew it was you," said TJ. "I'm surprised you called so fast."

"TJ, listen……. you are in Berlin now, but I want you to follow through on your wish to visit me here in Zurich. I want to hear your story. You don't sound anything like the guy who was full of life when I met him in Bora Bora."

"I don't want to bother you with my problems, Sophie. I don't want to depress you."

"I insist. Come to Zurich as soon as you can. I'll offer you a place to stay and some good company. I have a roommate, too. She will also be good company."

TJ thought carefully about Sophie's offer. He couldn't turn it down. He was leery at taking someone up on their hospitality after what had happened with the Green's in London. But Sophie was different. He had established an interesting bond with her in Bora Bora, and she was a kindred spirit.

"Okay, Sophie. I'll take you up on that offer. It will be a good thing. I need my good friends right now."

"Yes, you do. Okay…. get yourself a train ticket and let me know what day and time you'll arrive in Zurich."

"I will. Can't wait to see you. And thank you."

"We all have rough patches in life. I know you are a good person, and it's my pleasure to help you. I'll see you soon, okay?"

"Yes, see you soon. Bye."

TJ owed Sophie everything after that call. She singlehandedly gave him hope and altered the path that he was on. Going to Zurich and visiting her was an unplanned deviation from this failing new "TJ", but probably the best thing for him.

TJ decided to spend one more day in Berlin and finally sightsee like he had wanted to. He wanted to salvage something from this stay that had been an unmitigated disaster so far. He toured the city, seeing the Reichstag, Brandenburg gate, Holocaust memorial and all of the sites he could take in. He finished up his day and purchased his train ticket to Zurich, leaving the next day.

TJ boarded the train to Switzerland that following morning. His overwhelming thought was not to screw this stay up with Sophie. He needed to check all of his urges at the door, stop the drinking and try to recover himself as much as he could. This was an opportunity to once again change course. This new purpose he attempted did not succeed. It was a poor purpose to begin with, not something he was cut out for. He was now thankful that those failures happened. It was probably for the best, as he could have lost himself in that lifestyle and put himself at a lot of risk.

He sat quietly in the train as the German countryside passed by. This journey had had many ups and downs so far. TJ was hopeful and determined that his stay in Zurich would change things for the better.

BERLIN, GERMANY

Didn't take me long to screw up Berlin, did it, Journal? Holy crap. Am I impotent now? What a cruel irony to shell out money for sex and not be able to get hard. Then that stupid train and getting sick......I don't think I can properly take care of myself at this point. Thank God for Sophie. It's as if a guardian angel personally intervened. I can't screw this up. I need to be on my best behavior in Zurich. Maybe I can treat it like a bit of a rehab. And I desperately need to talk to Steven and Elizabeth. Journal, I'm going to try to turn this around in Zurich. I don't like the new me. He's a fuck-up. A sex addict. An irresponsible alcoholic. Time to get on the right path.

Chapter 20

"Hi TJ! So good to see you again." Sophie Kiebler said as she walked up and shook TJ's hand while he left the platform at Zurich's train station.

"A handshake?? That's all I get?" TJ said jokingly.

Sophie gave TJ a big hug and then introduced the tall blonde girl standing with her as Julia Gruber, her roommate.

"Welcome to Zurich, TJ," said Julia. "Is this your first visit to Switzerland?"

"It's my first visit to Zurich," said TJ. "It looks really beautiful."

"You've only seen the train station!" Sophie laughed at TJ.

"The train station is very beautiful. It looks……. clean." TJ was actually amazed at how clean it was. As they walked on to the street called Bahnhofstrasse, the scenery of Zurich became clear to TJ. It was all very neat and orderly looking. Trams passing by, people walking with a purpose and no sign of any dirt. Or even a bug. Not so much as an ant.

"We have a little bit of a walk to my car," said Sophie. "Do you want to stop and get some coffee first?"

"Sure," said TJ. They found a coffee shop, which there were many, about 50 feet up ahead.

"So, Sophie tells me you're on a bit of a tour," said Julia.

"You could say that."

"Where have you been so far?"

"Ireland, Scotland, England, France, Amsterdam, Germany and now here. Oh, and Niagara Falls in the US. This tour was not by choice. But it's happening."

"I know," said Julia, "no need to get into those details. You're here to relax. How did you and Sophie meet? In Bora Bora?"

"Yup, we were on a shore excursion together and talked. Then she showed off her bungalow the next day."

"Was that all the showed off?" laughed Julia.

"Sadly, yes," said TJ.

Sophie smacked TJ on the arm.

"This guy here thought he could do the Tour de France around Bora Bora. If I hadn't let him stop and rest, he may still be there now trying to finish that."

"I would have finished it. Don't flatter yourself."

They finished their coffee, walked for about ten more minutes and arrived at Sophie's car and headed towards the house where she and Julia lived.

Sophie and Julia lived in a small, Swiss styled home not far from the city. It only had two bedrooms, so TJ's new home was to be the couch. It's better than the Berlin park bench, he thought to himself. TJ dropped his things and sat on the couch.

"TJ, we are going to make dinner," said Sophie. "You just get comfortable."

TJ leaned up against the pillow on the couch and rested his head on the back of it. Then a thought hit him that he hadn't felt in a while. He was thinking about going home. He didn't care what the status of his relationship was with Paige. He just wanted to be near his kids again. He knew it would take a lot of work, but anything would be better than what he's been experiencing. He vowed to give it serious thought over the next few days here in Zurich and wanted to make sure to see what Sophie thought. From a woman's perspective.

TJ wondered how Paige would react if he offered to come home. That was a big mystery. Perhaps it would be better to just go and surprise her.

"TJ, so you want some beer or wine?" asked Julia.

TJ thought about it for a minute.

"No, water will be fine."

"Did you know the tap water is perfectly safe to drink here? Our water is very clean."

"Then one order of Swiss Tap Water, please," said TJ. That was the first time in a long time that TJ had turned down a drink. Progress, he thought. Things can be different here.

They all ate dinner and made small talk. It seemed like Julia was avoiding asking certain questions. Sometimes as she started to ask something, she glanced over at Sophie. Sophie never made any gestures, but perhaps she would have if the topic had gone somewhere it shouldn't have been. After dinner, Julie excused herself.

"I'll take care of the dishes and then head to the store so you two can catch up," said Julia, who once again looked over at Sophie, who just smiled at her.

Sophie remained quiet until Julia was gone.

"TJ…. why were you in Bora Bora? I mean, why did you go there, especially alone?"

"I could ask you the same question," said TJ.

"And I'll share why I was there. But you first."

"I went because I wanted to," said TJ. "I was looking for something, and in retrospect was already in the beginning stages of problems with Paige. I wanted to go and have an experience for myself. I tried to talk her into going, but when she didn't show the slightest bit of interest, I became determined to do it myself."

"What did you take away from it?' asked Sophie.

"It was amazing in one respect, but also the beginning of something bad."

"TJ, don't look at it as bad. Everything happens for a reason. If you had never gone there, you wouldn't be sitting here. Life is a tapestry of events. You will be okay in the end."

"Why did you go?" asked TJ.

"I just got out of a long-term relationship and the break up was hard. I loved him deeply but he fell out of love with me. I'm not sure why……. he never really explained it well. He just shut me out, and left me to wonder. So, after sulking for several months, I just decided to go reclaim myself and I had always wanted to see that part of the world. Plus, one of my good friends and her husband honeymooned there and highly recommended it."

"That's it?" asked TJ. "I thought there would be more to it."

"Nah," said Sophie. "Sometimes you just do it because you want to. No other reasons are necessary."

"Be honest……what did you think of me when you met me there? Did you even trust men at that point?"

Sophie laughed. "I thought you were hitting on me at first, and after my experience would have turned you down fast! But I realized right away that you were genuine, funny and had a desire to do things with your life. Taking that bike ride was a great example. You did it because you wanted to. And for you, I'm sure you were very proud of yourself when you finished it."

"You're right about that. Big accomplishment. I'll never forget the feeling of when I finished. And the pain."

"We'll talk more about what's happening with you right now, but not tonight. Enjoy your first night here. The TV is all yours. We never really watch."

Sophie sat on the couch with TJ as he scanned through the channels. "Not much for me to watch if I don't know German."

"Then learn German!" Sophie insisted.

"Easier said than done," said TJ. "This is a hard language. I did learn some swear words though."

"I'm not surprised that would be what you could retain." Sophie said, shaking her head.

TJ and Sophie scanned through some more channels, and TJ began to try and repeat some of the German he was hearing. This amused Sophie, who surely wasn't telling TJ how bad he was mangling it.

Sophie and Julia went to bed, leaving TJ on his own. He laid down on the couch and fell asleep. He had the best night of sleep he had had in a long time.

"Okay, TJ, let's talk," said Sophie.

Sophie had let Julia get off to bed on this, TJ's second day here. It had been a relatively quiet day, with TJ taking walks up and down the street on his own as Julia and Sophie tended to their day's business.

She continued. "Tell me what you want to tell me. What you feel like you need to tell me. I'm a great listener."

"Here it is in a nutshell………. things got progressively worse with Paige after I met you and after my trip to the South Pacific. Fights became more frequent; sex became less frequent and it finally became unbearable."

"So why are you here? Why are you moving through Europe?"

"I had to leave the US. The stress was unbearable. I was panicking. It was the only choice I felt like I had." TJ looked at Sophie, who appeared to have her next question prepared, but wasn't asking it. "I looked at it as a journey I had to take. Maybe to better myself."

"Better yourself to do what? What's your end goal?"

TJ thought for a minute. "I don't know anymore." He was disturbed that he didn't know that answer. There wasn't an end goal in mind.

"That's a problem. You need to understand what you want out of this. You're on a journey…. that's fine. Makes sense. But you need to set a goal and work towards it. Otherwise, you will keep wandering aimlessly. Honestly, TJ…. you didn't sound good when we talked and you didn't look good when we saw you at the train station. This journey you're on isn't the right one. Not with that kind of effect."

Sophie was right. She was making a lot of sense.

"I know," said TJ. "But I don't know what else to do."

"I will challenge you with something tonight," said Sophie. "Come up with your goal. Really think about where you want to end up. Tomorrow, Julia and I are going to take you to Lucerne and up Mt Pilatus. I want to have this conversation with you about your goal to help set you on your way. That will be a perfect, peaceful place to clear your mind and be philosophical."

"Okay, I'll do that." Said TJ.

"I'll leave you to it. Good night, TJ. Sweet dreams."

TJ laid on the couch with his eyes open, trying to figure out what it was that he wanted. The only answer that seemed firm in his mind was being at home with his kids. If nothing else, he would start there.

The cable car leading to the top of Mt Pilatus started its ascent. There was only one problem. They would be passing through the clouds to get to the top. So much for the scenic view, thought TJ. Although it's going to be cool to be on top of a mountain looking down at the clouds.

They arrived at the top. There weren't a lot of people there this time of year. It was bitterly cold and this view was probably known by Sophie and was part of her plan.

"It will clear up, don't worry," she said. "For now, there's a spot I want us to go to."

Sophie led Julia and TJ up a set of steps and to an even more remote place, where they would settle.

"You two get comfortable. I will go get us some hot chocolate from the cafe," said Sophie.

Julia and TJ got settled into spots, but couldn't quite get a conversation started. Julia was a strange bird, thought TJ. She really seemed to take most of her cues from Sophie.

"I am soooo cold," said TJ, literally trying to break the ice.

"I know. The hot chocolate will be great," said Julia.

They awkwardly smiled at each other and just waited for Sophie to return. TJ had his answer prepared for her when she joined them again.

Sophie returned after what felt like forever with a thermos and some cups and poured them each some hot chocolate.

"So, I've got my answer for you. My goal," said TJ.

"Excellent!" said Sophie. "Let's hear it."

"I want to return home. I want to be with my kids. Even if I don't get along with Paige. I want to be there with my kids."

"Okay," said Sophie. "That was easy enough. So why are you still here? Everything is in your hands. Start making this happen."

"I'm not sure where to start. Should I call home?"

"Yes, absolutely," said Sophie. "The sooner, the better. And don't be hesitant, TJ. If it's what you really want, then do whatever it takes."

As Sophie finished up her encouraging speech, the clouds started to dissipate enough so that there was a whole big enough to look through and see the town below. Perfectly timed, thought TJ. He was comfortable with his decision. Tonight, at the house, he would make contact with home, and take the first steps to ending this exile.

"Okay," said Sophie. "The hard part is done. Enjoy the view. And TJ, find your inner peace. Outward journeys can help, but inward journeys are sometimes even more critical."

TJ picked up the phone to make the call. The first time he was doing this with the intention of coming home. He was very nervous.

"Hello?"

It was Steven.

"Steven…. it's Dad. How are you?"

"I'm good. Where are you?"

"I'm in Switzerland, son. How is everything at school?"

"Everything is going good at school. Honor roll so far. Will you be coming home soon?"

"Yes, I believe so. Just need to take care of a few things."

"Good. Here…. Elizabeth wants to talk to you." TJ got excited to finally hear his daughter's voice.

"DADDY!!" screamed Elizabeth. "Where are you?"

"I'm in Switzerland, sweetie. Do you know where that is?"

"It's in Europe," said Elizabeth confidently. "What did you stay to Steven when he asked if you were coming home?"

"I said yes, sweetie. I just need to take care of a few things."

"Hooray!" said Elizabeth.

This call was doing more for TJ than anything else had on this trip. He was happy to finally talk to his kids, who seemed genuinely happy to talk to him.

"Sweetie, is your mother there?"

"No, she went out. Do you want me to tell her you called?" asked Elizabeth.

"Yes, sweetie. And I'll also send her a message."

TJ talked with Elizabeth for another 15 minutes. His daughter gave him a rundown of all of her activities at school and with friends. She didn't stop talking, and TJ didn't mind. He could have listened for hours.

After the call, TJ put a message together for Paige.

Paige. I hope everything is okay. I talked to the kids tonight. It was so good to hear their voices. Can I talk to you when you'll be there at the house alone? I wanted to see if you were open to a few things happening. Let me know.

TJ wanted to be careful where Paige was concerned. Trying to mend that fence would be delicate. He needed to be ready. To his shock, a reply came fast.

(Paige's reply) Hi TJ. Sure – we can talk. I've been hoping we could, you know. The kids miss you a lot.

(TJ's reply) I know. I miss them too. When would be a good time to call?

(Paige's reply) Day after tomorrow. When they are at school. TJ – how are you? Are you doing okay? Can you tell me where you are?"

(TJ's reply) I'm in Zurich, Switzerland. Visiting my friend Sophie and her roommate.

(Paige's reply) The girl from Bora Bora?

(TJ's reply) Yes, that one.

TJ got worried about where this was heading. Sophie caused an argument between the two of them. But TJ wanted to be honest.

(Paige's reply) Yes, I remember. You have a lot of international friends. All girls – lol!

(TJ's reply) She insisted I visited when she learned I was in Germany. I know, what can I say?

(Paige's reply) Germany, huh? Sounds like you've covered a lot of ground.

(TJ's reply) Yeah. I'll call you the day after tomorrow. Looking forward to it.

(Paige's reply) Me too. Bye TJ.

(TJ's reply) Bye Paige. Talk to you soon.

Paige Carlson looked back through the messages. She was trying to piece together TJ's journey and wondered why he was in Germany. Deep down, she wanted TJ to come home. But she wanted to be careful about giving him false hopes for their relationship at this point. It was too soon to be thinking about that.

TJ Carlson felt content. He had talked to his kids and had a dialogue with Paige that could lead to him going home. He still had two days before he would call. He decided to say goodbye to Sophie and Julia and head to Rome. A symbolic place for him to end his journey. He would mend fences with Paige and then reach out to Jim Keller from Rome. It was time to get his life together.

"Sophie, I can't thank you enough. My stay here was an absolute godsend. You've helped me course correct and that will lead to me hopefully getting my life back together." TJ was packed and ready to head back to the Zurich train station to head to what he hoped was his last stop, Rome.

"TJ, we were glad to help. There's always a reason you meet someone. It's never an accident. I will always be your friend, no matter what. If what we gave you here helps you to get your life back together in your eyes, then I couldn't be happier."

"Yeah, TJ, you're a pretty cool guy," said Julia. "Best of luck. Sophie will take you to the train station."

On the way to the train station, Sophie and TJ didn't talk much. TJ kept thinking about meeting Sophie on that excursion in Bora Bora. What a chance encounter it was. He could hardly believe he was here, in her car, having just spent a few days with her, and what a difference she had made in his life. Sophie was right, you meet people for a reason. This gave TJ a strong faith at that moment that everything was going to be okay.

"It's not goodbye, TJ. It's until next time. You keep me updated, promise? I want to know how all of this turns out. And you let me know if you get into trouble again."

"Thank you, Sophie. For everything. I'll miss you. I will always keep in touch."

TJ gave Sophie a big hug and kissed her on the cheek. TJ boarded his train to Rome.

ZURICH, SWITZERLAND

Hey Journal, it's me! The old me…. the old TJ. The one who was a father to his kids and a husband to his wife. Zurich was a gift from

God. Sophie is an angel. I'll never underestimate the power of having good friends. I feel refreshed and renewed and I'm ready to end this journey. Maybe I needed all of this to make me realize what was truly important. I'm nervous about talking to Paige. I don't know if she will take me back or if anything will ever be the same. But I have to try. For the kids. I can never lose sight of the fact that they are the most important people in my life. They need their father. I can be that man again. On to Rome! Journal – in our short time together, you've been helpful. Actually, putting my failures down in writing was like a gut punch. No offense, but I hope our relationship is coming to an end.

Chapter 21

TJ sat thinking about the last month as the train from Zurich sped towards Rome, which, in TJ's mind was to be the end of this journey. What a roller coaster ride it had been, where he had seen the very worst in himself and then managed to pull himself together through the help of a friend who he had a chance encounter with in Bora Bora and was there to help him in Europe. Paige seemed ready to talk to him. Or maybe he just wanted to finally end this. After Amsterdam and Berlin, he wasn't sure he could feel any lower. If that's who he really was, maybe it was best to go back and be that person he was with Paige, Steven and Elizabeth. It may not have been the real TJ Carlson, but maybe that was for the best.

Rome held a special place in TJ's heart. It was here that years ago he talked his friend Jim Keller into joining him on an out-of-country trip for the first time. Jim was really excited to be there with him, and they had a blast. They covered a lot of ground in a short period of time. This would actually be TJ's third trip to Rome. He always loves to tell a story from his first trip. On a journey to see family who lived overseas, TJ visited a friend who was studying in Rome. The stay was an overnight visit and the friend would be joining him. TJ hadn't slept for 36 hours prior to his stop in Rome, and was dead tired when he arrived. His friend, along with several others, attempted to take him on a whirlwind tour of Rome. At the Colosseum, which TJ could barely grasp that he was at, TJ leaned up against the walls of the historic structure. His friend tried to capture the moment:

"You're standing up against living history, man," said the friend.

"I don't give a shit," said a young TJ Carlson, while yawning loudly.

He kicked himself a hundred times that he blew the opportunity to enjoy that day and moment in Rome with his friend. When he returned with Jim Keller, their first stop was the Colosseum, which they spent hours at. As excited as TJ was about being back there, he was enjoying Jim's childlike approach to the place, as if he was enjoying every square foot of it, taking pictures of every nook and cranny that he was allowed to. He considered begging for the opportunity to go into the very bottom area where the Christians would battle the lions, which wasn't allowed at the time.

TJ was going to use these last few days in Rome to get himself completely straight, stop drinking, stop screwing around and try to become the man he was, for better or worse, and accept his lot in life as husband and father, friend and provider and try to grow old gracefully. He had a lot of damage to undo with Paige, but he was determined to undo it. He would go to counseling if necessary. He would go to meetings for alcohol addiction and sex addiction, which after this journey he was sure he needed help for. He would do anything to ensure that Steven and Elizabeth grew up with their father, a man who could be counted on and would always be there. TJ started to doze in his train seat.

TJ was walking in to his home after his arrival back in Fayetteville. It was a dark and foggy night, and TJ was a bit surprised he hadn't heard from anyone or received any messages after his arrival. The cab driver, who didn't say a word, or even look at TJ the entire time, drove off without even collecting his fare. Strange, thought TJ. I wonder if that guy was all there.

He walked into his house, shocked that the front door was unlocked this time of night. Everything had changed. All of the pictures of TJ were gone. In fact, all the pictures of the kids were gone. It didn't even appear that the house had any indication that children lived there. TJ got extremely worried.

"Paige?" said TJ, loud enough to ensure that Paige would hear. No response. Lights were on in the house, so someone was definitely home. His bedroom door was closed but he could tell the light was on in the room.

"Paige? You there?" asked TJ.

TJ heard a small bang in the room, and then what sounded like a cough. He walked to his bedroom door.

"Paige, I'm home. Where are the kids?" No response.

TJ Carlson opened the door. What he saw made him violently angry. A man was on top of Paige, thrusting in and out of her. Paige had her arms wrapped around his back, with her fingernails digging in to it, nearly drawing blood. She was moaning loudly, and looking like she was really enjoying it.

"Paige, what the FUCK??" screamed TJ. TJ ran over and put his arm around the neck of the man and pulled him back. Paige pushed the man away as he was being pulled back. It was Darkness. TJ threw a punch at the back of Darkness's head, which connected but did no damage. Darkness looked squarely at TJ.

"You're a fool," said Darkness. "You are a naïve, ignorant fool."

"Fucking my wife now? You said I'm supposed to trust you and that we would be friends, yet every time you show up, you are finding more sinister ways of making me feel like shit. I'm going to end this now." TJ looked for a sharp object in the room. He looked at Paige and was shocked at what he saw. She had heavy bags under her eyes and her hair was stringy and dirty. She gave TJ an evil look.

"He's more of a man than you ever were," said Paige. TJ noticed that Paige was holding a pair of scissors in her hand.

"Seriously, Paige? He's garbage. But if that's your type now, go for it." TJ re-focused on Darkness, who was standing there, now fully clothed and smiling.

"Understand something TJ," said Darkness. "I serve a purpose for you, whether you know it or not. I'm like your guardian angel. You just haven't figured it out. You will."

"Go fuck yourself," said TJ angrily.

"You're going down the wrong path," said Darkness. "You'll know that soon enough. Look at her. She's not worth it. She hates you. I'm not sure what you ever saw in her. She's cheap and easy. Not worth your time." With that, TJ lunged at Darkness, ready to strangle him. As he stepped toward him, Paige jumped to TJ's side, swung her arm around and stabbed TJ in the stomach with the scissors, which dug deep into his abdomen. Standing there, stunned, holding his stomach and watching blood pour out, he looked over at Paige, who was laughing.

"That's what you get, you bastard!" she screamed.

TJ was starting to fade and collapsed to one knee. Darkness kneeled down next to him.

"You remember this, dammit. I'm warning you. You listen to me. There's a reason I keep showing up. Stop being naïve and open your eyes." Darkness was talking to TJ not to scare him this time, he thought. This seemed different. As if Darkness was truly trying to warn him about something. He watched as Darkness walked over to Paige, grabbed her head, twisted it and made it crack loudly. Paige fell to the floor.

"Nooooo!!" screamed TJ, who then experienced a sharp pain in his stomach, faded to black and collapsed to the floor.

TJ woke up as the train came to a sudden stop. Angered by his dream, he punched the wall of the train, which attracted the attention of some of the other passengers. He was sick of this. He wanted these dreams to end. He wanted the nightmare that had become this journey to end. He steadied himself, got some coffee and stared out the window for the rest of the train ride to Rome.

The train pulled in to Termini Station in Rome. TJ had decided to stay at a hotel close to the Colosseum. Much like the Eiffel Tower was in Paris, the Colosseum was to be a beacon for him there in Rome. The hotel was within walking distance, and he began making his way out of the train station. He noticed a group of children, girls, that looked to be around the same age as Elizabeth. When they saw him, they all approached, obviously begging for money. TJ flashed back to the scene in Paris, being mobbed by the Bosnian women. These girls didn't look or appear like they could be dangerous, but he was certain there was an adult factor behind this. People who would use these children to collect money and then have the children turn the money over to them. A scummy business model, thought TJ.

As he looked at the girls who were all standing around him now, he couldn't help but think of Elizabeth. In a quiet moment in his mind, he thanked God that his daughter did not live this life of these girls, begging strangers for money. His heart wanted to reach out to each of them, but he knew that it wouldn't be looked at as an act of kindness. It would merely be a business transaction to some piece of garbage adult who's using these poor girls. The girls all had their eyes trained on TJ and their hands out. He looked in to some of their eyes. They were vacant. All were speaking Italian, which TJ did not understand.

TJ looked down and quickly moved his way through them. The girls followed him for a short time until someone new walked in to their vicinity. The whole event made TJ sad, but made him want to talk to Elizabeth even more.

It was early afternoon and TJ simply decided to spend the rest of his day at the Colosseum. No real plans there, just to be there. Later that night, he was going to call and talk to his family and let Paige know he is coming home. To let Elizabeth know he is coming home. He thought about the giant bearhug he was going to get from his daughter and that made him smile.

TJ walked around the Colosseum and saw a couple taking individual pictures of each other. He knew this feeling. Taking selfies of himself almost everywhere he went. He decided to approach the couple and offer to take a few pictures.

"Hi guys, would you like some shots together?" TJ said to the couple.

The couple looked quizzically at TJ, almost as if they thought he was a scammer. It didn't appear they had any intention of handing over their phone. TJ sensed that.

"Hey…. I can take it with my phone and then email it to you if you'd like." This seemed to warm the couple up to him a little bit.

"Sorry buddy," said the guy. "Can't be too careful here. We were nearly scammed by some goofy French guy trying to sell us necklaces so he could buy gas."

TJ laughed. "No worries, I'm not a scammer. I just know the feeling. I've been traveling alone for months."

"Really. Where have you gone?" asked the woman.

"Europe mainly," said TJ. "Sort of backpacking it around. Meeting old friends."

"I'm Ted and this is Meg. We're from Toronto. On a cruise. Rome today, then heading on to Greece, Montenegro, Croatia then Venice." Ted handed his camera to TJ and he proceeded to take several shots of Ted and Meg throughout the Colosseum, to which Ted and Meg would get shots for TJ.

TJ was getting good at befriending other couples on his travels. He'd done it several times now, but he was realizing that each new time he did it, he felt more and more alone without someone to share his experiences with. He decided he'd had enough of Ted and Meg. And other couples in general. He was looking forward to talking to Paige. And thinking of a future where he and his wife could experience these things together. He grabbed a drink, found himself a spot to sit, and pulled out a notepad and pen he had brought with him from his hotel. He began writing talking points. Preparing himself to try and take the first steps to put this all behind him.

"Yes, that's my husband's card," said Paige Carlson. "And where was this found?"

Paige listened intently.

"And this is located in Amsterdam?" she continued.

Paige buried her head in her hand as she listened. The conversation with TJ in Zurich went really well, but now she was getting an indication of where he'd been and what he'd been doing leading up to that.

TJ had lost one of his rarely used bank cards in a sex club in Amsterdam, where he had spent a week indulging in his sexual fantasies. Paige feared the worst when she learned the card was lost there. She had the name of the place. Now she would investigate exactly what kind of place it was. She pulled it up online and saw the offerings - Massage, oral sex and intercourse.

"Do you know if he showed up there often?" asked Paige.

"Ma'am, we are not at liberty to say. We just wanted to offer to return his property."

"Go ahead and cut the card up and throw it away," said Paige. "You won't reach him. He's not in the country right now."

"Okay, thank you ma'am."

Paige hung up the phone and immediately picked it back up to call Kylie. She had been right all along. Paige had been there holding that house together, taking care of the kids and struggling with everything and anything. TJ had been out there paying for sex in foreign countries. She was disgusted.

"Thank God you found this out," said Kylie. "I know you were hoping to reconcile, but now you know who and what you're dealing with.

"Can you come over here? He's going to call later. I don't want him to sweet talk me into anything. This is by far and away the last straw. He's a pig."

"Absolutely," said Kylie. "I'm there for you. Be over in a few."

Paige hung up with Kylie and steeled herself for the impending call with her husband. A man she no longer knew, who she hadn't seen for months and who she now didn't care if she ever saw again.

Kylie arrived at the house to find Paige crying.

"I really thought this whole nightmare was about to end," said Paige. "I was ready to take him back."

"God works in mysterious ways," said Kylie. "It was meant to be this way. Listen, get this behind you, okay. You need to prepare yourself to move on without him."

"I know," said Paige. "If I start to waiver when he calls, you get me straight."

"Gladly," said Kylie, smiling. "Where's the wine?"

"In the refrigerator. Let's down this one later tonight. Steven and Elizabeth are at school. I wanted to be alone this afternoon so I'd be ready for a long conversation with him. But thank God you're here."

"My pleasure," said Kylie. "Any man would be lucky to have you Paige. Don't let this guy ruin your life. He's no longer the man you married, and now he's someone you probably wouldn't even associate with."

At that moment, the telephone rang. Paige looked at Kylie.

"Do what you have to do," said Kylie.

30 minutes earlier

TJ Carlson sat in his Rome hotel room ready to make the big call home to hammer everything out regarding his return. He thought of many things he would say. He wanted to tell Paige that he loved her and he couldn't wait to talk to his kids. For the first time on this journey, he was starting to feel like himself again. The old TJ Carlson, before all of this chaos happened. He was excited about returning to his life. He now realized he had missed it. That the life path he was on wasn't leading anywhere good for him. Certainly not to the happiness he was craving.

He started to pack his things. He would get on the phone with Rose and get his final ticket booked back home. He was hoping that maybe this will be the end of Darkness, his nemesis in the dream world. But more than anything else, he wanted that bearhug from his daughter.

He was getting nervous as the time to call Paige approached. His heart was beating fast. He first like a teenager again, nervous to ask someone out on a date. But this was his wife. They had shared 15 years together and had 2 kids. For better or worse, he thought. And they've certainly made it through the "worse" part of that equation.

Excited, and happier than he had been for a long time, he picked up his phone and dialed home.

"Hi Paige. I'm so glad we're talking like this again. I've missed you and the kids terribly." TJ started out the call with his rehearsed first line.

"Hi TJ," said Paige. "What's on your mind?"

TJ was a little taken aback by that response from Paige, but undeterred.

He continued. "You know, I've experienced a lot of highs and lows the last few months. And I mean the lowest of lows. I think this was a journey I was meant to go on to make me re-appreciate everything I had there, that we had there, and make me cherish our relationship and our family. I'm sorry for everything, Paige. I hope you can find it in your heart to forgive me. I most certainly forgive you for everything. And I want to come home. I'm ready to come back home. I love you, babe."

Paige didn't respond right away.

"Babe…. you still there?" TJ was wondering what was going on. He had just laid it out there for Paige. He had served it up……but she wasn't hitting it back.

"TJ………all of that was complete bullshit," said Paige as Kiley raised her right arm up with a clenched fist in approval, "and don't think for a minute that by just uttering a few words and saying I love you will remove the stench of everything you've done over the last few months. How many girls have you fucked? Must be several in Amsterdam. They were apparently so good that you gave them a bank card as a tip. Fuck, you're such a piece of work. Why the hell would I take you back? I won't have you, and I don't even want the kids to be around the man you've become."

TJ was devastated. He was in shock listening to the bile that was coming out of Paige's mouth. How did she know about Amsterdam, he wondered?

"I'm divorcing you, TJ. I actually had everything drawn up just in case it ever came to this. We'll set up time for you to talk to the kids, but I warn you, don't you dare fight me for custody of them. You don't deserve it and our kids need to have a better example than you. When you get a free moment from whoring around in Europe, take the time to sign the divorce documents and then you can go out and fuck whoever you want, free of guilt, not that you had any to begin with. I hope these other nasty women you're getting……."

TJ hung up the phone. It was done. It was over. He didn't need to hear another word from Paige. The life that he had hoped to return to was now gone, never to return. TJ Carlson was a man without a wife, a job, his kids, his pride, his dignity his self-esteem and any notion of self-worth. Paige had just stripped all of that away from him in those few moments. And he deserved it. He deserved every bit of it in his mind. I'm such an idiot, he thought.

A complete fool. I won't even contest this divorce. Fuck it. Fuck everything.

"He just hung up," said Paige, "didn't even let me finish."

"You were amazing," said Kylie. "Didn't that feel good?"

"No, Kylie," said Paige. "That was the hardest thing I've ever had to do. Put yourself in my shoes and imagine having to do that to your husband. I wouldn't wish that on anyone, not even my worst enemy. I'm completely devastated." Paige started crying loudly. "Pour the wine, Kylie. I want to get drunk."

TJ had sat there staring blankly for several minutes, his phone still in his hand. He honestly didn't know what to do anymore. He was a man without a home and a man without a plan. And there didn't seem to be a lot of good options. Then, a stunning realization hit TJ. He began thinking back to his dreams where Darkness, while making his life a living hell in his dream, was also trying to deliver a message that TJ was not hearing. Could it be that Darkness was trying to warn him about this exact moment? Surely the dream involving Paige manifested itself in that cruel sendoff. But what about the other dreams? Especially the ones where he's claiming to be a friend and there to help. Next time Darkness shows up in my dream, thought TJ, I will not be as resistant and will hear him out. Perhaps Darkness is me. Or the man I'm becoming. And he wants me to embrace that? I no longer have anything to lose, so maybe I'll try and understand him, or perhaps me, a little better so I know what the point of all of this is.

TJ couldn't take being alone with his thoughts anymore. He wanted to numb the pain.

TJ wanted to get drunker than he had ever been. For the first time, he actually wondered if drugs would help. I now understand why people hand their lives over to something that numbs their pain, he thought. I can't imagine living like this anymore.

He spent the evening sitting alone at a table drinking as many glasses of scotch and soda as he could stomach. He felt like he was going to get sick. His pain wasn't being numbed. It was getting worse. "Fuck this!" he said out loud. "Give me my check please."

The waiter ignored TJ.

"NOW, GODDAMMIT!" yelled TJ.

The waiter looked at him angrily and went over and talked to the manager. They both walked over.

"How much?" said TJ with a quiet intensity.

"120 euros," said the waiter.

"You pay now and then get the hell out, you stupid drunk American," said the manager.

TJ threw the money at the manager and walked out. As soon as he stepped out of the bar, he screamed at the top of his lungs. He screamed a few more times until his voice started to get coarse. He sat down on the side of the road and started crying uncontrollably, his head buried in his arms which were resting on his knees. TJ had never cried this hard in his life.

He pulled himself together, purchased a bottle of wine from a general store on his way back to the hotel and proceeded to drink it until he passed out on his bed.

TJ was at his lowest point in his life. He played Russian Roulette with his marriage and lost. He wasn't sure what life he would go back to, if he ever went back. He just wanted to numb the pain. His mood was dark. All he saw was black. He wanted to leave Rome. A place that once symbolized good feelings and hope for TJ now represented everything dark and ugly. It's not the city, thought TJ, it's me.

"Rose, please book me a ticket from Rome to Helsinki, Finland." TJ hadn't talked to Rose Carter in quite some time.

"You're in Rome now, sweetie? How's everything?" Rose was in a happy mood.

"Just book the ticket, please."

"Oh…. okay. Everything okay, sweetie?"

"No, Rose, everything is not okay. Just please book the ticket. I'd like to leave today." TJ was annoyed at Rose's chirpiness on the phone.

"Wow, okay, sorry Mr. Carlson," Rose said formally. "I'll take care of that. Sorry if I intruded on your privacy."

"No intrusion, Rose. Just not in the mood for small talk."

"You don't sound good, Mr. Carlson. Pardon me for saying it. Especially considering the last time we talked. You don't sound like things are going well."

"They aren't. It's a long story. I'll tell you one day, I promise," said TJ, sounding a bit sorry.

"I'll hold you to that, Mr. Carlson. Call me again soon, sweetie. And take care."

TJ picked Helsinki because of the time of year. It was winter. He wanted somewhere that matched his vile mood. This time of year, Helsinki was cold and dark. Just like his mood. He wasn't really sure what he would find there or do there, but the idea of being in a dark room and moping sounded like a good plan. He had arrived in Rome with nothing but hope. He was leaving it a shell of a man.

ROME, ITALY

It's over. All over. My marriage, my hopes, my dreams, my life…. done. I fucked it all up. Journal, it's just you and me. I feel sorry for you having to capture this pathetic shit-show that is my life. I'm a cancer to everyone I know. I honestly don't give a shit anymore. I don't care if this flight to Finland goes down and crashes into a million tiny pieces. It would be a relief. Bring it on. I no longer have any fucks to give.

Chapter 22

This was a mistake, thought TJ, as he stood outside his hotel in Helsinki, Finland. Freezing cold, dark and gloomy, which is exactly what he thought he needed. Turns out it's better to be depressed while still being somewhat warm. He went inside and checked in to his room.

TJ was still reeling from the turn of events in Rome. One thing that comforted him in his exile is knowing he could go home at any moment. That was no longer an option. He was lost and had no idea what to do. And he knew he was dealing with an escalating depression.

Helsinki wasn't going to offer much in the way of distractions to get his mind off things. He had a couple of sites he wanted to go see, chief among them the Helsinki Cathedral. That was within walking distance. One-hour tops and then he would be done. He wasn't in the mood anymore to enjoy the things about travel that he always had in the past. It was early afternoon and already getting dark. TJ went to get alcohol. The rest of his day was to be spent in his dark room, drinking and wallowing in his depression. Just as he had envisioned.

As TJ returned to the hotel, he saw a man sitting against a wall with his head buried in his arms. Wow, that was me a few days ago in Rome, he thought. This man looked like hell. Dirty white hair, ratty clothes and multiple jackets on to obviously keep from freezing to death. Panic set in with TJ as he looked at this man. This could be me in the future, he feared. The parallels were striking. Something went wrong in this man's life that led him to that place. Probably a journey similar to the one I'm on. And that could be my final destination.

The man looked up at TJ, realizing he was being looked at. They locked eyes for a moment. TJ quickly walked away and the man began yelling at TJ. First, something in Finnish, then a very obvious English word......." money". TJ quickly moved on and didn't look back. Too much for me to handle, he thought. No matter what, I will never end up there.

The coldness of Helsinki was starting to become an obstacle TJ was hating to deal with. He wasn't prepared for it with the clothes he had, and certainly didn't want to shop for more. He got talked into trying a sauna by the hotel staff and they recommended a place. TJ wasn't sure what the big deal was about sitting in a room sweating, but at this point was willing to try anything. Supposed to be good for the body, and help sweat out the toxins. If there was one thing TJ had a lot of these days, it was toxins.

He arrived at the sauna and was given instructions. The place seemed pretty quiet and sterile. Almost eerily quiet. He placed his clothes in a locker, wrapped his towel around his waist and walked into the sauna room. To say that the heat was overwhelming at first feel would be an understatement. It was like stepping in to an oven. His level of discomfort was off the charts. He could barely breathe; it was so hot. There were several people in there as well, all sitting, naked, with their eyes closed. And they were all sweating profusely. TJ found himself a spot, resisting the urge to immediately leave. He wanted to stick this out and accomplish something here.

For a moment, as TJ looked around the room, he summoned a smile. Here I am, in a room that has to be close to the temperature of the sun with about 10 naked older Finnish men. It was one of those life realization moments where you sit and wonder how you ended up there. His smile was short lived. These Finns were tough, he thought. They don't look like this is bothering them at all. As for me, I need to get out of here before I die. This heat is too much, and the cold outside is too much. There's no happy medium, other than holing up in my hotel room for the remainder of my stay here.

"Mom, TJ and I are getting a divorce. I honestly don't know whether he is keeping in touch with you or has told you, but I just wanted you to know." Paige Carlson was finally breaking the news to family and felt like she had to reach out to TJ's mother.

"I'm sorry things couldn't be resolved, Paige. It's a shame. Especially for the kids." Ann Carlson knew this was coming but would have preferred to hear it from TJ. "When did you both make that decision?"

"I made the decision. TJ wanted to reconcile, but then I found out some of the things he'd been doing on his trip, and I felt like our differences were too great."

"So, he wanted to reconcile? That could have brought him home, Paige!" Ann Carlson became furious, which got the attention of Harold Carlson.

Ann continued. "Whether or not you intended to divorce him, the least you could have done was got him back here! Jesus! He's been gone for months and lord knows what his state of mind is now. Where is he?"

Paige was shocked at Ann's reaction. "I don't know, Mom," she stammered. "He was in Rome when we talked."

"And is he still there?"

"I don't know," said Paige. "He hung up on me and I haven't heard a word from him since."

"What did you say to him, Paige? Dammit! He needed to get back home!" Ann was on the verge of tears.

"Mom, I don't want to talk about the details of what I found out he was doing, but it was enough to ensure the end of our marriage. I'm sorry…. I should have thought through getting him at least to fly back here and doing things face to face." Paige wanted this call to end. She was feeling as if she had failed the Carlson's. She had the opportunity to get him home, but now may have spun him off deeper into whatever hole he was digging.

"Damn right you should have thought through that. I know his state of mind, Paige. If he was ready to reconcile and you slammed the door in his face, lord only knows what you've set in motion." Ann couldn't talk anymore. She was livid with Paige. She handed the phone to Harold.

"Paige, listen up. If you've made these decisions, that's fine. It's probably for the best. But if you have an opportunity to convince him to come home, then do what you have to do to make it happen. We're about ready to send Dean halfway around the world to get him. This whole situation is obviously having an effect on all of us, especially Ann. You have no further obligations to us other than to make sure we see those kids and ensuring that you do your part in helping to get him to come home."

"I understand, Dad." Paige was near tears herself.

"Good, just keep us informed." Harold hung up the phone. "That stupid woman."

"What did she say?" asked Ann.

"Nothing," said Harold. "I said my peace and left it at that. She blew it. He was ready to come home. I don't give a shit what he's been doing out there. Probably things for himself that he needed to do. But he needs to come home for those kids. Start leaving as many messages for him as you can, Ann."

Ann was thankful that Harold could keep his composure. They were hearing less and less from TJ, and were fearing the worst about where he was heading. Their biggest hope was that he and Paige would work it out. As long as that situation festered, they didn't see any hope that he would return.

Paige Carlson pulled herself together after the call to Ann and Harold. This is his fault, she thought. She wiped away the tears from her eyes. Of course, they'll take his side. That's their son. I know I'm right, and I don't care where he is or what he's doing anymore.

Kate – my situation is bleak. I'm in Finland, I'm depressed and I'm drinking heavily to numb the pain. I was ready to go home, but Paige blindsided me, told me she wanted a divorce, never to come home and basically told me to go to hell. I don't know what to do anymore. I'm completely out of hope.

Kate Ambrose was the only person TJ felt like reaching out to. She might be able to help him make sense of something. He was hoping that she'd be able to dissect his message and give him anything.

(Kate's reply) TJ, dude, you need to get back here to the US. Please come stay with me. For as long as you need to. I don't like the tone of your message at all. I've seen that before from past friends and believe me, it doesn't end anywhere good."

(TJ's reply) I appreciate it, but the last place I want to be is anywhere in the United States. But if I make that call, California is where I will go.

(Kate's reply) Am I going to need to come get you?

(TJ's reply) No. I just need to work things out. Don't worry, I won't do anything stupid.

(Kate's reply) I'm not so sure about that anymore. You sound bad, and I'm very worried.

TJ wasn't in the mood for this conversation any longer. He decided to send one last reply and then end the conversation.

(TJ's reply) Please don't worry too much, okay? I'll deal with everything. Thank you for being such a good friend. It means a lot to me.

TJ shut off his phone, but then turned it back on. He had one more message to send. He began composing a message to Steven, who was online.

Steven – I just wanted to let you know that I'm okay and that I love you and Elizabeth very much. Please give that message to Elizabeth for me, okay? Things between your mother and I aren't good at all. I will see you two soon, I promise. Please respond and let me know how you both are doing.

TJ put his phone back down. Kate had replied, but he chose not to read it. He closed his eyes and dozed off.

TJ woke up the next morning. He looked for a reply from Steven. The message had been read, but no reply. TJ was extremely sad that Steven did not even acknowledge his message. This spun TJ into an early morning depression that was paralyzing. He no longer cared about anything. He couldn't move from his bed. It was as if he weighed a thousand pounds. Every part of him ached. For the first time, he had a suicidal thought.

You know, thought TJ, I'm beginning to think that no one would care if I was gone. My own family doesn't. None of my friends seem to give a shit about me anymore. Maybe it's just better that way.

He caught himself quickly. As if that very thought jolted him out of his malaise. That was worrisome, he thought. At that very moment, a message arrived. This time, the message was from Neha Ganesh.

(Neha's message) TJ – where are you now? It's been too long since I've heard from you. Are u ok?

TJ debated whether to respond to Neha or not. After the way his day started, he thought it may be good to talk to someone who still cares.

(TJ's reply) Hi Neha. Things are bad. Paige is divorcing me. She wants full custody of the kids. I'm not in good shape. I can't go home anymore.

(Neha's reply) Oh my God! Where r u now TJ?

(TJ's reply) Helsinki, Finland. But I think I desperately need to leave here and go somewhere else. I'm very depressed and this place isn't helping.

(Neha's reply) I'm so worried about u. What about ur depression? And ur drinking?

(TJ's reply) Both out of control, I'm afraid. This morning I had some disturbing thoughts after my kids did not reply to my messages.

TJ was opening up himself to Neha, but he wasn't sure why. These messages were only fueling her worry and concern. TJ wasn't even putting on a brave face for his friend. He was baring his soul.

(Neha's reply) What kind of disturbing thoughts?

(TJ's reply) Honestly, that no one cared about me anymore and wouldn't even care if I was gone.

(Neha's reply) I'm scared TJ. I don't like that at all. I think it's time for u to follow thru on ur promise u made to me and come to India. I want to see u and show u that u still have people who care about u.

TJ thought about it for a few minutes before replying. It would be good to get out of Europe and be around someone who cares. After thinking about his time in Zurich with Sophie, his decision became very easy.

(TJ's reply) Thank you, Neha. I will come to India. Can I stay with you?

(Neha's reply) Yes, but not at my house. Somewhere near, within walking distance. Get here as soon as u can.

(TJ's reply) I'll leave tomorrow. And I'll see you soon.

(Neha's reply) Send me ur flight details and I will get u at the airport. Please take care until then. Can't wait to see u.

(TJ's reply) Can't wait to see you too. And thank you again.

"Hi Rose, its Mr. Carlson again." said TJ.

"How was Helsinki, Mr. Carlson?" asked Rose.

"Dreadful and cold."

"Oh, you should go there during the summer months. It is absolutely gorgeous. And you'll see Finns sunbathing everywhere. Even on the side of the road if there is space!"

"I'll keep that in mind," said TJ.

"Where to, TJ?" asked Rose.

"Please book me a ticket for Delhi, India, leaving tomorrow," said TJ. "Going there to be with a good friend."

"I'm glad to hear it. I'll take care of it and send you the information."

"Thanks, Rose."

"Mr. Carlson……. I look forward to booking that ticket for you back to the United States." Rose's voice wasn't as chipper this time. She was much more formal.

"Don't worry, Rose, that will happen eventually." Maybe, thought TJ.

TJ got himself mentally ready to move on and leave Europe behind. He had some good friends in India. And maybe, at this point in time, that was the medicine he needed.

HELSINKI, FINLAND

Winter in this place is miserable. Just like my life. Well Journal, another friend to the rescue. Sophie got me on the right track temporarily, so maybe Neha can do the same. Problem is, what right track is that? I have no destination. How long before I wear out my welcome in India? I'll never forget that homeless man. That shook me to the core. That's where I'm heading if I don't get my shit together. Or die first. I have blazed a trail of glory through Europe, but now it's time to go spread the love in India. I wonder if the spa girls will remember me there. What the hell, I have nothing to feel guilty about any more. The more women the merrier. Get ready Journal, looks like the party is just beginning.

Chapter 23

"Oh my GOD! TJ, it's great to see you!" Neha ran towards TJ as he walked out of the arrival's hall at Indira Gandhi airport in Delhi, India. She hugged TJ for long time, a hug that TJ really needed and really enjoyed. "TJ, you look bad. I don't want that to sound wrong, but you are very different than when I saw you last."

"I know," said TJ. "I was hoping this journey would do good things for me, but obviously it hasn't."

"You have bags under your eyes," said Neha. "Have you not been sleeping?"

"Sleeping has been helped by drinking, unfortunately. And several nightmares."

Neha looked at TJ and smiled big. "Everything will be okay. You have several people here looking forward to seeing you again. Raj is really excited, and some of his boys are looking forward to meeting you. And according to Raj, the girls at the Spa know you will be here soon. They are waiting for you."

More girls, thought TJ. Oh well, why not......what's stopping me now. "Haha.... I bet they are."

"They don't forget guys like you. They are used to seeing Indian men. To have a westerner is a treat for them. But TJ, please don't go there too much. I will get jealous." Neha gave TJ a coy look.

"Really?" asked TJ.

"I'm just kidding. You can do what you like. I'm here to be your friend in need. And it definitely looks like you need one."

Neha was right. Thirty minutes in to his stay in India and he was kicking himself for not coming here sooner. What a different vibe it was for him. And especially to be around friends again, who weren't judging him. They left the airport and Neha drove him to where he was going to stay. It was a spare room at her friend's apartment, but was within minutes of where Neha lived.

"I wanted you to stay here with my friend. He is rarely here as he travels a lot for work. It will give you some privacy and I'll be close by. And it won't cost you anything. He is happy to know someone will be watching his place." Neha showed TJ around the place and it was actually a very clean and nice apartment. The room TJ was staying in had a double bed, television and the place had wireless internet. Neha had really set TJ up well.

"TJ, please stay in India for as long as you need. Those other places have done a lot of damage to you. And when you're ready to tell me everything, we can start taking our walks again."

"That sounds wonderful, Neha. I'm looking forward to it." TJ was actually fighting back some tears as he looked at Neha. Considering where he had been in recent weeks and some of the despair he had felt, he was immensely appreciative of this woman standing before him, smiling at him. Right now, he would do anything for her if she asked.

"I'll go back to my house and give you time to unpack and unwind. I'll come get you for dinner. Me and you tonight, and then we'll have a group dinner either tomorrow or later in the week with Raj and his friends at his place." Neha left and TJ watched her walk back to her place out of the bedroom window. TJ laid down on the bed and sighed a deep breath of relief.

"I cooked dinner for us. We'll just eat here tonight and then we can take a walk. Is that okay?" Neha had shown up with a few Tupperware containers of food.

"Absolutely," said TJ. The last time he was in India, he hadn't really fallen in love with Indian food. The spiciness of most of the dishes was something that his taste buds were not used to and they simply would shut down on him, rendering that food and anything else as tasteless. But he was willing to try anything that Neha had prepared.

"I didn't add much spice this time. I remembered you did not like that."

TJ laughed. "Wow, you remembered. I'm sorry……. I'm just not used to all the spices."

"I know…. for us Indians, it's normal."

TJ and Neha ate dinner and Neha seemed anxious to take a walk. "I want you to tell me everything, TJ. And don't worry, no matter what, I will not think badly of you."

They finished and left the apartment. Neha took a few minutes explaining the route they could take. "This is very safe for the most part, but we should always be aware. You will look like a target."

"I've been a target, even in Europe," said TJ.

"But here, you will stand out," said Neha. "Just hold my hand as we walk."

TJ grabbed Neha's hand and they walked silently for a few minutes, just enjoying the views around them.

"Okay TJ, I'm listening. Tell me everything."

TJ thought about the best way to relate his story to Neha. He knows he had done bad things, but didn't want to hold anything back from Neha.

TJ started. "Things got really bad at some point with me and Paige. Now that I think about it, I can't really pinpoint where it started. But we started arguing more and having sex less. The lack of affection honestly was impacting me a lot. She would tease me sometimes with it, and then just frustrate me. I started to think about other girls. We started to argue about everything."

"What were the kids thinking?" asked Neha.

"We kept this hidden as best as we could from the kids," replied TJ. "Anyway, after Raj and the boys took me to the Spa here and I had that experience with those girls, I ended up looking at massages as a way to help satisfy my urges since Paige wasn't giving me anything."

"She wouldn't do anything for you?" asked Neha.

"Nothing," said TJ. "And I warned her where it could lead to."

"Go on," replied Neha.

"I ended up going on a few business trips. On a trip to Miami, I went to a massage place and met a girl named Mia. I visited her a couple of times. She was the first in the US to give me more than just the massage."

"Like what did she give you?" asked Neha. "More than the girls here?"

"Yes, but I'm not sure if she did that for everyone. She gave me oral sex and she let me touch her anywhere."

"Oh wow," replied Neha. "Do you still talk to her?"

"I did for a while after that. I even thought of going to Miami after I left. Mia had indicated she really liked me and wanted to try something outside of the massage parlor."

"Like dating? She knew you were married, right?"

"Yes, she knew my whole story up to that point."

"So, what happened with her?" asked Neha.

"Paige and I had had a really bad fight one morning. Something that really was one of the final straws to us at the time. In frustration, I texted Mia that day because I was stressed and told her that I wish I could have one of her massages. She replied and made several comments regarding some of the things we had done. Anyway, that night, Paige somehow got her hands on my phone and read that text message between us."

"Oh, that's bad," replied Neha.

"It was very bad. She accused me right there of cheating on her and told me we would never have sex again. Something in me snapped that night. I had to get away. I could no longer be in that house with her. One of our arguments had gotten violent. She threw a glass at me and then charged me. I didn't want the kids to get caught up in that stuff. I felt like I had to make the sacrifice and leave, for the sake of them and the sake of my health and mental well-being."

TJ looked at Neha. "What do you think so far?"

"I knew most of that," said Neha. "What happened after you left?"

"I drove up to Niagara Falls. I stayed there for a few days, trying to sort things out in my head. It just seemed like things were not improving and just getting worse. It was like my whole world was collapsing around me and I had to escape it. I had a bad conversation with Paige and then was having a hard time even trying to call home after that. I woke up one morning in a panic and felt like I had to leave the country. I left Niagara Falls, drove to New York City and then decided to go to Ireland. I started having strange nightmares before and after Niagara Falls. A person keeps showing up in my dreams, more like nightmares. I thought it was a manifestation of my stress, but recently it's like he's been trying to warn me about something."

"Is it someone you know?" asked Neha.

"No…. it's like someone out of a horror movie. Very evil and sinister looking. Anyway, I got very bored quickly in Ireland and then went to Scotland. I tried to enjoy the sights there and get those same feelings I get when I travel, but I think I was too tormented. From Scotland, I went to London. And that's where things started to go downhill."

"What happened to you in London?"

"My first day there, I got very sick. And my drinking was already getting bad. I couldn't reach my kids or they just didn't want to talk to me. This small scar on my forehead was a result of a tantrum I threw before getting drunk and passing out."

"Oh my God, TJ. You are lucky to be alive." Neha looked shocked. "What happened after that?"

"I ended up meeting friends of the family, who allowed me to stay with them. I got myself cleaned up and stopped drinking for a few days. Then one day, I met a girl in a park, who seemed interested in me. We went to lunch together, but then I must have said something to push her away. I'm not sure what. Anyway, I was missing female companionship, and coming so close there made the urges come back."

"Did you go find a massage place?" asked Neha.

"No……they weren't as apparent in London. I just decided to go drinking. I had a quick talk with a guy at the bar who convinced me that it wasn't the end of the world and to just keep trying. So, I went to the London Eye, already a little drunk, and met up with three girls there. One of them, an Asian girl named Fay, I really hit it off with. We hung out that whole night."

"Did you have sex with her?"

"That's a funny story. We did, but I don't remember it. We got so drunk, I blacked out, and wasn't even aware that we were doing it."

"How does that happen? Can you even function?" asked Neha.

"I guess so……I can never prove it, though. The next day though, we had sex three more times."

"Wow…," said Neha. "She must have really liked you. What happened to her?"

"She returned to the US, but not before letting me know that she was married and that would be the end of it."

"So, she just used you for sex. Haha! See, even girls can do that to guys!" Neha was laughing at that a little too hard.

"After that experience, I decided I wanted to experience that more. I stopped feeling guilty about being with other women and wanted to have as many sexual experiences as possible. In a way, that made me feel a bit renewed, like I had a purpose. That led to a disastrous visit to Amsterdam and Berlin."

"What do you mean…. disastrous?"

"I had a lot of sex with prostitutes, went to brothels and got drunk nearly every night and put myself in a lot of danger. I was out of my body and out of control. Fortunately, after Berlin, an old friend took me in and helped get me straight in Zurich. To the point where I was actually ready to go home to Paige."

Neha was very shocked when TJ had said what he did in those places. "I can't believe you did all that TJ," said Neha, "and I hope you don't have any diseases."

"Me too," said TJ. "All the prostitutes made me use condoms at least. Gosh, I'm sorry if this story is making you uncomfortable."

"No, it's okay," said Neha, "I want to hear it all. I'm understanding why you ended up where you are."

"I made the decision to try and reconcile with Paige. I went to Rome, figuring that was the last part of my journey. I was getting excited to see my kids and ready to return to my life. But then, stupidly, Amsterdam bit me in the ass. Somehow, Paige got a call from someone there that tipped her off to what I had been doing. When I called her from Rome, she tore into me and told me she wanted a divorce. I was devastated. I got drunk again every night, went to Finland, very depressed and near suicidal. Then, thank the lord, you sent your message. I'm not sure where I would have gone next."

"That's an awful story, TJ. I feel so bad for you. It looks like you have become very self-destructive in your behavior. But I understand why you did some of the things you did. Don't worry, I'm not judging you at all. I'm glad you are here and now I want you to get better."

Neha stopped their walk and gave TJ a long hug. "Thank you for trusting me with your story, TJ. I won't tell anyone else. Please consider staying here for a long time. I want to see you get better."

"I will, Neha. I already feel more comfortable here than I did anywhere else that I have been. Just promise we can keep taking these walks as much as possible. That was cathartic to tell my story."

"We can take a walk every night if you like," said Neha.

"I would love that," said TJ.

Neha's best friend, Priyanka Sankar, showed up for a walk the next night. Priyanka, or Pri, as Neha referred to her, was a very tall and slender woman with striking features. She had been friends with Neha since childhood. TJ wasn't sure why Neha had invited Pri for the walk this night. It was a bit awkward, as Pri really didn't say anything to TJ. She mainly just talked to Neha. Even though her friend was there, Neha still held on to TJ's hand.

After the walk, TJ had to satisfy his curiosity. "Neha, why did you invite Pri to join us tonight."

"She wanted to meet you. I'm not sure she believed you existed. I've told her a little about you. So, I told her to join us. Don't worry…. I'm not trying to hook you up with my friend." Neha laughed. "I think she'd be afraid to talk to you."

"Oh, okay," said TJ. "What did she think?"

"She didn't say. She'll tell me in private, then I'll report it to you."

TJ and Neha took walks for the next several nights. TJ was feeling a growing closeness between the two, fueled no doubt by the nightly hand holding as they walked. Neha hadn't indicated that she was romantically interested in TJ, but if she did, he would definitely reciprocate. She was a beautiful soul, and at this point in time, was saving TJ from himself. He resisted making any hints at anything romantic, for fear that it would ruin everything. Neha is different than the other girls, he thought. She was showing him true compassion. Sophie was similar in a way, but there is a lot more emotion involved here with Neha.

"Neha, I'm curious………have you ever had a boyfriend? Or seriously dated anyone? You've never really brought it up." TJ wanted to know a little bit about Neha now that she knew most everything about him. They were sitting in the apartment TJ was staying at after completing another nightly walk.

"No, I haven't," she replied. "I will wait for the right guy. I will not just settle for anyone."

"What is your type of guy?" TJ was curious.

"He must be caring and kind. He must be at least a little good looking. And not be like Raj and his friends," she laughed as she said the last part of that sentence.

"So, you've never had sex?" asked TJ.

"I've never even had a real kiss," said Neha. "Only in grade school, but those boys wouldn't have known what they are doing."

TJ looked at Neha for a moment. "Would you like a real kiss?"

"From you?" replied Neha.

"Yes. From one friend to another. Just so you can see what it feels like. No strings attached; I promise."

"I don't know, TJ. I don't think I can do that if I'm not in love."

"It's just a kiss, Neha. Nothing more."

"Why do you want to kiss me?" Neha asked.

TJ didn't want to admit it, but he was developing a bit of a crush on Neha. He improvised and gave a platonic response - "Because you have been so kind to me. And I want to give you something back. You've never experienced it before, so I give you the opportunity to try with me. Like I said, no strings attached. Just a kiss."

"You could just give me chocolates to thank me," said Neha playfully.

This was becoming a game of cat and mouse for TJ. He wanted to see if he could win her over and convince her to let him kiss her. If she didn't, it didn't concern him. He was just enjoying the game.

"No tongue," said Neha.

"Just a little tongue, Neha. It's all part of it." TJ laughed as he saw the disgusted look on Neha's face. "Hmmm……. you might really like it and want more."

"I doubt it," said Neha. "But we'll see. Okay, go ahead and kiss me. Just once."

"Excellent!" said TJ. "Okay, you have to do what I'm doing when we kiss. Promise?"

"Okay…. just nothing gross. And if you touch me anywhere else, I will slap you."

"Fair enough," said TJ. "Okay, get ready."

Neha sat there and closed her eyes. TJ held the back of her head with his hand and their lips met. TJ kissed Neha with a closed mouth. Multiple, quick but soft kisses. He then forced his tongue through her lips, which caused her to pull back.

"Do what I do…. you promised," said TJ.

"Fine," said Neha.

TJ moved back in and started kissing her again, and again forced his tongue through her lips. She opened her mouth and her tongue met his. They began French kissing, which Neha started picking up on quickly. The kiss became a bit passionate, thought TJ, as they hit the five-minute mark with it. Finally, Neha ended it.

They looked at each other. Neha looked a bit embarrassed. "What did you think?" asked TJ.

"I really liked it," said Neha. "I didn't like the tongue at first, but I got used to it."

"I'm glad you liked it. I enjoyed it too. You were unlike any girl I've ever kissed."

"How so?" asked Neha.

"It's like I was teaching you as we were doing it."

"You were," she replied. "How did I do?"

"You were great," said Neha.

Neha looked at TJ for a few seconds with a serious look on her face. "TJ…. I just want you to know that that right there was my limit. That kiss. I cannot do any more with you. I don't want to ruin our friendship, and my family would never approve of me being with a foreigner. Please don't be angry with me. I think maybe you are liking me now in a different way."

"Don't worry, Neha. I think of you as one of my very best friends. I will never pressure you into anything. I value our friendship, and I definitely don't want to ruin anything we have." TJ decided to keep any semblance of a crush to himself.

"Okay…. thank God," Neha said with a sigh of relief. She gave TJ another hug. "Thank you for the kiss, though. I will always remember that."

"Any time," said TJ. "If you want to keep practicing for your future husband, I'm here. No strings attached."

"You wish," said Neha. "Save your charm for your Spa girls. By the way, dinner with Raj and a few of his friends tomorrow night. Be ready…. I'm sure they have something planned for you."

TJ gave Raj an abbreviated overview of everything he told Neha. The empathy received from the two of them would be expressed in two different ways. Neha would be comforting and nurturing and Raj would……. well, he wouldn't be those things.

"Sorry you are going through all that, my friend. But now, you are in the right place. You are among friends!" said Raj, in an almost celebratory fashion. "Sunny…. this is TJ. TJ, this is my good friend, Sunny Gopal."

"Nice to meet you," said TJ.

"Likewise, Mr. TJ," said Sunny.

"I'll be right back, guys," said TJ as he spotted Neha.

TJ walked over to Neha who was talking to Pri. Neha had just shown up to Raj's house, and TJ wanted to be sure to greet her as soon as possible for going back to the guys. He saw Raj talking to Sunny and looking over at TJ. They all caught eyes. Raj smiled at TJ and gave a thumbs up sign.

"They are up to no good," said Neha. "I know that look on Raj."

"And it apparently involves me," said TJ laughing.

"Go be with the boys tonight, TJ. I've monopolized your time since you've been here." Neha gave TJ a hug and then she and Pri walked over to talk to some of their office mates.

Raj waved TJ back over.

"My friend, Sunny and I will have a surprise for you," said Raj, with the giddiness of a child. "It will make you forget everything, all your troubles."

"Is it the Spa girls? I've been anxious to see them again," said TJ, assuming that's what they had planned.

"Not this time, my friend," said Raj.

"Where we are going will make the Spa look like child's play," said Sunny. TJ couldn't help but be a bit turned off by Sunny's analogy, but he looked past it, as he was very curious as to what they had planned.

"What is it?" asked TJ.

"You will see when you get there. I will have one other friend join us. We will take a vacation! All your worries will be gone. You will never forget this." Raj patted TJ on the back and then proceeded to ask TJ about work. TJ broke the news that he had quit a while back. Sunny also made some small talk about work. TJ's focus on them started to fade as he paid more attention to what Neha was doing. He really wanted to go hang out with her, but she was willingly keeping her distance on this night.

TJ returned focus on Raj. "Are you going to give me any hints? When are we leaving? Will it involve girls?"

"My friend," started Raj, "it will involve some of the most beautiful women you will ever see in this world. Indian beauties. You will never forget what you are going to experience."

TJ was hooked with that last comment from Raj. He was excited once again to potentially have an experience similar to the one he had the last time he visited India, but at the same time concerned after his experiences at the brothels.

Several people at Raj's party had come up to talk to TJ. He began to feel a bit like a celebrity. Some were even taking pictures with him, for no apparent reason. TJ found a chair and sat by himself and enjoyed his beer. As he looked around the room, he felt as if he was definitely surrounded by friends. It was such a relief from the desolate landscape that Europe had become.

He watched Neha as she bounced from conversation to conversation. Part of him was comfortable with them always remaining just friends. But deep down, he had a strong affection for her. If she ever changes her mind, he thought, I would take her in a second. TJ had fought the urge to drink heavily in India, and Neha was certainly keeping him in check.

Neha walked towards TJ once she noticed he was alone. "So, what foolishness are Raj and his friends planning for you?"

"Indian beauties," said TJ. "Whatever that means."

"Oh lord," said Neha.

"Do you know what he has planned?"

"Yes, I do. You will like it a lot. He and his friends go there a few times a year." Neha had more to tell, by the look on her face, but she was holding back. "The girls you will see are very beautiful."

"Can you tell me anything else about it?" asked TJ.

"No, I'll let him have his surprise. You can tell me all about it when you get back." Neha excused herself and started back towards Pri. "Let me know when you're ready to go, TJ, and we'll leave together."

"My friend, it's all arranged. We will go this weekend and stay for three nights. Get a lot of rest!" Raj looked very excited. This place must be something special, thought TJ.

Neha and TJ had arrived back to TJ's apartment, and Neha looked like she had something to say to TJ, but couldn't quite force it out.

"What's on your mind, Neha?" asked TJ.

"Oh, nothing important," said Neha.

"Are you sure? I sensed it even back at the party that you were holding something back. Like you had details that you weren't giving me."

"Listen," said Neha, "I just want to warn you about what you're getting in to. Based on the stories you have told me about what you've experienced in Europe, I just fear that this isn't a good place for you to go. I think it's a kind of life maybe you are trying to escape. I just worry about you and don't want to see your situation get any worse."

"Don't worry about me, Neha," said TJ. "I appreciate it though. I know my limits and I will be very careful. Are these girls prostitutes?"

"No, they are not. They are professional dancers, but what they will do is a lot like it. You will have the opportunity to have sex there. Just be careful and be safe."

"I will," said TJ, who was now looking forward to this vacation with the boys even more. "We are going on the weekend. Can I see you tomorrow?"

"Sure. Good night TJ."

TJ wondered whether Neha was sad or jealous that TJ would be going to experience what he was about to there. She didn't appear to be either. Just concerned about TJ's well-being. Like a good friend.

Chapter 24

"TJ, I'd like you to meet Ashish Kapoor. He will be joining us." Raj had arrived at TJ's apartment with Sunny and his other friend, Ashish, for what was to be the boy's weekend out. The promise of Indian beauties was tantalizing TJ, who was now feeling liberated enough from Paige to not only feel not guilty about it, but to dive into it and enjoy it as much as possible.

"Nice to meet you, Ashish," said TJ. They all climbed into Raj's car and headed to the train station. The train ride to the resort they were heading to would take about 6 hours. A great chance to see the country, thought TJ. There was nothing about this weekend he wasn't looking forward to……the travel, the women and the camaraderie with Raj and his friends.

All four got settled on the train. Raj sat next to TJ, purposely it seemed, as he motioned for his friends to take the other two seats. Sunny and Ashish seemed to fall asleep fairly quickly after the train pulled away.

"That's a good idea," said Raj. "Get some rest…. you'll need it. You may not sleep tonight."

TJ laughed. "Sounds like I'm in for a wild time."

"My friend…. these girls are incredible. First, they will dance for us. And then, we will be able to party with them afterwards. That's the real fun part. Are you up for this?"

TJ started to tell Raj his stories from Amsterdam and Berlin, just to ensure Raj that whatever hedonism he had planned, TJ had experienced it tenfold. Raj listened in awe as TJ got very detailed with what he experienced.

"I need to go there," said Raj. "Those places sound amazing. But here, it will not cost you much. You will be stunned at how little we will spend."

"Honestly, Raj, you'd probably love it. I'm sure many men do and go there just for those reasons. Plan a trip there one day and I will join you." TJ was halfheartedly promoting those spots where he truly indulged his wild side. If he had been there under different circumstances, maybe it would have left a better memory.

"I know I would love it. Okay, we will plan that." Raj gave TJ a big smile. "It's good to see you again, my friend."

"It's good to be here, Raj." TJ really felt that sentiment. India had been a godsend for him.

"Neha seems to really like you, TJ. What's the story with you two?"

"Just good friends, nothing more. She's almost like a combination of mother and best friend, really caring about my well-being but encouraging me to do things like this with you guys. She's not like anyone I've ever met."

"She's a wonderful person," said Raj. "She's like a sister to me. She is very loyal to her friends."

"She is wonderful," agreed TJ.

"If she became interested in you, romantically, would you give it a try?" asked Raj.

"Certainly," replied TJ, "and wouldn't even think long about it."

Raj laughed big. "That's great my friend. You are liking Indian women. You will have the time of your life this weekend."

Raj leaned against the wall of the train and started to doze off. TJ decided it was his time as well. He was hoping Darkness would not pay him a visit. He hadn't shown up, oddly, since the train to Rome before the blow up with Paige.

After arriving at the train station, a never-ending cab ride over relentlessly bumpy roads had TJ feeling carsick and annoyed.

"Don't worry, my friend. It will be worth it," said Raj.

They arrived at a place called The Club Cabana. From the outside, it did not look like anything special. An unassuming structure with a dimly lit sign advertising who they were, with lettering that indicated that tonight was bikini night.

They walked in and were greeted by a man who led them to a table of four. TJ surveyed the place. No girls anywhere at this point and the tables were not even half full. The waiter brought a pitcher of Kingfisher beer to the table.

"The action will get started soon," said Raj. "Just sit back and enjoy the view."

TJ sipped on his beer and made small talk with Sunny and Ashish. Ashish, in particular, was curious about the United States. His goal was to one day get a job in either Los Angeles or New York City. TJ related stories of those cities, plus Miami and Las Vegas.

Suddenly, music started, and then about 20 women came out and started dancing on the stage and on the floor. They flirted with the occupied tables and everyone was really enthusiastically cheering for the girls. TJ was low key in comparison, really trying to understand what was going on. Most of the girls were Indian, he noticed, but there were some that obviously were not. They looked more Asian in features and one or two looked eastern European.

The music stopped after about 20 minutes, and Raj got up and walked over to the bar. He talked with a man at the bar for what seemed like a long time. He walked back to the table with a big smile.

"Drink up, friends. Everything is arranged," said Raj. He called for a toast and all four clinked their beer glasses. TJ was starting to feel a little like a deer in headlights, unsure of what was happening or going on.

"What is arranged?" asked TJ.

"You will see my friend. A special surprise just for you."

The four sat at their table for a few more hours, drinking beer after beer. TJ was getting drunk, but really wanted to hold back. He recalled his experience in London with Fay, and damned if he was going to miss this. It was close to midnight already, and he was already getting a little annoyed that whatever this big surprise was, it was taking an incredibly long time.

Finally, a man signaled to Raj and pointed towards a different part of the place. "It's time," said Raj.

They walked into a room that had two chairs and a couch set up. "TJ, that chair is yours."

TJ sat down as did the others. A few minutes later, six girls walked into the room. Five were Indian and one appeared to be Thai. Raj got up and pulled three of the Indian girls aside. They were to be TJ's.

The three girls walked over to TJ. They started to dance seductively around him. All three were wearing bikinis still. One of the girls sat in TJ's lap and kissed his neck. This is off to a good start, thought TJ. He looked over at the others and was shocked to see that Raj was already getting a blowjob from the Thai girl.

"You want?" said one of the girls to TJ.

TJ did not respond. He quickly removed his pants.

"Get comfortable," said the girl.

TJ reclined back and watched as the girl took his now very hard cock into her mouth. The other two girls got close and watched as the first one did her thing. Then the first stopped and let the next one have a turn. The three switched turns consistently, each time increasing the intensity of it. Finally, one had it in her mouth while another began licking TJ's balls. That was too much for him, as he came nearly in an instant once that started happening. An intense orgasm, which the girls helped by continuing to stimulate him as it happened. His lack of ability in Amsterdam and Berlin seemed to now be a distant memory.

TJ was exhausted after that. He looked around at the others. It seemed like the same thing had taken place with each. The only difference was that Raj had apparently arranged for three girls for TJ while the others each had one. What a friend, thought TJ.

All of the girls left the room. "That was amazing," said TJ to Raj.

"That was just the beginning, my friend," said Raj. The girls are going to get more drinks. They are ours for the night. The main event is coming up."

The girls all returned with prepared cocktails, and all sat around and drank. Raj did a lot of the talking, telling stories about TJ, saying that soon India would be his home. "He will never want to leave!"

TJ had lost a bit of his earlier buzz thanks to slowing down while he was at the table and then not drinking for the last hour while they were in the room. But these drinks were strong and having an instant effect. The three girls sat around TJ, each touching or rubbing his arms and legs. After a few more drinks, Sunny and his girl left the room. Then Ashish as well.

"Go with your girls, TJ," said Raj.

The girls grabbed TJ's hand and led him to a different room, one that had a bed and a number of liquor bottles around. One of the girls poured TJ another drink. Against his better judgment, he took it and drank it. TJ was high as a kite now and climbed up on to the bed.

"What happens now, girls?" asked TJ.

Each of the girls removed their bikinis and were completely naked. They climbed up on to the bed and each helped TJ remove his clothes. TJ's hands got very busy as he started touching each of the girls, feeling their breasts and their asses. The girls began kissing TJ on his chest, neck and stomach. They were not touching his cock yet, but they were purposely rubbing against it as they kissed him. TJ began licking one of the girl's nipples as he squeezed her breasts, and then worked his way around to each, determined to get all of them. TJ was barely in control of himself as the alcohol and his current situation combined to create this surrealistic scenario playing out for him.

One of the girls rolled a condom on to TJ's cock and then sat down on him, grinding back and forth and up and down. The other two girls were kissing his neck and his nipples. TJ was in ecstasy…. quite possibly one of the greatest feelings he'd ever experienced. As each girl was ready to have sex with TJ, a new condom would be introduced. Even in his drunken state, TJ was thankful these girls had their wits about them. TJ had sex with all three for the next hour, with the other girls always continuing to touch or kiss him. He came twice more during that time, before he'd had all he could handle.

He relaxed in the bed, very drunk and very tired, and the girls began massaging him. When TJ opened his eyes again, the girls were gone. I must have fallen asleep, he thought to himself. What the hell happened last night, he wondered, knowing fully what happened. Then there was a knock on the door.

"TJ, lunch." It was Raj. And apparently, it was already lunchtime.

"How was your night, my friend?" asked Raj.

"I can barely describe it," said TJ. "It was like all of my wildest fantasies coming true at once."

"I told you. We have a few more nights here. You'll get that a few more times, but only one girl, okay? Have to watch the budget…. hahaha."

TJ was definitely okay with hanging there a few more nights. "What's our plan today?"

"Sleep!" said Raj. "Our day will begin at night."

TJ went back to that room after lunch and tried to sleep some more, but had a difficult time. He wondered which girl he would get tonight, actually hoping to try some different ones.

TJ and the boys went through the same routine each night. The bar for several hours, the combined room and then everyone off to their private rooms where they had whatever sexual fun they wanted. TJ got his wish and tried two different girls. Mixed in with the drinks was now a variety of food that they were enjoying each night. Eating, drinking and sex without abandon was the theme of this weekend getaway.

TJ indulged in drinking more and more each night, caring less about the effects, and ate the food in abundance. He became an uncontrollable glutton. He could only imagine the days of Caligula in Rome being like what he was experiencing.

The morning of their return back to Delhi also happened to be the last night of their parties. They did not sleep before preparing to get on the train and start their way back. TJ had fallen asleep only to be jolted awake by Raj.

"Time to go, my friend. Our cab is waiting." Raj seemed impatient. Or maybe he was unhappy that his vacation was done. As quick as TJ tried to move, he was in pain. And still very drunk. Each step, each muscle movement, seemed to be a challenge.

The cab ride back to the train station was brutal. It was hot in the car, and it smelled. No doubt the combined funk of all four of the boys, fresh off their night of partying. Each of them looked to be dozing off effortlessly. But TJ was still in pain. A pain that stretched from his waist to his neck, stabbing pains in his back and a growing headache. He tried his best to doze off in the car but couldn't. Each bump in the road rattled TJ's body. He was growing increasingly nauseous, something he contributed to being carsick. Oh God please, don't have me throw up in this car, he begged to no one in particular. It smells bad enough already.

They finally made it to the train station. Raj, Sunny and Ashish looked unaffected by the night's past, but with TJ, something was seriously wrong. They got on the train and in to their seats. The other three once again managed to doze off even before the train left the station. But TJ was now in intense pain. A pain eclipsing that of what he felt in London. He thought he knew where this was heading, so he went and barricaded himself in the bathroom. As much as he tried, he could not force himself to throw up. He laid down on the dirty bathroom floor. Tears were forming in his eyes. The pain in his stomach was now overwhelming him and he felt as if he was losing control.

Finally, and without much warning, he vomited multiple times while he was laying on the floor. This was it, he thought. But it wasn't. The pain in his stomach intensified and he remained doubled over in the floor, dry heaving. The stomach pain was now joined by a lower back pain, which, to TJ's horror, was about to be uncontrollable diarrhea. He had no strength to get up to get on to the toilet seat. He gave up, and just let it happen. It went on for minutes. TJ could only imagine the scene he was leaving here in the bathroom of an Indian train.

He thought that with everything that happened, he would start feeling some relief. But there was something very severely wrong with him. He continued the dry heaving for hours as well as the diarrhea. He felt his heart beating faster and faster and his head pounding.

Oh my God, thought TJ. I'm about to die. TJ closed his eyes, and passed out there on the bathroom floor.

Chapter 25

TJ was barely able to make out her face. Unable to move, unable to speak, unable to feel anything but pain, he sooner would have shut his eyes and drifted back away. But he could sense that someone was there watching over him. This gave him only a minor comfort, as he really didn't know anything else that was going on around him. He didn't even remember how he got to this place or what led to his current state. Everything was a blur. The only thing real was the intense, searing pain in his stomach, back and head, paralyzing him and confining him to where he was. TJ closed his eyes, and drifted back off.

"I think he briefly woke up," said Isha Ganesh, Neha's mother. "Were you able to get him any water?"

"No, none," said Neha. "He opened his eyes and I think he looked at me, but I'm still not sure he's aware of what is going on."

"Tell me again, how did this happen? I know sometimes foreigners can get sick here because of the food, but this is far more than that. Where exactly was he with your friend, Raj." Rahul Ganesh, Neha's father, was adamant to know how TJ ended up in such a state. Neha was hesitant to tell her father about TJ's getaway with Raj. She herself really didn't know the details. All she knew was that she received a panicked message from Raj from the train and that they found TJ near death in the bathroom. Raj didn't even stick around after they arrived and Neha and her parents retrieved him, cleaned him up and brought them to their home.

"They went to a place that he and his friends go for vacations. I didn't ask for the details. I trusted Raj." Neha sensed that her father wasn't quite buying her explanation.

"Well, that was a big mistake, trusting that idiot. You were the one that asked him to come here. He should have been your responsibility."

"TJ is a grown man and can make his own decisions. But I understand what you mean. From this point on, I will not leave his side." Neha felt guilty about TJ. She looked down at his lifeless body. I should have given him a much firmer warning, she thought. But even she couldn't have imagined that this was the state that Raj and his friends would return him in.

"Good," said Rahul. "My friend is a doctor and will do me a favor of coming here to check on him and give him fluids. I will trust you to watch over him and make sure he gets better. And find out from Raj just what the hell happened."

"We will both watch him, Rahul," said Isha. "Neha will surely need to sleep…. we will take turns."

Neha picked up her phone and called Raj. It had been 3 days since they returned, and so far, he had been unreachable. She tried to call, but no response. She left him a voice mail.

"Listen, we need details of what happened to TJ. He's very sick, and my father is blaming you. You don't want him on your bad side. You just need to let me know what happened. Call me back as soon as you can. I have not told my family where you were that weekend, and I don't plan to. But you owe it to me, as the one who is taking care of him, to explain this."

Neha feared losing TJ for many reasons. He was one of her best friends, but more than that, he was a father to young kids and she was sure his family was missing him after all the time he had been gone. It scared her to death to think that she may be the one to have to message his family that he had died in India. And that she could have potentially prevented it.

Raj finally called Neha back. He asked her to meet at a coffee shop. Neha arranged for Isha to watch over TJ for a few hours and went to get her details.

"There's not much I can tell you," said Raj. "He got up from his train seat, and we didn't see him again the entire trip. We were all asleep."

"But what did he do while you were there? Did he eat anything he shouldn't have? Were drugs involved?"

"No, no drugs," said Raj. "I never would have allowed that to happen and I don't do that myself. There was just a lot of eating, drinking and time with the girls."

"Who made the food and drinks, Raj? Could they have potentially added something to those that you wouldn't have known about? Listen, what you did was illegal and who knows what kind of awful people are behind it and the things they are capable of. Especially to a foreigner."

"We have been there many times, Neha. I know those people and they wouldn't have done that. TJ had a great time from what I can tell, but he did seem off the morning we left. But none of us had slept. I thought he was just tired."

"We may have to get more details regarding the food and drinks, Raj. TJ's in bad shape, and we aren't sure he's going to survive. Our family friend is checking up on him, and he says it's a very touchy situation right now. He has a high fever and hasn't really come to the whole time. He has a family, Raj. If he dies here, we have to explain that."

"Oh God!" said Raj, realizing the gravity of the situation. "I never meant for this to happen. I'm so sorry."

"Don't apologize to me," said Neha. "But if I ask you for something, you get it. I am going to put everything aside and watch after him until he recovers. If you are his friend, then you will help me when needed."

"Just tell me what you need and I'll get it. Can I come to visit?"

"No, it's best that you don't. My father blames you for this, and you would not be very welcome in the house right now."

"Why does he blame me? I didn't make TJ do anything he didn't want to," said Raj angrily.

"You took him to the place. That's enough. If he had just stayed around here with me, this surely wouldn't have happened."

"Fine, Neha. I refuse to take the blame for this, though."

"Where my father is concerned, that's not your choice. Just stay clear. I'll keep you updated on TJ. Can you at least tell me the meals that were prepared as well as the drinks?" Neha wanted to wrap this conversation up and get back to TJ.

Raj gave Neha a rundown of the meals they had and the type of drinks that were made. Neha made notes and then bid farewell to Raj, who was extremely shaken up by everything.

"Please give TJ my best wishes to recover," said Raj as Neha was leaving.

"Sure," said Neha, and she headed back home.

"So, my friend, it's quite a mess we've gotten ourselves into, isn't it?"

TJ and Darkness were sitting in a desert. Nothing around except for sand, and two camels. They had mats on the desert floor and they were both sitting cross legged across from each other. It had been awhile since Darkness had graced TJ's presence in his dreams. TJ decided to be less combative this time.

"Without a doubt," said TJ. "It's bad."

"Even I'm impressed with how you screwed this one up," said Darkness, with a laugh.

"Whatever," replied TJ. "I'm still not even sure what I did. Or where I am."

"Then you need me now more than ever," said Darkness. "Are you ready to listen?"

"Actually, yes," said TJ. "Please tell me what this is all about. I'm dying to know."

"Well, the point is that you are ready to listen. That's progress. But rather than tell you, I will show you."

TJ and Darkness were standing in TJ's house. Things were different. TJ looked over to Darkness, who had vanished. All of a sudden, Elizabeth, who looked a little older now, came running out of her room.

"Daddy!" she yelled.

"Yes, sweetie!" said TJ, excitedly.

Elizabeth ran right through TJ and into the arms of a man TJ did not recognize. The man hugged Elizabeth and kissed her on the cheek. Paige joined the two of them and kissed the man.

"What the fuck is this?" yelled TJ, looking for Darkness. "Get me out of here, you bastard."

TJ was forced to watch this scene unfold. He kept reminding himself that this was not real and his anger towards Darkness returned.

"I will never listen to you," said TJ. "You might as well throw your worst at me and get it over with."

TJ and Darkness were now in a metallic room, filled with computers. A very sterile environment, and with monitors in the back ground. Medical monitors.

"This is you, TJ. These monitors are you……. you are on the brink. Not sure if you realize that."

"Why show me that…. with my daughter and some strange new guy she's calling her daddy. Out of all the shit you've subjected me too, that's probably the worst."

Darkness looked at TJ with some confusion. "You are creating that future, TJ. All the evil that you think I represent; you're bringing that on yourself. It's no coincidence that I showed up when I did. Everyone battles demons. You've welcomed yours, and there are consequences for that."

"I don't get it," said TJ. "I'm a good person, deep down. I want everything to be righted, but I seem powerless to do it."

"Are you a good person? What did you do to end up where you are? Those demons control you now. You've given in to them and aren't fighting anymore."

TJ noticed that the monitors were starting to show signs that his heartbeat was stopping.

"What is that?? Am I dying?"

Darkness looked at TJ. "Uh oh…. that's not good."

"What do you mean? What's happening??" TJ was getting frantic.

All of a sudden, a bright light appeared, just as TJ had heard would happen at death. He stood mesmerized at it, unable or unwilling to move. It was a peaceful feeling. Then the bright light began to fade and an image of someone began to appear. TJ tried hard to focus.

"TJ….TJ……. can you hear me?" Neha noticed TJ's eyes opening and focusing on her. "TJ…oh God, I hope you can hear me."

TJ looked hard and tried to focus on the person in front of him. He still felt very numb, unable to move, and unsure whether this was real or still a dream.

It's Neha! TJ finally focused to see Neha's face looking back at him, sweetly, but with a lot of concern. She was talking, but he could not hear what she was saying. It comforted TJ to see her face. He closed his eyes again and faded back out. But not before a small smile appeared on his face. Neha noticed the smile.

"Mom!! I think he recognized me! He focused on me for a few minutes and I think he recognized me and smiled."

"That's wonderful!" exclaimed Isha. "Maybe he will come out of this soon. I'll have your father let the doctor know."

As the next two weeks passed, TJ would come around several times a day, but was still too weak to move. The doctor was ensuring he would get his fluids and nutrients, but he was losing weight. The one thing that he would always see is Neha, who was always sitting there by the bed waiting for him to focus on her.

Finally, when TJ opened his eyes one day, they did not close after a few minutes again. The focus on Neha became an intense awareness that he was at her house laying on a bed. He was able to feel his arms and legs. The pain in his stomach, back and head were gone. His eyes remained wide open, and this time Neha knew there was something different.

"TJ? Can you hear me?" said Neha excitedly.

"Yes," said TJ.

"OH MY GOD!! THANK GOD!!" Neha stood up and yelled for her parents, then leaned over and gave TJ a hug. "We are so happy. You were so sick. We were worried you would not survive. There were a few moments where we thought we had lost you."

"What happened?" TJ said, summoning strength to project his voice.

"You were very sick when you were on the train coming back from your weekend getaway with Raj. You had a bad case of Dengue Fever and also food poisoning. You are lucky to be alive. I hope that everything is okay with you. We will have our doctor check you out to be sure."

TJ processed that information. He still couldn't remember much of what happened towards the end of the getaway or how he ended up here.

"So, you've been taking care of me? I think so, because I always would focus on you."

"Yes, between me and my parents and our doctor, we have been taking care of you. We wanted to make sure you recovered. And I thought maybe you were noticing me."

"I was never sure whether I was dreaming or not. But your image always comforted me when I saw it."

"I know," said Neha, smiling. "You even would smile at me."

"You were my guardian angel. That's what I was thinking. I owe you my life." TJ tried to get up and move towards Neha.

"Oh, don't move yet. This will take a bit of time. You need to try and eat some food first. You need to gain weight. You will be shocked when you see yourself in the mirror."

"How long have I been out, Neha?" asked TJ, now concerned, both at how he will look and how much time has passed.

"You need to be prepared to hear this." Neha looked at him with seriousness. This obviously meant a decent amount of time had passed. TJ braced himself.

"How long?"

"It's been three and a half weeks. Almost a month. It took a week before you even opened your eyes just a little. It was very bad." Neha leaned over and hugged TJ again. "I am just so thankful we didn't lose you."

Once again, TJ processed his situation. Nearly a month that he'd been out of it. Nearly a month since anyone, including his kids, had heard anything from him. He tried not to let the situation overwhelm him, but he was having difficulty controlling his emotions.

"People must wonder what happened to me," said TJ. "You didn't by chance check my messages or anything?"

"No, I didn't," said Neha. "You had a lock code on your phone and I did not know any of your contacts."

"That's okay. I need to send messages as soon as possible." TJ wanted to get a message to Steven and Elizabeth right away. He wanted to make sure they knew he had not forgotten them.

"For now, get some rest. I'll bring you your phone. I did keep it charged for you." Neha brought TJ his phone, and he placed it on the table next to his bed.

"Neha, I don't know how I'll ever be able to repay you and your family for this. You saved my life."

"TJ," said Neha, while stroking TJ's hair, "the fact that you are alive is the only repayment we need or want. I'll leave you alone for a bit so you can look at your messages."

TJ got into a more upward position in the bed, and prepared to view his messages. To learn who was concerned about him. And who wasn't.

TJ was not surprised by most of what he saw. Seven messages from Kate Ambrose, initially joking that maybe he had died, and then getting seriously concerned that he had. Five messages from his mother, one threatening to send Dean looking for him. At this point, Dean could be on his way. One message from Sophie wondering how everything went with the phone call in Rome. There was one message from Steven, noting that he hadn't heard from him in a while.

Then there was a message from Paige. TJ saved it for last, and responded to all of the others first. TJ explained to his mother that he had gotten sick in India but was recovering now. He gave a vague explanation to Kate and a summary of what happened to Sophie. He told Steven that he had lost his phone for 2 weeks but had now recovered it. Finally, he opened the message from Paige.

I don't know where in the world you are right now, but sign this and send it back as soon as possible.

The message contained divorce papers. Reality slapped TJ in the face again. As he read through it and absorbed the terms – Paige got the kids with visitation allowed by TJ, he was to pay child support and alimony with money he wasn't making and the house belonged to Paige as well. TJ had neither the strength or mental disposition to fight Paige on any of it. Who fucking cares anymore, he thought, thoroughly defeated? He suddenly realized why he was in India and portions of what led him there. He put his phone down and laid back down on the bed. He wondered if he would have been better off not making it through his sickness. Maybe that would have been easier.

The next few nights, Neha helped TJ get up and around. He was eating again and starting to regain some strength.

"Soon we will start taking walks again," said Neha.

"Okay," said TJ. "I'm ready when you are."

"Do you want to try one tonight?"

"Sure. We can just walk slow."

Neha noticed that TJ seemed very sad after reading his messages but was shy to ask him what had happened. Tonight, on their walk, she wanted him to open up.

They started out, walking down the sidewalk by the house, holding hands. TJ felt very weak. "We'll need to stop or sit every so often," he said.

"TJ.... you seem very sad since reading your messages. What happened?"

"Paige sent the divorce papers. The kids barely messaged me, and Steven never responded back to my reply. None of my friends other than Kate or Sophie messaged me in those 3 weeks and most haven't even checked up on me in months. I truly have nothing to go back to."

"I'm sorry…. I don't know what to say. You can stay here as long as you want."

"Neha, I think I've burdened you and your family long enough."

"Don't ever say that," said Neha angrily. "You are no burden. We had a duty to take care of you and I would have done that no matter what."

"By the way……what ever happened to Raj? Did any of them ever get sick?"

"No, they didn't. Raj was not allowed to visit the house. My father would not let him. He blamed him for you being in that situation."

"Oh wow…. don't blame Raj. It's not his fault. It was all mine. I was careless and didn't take care of myself. I was letting my wild side take over again. Honestly, and this is sad to say, I had fun with him there. It's sad because that seems to be my only way of having fun. That's a sad life."

"TJ, you are sounding depressed again. Promise me you will take care of yourself. Please know that there are people in this world who care about you."

"But if I'm not one of them, it doesn't mean a thing. I'm sorry…. I'm just in a bad mood. Maybe if I just get this divorce over with, I can move on." TJ looked at Neha, who was looking down at the ground.

"Neha, can I ask you a question."

"Sure, go ahead," she replied.

TJ decided it was time to test whether or not he and Neha could be anything more than friends. If so, TJ would extend his stay in India in an effort to develop their relationship. If not, it was time for him to move on. He did not want to be a burden any longer to her family.

"Do you ever think we can be more than friends?" TJ asked the question with nothing to lose. "If you have the interest, I want to stay here to work on that with you."

Neha had been dreading this question from TJ. They had talked about it before and she was sure she made it clear it could not happen. Her parents would not approve of it. She wasn't sure how best to respond to him without being seen as another disappointment for him.

"TJ……. I don't know how I can say this, but……."

"There's no need," said TJ, cutting her off. "You just did. It's okay. It was worth a try."

"I was just going to say……. I can't. If it was possible, I would say yes. But it's not that easy."

"I understand. Don't worry, you will always be one of my closest friends and I will never forget what you've done for me here."

"I'm just afraid that I am another disappointment for you," said Neha, now crying.

"No, deep down I knew that would be your response. But if I didn't ask, I would have never known."

TJ and Neha stopped their walk and turned back. They did not say another word to each other that night. TJ was unable to sleep. The feeling was hitting him again. The feeling that it was time to move on. His time in India, once promising, can now also be qualified as a disaster. He needed to regain his strength. That strength would lead towards his goal of leaving India and moving on to his next stop.

For the next few weeks, TJ and Neha walked, TJ ate well and regained his strength. Neha was a little more reserved in her conversations. TJ had not shared his desire to leave with her yet. But tonight's walk would be that night.

"Neha…. I just wanted to let you know that I will be leaving soon."

"No, TJ, please don't leave here. I don't think you are at full strength yet." Neha was shaken up at TJ's sudden announcement.

"I have to go. It's time. I'm no longer comfortable being here. It's nothing against you or your family. But I have to find my way. And I'm stuck here right now, with no hope of progress."

"Is it me?" asked Neha. "Because I can't be with you?"

"No, that's not it. I……. I just need to go."

Neha was silent for a long time.

"TJ…. please promise to take care of yourself."

"I will. Don't worry."

The walk once again turned silent. TJ knew that Neha was blaming herself for him wanting to leave. But there was no other option for him, he thought.

Back at the house, TJ informed Neha he wanted to go back to his apartment to start getting his things ready.

"Bangkok. I want to go from Delhi to Bangkok."

"Okay, TJ," said Rose Carter, TJ's personal travel booker. "You must have enjoyed Delhi…. you had quite a long stay there."

"Yeah," said TJ, not wanting to get in to details.

"What will you do in Bangkok?" asked Rose.

"Have fun," said TJ.

TJ signed the divorce papers. He wanted to stab the papers over and over with his pen, making the papers bleed. He couldn't believe it had come to this.

He was at an internet café, which faxing service was also an option. He watched as each piece of paper made its way through the fax machine. When the final piece went through, he slammed his rupees on the counter, did not wait for change and left the café.

"Fuck it all," said TJ, loudly, to himself.

Neha had arranged a goodbye party for TJ, at a neutral site, which was her friend Priyanka's house. This way, Raj and his friends could also attend. Raj had not talked to TJ since the getaway, but he made sure he relayed messages to Neha to give to him.

"My friend, I am so sorry. I could never have imagined things would turn out the way they did." Raj sounded very upset.

"Don't blame yourself……. none of it was your fault. That trip was the most fun that I had here."

"I'm happy you enjoyed. If you ever come back to India……"

"I'll just stick with the Spa girls," said TJ, cutting Raj off.

"Good bye, my friend. Take care of yourself. I want to see you again. Maybe we can meet in Amsterdam!"

"Sounds like a plan," said TJ.

"TJ, I will take you to the airport tomorrow," said Neha.

Neha hadn't said much to TJ at this party. She had looked very sad all evening.

"Okay…. thanks," said TJ.

"TJ…. please tell me you aren't mad at me."

"I will never be mad at you. Don't ever worry about that. I consider you my best friend in the world. Nothing will ever change that. I'll never forget what you've done for me. I love you and I always will."

TJ hugged Neha tightly and she began crying on his shoulder.

"I will miss you, TJ. I've gotten used to you being here."

"I'll miss you too, but I promise we will see each other again. Hopefully in much better circumstances."

TJ and Neha arrived at Indira Gandhi Airport in Delhi. Neha had held TJ's hand tightly the whole car ride. This was going to be a sad goodbye, but TJ just wanted to get it over with. His mood had once again darkened over the last few days.

"TJ, take care, please. Keep messaging me."

"I will, don't worry."

"What will you do in Bangkok?" she asked.

"I will just tour around. It's somewhere I've always wanted to go."

"Be careful there. I've heard some bad things, and there are many temptations there."

TJ's intentions in Bangkok were not noble at all, and he wasn't being honest with Neha. He chose Bangkok because of that very reputation. He was going there to have fun. To celebrate his divorce and his new, unquestioned freedom. He had nothing left to lose. Only to make himself feel better. To look for that comfort in women and alcohol.

"I will definitely be careful."

"Good. I love you, TJ." Neha's eyes were very wet and tears were rolling down.

TJ and Neha walked to the airport entrance.

"Goodbye, Neha. Thank you again."

"Goodbye, TJ." Neha hugged TJ tightly and then stood and watched as TJ walked in to the airport. TJ gave one final look back and blew Neha a kiss.

His time in India was done. He begins his Asian adventure a newly single man, with no direction, no goals and no reservations.

DELHI, INDIA

Actually Journal, this could just as well-read Delhi, India and the seventh layer of Hell for all I've been through here. I now have absolutely nothing. The divorce papers spell it out. I should have wanted to contest it, but deep down I know I'm so fucked up and such damaged goods, I had no leg to stand on. What can I say about India? Neha saved my life. Not that it was worth saving. I indulged in my wildest of fantasies and then nearly got myself killed again. Only her kind heart and loving nature pulled me through. Why would she have wanted me? That was so stupid to even ask. I risked ruining a friendship and probably looked like a fool for even bringing it up.

Journal, to this point I have refused to acknowledge Darkness in this space. I can't allow a dream to permeate my life. But in this case, my life has permeated my dreams. Whoever Darkness is, and whatever he's trying to tell me, he may just be the only thing in my life making any sense.

And now, on to Bangkok! A perfect place for a sex addict and alcoholic to get on the mend. Cheers!

Chapter 26

What drives a person to the brink of despair? To the point where their own life is no longer of value to themselves and the most logical choice to them becomes to just end it all? For TJ Carlson, the endgame took a long time to come about, and a series of events sometimes of his own making and sometimes beyond his control made it all seem like that choice was his logical choice.

Upon leaving India, TJ embarked on another self-satisfying journey through Asia. An empty and morally bankrupt effort that did nothing but give his demons seats at the table and further control of his life. TJ continued his journal with his travels through Asia, becoming increasingly reliant on it and almost treating it like a real person he was talking to. Sadly, one that would never respond back. These Asian journal entries show the final descent of a man, a good man, whose choices and decisions led him to one last fateful decision.

BANGKOK, THAILAND

(Journal Entry #1) I arrived in Bangkok a few days ago. This place was everything I thought it would be. I've made a few new friends at some massage parlors close by. It seems that for the right price, they are willing to do anything. The one willing to do both oral and full on sex has won me over. Later tonight will go and see some of the famous "shows" that I've heard about. Good times.

(Journal Entry #2) I tried messaging Steven again, but the kid doesn't seem to want to respond. I'm sure Paige has told him a bunch of shit about how much of a prick their father is. Well, fuck her. I'll get the record set straight with him one day. Today, I took a trip to Ayatthaya to go see some sights. I was initially interested and then bored witless. Couldn't wait to get back and visit my Thai beauty at her "office". She is really taking care of me well. Next time, she told me to get some drinks and she will come to me. Outstanding. Life is good.

(Journal Entry #3) Sandy (I'm not sure that's her real name) came to my hotel last night. We got hammered and had fun with each other. She's costing me quite a bit though. Sad that I have to pay for this, but have no other choice at this point. She did drugs while she was here. I was a bit shocked. She offered some to me. I said no, but was admittedly tempted. Anything to dull the pain.

(Journal Entry #4) Getting sick of this shit. Feeling depressed again. Don't feel like going anywhere or doing anything. My only two options seem like drinking and sex. And I'm even getting tired of that. Fuck my life.

(Journal Entry #5) Writing this journal is starting to depress me. It's probably a good thing I didn't re-read all the shit I've written on this trip so far. I probably would have put a gun to my head and happily pulled the trigger after re-reading it. Not going anywhere today. Another bed and TV day.

(Journal Entry #6) Getting the hell out of Bangkok. Leaving tomorrow. Spent nearly two weeks here and have little to show for it. I think it just made things worse. The girls here don't care about you unless you keep spending more money on them. I just hope I'm not leaving here with any unwanted "souvenirs".

I called Rose, and will head to Singapore. Will try to get my shit together there and message the family again. Thanks for indulging me, Journal. Some lucky person will have a field day when they get their hands on you.

SINGAPORE

(Journal Entry #7) What a strange place this is. It is very clean and orderly. The anti-Bangkok. It's fascinating. I don't think I saw a speck of dirt anywhere. I will spend today attempting to reach out to my kids. I'm missing them terribly and getting this sick feeling that Paige will not let me see them again. If that's the case, there is no reason to live. I despise that woman.

(Journal Entry #8) I got fined today! Twice! What the hell?? I get wanting to keep the place clean but that is a bit extreme. Just because I bring a fucking drink on the subway, I get a fine. No women here, but I'm still paying out the ass. This is going to be a short stay.

(Journal Entry #9) Dear Journal – you must think I'm a complete idiot by now. I think I'm going mad. Steven absolutely will not respond to me. I thought I raised him better than that. To make things worse, my own mother's responses to me are getting shorter and she seems really annoyed with me. Great. I truly have no one anymore. I haven't heard from Neha since I left India. Or Kate. Feeling abandoned. Feeling alone. Feeling worthless. I can only escape into the arms of the women I pay for. If that's all I have, so be it. I don't know how much I drank today. It doesn't really matter. I can't keep living like this much longer.

(Journal Entry #10) Today I had a brilliant idea, Journal! I'll go to Hong Kong. Maybe I'll try to find Irene, or at least make up for the only other miserable trip I had there. Redemption, here I come!

HONG KONG

(Journal Entry #11) Arrived in Hong Kong today. A very sobering return. Many years ago, I was in love with a girl here, Irene, who crushed my heart into little pieces. She didn't have the decency to even break it off with me before I arrived here. She let me travel here, and then broke up with me the first day, leaving me two weeks to mope around here like a fool. I would love to find her and thank her for that. I owe her for that chapter of my life.

(Journal Entry #12) I sent a message to Irene. That was dumb. I don't know what the hell I was thinking. If I let her see me now, she'll be thankful that she broke it off. I'm a shell of what I was. She's apparently married and has four kids. Good for her, the

lousy bitch. I still need to redeem myself here somehow. My trip here will not be complete until I do. Any suggestions, Journal?

(Journal Entry #13) I hate being here

(Journal Entry #14) Got extremely drunk again last night and spent the morning throwing up. What the hell is wrong with me. Couldn't leave my hotel room. No messages from anyone.

(Journal Entry #15) Redemption is mine. Picked up a prostitute last night and had sex. Take that, Irene. I can leave Hong Kong now that I have righted all wrongs and made up for my miserable trip here by banging a hooker. Good work, TJ. I'm awesome. And really and truly pathetic. Journal…. just shoot me and get this over with.

MANILA, PHILIPPINES

(Journal Entry #16) Arrived in Manila in hopes of visiting a good friend I made here. I need to stop it with the prostitutes. I need to stop it with the drinking. But I'm not sure if I can. It seems to be all I have.

(Journal Entry #17) Stayed at a bar drinking last night and made a new friend. A "ladyboy" named Jepoy. I was leery at first, but actually enjoyed talking to him (her?). The people here are exceedingly friendly. My friend doesn't seem to have time for me. Busy with work. Looks like I'll be hanging out with my old friends – women and alcohol.

(Journal Entry #18) Today I am paralyzed with depression. It is pouring rain outside. Apparently, a typhoon. There is flooding on my streets. I can't go anywhere. Journal – I don't know where all of this is heading, but I am losing hope. I wish something positive would happen in my life. There is nothing for me to hold on to anymore. I've burned through it all. Soon, I'll be out of money and won't be able to afford to do anything. My God - I may end up like that guy I saw on the street in Helsinki. I'd sooner kill myself than suffer that kind of life.

(Journal Entry #19) Went for a massage today. The girl was really nice and friendly. Even she could sense that I was sad and depressed. She tried to make me feel extra good. I appreciated her for that. Still can't shake the depression.

(Journal Entry #20) I need to stop myself before it's too late. I need to find the old TJ. I hope he's not lost forever. On to Malaysia, Journal. Let's see if I can avoid temptation for once.

KUALA LUMPUR, MALAYSIA

(Journal Entry #21) Decided to do something touristy again. I want to go see the Petronas Towers. Maybe if I can focus on those kinds of things again, I can re-discover who I once was. The man who used to get a joy and a special feeling about being in certain places in the world, seeing different cultures and marveling at the world's wonders. I'm done with the women and alcohol. I always feel like such a piece of garbage afterwards.

(Journal Entry #22) Went to see the towers. It was impressive, but I felt brutally alone. It's because I am alone. Except for you, Journal, but you aren't really helping much. I wish I had someone to share all of this with. I need the alcohol for the pain and the women for the companionship. That is my sad fact. Time to get drunk tonight.

(Journal Entry #23) Sorry Journal – it's been a few days. I've been in an alcoholic haze. It has been weeks since I have heard from anyone. I can only conclude that everyone has given up on me. Well, fuck them all. I don't need any of them. I can only rely on myself. And I'm not even sure I can do that. I hate my life and what it has become.

(Journal Entry #24) Another night and morning of drinking and puking. Time to get out of here. I need to go detox on a beach or something.

BALI, INDONESIA

(Journal Entry #25) Decided that Bali might be a nice place to detox and relax. Arrived just a few minutes ago. Will go find a beach and just set up camp there. Staying in Kuta so I can just walk to the beach each day.

(Journal Entry #26) The beach day was nice but incredibly boring. While lying on the beach, all I thought about was getting drunk and getting laid. Sad. I'm a sad human being.

(Journal Entry #27) I did it again. I couldn't help it. I found a place here where the girls will give massages and have sex with you. I couldn't help myself. The urge was too powerful. I'm so pathetic. Everywhere I go, this is what it comes to. I don't deserve anyone's care anymore. I'm a terrible human being and am doing no good for anyone.

(Journal Entry #28) Getting the hell out of here. Called Rose and had her book me to go to Sydney. I don't know what I will do there. I just want this depression to go away. I wish you could talk, Journal. You're the only friend I have left.

SYDNEY, AUSTRALIA

(Journal Entry #29) Here I am in Sydney again. Walked down to the Opera House. Just stood there and stared for a while. Started thinking about where I can find women again. This is no way for me to live.

(Journal Entry #30) I got a message from Steven. He said he hated me. He hated me because I hurt mommy and left them. That's why he's not responding to me. He hates me. My own son hates me. Oh, and apparently Elizabeth hates me too. My kids hate me. I no longer have anything to live for.

Dear Journal – this is my final entry on this disastrous and god-forsaken journey. It has been a journey straight to hell. It has shown me that I no longer matter. I'm sorry to all of those I have disappointed and let down, which is an endless list. I'm sorry that I have failed as a person, and to my kids, that I have failed as a father.

TJ re-read all of his journal entries over and over. A sad tale, to be certain. He was absolutely devastated at his message from Steven. It had stripped his will to live. He had no one to blame but himself for everything that had transpired leading to this moment. A line had been crossed in this journey. His behavior had been self-serving, but it wasn't until now that the final and most harsh consequence had taken place. He lost his kids.

TJ had made another big, and perhaps final decision. One he never thought he would make. One that he had criticized others for resorting to. One he thought was a coward's way out.

TJ decided to end his own life. He decided to kill himself to end the pain that only alcohol seemed to numb.

Now that he had made this decision, TJ decided he was going to do this his way and go out on his terms. If he was going to end his life, he wanted to do it in the most perfect place in the world.

"Rose, I'd like to book one last trip. To Papeete, Tahiti."

"Last trip, Mr. Carlson? You are going back to the USA eventually, right?" Rose Carter seemed very concerned at TJ's request.

"Don't worry about that, Rose. Please book the trip for me."

"Okay, Mr. Carlson. This has been quite a whirlwind recently. You've almost used up your points."

"I know, Rose. It's okay. Thanks for everything." TJ hung up the phone and began packing his things.

TJ felt at peace with his decision. He had no other options left. He was running out of resources and places to go on this journey to nowhere. He had lost everything that meant anything to him. He picked the one place in the world where he truly felt that it would be the last thing he wants to see.

TJ was going to Bora Bora. To end his life in one of the most beautiful places on earth.

PART 4:

ENDGAME

Chapter 27

It was just as he had remembered. The sights and the smells and the scenery of Papeete, French Polynesia. TJ knew he would be back here one day. But not like this. Not as a failure in life. Not coming here to end everything.

The flight from Sydney to French Polynesia was brutal. TJ was an emotional wreck the entire trip. A continuous replay of all of the mis-steps, mistakes and bad decisions played over and over in his mind. He always had the power to stop what he was doing. But he never did it. He let it get to this point. The point of no return.

TJ had arranged a local flight to Bora Bora, and from there was going to stay in the same resort and the same bungalow where he had hung out with Sophie. There was a perfect stretch of beach where he wanted to spend his final days. As he sat in the airport waiting, his thoughts turned to daydreams of the potential reactions of others when they come to learn what he had done. His parents would surely be devastated. His friends would be extremely sad, and friends like Kate and Neha may be angry at themselves for not pushing harder. His ex-wife and kids……. well, they would be the saddest of all. They all rejected him, and this was the consequence.

TJ boarded his plane to Bora Bora. He watched out the window as the lush green landscape of French Polynesia passed by below and as the unmistakable island outline of Bora Bora came in to view. This would be the last flight I will ever take, he thought. It was an uneasy peaceful feeling.

He arrived in Bora Bora. A fleeting moment of happiness overcame him to be back in a place that meant so much to him. But any thoughts always ended with what he was there to do.

TJ had not made the decision lightly. He was sure now it was the only way out. He continued thinking on the taxi ride to his resort, and with every moment of thinking, the weight on him grew heavier.

"Welcome back, Monsieur Bike Rider," said the very familiar gentleman at the front desk. "Your bungalow is ready." TJ remembered the man as the guy who greeted him at arrival on his bike ride.

"Thanks. I can't believe you remember me," said TJ.

"I have a photographic memory," said the man. "Enjoy your stay here."

TJ walked to his bungalow, took a deep breath, and then went inside. This is where it's going to happen, he thought. It's a perfect place to do it. He remembered being in this exact room with Sophie, except now it was empty of her stuff and was his alone.

TJ dropped his things and sat down on the bed. The heaviness of his heart was too much. He laid down and cried.

TJ walked over to the beach the next morning and found himself a spot under a palm tree. He laid out his blanket and dropped his backpack. He had brought enough with him to last a day in this spot, and there was a bar/restaurant joant close by to grab his meals. Today would be a day of planning. Potentially his last day on this Earth. He had two goals to accomplish. Number one – messages to family and friends, and number two – determine the best way to end it. The second goal was a morbid one, and TJ could barely stomach even thinking about it. But he knew he had to. He wanted to go peacefully….in his sleep somehow.

The messages were also hard to determine. What could he possibly say to his friends and family to make them understand? He jotted some notes down in a notebook, making a list of people. All of them would get an individualized letter from him. Including Paige and the kids. The notes he jotted down were about the pain that he had caused everyone and how this journey had made him feel like a failure of a human being.

About 30 minutes later, with the notes being written in lesser intervals, TJ put the notebook away. That exercise was particularly difficult. He would need to come back to it. He would give himself the time he needed and wanted to make sure he did it right.

He put the bad things aside for now and went over and got himself a beer and a hamburger. The remainder of the day consisted of one beer after the other until TJ was feeling very sleepy. And then it hit him. This would be the way he would go – buy some sleeping pills, take several more than he should, and drink heavily. Once asleep, he wouldn't feel a thing.

Once that realization hit, he packed up his things and ended his day at the beach. He stopped by a pharmacy and bought some sleeping pills and a 12 pack of beer. These would get stored in his bungalow until the right time. Whenever that time may end up being.

TJ sat in his bungalow and had pulled out his notes he had made at the beach. It was time to sit down and start writing his letters to home. He made the mistake of starting with Elizabeth. She was the person he felt like he loved the most in this world. Her rejection and hatred destroyed him. He started to write:

To my beautiful daughter Elizabeth,

Daddy wants you to know how much he loves you, and that I'm so sorry that I cannot be there anymore. Just know that I will always be watching down on you as you grow up into what I'm sure will be a beautiful young woman.

TJ stopped there and began crying uncontrollably. He folded up the letter and put it in a folder in his desk. He was not up to this right now. He would have to do it eventually, but emotionally, at this point, he couldn't handle it. He decided to go out and get drunk instead.

TJ went to a bar near the resort. He sat alone at the bar and nursed a few beers. A couple of locals walked in with some tourists. TJ wasn't sure what to make of that, as he had never noticed that dynamic before. The locals appeared to be guides as they were telling the tourists, a few western couples, to grab a drink and then they would continue on. It was close to the end of the day, so TJ wasn't sure where they were heading after this, but he was curious. He decided to go and approach one of the guides.

"Hi there – are you leading them on a tour?" asked TJ.

"It is now a tour to sample some of our best drinks!" laughed the local. "Are you on something similar?"

"No, but it sounds like my kind of tour," said TJ.

"Then why don't you join us, my friend. My name is Bill. I'm happy to be your guide, just a small tip for me is all I ask."

"Bill? Is that your real name?" laughed TJ.

"I picked a name easy for everyone to remember," said Bill. "We are finishing up the day at Bloody Mary's. Care to join us?"

"I would love to," said TJ. "That's one of my favorite places."

"Oh, so you've been there before. Did you see any celebrities?"

"Nope, but maybe we will get lucky tonight." TJ was happy to have latched on to Bill and his group, and the distraction that it was bringing. "I'm in, Bill. Just let me know when we are heading that way."

Bill's group finished up their drinks and he gathered them all together, introducing TJ as their newest member. The group shouted "Hi, TJ" in unison, and then they made their way to Bloody Mary's.

TJ loved Bloody Mary's. It was probably his favorite place on Bora Bora. He and the group were welcomed by the staff, who recognized the guide. I'm sure that "Bill" is compensated nicely with each group he brings in, he thought.

TJ sat down alone at one of the tables and ordered a drink. He always kept a lookout at the entrance. Who knows when a celebrity will walk in.? TJ got lost in thought as he sipped his fourth glass of wine, laid his head on the table, and then began to daydream.

"Can I join you?"

TJ looked up. Holy shit……it's Matt Damon! TJ lucked out…. a celebrity had joined him here at Bloody Mary's…. finally!

"Absolutely," said TJ excitedly.

"What are you drinking?" asked Matt Damon.

"Pinot Noir……from Australia."

"Let me order you one of my favorites. It's called Mary's Mai Tai." Matt Damon called over one of the waiters, who rushed over once he saw it was a celebrity. "Two Mai Tai's my friend…. strong. My friend here looks like he needs a strong one."

"Thanks, Matt Damon. Why join me……just wondering." TJ was curious as to why Matt Damon picked him to sit with.

"I can tell when people are having an issue they are trying to work through. It's written all over your face. Want to talk about it?"

"Not really," said TJ. "I don't want to bore you with my problems. I'm sure you deal with enough of your own."

"I'm a person, too, first and foremost. There's a reason I love coming to a place like this. People don't mob you…. they may ask for a picture or autograph, but they are laid back. You don't have to give me all of the details. Just a little of what's on your mind." Matt Damon stared at TJ and waited for him to start talking.

"Okay, well if Jason Bourne wants me to talk, I'll talk," laughed TJ. "My life has thrown me too many curveballs, and I've lost the ability to cope with it. I've lost hope. I came to the one place in the world I love the most. And I'll never be leaving, if you catch my drift."

"I think I do," said Matt Damon. "Listen, I'm not a therapist or counselor, or anything. I'm just an actor. So, I'm not qualified to give you any advice. But I'll say this…. don't give up on life. It's the only one you have. Fight whatever it is you're going through. You a religious man?"

"Not particularly," said TJ. "But I believe in a higher power. But I think that higher power has abandoned me."

"It doesn't matter," said Matt Damon, "good things will happen to good people. Those that fight, those that persevere and those that never give up will always win in the end. Whatever it is that you're battling, don't let it defeat you. There's always a way."

"Thanks, Matt Damon. I'm glad you joined me here. I'll think about what you've said."

"You do that," he said, "and hang in there. Best of luck. Never give in." Matt toasted TJ a final time and left Bloody Mary's.

TJ snapped out of his daydream, and laughed at the absurdity of it. His first time to meet a celebrity, and that was in a daydream and the celebrity gives him life advice. Or maybe that was my subconscious giving me a message. He laughed at himself again, looked down at his drink, and then quietly wondered if his drink had been spiked.

TJ continued drinking at Bloody Mary's and mingled with the guests and staff. Everyone was relentlessly positive and upbeat. And TJ must have had the word "problem" written all over his face. People were diagnosing him within minutes, and trying to get him to open up. They wanted to hear his story, but TJ did not want to tell it. Finally, he'd had enough of the evening. He tipped Bill, said goodbye to everyone, and left Bloody Mary's.

On his way out, he stopped by the wall of celebrity names. He scanned through them and found the name he was looking for. Matt Damon.

"Thanks Matt," said TJ to the celebrity name wall. "I'll take it under advisement."

Back in the Bungalow, TJ pulled out the paper where he was writing his letters. He pulled the one out he had started to Elizabeth. He read his first few words over and over again. Sadness overwhelmed him. He couldn't bring himself to write anymore. He folded it back up and put it away.

TJ was certain of what he wanted to do when he arrived in Bora Bora. But the place had a vibe about it. He felt it changing him a little bit. Even though he had a great time this evening, it was just a passing thing, and there's no reason why everyone shouldn't be in a good mood. They were in Bora Bora. TJ Carlson may well have been the saddest person on the island.

TJ decided he didn't want to think about it anymore. He'll see another sunrise tomorrow and see what the day brings. He laid down and fell asleep.

TJ was sitting on an abandoned beach. He was sitting there, on his beach blanket, just watching the waves roll in. It was a peaceful feeling.

"Big decisions, huh?" said Darkness, who appeared out of nowhere behind him.

"Yeah," said TJ, not really fazed that Darkness had shown up.

"You'll make the right ones, don't worry. The end of your journey is near. Can't you feel it?" Darkness wasn't speaking menacingly to TJ this time. There was something different.

"I suppose this journey will end when I make it end."

"Right," said Darkness. "You'll know when it's time."

"Who are you?" asked TJ.

"Once again, I'm a manifestation of you. You've needed me. Whether or not you realize it, I've been trying to help you. The brain works in ways you can never imagine. There's more to existence than just waking up and dealing with life's problems. You've been short-sighted the whole time."

"You'll excuse me if I don't take to being mutilated and killed by you in my dreams and expect to extract advice out of that."

"It's not advice I've been trying to give you." Darkness was being very coy, trying to lead TJ to an answer.

"Then what is it then? Why do you keep showing up? I've never had anything like this in my life. I'm keenly aware that I'm dreaming right now, and this setting is not real. But something about you is real. And I want to know what it is."

"The fact that you know this is a dream, and you have the ability to recognize that, is a big step. This is all in the mind, TJ. Your mind. As soon as you figure it all out, I'll be gone for good. And the TJ Carlson in which I've been manifesting myself will also be gone for good."

"Gone for good. Is that what this is all about? Killing myself? That's what I'm here for, right?"

"Wake up, TJ," said Darkness. Darkness pulled out a gun and fired a shot at TJ, temporarily making everything go black.

TJ woke up in the bungalow, taking a few minutes to orient himself with where he was. He stood back up, walked over to the area of the bungalow where he could look down in the water and watch as the fish swam by.

The dream with Darkness fascinated him, far more than the others. He was lucid in this one. He was keenly aware that he was dreaming. It seemed that Darkness was getting frustrated with him in this dream. As if TJ was close to figuring him out, but couldn't quite do it. For the first time, he looked forward to seeing Darkness again in a future dream.

He put his plans of suicide on hold, temporarily. The despair he had felt upon his arrival in Bora Bora was being replaced. It was being replaced by a curiosity of a potential bigger answer to everything he was going through. He was willing to give that a few more days. After all, Matt Damon was right – you only have this one life.

TJ stared at the fish for another hour, then went outside of his bungalow, set up a chair and watched the sun rise.

Chapter 28

The sunrise was accompanied by some ominous looking clouds that were off in the distance, but unmistakably heading in the direction of the beach. Dammit, thought TJ. He was looking forward to just trying to clear his mind, if he could, while enjoying the view. Stubbornly, TJ just sat there, refusing to budge as the now full on storm was heading his direction.

TJ entertained the thought of just lying there and letting it rain on him. So what, he thought. So, I get a little wet. It began to sprinkle on him. Then it got heavier. Then it became a downpour. His mood began to turn foul the more he got pelted. "FUUUUCK!!", yelled TJ as he began to pack up his things to run back to the bungalow.

Inside the bungalow, he threw his things on the floor and paced around for a minute. TJ had no idea what to do with himself on this day now. Then he decided. It was time to drink, and drink heavily. If this day was going to be ruined by rain, he figured what better way to make it go by quicker.

TJ purchased four bottles of wine at a nearby grocery store. The smiling, young Polynesian man at the register tried to make small talk with TJ.

"Looks like sir is having a party today," said the young man, as he carefully packaged the wine bottles into a box.

"My friend, it is a party of one," said TJ, smiling back at him.

"Oh, you are not here with your wife?' asked the young man inquisitively, unaware that he had just touched a nerve.

TJ felt a wave of sadness hit him. He wasn't here with his wife. He no longer had a wife. Or kids, for that matter. The reality of why he was here in Bora Bora crashed down on him like a ton of bricks. He felt heavy, and his eyes began to water.

TJ just glared at the young Polynesian man, who seemed a bit taken aback at the mood change in TJ. The man did not say anything more to TJ and just let him grab the box of wine bottles and watched him as he left the store.

TJ got back to his bungalow, grabbed a bottle of wine and fell forcefully on to his bed. He didn't bother to get a wine glass. He opened the bottle and just started drinking it, in big gulps. He repeatedly took the swigs from the bottle until he started to feel a bit buzzed. As this state was setting in, TJ's mind began to race. I'm here to kill myself, he thought. He pulled out his journal and read through a few of his early passages. Once he got to his upbeat entry after Zurich, he threw the journal across the room towards the kitchen, where it careened off of the refrigerator and almost in to the trash can.

He downed the bottle with more intensity, but his buzz wasn't increasing enough to numb his pain. He polished off this bottle and then stumbled over to grab another. He opened it and began drinking it like the other one. TJ wanted this pain gone. Alcohol was seemingly his only hope.

About a quarter of the way through the second bottle, TJ was feeling drunk. But more than drunk, he was feeling angry and sad, a combination of emotions so brutal that even the increasing volume of alcohol wasn't stopping it from building up. TJ replayed all of the events that led up to this very moment over and over in his mind, something he couldn't stop and something that was increasingly enhancing the pain, which was now settling in his head and his heart.

Overwhelmed now with negative emotion and pain, TJ finally gave in. "It's time," said TJ calmly. "The endgame is here." TJ was going to end his life.

TJ could barely stand up, and he fell to the floor as he tried to make his way over to the sleeping pills and the beer he had bought for this very moment. He crawled over to them, managed to grab the bottle of pills, then crawled back to his bed. The wine he had bought was right next to the bed, so he decided to keep rolling with those.

TJ had no idea how many pills it would take, so he poured ten of them on to the bed. I'll just shove all of these in my mouth and chug them down with wine, he thought. TJ looked at the pills, and somewhat obsessively lined them up in a neat order. He temporarily became more fascinated by doing that with the pills than swallowing them. He drank some more wine, trying to dull the increasing butterflies in his stomach.

TJ had sometimes wondered about death. It was the great unknown, and the thought of what could happen to him after he died terrified him. He wanted to believe there was a heaven, but what if there wasn't? What if there was nothing? And what if Hell was real. At this point, TJ felt like he had certainly done enough to warrant being banished to Hell for eternity. Sadly, for TJ, life on Earth had become his own living hell, and the actual Hell couldn't be much worse.

"It's time to find out," said TJ, as he determined he was ready to do this. He grabbed one pill and chugged it down with a glass of wine. The combination of trying to swallow the pill along with downing a huge glass of wine sent TJ into a choking, coughing fit. But the pill finally went down. He composed himself and grabbed another. He approached it a little more carefully this time, and successfully swallowed the pill without choking on it. He kept going. A third pill. Then a fourth pill. By the time TJ got to the fifth pill and swallowed it, he began to fade. Everything went to black. TJ keeled over face first onto his bed, his wine bottle slipping out of his hand, empty enough that none was spilling out on to the bed. The remaining pills sat next to TJ's head, not needed for the task at hand.

A bright light. TJ had heard about this phenomenon from people who say that they had near-death experiences. And there it was! I did it, thought TJ. He wasn't feeling any pain. The light dominated him, and his only urge was to walk towards it. TJ began to move briskly towards the source of the light, unaware of what it was he was actually walking on. He didn't care. I have to get to that light, he thought with a sense of purpose.

Then the light began to fade. "NOOOO!" yelled TJ. It began to get darker, the light in front of him dimming as if being slowly turned off by someone. Finally, everything faded to black and turned cold. TJ felt a shiver go through his body. He feared what would happen next. He feared he was in Hell.

"Expecting someone?" TJ heard those words, coming from a voice he knew all too well.

"Well fuck, I am in Hell," said TJ, with a palpable disappointment that Darkness was who greeted him in his death.

"It's your own Hell, TJ. You and you alone have created this. You and I now have eternity together. And you can't wake up from this!" Darkness said his last line with a segue into a sinister laugh.

This didn't feel right, thought TJ. It was too much like his dreams and every other encounter with Darkness.

"I'm not dead, am I?" asked TJ, calmly.

Darkness finally showed himself, a spitting image of TJ, but with deep bags under his eyes and a dead stare. "You can't even do that right," he sneered. "You could have just put a gun to your head and a bullet in your brain. You could have hung yourself. But no, you took the easy way out. Again. Wanting to die a painless death, in your sleep. You coward."

"Well let me wake up and I'll try harder next time," said TJ. "I'll be sure to leave behind blood, guts and gore, so that everyone can remember me that way."

Darkness moved closer to TJ until they were eye to eye. Neither flinched.

Darkness broke the silence. "Do you honestly think this is your answer? If it is, then do it right. But keep this in mind. Killing yourself solves the problems of only one person – you. What about your kids? Are they not worth trying to win back? Do you realize the damage you'll do to them by killing yourself?"

TJ listened intently. He tried forming his response, but couldn't.

Darkness continued. "You don't care, because you tried going through with it. You didn't think about them. Or your parents and your brother. Imagine everyone's reaction when they find out you're dead. You think they don't care about you anymore? Bullshit! They are worried sick about you, and with good reason."

"Why are you doing this?" asked TJ. "Why are you acting now like you care, like you have my best interests at heart? You were part of what drove me to this. You showed me everything in this world that was awful and heartbreaking to me. You fucked my wife, stole my kids, killed me countless times, all in the name of helping me. Well you did help me…. you helped me to realize I was worthless and that this was my endgame."

"I'm you, TJ. Never forget that. You can make me go away. Either kill yourself right or get your shit together. Those are your two options. Because if you keep occupying this space that you're in, you will never get rid of me." Darkness stepped back, waved his hand up in the air, and the light started to come back.

"Fight it, TJ. Or the damage you've done will become permanent to both you and the ones who care about you." Darkness vanished, and as he faded, flames erupted all around TJ. He could feel the intense searing heat and watched as his skin began to boil and blister. TJ screamed and panicked. Maybe he was in Hell after all.

"HEEEEEEEEEEEEELLLLPPPPPPP!" yelled TJ. The heat engulfed him and he watched as the flames disintegrated his body. He faded to black once again.

It was blurry. TJ slowly cracked open an eye, but everything was out of focus. He couldn't feel the rest of his body. He didn't know whether he was dreaming still, or actually awake. Suddenly, and with a violent spasm, TJ threw up all over the bed. A vicious red color, which TJ didn't know whether it was wine or blood. Multiple spasms, as TJ emptied out everything that was in his stomach and what felt like all of his other internal organs. This took place for the next thirty minutes until TJ finally was able to calm himself and focus.

The first thing he noticed, albeit now covered in his red vomit, were the remaining five sleeping pills there on the bed. His head was pounding and he could barely handle the light in the room.

"Holy shit," said TJ, quietly and struggling to get the words out. He let some time pass by before he fully tried to move. Finally, he pushed himself up, opened his eyes and surveyed the room. It took him a minute to remember where he was in this world. He saw the wine bottle on the bed, sitting out of reach of where he had just emptied his stomach. "Now what do I do?" muttered TJ to himself. "I just failed at the main reason I came here."

TJ sat quietly in his room for the remainder of the day, lost in thought. His fresh encounter with Darkness was vividly in his mind, as were two of his words. *"Fight it."* He thought about Elizabeth. At that moment, TJ realized that his daughter would have been devastated if he had been successful at what he just attempted. His son and his family too. His relatives, his co-workers, his friends…. some of whom really went out of their way to help him. TJ's sadness and anger were now being replaced by another feeling. Guilt.

TJ woke up the next morning, still feeling a bit weak from the previous day. He was not feeling sad or angry or even guilty any longer. He was feeling relief that his attempt the previous day had failed.

He spent the day exploring Bora Bora, hopping a cab to take him to different spots. He asked the driver to stop at one of the beach spots he took a rest at during his bike ride around the island. He found the same tree that he rested up against and slowly got back into that resting position. Right at that moment, he saw a man and a woman pass by on bicycles. Just like TJ did a little over a year before. TJ then did something he hadn't been able to do earnestly for a while. He smiled.

Chapter 29

TJ looked outside his bungalow and caught the beautiful sunrise. This place was wearing him down. Ever since his recovery from his failed suicide attempt, he was finding it increasingly hard to be depressed. But no matter what, and no matter how picturesque and paradise-like this place was, that alone did not solve the mess that TJ had created for himself.

He decided that today would be a beach day. More time to clear his mind and find his answers. He prepared for his day, but when he pulled open the drawer and saw the notes he had been writing, he closed it quickly and left them. Those notes had become a sort of venomous poison to TJ. He was afraid to touch them.

TJ headed over to the beach, found his spot under a palm tree, and got comfortable. He looked over to the bar and saw Martin, the bartender who he was getting to know very well. Martin waved and made a hand signal that said "want a drink"? TJ gave him the universal signal for yes – a thumbs up.

"Steven…. have you heard from your father recently?" Paige was curious, as Steven usually brings it up when he hears from his dad.

"It was the other week," said Steven, barely paying attention while he played his computer games.

"What did he say?"

"The same as usual. Mom, I know you hate him now, and so do I. For leaving us……and I told him that. I said that both Elizabeth and I hated him."

Paige felt a chill come over her. She was shocked that Steven had done that.

"Oh my God Steven……. you should not have done that." Paige's voice was shaking. She knew deep down that TJ never wanted to lose the love of his kids. That would destroy him.

"Why? He's never coming back, right?"

"Steven, no matter what goes on with your father and I, he loves both you and Elizabeth more than anything in this world. To send him a message like that may have done a lot of damage to him. You should have talked to me first." Steven looked curiously at Paige, who looked on the verge of tears.

"What should I do?" asked Steven, now fully engaged in the conversation.

"Please apologize to him. And ask him to come home to see you and Elizabeth. Do that right now, please."

"Okay," said Steven, "but how should I feel about all of this….and him……I'm confused."

"He will always be your father. And he will always love you. He'll get over what he's going through and be there for you two again. Your feelings for him should not change or be affected by what's going on with him and I. Sometimes, adults can be childish, and it's always the kids who are impacted. Just send him a message…. soon."

Steven sensed that Paige was panicking a bit, and now Steve was beginning to worry if he had done something really wrong. He quickly put together a message for his father:

Dad – I'm sorry about the message I sent the other week. That was wrong. Elizabeth and I don't hate you. We really want you to come home. We both miss you so much. Please come home soon.

"Dean, I'm not sure where he is now, but when we find out, get ready to go get him. I haven't heard from him in weeks, since he was in India. He mentioned being sick. I'll keep messaging him to find out where he is, and then be ready to go." Ann Carlson was a nervous wreck. Not a word from TJ in weeks. It's as if he dropped off the face of the earth. She had had enough and was preparing Dean to go get him."

"Unless we know for sure he is staying where he is, I'm not sure it's a good idea. I don't particularly want to go on a wild goose chase for him all over the world." Dean was less than thrilled about the prospect of getting his brother, but was extremely worried about his mother's state of mind.

"Dammit, we need to get him back here. I don't like this at all. Lord only knows where he is now, and how he's reacting to the divorce."

Harold Carlson was listening, but for once, not chiming in. He usually tried to talk Ann down, to have some faith in their son that he would do the right thing. But even he had lost hope in TJ that he was still in his right mind. The giveaway was Paige's comment about what drove her to reject him…. his behavior in Europe. Harold could sense that other women were involved, and if that's the path TJ was heading down, it was not a good sign.

"Alright," said Dean, "let me know if you hear anything."

TJ Carlson had fallen asleep underneath the palm tree. Despite a little bit of shade, he was still getting a bit sunburned.

Tehani Rey was a gorgeous Tahitian girl in her late 20's. She had long, flowing black hair, and light brown complexion and usually wore traditional Polynesian outfits that accentuated her very fit body. Tehani and Martin, the bartender, were friends. On days that she would go to the market or run some other chores; she would always make it a point to stop by for a quick chat. Martin was a family man, and had a Tahitian wife, who happened to be a friend of Tehani's.

On this day, she couldn't help but notice a westerner laying on the beach under a palm tree, turning new shades of red.

"Martin…. what's with the guy over there?" Tehani asked.

"That's TJ…he's become like a regular here," replied Martin.

"I wonder if he realizes he's becoming a bit lobster-like."

"Probably not," said Martin, "he had a few beers then dozed off. He's a bit of a mystery. I don't really know his story."

Tehani looked over at TJ, and mulled whether or not to go over and warn him about how red he was getting. She was fascinated by westerners, but other than Martin, hadn't really spent much time talking to one.

"You should go warn him," said Martin. "Although when he sees you, he might think that he's dreaming."

"Awww…. thanks. Because I'm so pretty, right?" Tehani laughed. "Do you think he has sunscreen with him?"

"Are you going to offer to rub it all over him?" asked Martin, jokingly.

"Come on…. you know me better than that. I'm just being a good host here. I'm sure he'd appreciate it. Is he nice?"

"It seems so," said Martin. "Why?"

"Just wondering. Sounds like you know him a little anyway." Tehani went to a store next to Martin's, and picked out a small tube of sunscreen.

"My good deed for the day," said Tehani toward Martin. "Here goes."

Tehani walked over towards TJ. She leaned down and nudged his shoulder to try and jostle him awake. It took a few minutes, but TJ started to wake up.

TJ was groggy, but was a little stunned to see a gorgeous Tahitian girl bent down, looking at him, trying to wake him up.

"Sir……sir……are you awake?" asked Tehani.

"Yes, I am now," said TJ.

"I couldn't help but notice that you were probably getting more sun than you were intending. You're starting to burn."

"Oh….," said TJ, now examining his skin and noticing how red it was getting. "Crud, I must have fallen asleep."

"Looks that way," laughed Tehani. "I brought you some sunscreen. I wasn't sure you had any. I asked my friend Martin over there whether or not he knew if you had any and he wasn't sure."

"Wow, that was really nice of you. Thanks." TJ took the sunscreen and started to put it on as Tehani watched, smiling. "I guess this might be a little too late, huh?"

"Well, at least you won't get burned more," said Tehani. She wondered to herself whether she should offer to put some on his back, the only part of him that wasn't burned.

"True," said TJ. "I know this may sound awkward, but can you put some on my back? If you're not comfortable with that, I understand."

"Maybe I'll ask Martin to come over here and do that for you." Tehani looked at TJ for a reaction, and saw a look of disappointment. "Haha – I'm just kidding. Sure, I will help you with that."

Tehani rubbed lotion on TJ's back. She has soft, smooth hands, thought TJ. TJ began thinking of ways to continue this conversation with Tehani. To him, she was a sight to behold. She was gorgeous. An exotic beauty, who also appeared to be generous, kind and friendly.

"What's your name?" asked TJ.

"My name is Tehani Rey, TJ."

"That's a beautiful name. Tehani. And how did you know my name already? Either you are psychic or Martin gave you a briefing on me."

"Of course, it was Martin. And that's pretty much all he knew about you. Said you were a bit of a man of mystery."

"I like it that way," said TJ. "Being mysterious…. keeping people on their toes."

Tehani looked at TJ. She was becoming increasingly curious about this man. He seemed nice and friendly. She didn't want this conversation to end. She had a lot of questions and wanted to satisfy her curiosity.

"TJ…. can I join you here for a drink? It's the least you can do for me after me spending my hard-earned money on sunscreen for you."

TJ's face lit up. "Oh, absolutely! What will you have?"

"Anything…. surprise me. Just don't be cheap and bring me tap water." Tehani laughed and got comfortable on TJ's beach blanket.

TJ walked over to Martin, who he noticed had a smirk on his face.

"What's that smile for, Martin?" asked TJ, also smiling.

"You know why. She's really a sweet girl. And she was very curious about you."

"Really?" asked TJ. "Why is that?"

"I'm not sure. But don't look a gift horse in the mouth. The fact that she's still there talking to you should tell you something."

TJ ordered two beers from Martin, and set back towards Tehani. He could not stop staring at her. She was so beautiful, and just the sight of her gave TJ goosebumps on a hot day.

"Here you go," said TJ.

"Thanks," said Tehani. "Okay, mystery man, what's your story?"

TJ thought for a few seconds about opening up to Tehani. She may reject a very sad story. But at this point, he had no other stories to tell and didn't have the energy to make one up.

"Honestly, I'm here because I have nowhere else to go. I'm now divorced, can't go home and don't know what to do with myself. Being here gives me a sense of peace that nowhere else in this chaotic world gives me."

Tehani studied TJ for a minute to process what he just said.

"Why can't you go home? Where is home?"

"Home used to be in the USA…. North Carolina. My marriage ended badly and, unfortunately, the kids were impacted." TJ studied Tehani to see if it looked like she was looking for a way out of this conversation.

"That's sad, TJ. I'm sorry. How are you doing now? Is being here helping?"

TJ was pleased that Tehani didn't flinch and was still talking to him. In fact, she was looking at him with empathy.

"You know, it is. I find it really hard to be depressed here. It's such a paradise and everyone here is so amazingly friendly."

"Do you have anyone you can talk to? What about your friends and family?"

"I've had friends who have helped me along the way. As a matter of fact, I stayed with friends in Switzerland and India. It was nice of them to host me, but I felt like a burden to them in certain ways."

"I'd love to hear more about them, TJ. I hope you're okay talking to a complete stranger here." Tehani was very interested in TJ's story. There was something about him that was fascinating her. How could this seemingly nice and handsome man have gone through something like he was describing?

"Sure, I'll tell you as much as you can handle hearing. Cheers." TJ toasted with Tehani and debated with himself on how best to frame his story if he was going to talk to her more. There were elements, such as the brothels and prostitutes, that TJ was certain would turn her off. She seemed so nice, and he didn't want to ruin whatever was happening here.

Tehani knew her time was running short to continue her conversation with TJ, even though she really wanted to. She had to get to the market and then get back home. She could tell she was dealing with a bit of a lost soul. But her heart was reaching out to him. She really wanted to hear more. She wanted to open him up. She wasn't sure why, but she felt drawn to him.

"TJ, I'm going to need to run over to the market and then get back home before my father and brother wonder where I am."

"Oh, okay," said TJ, a bit disappointed.

"But listen, I will come back here again tomorrow and will not have other chores to do. Will you be here?" Tehani gave TJ a sweet look, and he got lost in her beautiful, brown eyes.

"Yes, I'll be here," said TJ. "I'll come here around 9:00am."

"Okay…. you promise to be here?" asked Tehani. "I want to hear more of your story."

"Definitely, I will be here, especially if you'll be showing up again." TJ gave Tehani a big smile as he said that last line. He hoped beyond anything that she would show back up the next day.

Tehani got up and headed to the market, looking back at TJ and waving several times. Martin watched the whole thing unfold and gave TJ a thumbs up and laughed.

TJ sat on his beach blanket for a little longer just staring at the ocean. He wasn't sure what he had done to earn the gift that was the visit from Tehani today. He quietly looked up to the sky and muttered under his breath: "Thank you."

TJ had a different feeling about him that evening and couldn't get Tehani off his mind. All of the drama that usually went into his evenings there was absent on this night. He relaxed comfortably in his bungalow and thought of ways to tell his story to Tehani the next day. If she truly showed up. TJ decided to go to bed early so he could get to the next day as quickly as possible.

"Don't do it to her. Don't make her another one of your victims. Don't pull her into this." Darkness was sitting with TJ on a rock, overlooking a pond, where the two of them were fishing.

"What are you talking about?" said TJ. "And who are you talking about?"

"You know damn well who I'm talking about. Don't give her damaged goods. Leave her alone. She doesn't deserve that."

"You know what, you can kiss my ass. I'm done trying to figure out your cryptic messages. Again, I'm aware that I'm dreaming, and who you are, but I still don't know what you represent. But I'm beginning to think that ultimately you aren't my friend. I need to defeat you. Somehow, someway, I need to purge you from my life."

"What makes you think I'm not a friend?" asked Darkness. "I'm the only friend you have right now. I saved your life once already"

"No, you aren't. You are still making me feel the worst things about myself. You reinforce the notion that I'm worthless, and that even will tarnish someone like Tehani. What message there should I be latching on to that would make me think that you are anything positive for me?"

"Excellent," said Darkness. "You're getting it. And you're right, you have to defeat me, which means you have to defeat yourself. It won't be easy. You don't have the control you need to do it."

TJ opted to throw a punch at Darkness to test whether he could fight. Darkness vanished before the punch could hit him.

"Get real, TJ. That's not how you're going to do it. You have to find the right kind of strength. You don't have it in you. Just kill yourself and get it over with." Darkness and TJ were now at the ledge of a tall building. TJ was teetering on the edge about to fall. Darkness was cheering him on.

"Come on, TJ, do it. Jump! You know you want to. It's your only way out of this mess you've created."

TJ looked over the edge and looked back at Darkness. "You're right," said TJ. Then TJ stepped off the ledge and began a free fall to the ground.

Then suddenly, he was back on top of the ledge.

"I'm not going to make it that easy for you," said Darkness, menacingly.

"What the fuck do you want from me?" yelled TJ. "Let me end this dream and wake up!"

"Don't pull her into your chaos, TJ. Don't do it. I'm warning you."

"She'll probably run away herself," said TJ. "After getting to know everything about me."

"That's my boy. You got it." TJ was pushed off the ledge and freefell to the ground. Upon impact, he woke up in his bungalow with a spasm.

"Fuck!" he yelled out. I let him beat me in the dream, he thought. I gave in. Next time, I'll figure out a way to defeat him. But the seed was planted. Darkness was right. Tehani seemed to be so nice and sweet.... what good could come to her in getting involved with damaged goods like TJ. His excitement for the day became tempered by the fact that he knew nothing would likely come out of this meeting with Tehani. He shouldn't allow it.

TJ headed off to the beach at 7:30am the next morning. He was up early anyway, and the beach was the only place he needed to be that day. He was nervous about Tehani showing up. Could they recapture what semblance of a spark they had the previous day? Would she even show up? He set up his beach blanket and got comfortable.

9:00am arrived, and no sign of Tehani. As each proceeding minute passed, TJ became more and more disappointed. He figured maybe she had second thoughts about coming back to hear more of this stranger's awful and sad tale. He laid flat and closed his eyes.

"Wake up, sleepyhead," said Tehani, jolting TJ into alertness. "Did you even leave here yesterday, or did you sleep at the beach?"

"Nah, I left after you did, but I came here early this morning." TJ was ecstatic that Tehani showed back up. And one look at her this morning showed that she took some time getting ready. Another beautiful Polynesian outfit and full make up. Not exactly beach attire. She looked stunning, making TJ wish he had taken more time to prepare himself that morning.

"Sorry, I'm late," said Tehani. "I got grilled by my brother as to where I was going looking like this."

"What did you say?"

"I told him sometimes a girl just wants to look nice."

"Did he buy that?"

"I don't know. It doesn't matter. Okay, let's pick up where we left off yesterday."

"Before we do that, Tehani, I just want to ask you something."

"What is it?" asked Tehani.

"Are you ready to hear this? I just want to be sure. I'll share it with you, but I don't want to ruin…….. well…….. whatever early connection we have. Because I'll admit…. I thought about you all last night after our conversation."

"It's okay," said Tehani. "I want to hear it all."

TJ told Tehani the story of the things that led to the breakup of his marriage, specifically focusing on the lack of closeness and intimacy of the final years, Paige's seemingly falling out of love with him and ultimately what made him leave the country.

Tehani took all of it in, letting TJ talk.

"I'm sorry you had to go through all that. You must have been so stressed every day. I can see how you would need to leave to cope with everything. What happened after you left?"

TJ told Tehani the story of some of his adventures in Europe, focusing on the failed attempts to call home or message his kids, and also about the drinking, but he omitted anything to do with sex. His encounter with Fay and his time at the brothels in Amsterdam and Berlin. He talked at length about his stay in Zurich,

"This friend in Switzerland…. did she help?" asked Tehani.

"Yes, quite a bit," said TJ. "I was actually ready to go home after that."

"What happened?" asked Tehani.

"Paige rejected my offer to come home and said she wanted a divorce. After that, I had no home to return to. I went to Finland after that. Then my friend in India invited me there."

TJ explained the trip to India, covering the food poisoning and Dengue fever, but not revealing how and why that happened.

"Oh my gosh," said Tehani. "You've been through so much. I can see why you are in the mental state you are. What happened afterwards? After India? What led you here?"

TJ explained his travels through Asia, again concentrating on the drinking and not the sex.

"When I ended up in Australia, I was really in bad shape. Then I got the worst possible message I could have ever imagined getting."

"What was the message?" asked Tehani.

"I got a message from my son saying that both he and my daughter now hated me." As TJ said it, tears formed in his eyes. "It destroyed me. It left me with no hope. I felt useless, worthless and like I had nothing to live for."

Tehani reached her hand over and wrapped her fingers into TJ's, now holding his hand tightly. The instant Tehani did that, TJ felt a shiver go through his body. That was it! That was a spark, he thought. He had never felt that with anyone before. It was beyond description.

"TJ, wow, I am so sorry about your kids. I'm sure they will come to understand you one day, and everything will be okay." Tehani smiled sweetly at him and her thumb began rubbing the back of TJ's hand. TJ squeezed Tehani's hand, causing her to give him a coy look.

"I hope it's okay," said Tehani.

"It is," said TJ. "Don't let go."

"TJ, that story was heartbreaking. It sounds to me like you are a guy who tried to make everything work, and when it didn't, you tried to cope the only way you knew how. Your kids will appreciate you one day again, don't worry. You know, the fact that you opened up to me like that tells me a lot about you. You are a kind soul. You have treated me with nothing but respect these last two days. I find myself wanting to know more and more about you."

TJ knew something special was happening here. But he also knew there was a part of the story he still wasn't telling. But he would do just about anything to make sure this conversation and interaction with Tehani continued.

"I feel the same about you…. wanting to get to know you better. You look so beautiful today. Can I take you out tonight? On a date? I want to get out of my beach clothes and look good for you. I feel like I look like a slob.”

“Yes, we can go out tonight. On a date, if you want to call it that. And you would look just as handsome dressed up as you do now.”

“I’ll take you to Bloody Mary’s tonight. Is that okay?” asked TJ.

“That’s really expensive,” said Tehani. “Are you sure?”

“Yes,” said TJ. “That is one of my favorite places in Bora Bora, and I can’t think of anywhere else I’d rather take you.”

“Okay,” said Tehani. “Let’s meet back here and we’ll walk over there. See you at around 4:00?”

“Perfect,” said TJ. “See you then.” It was 2:00pm now. TJ was shocked at how much time had passed. Time seemed to fly by when he was with her. And now, he could take her on a proper date. He headed back to his bungalow, anticipating the night ahead.

So many scenarios played out in TJ’s mind. She was still there, and she wanted to see him again. He prepared for his date with Tehani in his bungalow, determined not to do or say anything on this night that would mess it up. It had been a long time since a date had gotten him excited. This may have been the first since Paige. He recalled his nervousness aboard the cruise ship with the Vahine when he took her out to dinner. This was different. Tehani was under no obligation to be with him……it wasn’t part of her job.

TJ bought Tehani some candy, as he wanted to give her something like a gift. He shot down some corny lines in his head about her being sweet.

The time had arrived and he made his way to the beach to meet her. She was already waiting there, talking to Martin.

"Have a nice night, you two," said Martin as TJ approached.

"Thank you, Martin," said Tehani.

"I'll expect an update tomorrow," Martin shouted as they walked away towards Bloody Mary's.

TJ debated as they began walking whether to hold Tehani's hand. In what he considered a slick move, his hand brushed against hers as they walked. Tehani grabbed his hand and held it. It worked! TJ was proud of himself, and extremely proud walking hand in hand down the road with this incredibly beautiful girl.

"I got you something," said TJ. "Some chocolate covered mangos."

"Mmmm…. I love mangos. And chocolate. Nice work. That will be our dessert."

The two did not say much to each other as they walked down the street. They were both nervous. TJ wasn't sure where to pick up the conversation after spilling his guts at the beach for days. He was tired about talking about how awful things had been. Since meeting Tehani, he hasn't been able to think about anything else but her.

They arrived at Bloody Mary's and found a table. They enjoyed a nice dinner and a few drinks. TJ was going lightly on his drinks. He had no interest in getting drunk.

"TJ, can I ask you something? Related to your travels?" Tehani was looking at him playfully, but with some curiosity.

Uh oh, thought TJ. This is likely to be a question about girls. He hadn't told the full story of his journey and the crippling sex addiction he developed.

"Sure…. what is it?"

"When you were in India, why didn't you and your friend there become something more? She seemed to care a lot about you."

Whew, thought TJ. I can answer that one.

"I believe it was cultural. Her parents would never have allowed the relationship. But I consider her a very dear friend and if it wasn't for her, I may not even be here right now."

"Did you meet any other girls on the journey? That interested you?" Tehani was slowly getting to her point.

TJ thought for a second about the best way to answer this to get out of this line of questioning.

"I met some people, but none that meant anything. My true friends were Sophie and Neha, and they are the ones that helped me through the roughest times."

"I see," said Tehani. "I just wanted to make sure you didn't have any other girls waiting for you somewhere." Tehani laughed, but TJ was caught off guard by her comment. It seemed like Tehani was interested in this becoming a lot more.

"Nope, no need to worry. No other surprises out there," said TJ. "I'm all yours."

TJ wished he could have taken those last three words back. That was very forward, he thought. It was only the third time they were seeing each other, and he just verbally committed to her. He studied her for her reaction.

Tehani looked at TJ and laughed. "Okay, good to know. And don't worry about me. I also don't have any crazy ex-boyfriends still hanging around."

"Thank God," said TJ. "Then I won't have to be ready to beat someone down if they show up."

"TJ…. I hope some of this talk isn't scaring you. This is really new for me. It usually takes me a long time to get to know and like a guy. But with you, there's something different going on. I feel like I already know you. Like we've met somewhere before. I really like being with you. I hope you're planning to stay in Bora Bora for a while."

"It's not scaring me. As a matter of fact, it's……well……. not quite sure how to say this without sounding dramatic……. but it's saving me. I'll just leave it at that." TJ came to a realization at that moment that all of the reasons he came to this place were now far from his mind. He was suicidal and had lost hope. This girl was giving that back to him. He was starting to feel something strong for her.

"Tehani," TJ continued, as he grabbed her hand, "I have no plans to leave Bora Bora. I would like to see what we can develop into. I will not pressure you to do anything. I'm happy just talking to you and being with you. If I could see you, even for a little while, every day, then I would look forward to waking up every day. Like I have been the last few days."

"Oh my," said Tehani. "My heart is beating fast."

TJ's was too. This date was turning out better than he could have hoped for. He stared at Tehani, and she stared back. No words needed to be said.

"Want to go back to the beach? It's beautiful there at night." Tehani smiled at TJ, and TJ quickly agreed.

They walked hand in hand back to what was becoming TJ's spot at the beach.

"I don't have my beach blanket," said TJ.

"It doesn't matter," said Tehani. "It's just sand. You sit right here."

Tehani positioned TJ sitting cross legged, and she sat the same way opposite from him. Her hands grabbed on to TJ's hands.

"I really like you, TJ. You are kind and funny. You are handsome. You are a gentleman. Be good with my heart." Tehani was stepping this up a level. TJ couldn't believe this was happening so fast.

"Of course, I will," said TJ. "For me, it will be the thing that I treasure the most."

"You can kiss me now, if you want," said Tehani.

TJ slowly moved towards Tehani. He stroked her cheek with his hand, and then moved it to the back of her head. Their lips met, in a series of small, quick kisses. Finally, the kiss became continuous, and very passionate. Their tongues met, swirled, exploring each other's mouth with increasing intensity. Tehani was gently moaning the longer the kiss went and as the kiss became more passionate. TJ was careful not to advance it any further by attempting to feel her breasts or anything else more sexual. Instead, their arms just wrapped around each other, and they got lost in their first kiss.

TJ had never experienced a kiss like that. It was the best kiss he had ever had. No contest. Paige had never kissed him like that. Much like the time where they first held hands, TJ felt that same spark when they kissed. It was like magic. It did something to his body that he wished he could have bottled up and sold.

"That was amazing," said TJ. "Easily the greatest kiss I have ever had."

"Same here," said Tehani. "You are a good kisser."

"This night was perfect. The best night I think I have ever had," said TJ.

"We can stay here for another hour," said Tehani. "Then I'll be expected home."

"Okay," said TJ. "How should we spend our hour?"

"More kissing, of course," she said playfully.

TJ and Tehani kissed for the next hour, which made the time fly by at lightning speed. TJ didn't want to leave. He didn't want to not be with her.

"Let's meet again tomorrow, TJ. We can spend the day together. I'll take you with me to some of the places I like to go."

"Sounds perfect," said TJ. "I can't wait."

TJ walked Tehani back close to her house. "One more for the road?" asked TJ.

"Without a doubt. Good night TJ. See you tomorrow." Tehani hugged and kissed TJ, then made her way to her house. TJ walked back to the resort and to his bungalow. On cloud nine, walking on air.

TJ sat up in his bungalow for a while thinking about the evening, and thinking back to just a few days ago when he was thinking of different ways to kill himself, had even bought the items to do so and even failed in an attempt to do so. The 12 pack of beer and the sleeping pills were still in the bag that he had put them. He decided to just leave them there. He also pulled out the letters he had begun writing. It had become a ritual for him to simply fold those letters back up and put them away, unable to do anything further with them.

TJ knew that what he had with Tehani was saving his life. She alone was preventing him from completing the task he returned to Bora Bora for. If they failed, or if she broke his heart, he would be right back in that place again. He tried not to let his thoughts go negative, but his demons were apparently strong.

He took the notes and the beer and the pills, and he placed them out of sight. He didn't want any reminders. Look to the future, not the past, he thought. Tomorrow, he will spend the day with a beautiful girl, who liked him and genuinely wanted to be with him. He would make the most of that day, and every day that they have together. And for the immediate future, he certainly was not going to leave Bora Bora.

Chapter 30

TJ Carlson had carved a path of sex and debauchery through Europe, India and Asia. Yet, none of those experiences affected him as emotionally as simply kissing Tehani that previous day. It was those kisses that were entrenched in his mind, taking up residence and building a house. Considering the emotional lows he had been through, this high was like a drug permeating his entire body. But TJ was scared.

He was a man with a lot of baggage. Tehani didn't know the full extent of it yet. She was flirting with and being sweet with a man who was doing everything in his power to portray the best side of himself and not let that awful, miserable side back out. That side still existed. All of TJ's worldly problems hadn't gone away because he met a gorgeous Polynesian girl. The darkness was still trying to control the light. This was TJ's battle.

TJ tried to bury any negative thoughts. It was time for him to prepare for his day with Tehani. She was leading the way today and TJ would be along for the ride. He spent a lot of time fixing his hair just right, picking out his clothes for the day and deciding what, if any, cologne to wear. And, most importantly he thought, plenty of breath mints in the hopes that there was more kissing to come.

TJ laughed to himself at the thought that he was excited and nervous about kissing a girl. "What am I, 12?" he said aloud. Lost in that train of thought, there was a knock on TJ's bungalow door.

Tehani Rey was standing there, in a beautiful red and white colored Pareo with her black hair flowing down half hanging in front of her shoulder and half behind her shoulder. Next to Tehani was a moped.

"I remembered you mentioned you rode a bicycle around this island, and nearly died in the process," laughed Tehani. "Today, we are going to do this the right way."

TJ smiled. "What do you mean?"

"We are going to re-create your ride around the island on this moped!" said Tehani with a bright smile. "And I'm driving."

TJ was taken aback that she had planned something so perfect. That bike ride is one of TJ's greatest memories, not only of Bora Bora, but of his life. "Can we fit?" asked TJ. "On that moped……both of us?"

"It will be a tight fit," said Tehani, and then she looked coyly at TJ. "You'll have to hug me tight from behind so you won't fall off."

"I think I can handle that," said TJ, thoroughly excited at that prospect. TJ and Tehani walked the moped out on to the road and began their journey around Bora Bora.

TJ was half paying attention to the scenery as it passed by. He was hugging Tehani around her stomach, carefully trying to not touch her breasts. He wanted to, but it didn't feel like it was the time. I need to behave, he thought.

Tehani pulled the moped off the road and down a driveway to a place TJ recognized. It was a little shop where they made and sold Bora Bora themed Pareos and also served some amazing pineapple and mango.

"I've bought a few of my Pareos from here. I thought you might like to see how they are made," said Tehani, sweetly. TJ didn't let on that he had been here before. "Absolutely," said TJ, as they watched the older Polynesian women create the dresses and add the color patterns using pre-made molds.

"Tehani, what are your favorite colors?" asked TJ.

"I love purple!" said Tehani.

TJ walked over to one of the Pareo makers and requested a purple and white Pareo to be made for Tehani. "Of course, handsome," said the Polynesian women. "She's lovely." TJ returned back to Tehani.

"Okay, what are you planning?" asked Tehani, curiously.

"Just a little something special for you. I hear the fruit is amazing here in the South Pacific. Can we get some while my, um...., plan unfolds?"

TJ and Tehani had a huge serving of mangos and pineapples, and while they were eating, the Pareo maker brought over a bag and left it with TJ. She smiled and walked away.

"For you," said TJ. Tehani looked inside and saw the purple and white Pareo.

"Awww.... purple. How did you know??" laughed Tehani. She leaned over and kissed TJ on the cheek. "I love it. I'll wear it on our next date."

Yes!, thought TJ. A next date. Something as simple as the prospect of another date did TJ's soul good and would be a weapon in fighting off his demons.

Tehani took TJ on a long moped ride, and then they finally stopped near a remote beach. "This is one of my favorite spots. Very few people come here." Tehani rested the moped up against a tree. "Let's go for a walk along the beach."

"Tell me more about your friends," said Tehani to TJ as they held hands walking along the beach with their feet in the water. "Especially the two you stayed with on this trip."

"Okay, sure," said TJ, as he wondered who to begin with. "Let's start with someone I haven't told you about. Her name is Kate Ambrose. I've known her for a good chunk of my life, although we didn't fully reconnect until a few years ago. She's the kind of friend who supports you through good and bad. No matter what problems I have in my life, she gives an unfiltered opinion on the matter, but never does it in a way that's insulting. I love her to death. She has consistently offered me a place to go if I needed. I probably should have taken her up on her offer, but if I had, you and I wouldn't have met."

"Did you ever have romantic feelings for Kate?" asked Tehani.

"None at all," said TJ, decisively. "She's like a sister. And her nickname for me is Dumbass."

Tehani let out a belly laugh. "I'm sure you earned that nickname."

"I think that's Kate speak for Buddy," said TJ.

"Oh…. okay. Sure," said Tehani, smiling.

"Then there is my friend, Sophie, from Switzerland. I actually met her here in Bora Bora the first time I was here. It was on an underwater walk. She is like a female version of me," said TJ thoughtfully. "We are on the same wavelength with our love of travel and adventurous spirit. She did her best to help me out when I was in Switzerland by giving me a place to stay for a few days, and I can't thank her enough for that."

"And then you know about Neha," TJ continued. "Met her for work…. her and her friend, Raj. We became very good friends as well. I got very sick when I was in India, and she and her mom nursed me back to health."

"What caused your illness?" asked Tehani. Uh oh, thought TJ. I'm going to need to leave a lot of detail out here.

"It was a combination of food poisoning and Dengue fever," said TJ, confidently, so as trying to hide the deeper story.

"Well these three ladies sound like they mean a lot to you for various reasons. You have them spread out all over the globe, too, Mr. International!"

TJ wanted nothing more than to stop and kiss Tehani again. He stopped walking, and she stopped as soon as he did. TJ leaned in. Tehani closed her eyes and they exchanged another passionate kiss, hugging each other tight as the water from the ocean crashed into their feet. In that moment, time stopped for TJ.

Their last stop of the day was at a small outside bar on a more popular beach. Tehani had ordered them a couple of drinks. She was quietly sipping hers, just staring at TJ and smiling.

Tehani looked seriously at TJ. "TJ….is it okay that I have my library card?"

TJ looked confused. "Say what now?"

"My library card. Is it okay that I have one?"

TJ shrugged his shoulders, still confused. "Sure, I guess. Why?"

"Because I'm totally checking you out." Tehani stared at TJ, waiting for a response.

TJ slowly got it. "OH MY GOD! Was that a pickup line??" Tehani smiled. TJ busted out laughing.

"Nice one," said TJ. "Okay, I've got one too. Do you have a Band-Aid?"

"No," smiled Tehani. "Why?"

"Because I just scraped my knee falling for you!"

Tehani laughed. "Okay, let's do this."

"Do you believe in love at first sight? Or should I walk past again?" Tehani seemed to be getting a bit tipsy with her drink as she could barely say these without laughing.

It was TJ's turn. "If you were a booger, I would pick you!" This caused Tehani to spit out a little of her drink.

This was a full-on contest of silly pickup lines.

Tehani: "Treat me like a pirate, and give me that booty."

TJ: "Do you work at Subway? Because you just gave me a foot-long." With that, TJ wondered if he had gone too far. But Tehani kept laughing, and she upped the ante.

Tehani: "Hey baby, can I sit on your lap and we'll talk about the first thing that pops up?" TJ was loving this. The bar was raising. He went in for the kill.......

TJ: "After tonight, there will only be seven planets. Because I'm going to totally destroy Uranus."

Tehani looked shocked at that last one, and then started to chuckle. "Oh my God, you win. I can't top that one!"

TJ was loving Tehani's sense of humor. "Tehani, you are both beautiful and funny."

Tehani smiled sweetly at TJ, then her eyes got big. "Destroy Uranus!" she said loudly. "Awful!!!" Tehani then busted out laughing again, causing TJ to do the same.

The day finally had to come to a close and once again, TJ was at Tehani's house dropping her off. He had been looking forward to this moment again. He wanted another passionate kiss.

"TJ, today was amazing. I'm so glad to get to know you even more. I'll see you again tomorrow, if that's okay with you."

TJ couldn't say yes quickly enough. "I never want this date to end," said TJ, looking into Tehani's brown eyes.

"Your best line yet," said Tehani, as she swiftly moved in for the kiss. Tehani's hands, initially wrapped around TJ's back, moved down to caress his butt. TJ stayed good, and just let himself enjoy the kiss. A very passionate kiss that upped the intensity from the previous night.

Tehani pulled back, stared at him, and said "See you tomorrow, TJ." She started walking back to her house. TJ then heard Tehani say "Destroy Uranus" followed by another audible laugh.

TJ smiled and started back to his bungalow. The perfect day, he thought. "I think I'm falling in love with this woman," he said, softly, shocked that he was feeling this way. He stayed lost in that thought all the way home.

Chapter 31

Inseparable. That is the best description for TJ Carlson and Tehani Rey since their first kiss on the beach. As they spent more time together, TJ grew to love what appeared to be a sarcastic wit about Tehani's sense of humor, which is something that they shared. Her observations made him laugh, and even grocery shopping at the market became fun. She would pick up oranges and melons, and judge their overall quality by comparing them to her breast size. TJ would respond in kind by performing a similar test with bananas.

Their days started to blend together, with the combination of activities including going to the market, spending time sitting at the beach, visiting local stores, going to Bloody Mary's and going to different spots on the island by way of moped and taking pictures of each other.

TJ had not been this happy in a long time, so long he really couldn't quite remember. As much as he enjoyed being with Tehani, he was always nervous that if she found out more details about him, this beautiful and blossoming relationship would end. He was also concerned about himself and his health. If his relationship with Tehani turned physical, he couldn't be sure he didn't catch something during his travels. While being happy, he was also scared to death. If this relationship with Tehani fell apart, TJ might be in even worse shape than he was when he landed in Bora Bora, a thought he could not fathom.

Tehani was beginning to notice some of this weight on TJ's mind. There would be times when the happy look on his face went away or he went quiet. She was reading his signs and his body language. On occasion, she would question TJ which would quickly lead to a mood swing from TJ. He was getting concerned that she was noticing.

One afternoon, Tehani and TJ were sitting in his bungalow. Tehani had decided to ask TJ what's been on his mind. TJ wasn't prepared for the line of questioning.

"TJ……. I need you to do something for me," said Tehani.

"What is it?"

"Talk to me. I think you still have things on your mind. I feel you pulling back at some times, and it's things that really seem to be bothering you."

TJ wasn't sure how to handle the request from Tehani. He did not want this to end.

"Honestly……. there are things I haven't shared because I don't want to burden you with them. You are so kind and you make me so happy. I just don't want to ruin it. And I fear it will."

"Dammit, TJ, give me some credit. Why don't you think I can handle it? Why would anything you tell me ruin what we are building?"

"Because it's bad. Very bad," said TJ with a sigh. He was going to go the rest of the way with this. It was do or die time. If this was meant to be, he thought, she had to know everything. And if she accepts me, then we have something. If she leaves, then my life is truly over. These next few minutes would be a matter of life and death.

"Okay. Let me show you something." TJ walked over to the drawer and he pulled out the letters he had started. The ones he was incapable of finishing. He walked over to Tehani and handed her the folder.

Tehani took the folder and looked up at TJ. "What is this?"

"Just read the first letter. It was to my daughter."

Tehani took several minutes just staring at the letter. TJ knew she was thinking through what she would say next, as that letter only contained a few sentences. She finally looked at TJ. "Is this……. a suicide note to your daughter?" Tehani seemed to be in shock.

TJ hung his head down and did not respond.

"TJ……why? Were you planning on committing suicide? Here?" Tehani's question was asked with a sense of urgency.

"When I arrived here………. yes. I was in such bad shape. I truly did not want to live anymore. These last seven months have destroyed everything about me. But then………. you showed up at the beach that day."

"I don't get it TJ. What drove you to this point? You've told me the story….at least most of it, I think. Why decide to kill yourself?" Tehani wanted an answer to this question. In her mind, if she was able to extract the rest of TJ's secrets, then he could fully heal.

"I lost my sense of worth. I did not like who I was becoming when left to my own devices and whims. The demons seemed to take over, and I did things to satisfy myself that in the end only made me feel worse."

"What kind of things? What could be that bad? You didn't hurt or kill anyone, did you?"

"No, of course not, unless I'm counting myself."

"So, what is it, then? What could have been so bad that you were writing this letter to your own daughter letting her know she'd never see her father again?"

TJ realized he was unable to answer that question. Other than to explain that it was depression.

"I think it was a slowly escalating depression. It was taking over. Maybe I wasn't in my right mind."

"It certainly sounds like it," said Tehani, looking disappointed.

TJ felt that he was losing her, and decided it was time to finish this story.

"You want the rest of the story……here it is. Along with the depression was a serious problem with alcohol and a sex addiction. I couldn't begin to count the number of bottles of wine and beer that I drank. There were nights that I blacked out, there were nights that I woke up the next morning sick as a dog. And I would always solve my problems by drinking. And the sex……. everywhere I went, I was overcome with the urges. I ended up getting dozens of erotic massages, had one-night stands with strangers and visited brothels and had sex with prostitutes. All over this world. Each time I got drunk again or had sex again, I felt like less of a good person. Like an animal who was just feeding his urges. I stopped caring about everyone and everything, and they stopped caring about me. And now, Jesus Christ, I've met a goddess here in Bora Bora who genuinely seems to like me, and I am falling hard for her, but I am scared to death of losing you. I'm scared right now that you are going to get up and walk out that door. And I wouldn't blame you. I'm so damaged. You don't deserve that."

TJ sat down on the bed and started to cry uncontrollably. Tehani looked at him. She knew she had just heard the worst of the worst. This is what was holding him back. She remained quiet until it seemed like the right time.

TJ composed himself and looked over at Tehani. "I'm amazed that you're still here."

She moved over closer to him. "TJ……I don't care about any of those things you did. The only thing that will drive me away is your outright rejection of me and my feelings for you. I feel really bad about what you've experienced, but if you hadn't gone through that hell, you and I never would have met. Try looking at that bigger picture. God always has a plan. Sometimes you can't see it when you feel like you are at the bottom, but I beg you now to try and see it. Defeat these demons you're battling. Don't let them ruin this. Be a man and re-take control of your life. I can't do that for you, but I guarantee you, if you do that, I will be right there for you."

TJ looked straight ahead, really thinking hard about what Tehani was saying. He looked over at her and smiled.

"Listen…. I will be at the spot that we met at 10:00am tomorrow morning. If you want us to keep pursuing what we have started to build, you show up there at 10:00am. If you would rather to continue battling your demons and let them control you, don't show up and I'll move on with my life. Please don't let the demons win, TJ. I think we are destined to be together. Take care, tonight. I'll leave you alone with your thoughts." Tehani walked over and kissed TJ on the forehead and then left the bungalow.

TJ sat motionless for the next 30 minutes, running through that conversation in his head. He fully expected that Tehani would reject him at that point. But she didn't. Why? TJ couldn't make sense of this girl. What was it about him that was keeping her around? Almost everything she knew about him was either bad, sad or worse. He had told her of his sexual misadventures. She didn't flinch.

"What have I done to deserve her?" TJ asked out loud. "I've been an awful person, done terrible things and yet she is still wanting to be with me. I don't deserve her."

TJ paced around his bungalow for a while. It was nervous energy. He wanted Tehani, and by all appearances she wanted him too. The more he paced, the more the realization set in. Happiness was there for the taking. It was being offered to him by a beautiful, kind and caring woman who had seen the worst side of him and yet still offered happiness to him. He would be the biggest fool who ever lived if he rejected that. He had to take happiness when it was right in front of him asking to be taken.

TJ stopped pacing. Slowly, the scowl on his serious face turned to a smile. This was his moment. The moment where he was going to shed the weight of his past and seize the future. He didn't know what the future would hold with Tehani, but he was willing to take a chance. She was becoming his salvation, and more importantly to TJ, the purpose of his long journey. She was it. She was the reason he went through this. If he hadn't gone through all of the highs and the lows, he never would have met her on the beach that day. She saved his life……. or perhaps she was merely the destination of the road that he traveled.

TJ went to the desk and pulled out his suicide notes. He tore them all up into hundreds of pieces. It was a cathartic exercise. He felt that weight dropping off of him. He picked up a pile of the torn paper and threw them around the room, feeling adrenaline each time he did it. He gathered up all of the shreds of paper and took them over to the toilet. He dumped handful after handful and flushed them down the toilet until every last piece of paper was gone.

TJ went to the closet where he was storing his beer and sleeping pills. He took the pills over to the toilet and poured them all in. Once again, he flushed the toilet and watched them all get sucked away. He then walked over to the sink with his 12 pack of beer. One by one, he poured the beer down the sink until he got to the last one. He took that beer, walked over to his comfortable bungalow chair and sat down.

He held the can of beer up to the sky. "A toast to you," said TJ, "for giving me the strength to defeat my demons. For putting roadblocks in my way in my path of self-destruction. For bringing Tehani Rey into my life. For revealing the purpose of this journey. Thank you."

TJ slowly drank his beer and was now planning out his meeting with Tehani the next morning. Without a doubt, he would be there. And he wanted to make sure she knew he had chosen her over his demons and he was in it for the long haul with her. It was 11:00pm now.... he had 11 hours before he was to meet her at the beach. He wanted to sleep the time away, but adrenaline was preventing that.

He pulled out a blank piece of paper. He would have a special letter prepared for her. He wanted her to always know how profoundly she had changed his life.

Tehani,

I don't know how I can say all of the things I want to say to you. But here are a few things you should know:

You are the most beautiful woman in the world to me

You have the kindest soul of any person I have ever met

I am the luckiest man in the world

I love you

A million times over

I love you

TJ climbed into his bed, determined to get a little sleep before the next morning. He forced himself to lay there until he finally dozed off.

TJ was sitting at that exact spot on the beach where he was to meet Tehani. He lay down on his beach blanket and closed his eyes.

"Waiting for someone?" asked Darkness.

"Yup," said TJ.

"Do you really think she will be here? After everything you told her? You must think she will easily forget all of that. I don't think she will. She'll probably realize you're too damaged, and probably full of disease."

"Awwww....is that what you're hoping? Once again, fully aware that I'm dreaming. I'm glad you showed up." TJ locked eyes with Darkness. "You told me I needed to defeat you. I already have."

"What makes you think that?" asked Darkness curiously.

"Because I decided that. You're me, right? You represent me if those demons I battled overtook me and controlled me. I'm choosing happiness over being accompanied by these demons who control my mind and my thoughts. Those demons that nearly killed me. And you were their eager spokesman. Egging me on. Driving me towards oblivion. Planting the seeds in my mind that I deserved every bad thing I was willing myself to do or allowing myself to feel. Giving me only destructive advice. Capitalizing on my depression. Well fuck that. Tomorrow morning, my life will begin again. Without the demons and without you. I will start living my life again looking to the future and not buried in the past. What do you think about that? It's time for you to leave."

"Nicely done, TJ. I was more than happy to be there while you wallowed in self-pity. You deserved me and everything I represented. Good luck. I hope you never see me again, but just know what it takes to bring me back. If you come calling, I will be there." Darkness stood up, walked away and vanished. TJ assumed he would wake up at that point, but was still dreaming.

"What's left?" yelled TJ. "Bring it on!"

He sat there and waited, but nothing happened. TJ laid back down on the beach blanket and closed his eyes.

When his eyes opened, TJ was back in his bungalow on his bed. Am I still dreaming, he wondered? He looked at the time – it was 5:00am. He got up and paced around. Everything seemed real. Including the dream he had just experienced. The dream where he had just apparently defeated Darkness. Another huge step to changing everything about this journey.

TJ decided to stay up and get himself ready. He wanted to look good, smell good and be ready to profess his love to Tehani. To commit to exploring a future together. He wanted to go to that beach right at that moment, but he still had about 5 hours to go.

He finished preparing and had some coffee and breakfast. He simply couldn't wait any longer. It was now 7:30am. He could wait for two and a half hours at the beach for Tehani. He finished getting ready and headed out the door, filled with excitement, nervousness and with a butterfly loaded stomach.

TJ got close to the beach. It was now 7:50am. As he zeroed in on his beach spot, he was shocked. He couldn't believe his eyes.

Tehani was already there. Waiting for him. She had a bottle of champagne and two glasses. She had prepared a bowl of fruit. She hadn't noticed him yet. TJ was overwhelmed. He knew that she was putting the same amount of importance on this meeting as he was. He walked slowly, waiting for the moment that she would notice him.

Finally, she looked his way. Once she saw TJ, she flashed a big smile and stood up. TJ picked up his pace. Tehani held out her arms. TJ walked to the spot, dropped the bag he had brought with him, and hugged her tight. He kissed her neck, then her cheek, then a long passionate kiss on the lips.

"You're early," said Tehani.

"So are you," said TJ.

"Thank God you're here. I prayed the entire night you would show up. I could barely sleep. I love you so much, TJ. I can't imagine my life without you now."

TJ's eyes watered. He thought about giving her the note, but that would pale in comparison to how she just poured her heart out.

"I love you too, Tehani. I look forward to every day with you. I want you. Today, tomorrow and for the rest of my life."

They hugged and kissed again. Tehani was crying noticeably as they hugged.

"I'm just happy," said Tehani. "Come on, let's toast us and enjoy our day."

They sat down and drank some champagne and ate some fruit.

"I wrote you a short letter," said Tehani. "Just open it when you have a moment alone."

TJ smiled. It was time. "I also wrote you one," said TJ.

Tehani laughed. "I think we must be soulmates."

"Tehani?" asked TJ.

"Yes," she replied.

"I love you."

Chapter 32

Mom – I know it's been too long since I sent the last message. But I just want you to know that everything is okay. It's more than okay. I'll be calling the house there in the next few days. I have an amazing story to tell.   – TJ

TJ Carlson was full of life again. He felt it in every fiber of his being. He had heard clichés about having an extra bounce in his step, or even getting one's "groove" back. But for him, these were very real. One night ago, TJ and Tehani Rey professed their love for one another. TJ slayed his demons. He chose happiness over despair and had a future he was now very much looking forward to.

There was only one potential remaining problem that TJ needed to sort out.

TJ was concerned about his sexual activities in Europe, India and Asia. While he sometimes protected himself, it wasn't all the time. He had to know, before he and Tehani make love for the first time, which he knew would be happening soon. He had to know whether he had picked up any sexually transmitted diseases along the way. He was on his way to a doctor's office on this morning to hopefully get himself a clean bill of health.

The thought of it was making him nervous. What if he had? And it was something he would have a hard time getting rid of? These thoughts kept bouncing in his head along the way to the doctor. He was going to invite Tehani to his bungalow tonight, and he really wanted to give himself peace of mind. I will accept the consequence of my actions, he thought, but I hope that this turns out to be negative.

TJ met with the doctor and explained the situation. The doctor seemed enthralled with the story TJ told about his adventures. He administered the tests and TJ waited patiently for the results. Finally, the doctor called him back in.

"First of all, my friend, God is smiling down on you today. Everything turned out negative."

TJ exhaled. He quietly thanked God for the result, and then thanked the doctor.

"You don't know how happy I am to hear that," said TJ. "I was careless and should have known better. You said first of all………is there something additional?"

"Yes," said the doctor. "You need to stay clean, TJ. The illness you had in India and the amount of drinking you have been doing have likely weakened your immune system. This is a tropical environment still, and you need to be very wary of diseases like Dengue. If you get one here, you may not have the strength to fight it off."

"I understand," said TJ.

"Eat a lot of fruit, take vitamins, exercise…….and let that lady friend take good care of you. She will surely know what to do." The doctor smiled at TJ and told him he was free to go.

Tehani knocked on the door to the bungalow, which was now without a speck of dirt. TJ had spent hours preparing for Tehani's arrival. This would be the first time they laid eyes on each other since they admitted their love, and was day one of their future together.

"Good morning, baby," said TJ. "Come on in."

"Wow, look at this place," said Tehani. "Who cleaned it for you?"

"All me……are you impressed?"

"As always," she replied. "You never cease to amaze me. What would you like to do today?"

"Anything you want," said TJ. "We could go for a walk, head back to the beach, go grab some coffee or just hang out here in the bungalow."

"Let's just stay here in the bungalow," Tehani said nervously.

That was the answer TJ was hoping for. By her response, he thought maybe she had something more on her mind. "Perfect," said TJ. "I actually bought us some drinks and snacks just in case."

TJ sat down on the couch next to Tehani. They moved towards each other and started kissing. It was as passionate as their kisses had been before, but this time, Tehani's hands were doing more exploring. She slid her hands up TJ's shirt, rubbing his back as they kissed. TJ did the same, but kept his hands outside of her dress.

They stopped kissing and Tehani pulled back and stood up. She untied the straps on her dress and removed it, while staring at TJ to watch his reaction. Now in just her bra and panties, Tehani sat back down on the couch.

"TJ," she said shyly, "I am ready to show you my love. But before we do anything……I just want to know……. if you are ready."

TJ was reading between the lines on that question, and was now thankful that he had made that doctor's visit.

"Very much so. This morning, I visited the doctor. I thought we may be getting close to new steps in our relationship, and I wanted to make sure that I was………clean. And I am."

"Okay. Thank you for doing that. And I'm happy that we don't have to worry about those kinds of things."

"I would not have done anything until then," replied TJ.

"Where were we then?" asked Tehani.

They started kissing again and Tehani removed TJ's shirt. She began rubbing his chest, while TJ fumbled to remove her bra. Never the easiest of things to do. As he unhooked it. He moved his hands underneath her bra, cupping her breasts, gently squeezing them and softly pinching her nipples.

"Kiss my breasts, TJ. I love that."

TJ kissed Tehani on the lips, then slowly moved down to her neck, playing with her breasts as the kisses moved closer. Her nipples were very erect and inviting TJ's mouth. TJ took one in his mouth, sucking on it gently and flicking it with his tongue and swirling his tongue around it. Tehani moaned, obviously enjoying it, and her hands made their way to grab TJ's now very hard cock. She attempted to unbutton his pants, but TJ stood up and removed both his pants and underwear in one quick motion.

TJ licked and sucked both of Tehani's breasts as she stroked his cock. He then began to start kissing Tehani down her chest and stomach. She began breathing heavier knowing what was about to happen. TJ removed Tehani's panties, already wet, to reveal a cleanly shaven pussy. TJ didn't hesitate……he quickly buried his mouth on Tehani's pussy, licking her clit and taking it into his mouth. He ran his tongue up and down her pussy lips and then inside her pussy. Tehani was grabbing on to TJ's hair, arching her back and lifting her hips. TJ could tell she was close. He concentrated on her clit and kept sucking it until she finally came. Tehani collapsed her hips back down on the couch and looked to be out of breath.

"That was amazing," said Tehani. "You are so good at that. Now…. you get comfortable on the couch."

TJ sat on the couch and Tehani kneeled on the floor, between his legs. She ran her tongue around the tip of his cock while she continued to stroke it. In quick motions, she took his cock into her mouth. She was getting TJ close, and he decided to stop her before it was too late.

"Let's make love, right now," said TJ.

Tehani climbed on top of TJ, letting the length of him go inside her. TJ wrapped his arms around her and they kissed passionately as she grinded on him back and forth. It did not take long before TJ came. But she did not want to stop, and he did not want her to stop. She kept going, faster and faster, and TJ knew she was about to have another, rather intense, orgasm. And so was he. They perfectly timed climaxing together, and Tehani collapsed again on TJ, burying her head in his shoulders.

She pulled her head back up and kissed TJ on the lips.

"I love you," she said softly.

"I love you too."

"I'm surprised it took you so long. I thought you were about to lose it when I was going down on you."

TJ smiled at her and held up two fingers.

"Twice?? Really? Wow……. good job." Tehani laughed.

They spent the rest of the afternoon and evening in the bungalow, cuddling in TJ's bed and making love. TJ was amazed that he could just lay there with this girl, watch time fly by and be nothing but happy doing it.

Tehani needed to head back to her house. But she had a bombshell for TJ before she left.

"TJ……. it's time for you to meet my family. They want you over for dinner tomorrow night. You may get a lot of questions."

"Oh lord…….do I need to prepare?" asked TJ. "Am I going to get grilled? And then barbecued?"

"No, but just be ready. They would be hard on a Tahitian guy, but even more if you're an American."

"I'll be happy to meet your family tomorrow. I'll be at my best, don't worry."

"I'm not worried. I know they will like you." Tehani kissed TJ and then headed home.

"So, when will this gentleman be here?" asked Afa Rey, Tehani's father. Afa was an imposing figure. A large man with a sense of swagger and a good sense of humor. He was planning on putting TJ through the ringer on this evening, and then letting him off the hook. Afa was not concerned that Tehani was bringing a Westerner to the house. He trusted her judgment and knew that she did not suffer fools.

"He'll be here in an hour. Daddy…. go easy on him please. You and Fara both. I know he'll be nervous." Tehani was getting ready for TJ's arrival and preparing the last few things for their meal.

Fara Rey, Tehani's brother, was much younger than she was, by almost 9 years. He was looking forward to meeting TJ, as he had not been in contact at all with Westerners. He had seen plenty on the island, but this would be his first chance to get to really talk to and get to know one.

"I'm looking forward to meeting him. I'm curious as to why he would have picked you out of all the girls on this island. He must have impaired taste." Fara laughed and waited for his sister's response.

"He has immaculate taste, dumbass. He picked the best of the best."

"That's true, he did," Afa interjected. "There's no better catch on this island than my Tehani. How long have you known him again?"

"That's not important, daddy."

"It's only been a short time, hasn't it? Are you sure about him?" Afa wanted reassurance from his daughter that she really knew what she was doing.

"Let's just say it's a strong feeling I have when I'm with him. Like this is meant to be. It's hard to explain. You will know when you meet him."

"Why….am I going to fall for him, also?" laughed Afa, causing Fara to also laugh out loud.

"You two are idiots. Please don't embarrass me." Tehani stopped paying attention to her father and brother as they walked through what they would do if TJ fell in love with either one of them.

Finally, there was a knock on the door. It was TJ. Afa insisted he would get the door. Tehani relented and watched in apprehension as her father approached the door.

TJ had braced himself for this moment. He was very nervous, but was determined to be himself. He figured Tehani's family must be as nice as her, and if she endorsed him, they would give him the benefit of the doubt.

The door opened. A rather large man opened the door and stared at TJ. He was expressionless and was waiting for TJ to talk.

"Good afternoon, sir. I'm here to join you and Tehani for dinner tonight. I'm TJ, and you must be Tehani's father."

"Indeed I am. You can call me Afa. Although I like the word "sir" as well. We'll see how it goes tonight. Please come in."

"Thank you. It's a pleasure to meet you." TJ entered the house and saw Tehani standing there with a nervous smile on her face. TJ winked at her. He re-focused on her father. "And thank you for allowing me in your home."

"I love my daughter with everything I am, and if she insists that you are a good, kind man, then you are welcome in my home. Have a seat. We will get everything prepared." Afa led Tehani into the kitchen. A younger man approached TJ and sat down on the couch next to him.

"Hi, I'm Fara, Tehani's brother."

"Nice to meet you, Fara."

"Excuse my father. He's just giving you a hard time. He likes to joke with people. He's very friendly." Fara talked to TJ with a glimmer in his eye, like he was fascinated by him.

"I would expect nothing less from a father with a daughter he loves so much. He wants nothing but the best. Can I ask you a question? I've been shy to ask Tehani, because she never mentions it."

"What is it?" asked Fara.

"Your mother. Tehani hasn't mentioned her. She has only talked about Afa and you."

"Our mother passed away many years ago. She had cancer. Tehani doesn't like to talk about it. She was absolutely devastated. So was my father. Me too."

"I am so sorry to hear about that. My deepest condolences to all of you for that loss. I'm glad I asked you about it."

"It's good that you asked me. If you had brought it up randomly during dinner or conversation, the mood would change here quickly."

"Thank you, Fara. I can see already that Tehani has a great home and family."

"Now let me ask you something. Why my sister? I'm just curious." Fara was in all likelihood helping TJ to warm up for a grilling from Afa later in the evening.

"She's amazing. The most beautiful woman I have ever met. The day I met her very much changed my life. And she has a wonderful personality to match."

"Do westerners like Polynesian girls? Do you think the women would like us Polynesian guys?"

TJ laughed. "Ah ha……Fara, I think you are interested in getting set up with one of my friends."

"I'm just curious," said Fara. "I've never had a chance to really meet or talk to any Americans or Australians or Europeans."

"I find Polynesian girls to be beautiful, your sister being the most beautiful one. You're a handsome guy. Next time you see some western women who don't have a guy with them, go up and say hi."

"I'd be too shy to do that," said Fara.

"You never know unless you try," said TJ, who then noticed Tehani and Afa emerging from the kitchen with food. TJ got up to help, but was asked to take a seat at the table.

"You are our guest," said Afa. "Let us show you our hospitality."

Tehani sat down next to TJ at the dinner table and grabbed his hand underneath the table. He looked over at her and she smiled sweetly at him.

"So, TJ………. what are your intentions with my daughter? Now that you have captured her heart. What do you plan to do with it?" Afa opened with a question TJ was prepared for.

"I will treat it as my most valuable gift that I have been blessed with," said TJ. "Your daughter is the most special woman I have ever met. She is amazing."

"Whoa hoah……. good answer TJ," said Afa, laughing. "I think you were prepared for that one. How long are you going to be on our island, TJ? Are you planning on leaving any time soon?"

"No, sir. I have no plans to leave."

"I understand you are staying at that resort close by. That is very expensive. How much longer can you afford that?"

"I don't know. I hadn't thought about it. I suppose an apartment or something would be a better option." TJ knew he would have to leave that resort soon. It was costly, and if he had no plans to leave Bora Bora any time soon, not only would he need to find somewhere cheaper, he would need to find a way to start making some money.

"Do you have any source of income? Or are you already a millionaire?"

"I had some significant savings that I tapped into, sir. It's been enough to this point." TJ was getting nervous at this line of questioning, as it was possibly leading to a discussion of how he had spent the last several months.

"My concern is how you will be supporting my daughter. Don't worry, TJ, I know a bit of your background regarding your ex-wife and family. That doesn't matter to me, but Tehani does. I don't want her to be put in a position to support you."

"Don't worry, sir. I won't put her in that position. I've actually been thinking of things I could do here for work. Under the table, of course, since I can't actually get a job here."

Afa was silent for a few minutes as everyone focused on eating. TJ glanced over at Tehani, who shot a glance back. She mouthed "I love you", making TJ smile.

"Okay, son, I have an offer for you. We have a room here at the house. You can stay in that room for now. All I ask is that you help with things around here. And continue taking good care of my daughter. You slip up there, and you're out on your ass." Afa looked seriously at TJ, waiting for his response.

TJ thought about it for a minute. This was a big, and unexpected, step. This would definitely provide relief on his finances and have him with Tehani every day.

"Thank you, sir. I accept. I can't tell you how much this means to me. I will also look for work, so I can chip in for food and other things."

"I can help you there as well. You seem to know this island very well. There are many of us that are asked to lead special tours when visitors arrive, separate from the organized ones. I can get you connected there, and you can help lead some tour groups, providing commentary with a unique perspective."

"That sounds great," said TJ. "I would love that. Can Tehani be my partner, so they also have someone local?"

"You are already a local, son," laughed Afa. "But yes….and that way, Tehani can keep her eye on you."

"Perfect," said TJ. "Thank you again. Tehani, your family are just as amazing and kind as you are."

Tehani smiled and then turned serious. "TJ, there's one more thing you need to know about our family." TJ knew where this was heading, as he watched the mood on Afa's face change.

"I have already told him," said Fara. "It's okay……nothing more needs to be said."

TJ nodded to everyone. TJ raised his drink. "A toast to all of you. May God bless your entire family. He has already blessed me by allowing me to meet you."

Afa looked at Tehani. "He's okay, Tehani."

Tehani smiled big. "I know he is. TJ, we'll just take care of the dishes and then we can talk about you getting your things moved here."

TJ sat on the couch alone while everyone did the dishes, amazed once again at the turn of events of the evening. It had been a whirlwind few weeks. The positive things in his life were starting to build on each other, and he was deeply grateful.

TJ returned to his bungalow for what would be his last night there. This place represented the lowest of lows and highest of highs to him. He was ready to end that story and look to the future. He began packing his things. He only had one other thing he needed to take care of this evening. A promise he needed to fulfill.

He had sent a message to his mother the previous day, which elicited an ecstatic response. She was anxiously awaiting his call.

"Hi Mom," said TJ, as soon as Ann Carlson answered the phone.

"TJ…. thank God! Hold on, I'm putting you on speaker phone. Your father and brother are here."

"Hi everyone."

"Where are you?" asked Ann.

"I'm in Bora Bora," TJ replied.

"Nice!" shouted Harold. "I should have known that's where you'd end up."

"How long have you been there, son? Why haven't we heard from you in so long? You can't imagine how worried we were."

"I can imagine," said TJ, "and your worries were well founded. I was in bad shape when I arrived here. Very bad shape."

"What do you mean?" asked Ann.

"I'd rather not get into it. It's a story for another day. But now, things are very much looking up, and I'm taking steps to rebuild my life."

"What happened there in Bora Bora to change things? Did you meet someone?" asked Ann.

"Yes, I've met someone very special. She changed everything. She helped turn me around. She very much saved me from an abyss. Her name is Tehani."

"Tahitian girl?" asked Harold.

"Yes. Absolutely stunning and beautiful. The most beautiful woman I have ever met."

"So, what are you two doing there? When are you coming back here? Your kids miss you deeply, son. They need to have you back."

"I know," said TJ. "I need some more time here. I don't want to come back there without Tehani."

"What are you saying, son? How long will that be?" Ann sounded concerned at the vagueness of TJ's plans.

"Just give me more time. I still need to get myself more straightened out before I come back. But I want to arrange a conversation with the kids. Can you have them there at the house? I want to call on video and talk to them."

"Yes, of course we will do that. TJ……. please stay in touch each day. And give us numbers and addresses of where you are. We don't want to go through this stretch of not knowing again."

"I will. Listen, I will be moving in to Tehani's family home for now and doing a bit of work to try and rebuild some funds. I'll send you their address and phone number."

"Wow, moving into her home? This must be very serious, son." Ann sounded shocked at that revelation.

"I met her family tonight. Her father offered me the place to stay so I wouldn't have to keep paying for where I am staying now."

"Well, I for one cannot wait to meet this woman who has had such a significant impact on your life. I'm assuming Paige and the kids don't know about her yet."

"No, I haven't talked to them in a long time. I really want to talk to the kids soon."

"Yes, of course, son. We'll arrange it. We are all glad you are okay. We hope this is the beginning of the end of this journey you have been on."

"It certainly seems that way, mom. I am looking forward to it ending as well."

TJ and his parents ended the call, and TJ felt another sense of relief in re-connecting with the world he left behind. He put together messages for Neha Ganesh, Kate Ambrose and Sophie Kiebler:

Hi there – just messaging to let you know I'm okay. I made it to the other side of the tunnel. Thank you for supporting me. I'll never forget it.

He then put together a message for Steven:

Steven – Grandma is going to arrange a video call and will be asking that you and Elizabeth be there at the house for it. Make sure you are there. I want nothing more than to see both of your faces again. It's the most important thing in the world to me right now. I love you both.

Chapter 33

"Come on, kids……your dad can't wait to talk to you," said Ann Carlson hurriedly as she expected TJ's call at any moment. It would be the first time that Steven and Elizabeth Carlson would be talking to their dad in months.

"I wonder if he looks the same," said Elizabeth, as she checked herself in the mirror to make sure she looked pretty. "I wonder where he's been."

"I hope he's not still mad at me," said Steven.

"I'm sure he's not, honey. Don't worry about that. Your father has been through a lot, and he's missed you two very much." Ann signed in to the computer and waited for TJ's call.

TJ Carlson was nervous as he prepared to call home and see everyone for the first time in what seemed like forever. Tehani rubbed his shoulders and kissed him on the cheek, then left him alone in his room.

He wasn't really even sure where to start. What could he possibly tell them to explain away these many months of him not being there? He wondered if the kids would look more grown up now. After this, he knew the urge would be incredibly strong to see them again. He had already started future planning, but they were seeds planted in his mind that he needed to let grow.

He signed in to the computer and dialed Ann Carlson.

"Oh my God, son. You look good. Better than I expected. Thank God we are here talking to you. We love you so much." Ann Carlson was fighting back tears as she saw her son on video.

"Thanks Mom. I'm sorry for all the heartburn I've caused. I love you all too." As TJ opened the conversation with his mother, a smiling Elizabeth peeked to the side of the camera to see her father. As soon as TJ saw that, he felt overcome with joy and couldn't control his smile. Ann Carlson knew what was happening, and knew she needed to hand over the spotlight.

"I think someone here is really wanting to talk to you," said Ann as she stood up and set Elizabeth up in the chair. Elizabeth had a big grin on her face, and seemed fascinated by looking at her father.

"Hi, sweetie. Daddy loves you," said TJ.

"Hi Daddy!! I love you too. Where are you?"

"I'm in a place called Bora Bora, sweetie. I showed you pictures of it when I went before, do you remember?"

"Not really. Are you coming home soon?"

"Yes, sweetie, I am."

"Hooray!" yelled Elizabeth. "Daddy, when you get home, can you take me to the movies?"

"As many movies as you want."

"Okay, I'll make a list," she said happily.

"Great!" said TJ. "How are you, sweetie?"

"I'm okay, Daddy. I just miss you. I miss our bedtime stories."

"I know....so do I." TJ sensed some sadness in Elizabeth and knew he needed to get back there for her. "Listen sweetie, Daddy is going to finish things here, then I will come home. I will set things up so that Steven will receive messages to you and you can respond until then, okay? Every day I will send you something."

"Okay Daddy. I can't wait to see you."

TJ and Elizabeth engaged in some more small talk that in TJ's mind could have gone all night. He was completely satisfied talking like this to his daughter and didn't want it to end. Finally, Steven interrupted Elizabeth and asked for time to talk. Elizabeth begrudgingly gave over the computer to Steven.

"Hi dad," said Steven.

"Hey son…. how is everything?"

"It's okay. Listen, I wanted to say I'm sorry for that message. I was just angry, but I shouldn't have done that." Steven seemed genuinely upset as he said that apology.

"Son, you had every right to be angry. Don't worry about anything. I would have been angry too. You and Elizabeth did not deserve to go through this. I am so sorry."

"It's okay Dad. I understand now. Everything is fine, and we can't wait until you get home."

"Me too, son."

TJ and Steven also carried on some small talk for a while, not one of Steven's strong suits. TJ let him off the hook.

"Son, I'll be messaging you both quite a bit before I come home. For both of you. I just ask that you stay on top of those, okay?"

"Sure, dad. No problem."

"Okay, good. You can put Grandma back on."

Ann Carlson got back in front of the computer. "Bet that felt good," she said.

"It gave my soul something it desperately needed. I couldn't be happier."

"I can't wait to meet Tehani. What are your plans?"

"Not sure yet, but I'm working on something. I'd love for the two of you to talk like this soon."

"Whenever she's ready, son," said Ann. "Here's your father."

Harold Carlson leaned over Ann, leaving himself about half cut off on the camera. He didn't care. TJ knew this would be short and sweet.

"Hi son, Bora Bora again, huh? And bagged a Tahitian girl this time. Nicely done. Can't wait to meet her."

"Hands off, you pervert," laughed TJ. "She's amazing."

"I'm sure she is. Say hi to your brother."

Dean Carlson leaned down next to Ann. "Hey douchebag, I was nearly sent all over this planet to look for you. Get your ass home."

"Will do, sir," said TJ.

That was all from Dean. TJ laughed. He wrapped up the conversation with his mother and before he was about to hang up, he asked his mother to wait a second.

TJ waved Tehani into the room. "Please come say hi to my mom," said TJ.

Tehani walked slowly and nervously into the room. TJ sat back down and had Tehani sit on his lap.

"Mom, I'd like you to meet Tehani Rey."

Ann Carlson smiled. "Hello young lady."

"Hello, Mrs. Carlson," said Tehani. "So nice to finally meet you."

"Likewise. I look forward to getting to know you. You both take care."

TJ ended the call to home and immediately hugged and kissed Tehani. "I needed that more than anyone can ever imagine."

"I know you did," said Tehani. "I'm so happy for you. I hope your kids will like me."

"They will. Don't worry. Everyone will like you."

Tehani kissed TJ again and went to fix them both a celebratory drink.

The days passed and TJ settled into a groove of work, quality time with Tehani, keeping in touch with family and friends and getting in good with Tehani's father and brother. On this day, TJ had set up a meeting with someone that would play a very important role with his future plans in Bora Bora. The lady was in her mid-40's, very classy, and looked like she knew everyone on the island.

"Mr. TJ, don't you worry about a thing. We'll make this happen and it will be something you will never forget."

"Thanks – I want you to make sure it's great, beyond my wildest dreams."

"That's my job," she said.

"Good. I'll be talking to you very soon."

TJ didn't usually make it a point to corner Afa Rey and talk to him alone. He definitely had something on his mind and only Afa Rey could offer him advice.

Afa had grown to like TJ, as it appeared he worked hard, treated his daughter well, and showed him respect. On this night, he was not prepared for what TJ had cornered him about.

"Tehani, let's go to Bloody Mary's tonight," said TJ matter-of-factly.

"Okay," she said. This was not an uncommon request from TJ, as once every few days, TJ would ask her to go there to unwind and grab a drink.

They made their way there and settled down and ordered a drink. All of a sudden, Afa Rey walked in, looking disturbed.

"Tehani……I need to speak with you." Afa seemed upset, which alarmed Tehani. Tehani looked at TJ, who also seemed a bit shocked.

"Do you know what this is about," asked Tehani.

"No…. but now I'm worried. He really looks upset."

Tehani got up and headed towards the door, where Afa was standing.

"Daddy, what is it?" she asked.

"It's about loverboy over there. We had a very interesting conversation." Tehani and Afa stepped outside.

"Listen, you are a big girl, and I know you can make your own decisions, but I'm not 100% sure about him. I still don't feel like you know him very well and yet you are getting so serious."

"Where is this coming from? Why now? And how did you know we were here?" Tehani seemed puzzled by this uncharacteristic behavior from her father.

"It bothered me enough that I had to come here, to bring you back home. Let's go. We will continue this conversation at home."

"No.... you haven't explained this to me. I don't mean to be disrespectful, but up until now, everything has been fine. You have welcomed him into our home, gave him work and almost treated him like a son. What did he do wrong?"

"I don't have to explain myself to you, Tehani. Let's go now."

"Fine," said Tehani. "But I'm going back in there to let him know."

As Tehani walked back in to Bloody Mary's, she figured out what her father was talking about.

Arranged on the floor were tiare flower petals that spelled out "Tehani, will you marry me?" TJ knelt down next to the flower petals holding out a ring towards Tehani. Tehani started to cry. She looked back at her father, who was standing there smiling. Afa nodded his head at her.

Tehani walked slowly towards TJ, smiling and crying. She took some flower petals from the word "Tehani" and spelled out "Yes". TJ watched and also started to cry as he realized what she was doing. As soon as she was done, she put her finger out and TJ put on the ring.

"I love you TJ. I will be proud to be your wife." Tehani hugged TJ and they kissed. The patrons at Bloody Mary's erupted in applause, and TJ and Tehani posed for pictures for everyone.

On the way home, as they walked hand in hand, Tehani leaned her head on TJ's shoulder.

"That was brilliant. The way you did that. But my father is a terrible actor."

TJ laughed and agreed. "I actually didn't think he was going to pull that off. I had a talk with him about it, and he seemed like it was going to be easy for him, but I knew you wouldn't believe he was angry at me."

"I didn't. But I didn't expect what you did. That was wonderful and perfect. Just like you." Tehani kissed TJ on the cheek and TJ swore he could see Tehani skipping as she walked.

TJ revealed to Tehani a few days later that he had already started talking to a wedding planner. "I met her before I proposed, because I didn't know much about Polynesian weddings and wanted to get something going."

"That's okay. Do you mind if I take it from here? I know exactly what I want."

"Sure," replied TJ. "I'll get her number for you."

"Thanks. Love you." Tehani took the number and walked out of the room.

Unknown to TJ, Tehani had cooked up a plan to get three of TJ's best, and most supportive friends, to attend and be part of this wedding. She wanted to shock TJ with a few of her bridesmaid selections. She put together a message to send to Sophie Kiebler, Kate Ambrose and Neha Ganesh. She wanted to not only invite them to their wedding on Bora Bora, she wanted to have them be a part of her bridal party. Tehani had discussed the plan with Afa, who had agreed to help all three get to Bora Bora.

Tehani thought a lot of those three girls. Because at one point or another on TJ's rough journey, the three of them tried their very best to help TJ through it and gave him a world of support. If it hadn't been for them, perhaps TJ never would have made it to Bora Bora to begin with.

Tehani was excited as she got positive responses right away from Kate and Sophie. She swore them to secrecy. It took a little more persuading with Neha.

Tehani – thank u so much for the invitation. I looked up Polynesian weddings and saw the outfits the bridesmaids will wear. I can't do it if I will need to wear that. But if I can wear a traditional Indian outfit, I will be okay.

(Tehani's Reply) Hi Neha – yes, you can wear whatever makes you most comfortable. All that matters is that you are here with us.

(Neha's Reply) Okay, count me in. Thank God TJ found you.

Armed with a bridal party, and the contact information of the wedding planner, Tehani Rey set off to plan her perfect wedding.

Their wedding day had arrived. TJ had not only spent the 6 weeks since the proposal planning the wedding with Tehani, but rebuilding relationships back home. He followed through on his promise to message or talk to his kids each day and also kept close contact with his parents. TJ had not yet introduced Tehani to Steven and Elizabeth yet. But Tehani had built a close relationship with Ann Carlson, who assured Tehani that it was okay to wait where TJ's children were concerned.

TJ's outfit had been prepared for him. A white shirt with colorful vertical stripes, white pants and sandals. The wedding was to take place on the beach where they met, which was TJ's only condition for the ceremony. He took his time getting dressed, all the while reflecting on where his journey had brought him.

Tehani saw her white dress hanging there and was excited to put it on. At Afa's request, Tehani was wearing a conservative dress. However, the bridesmaids were anything but conservative. Kate Ambrose and Sophie Kiebler were putting on their grass skirts and coconut shell bikini top, and laughing it up.

"Oh my God! I can't believe I agreed to this," said Kate. "No one wants to see this much of me, and I can't believe my tits fit in these coconuts!"

"You look great," reassured Sophie. "How do I look?"

"I wish I had your body," said Kate. "Then I would look as hot as you do."

"You both look great," said Neha Ganesh, wearing a traditional Indian Sari dress.

"How come she gets off not having to wear this?" asked Kate.

"It was a condition," said Tehani, as she got her dress on. "She was a tough negotiator."

Tehani was finally ready, and she turned around to show her three bridesmaids.

"Stunning," said Kate. "You are gorgeous." Sophie and Neha nodded their heads in agreement.

"Thank you all. For being here for me, and for TJ. He will be so happy to see all of you. One last hug before we head out there."

The girls had a group hug. One by one, they would walk out on to the beach after TJ and his groomsmen, Martin the bartender and Fara Rey, Tehani's brother, had gotten themselves in place. They were all looking forward to surprising TJ one by one.

The bridesmaids all watched out the window as the groomsmen and TJ all got themselves in place near the priest. The priest was wearing a white robe with a colorful head dress and neck adornment. All of them looked at each other as TJ walked up to where the altar was.

"I'm sure you both have incredible stories to tell about him," said Kate to Sophie and Neha.

It was time. The music started playing that was to usher the bridesmaids and Tehani to the altar. The girls had picked their order. Neha would go first, followed by Sophie and then Kate.

"I'm nervous," said Neha. "I hope I don't trip as I walk out there."

The girls laughed and then indicated to Neha that it was time to walk out there.

TJ stood anxiously at the altar. Tehani hadn't told him who her bridesmaids were. He never really met any of her female friends, and he was very curious. The music hit, and TJ turned to face the area where the bridesmaids and then Tehani would emerge. His jaw dropped as he saw the first bridesmaid emerge.

It was Neha! TJ's open mouth turned into a big smile, and he was overcome with happiness. Neha smiled shyly at him as she walked to her position. As she stood still, she blew TJ a kiss. TJ put his hand on his heart and smiled at her. Tehani had delivered a shocker. Then she delivered another one.

Sophie Kiebler emerged, wearing a quite revealing outfit, but looking absolutely amazing. She gave a thumbs up sign to TJ as she got into her position. She grabbed Neha's hand, who laughed at TJ's reaction to the both of them being there. Then, the biggest surprise of all.

Kate Ambrose emerged, and strutted towards the altar like a supermodel, making TJ laugh hard and providing a show for all the Rey family friends who gathered. Fara Rey seemed especially enamored with Kate as she took her position. Kate grabbed Sophie's hand. Then all three walked towards TJ.

TJ stepped forward to meet the girls, and all four embraced in a touching group hug, eventually pulling into a huddle directed by Kate.

"You have found an amazing woman, TJ," said Kate. "She loves you with everything she has. You deserve her and the happiness she will bring you. Don't ever make her cry with sadness, or the three of us will kick your ass."

TJ laughed and assured the girls. "No need to worry, this girl will be treated like a queen and I will love her until the end of time. Thank you all for being here. I can't begin to tell you how shocked and happy I was to see each of you. And how amazed I was that Tehani was able to keep this a secret."

"Congratulations, TJ. Super happy for you," said Sophie. "And I wouldn't hesitate to come back to this place, where we met."

"Now, go marry that girl, dumbass," said Kate. "We have enough time to BS after this is done."

"Yes, ma'am," said TJ with a salute. He returned to the groom's position, then all eyes were where Tehani was to be led to the altar by her father.

"Are you ready, my daughter?" said Afa.

"Yes, daddy," said Tehani, with one last look in the mirror.

"I'll be proud to call him 'son'," said Afa.

Tehani emerged arm in arm with Afa Rey and they made their way to the altar. Afa was dressed in full Polynesian dress, casting an imposing figure as he approached TJ with a serious look on his face. He stuck out his hand. TJ proceeded to get the most painful handshake he had ever received. Afa smiled at TJ, then took his seat in the front row.

A dance performance took place as the party watched, featuring young and older teens performing a traditional Tahitian dance. Once the performance was complete, the priest had TJ and Tehani join hands.

After reciting a few words, the priest turned to TJ.

"Do you, TJ Carlson, take this woman, Tehani Rey, to be your wife?

"I do," said TJ.

"Do you, Tehani Rey, daughter of Afa Rey, take this man, TJ Carlson, to be your husband?

"I do," said Tehani.

"Then by my powers, I now introduce to everyone the new bride and groom and newest members of our Bora Bora family, TJ and Tehani Carlson."

Everyone stood up and cheered as TJ and Tehani kissed.

"I love you, TJ," Tehani whispered in his ear.

"I love you too," mouthed TJ. "Mrs. Carlson."

They kissed again, then turned to face everyone. It was all cheers and smiles, then the performers came out again and performed another dance routine.

The reception was to begin at nightfall on the beach, where they would enjoy a full Polynesian meal and performances by fire dancers. TJ made it a point to go and personally thank Neha, Kate and Sophie for being there and for the role that they played in his journey, keeping him afloat, and letting him know that he still had good friends who cared about him.

Kate Ambrose's evening became dominated by Fara Rey, who was obviously smitten. Kate was still wearing her bridesmaid outfit, while Sophie had changed into a Polynesian style outfit, she had bought on her first stay there.

"It's become strangely comfortable," said Kate. "Not often I get to let it all hang out like this." Fara, her admirer, certainly seemed to agree.

Neha sat quietly at a table, but she was joined there by Afa. Afa kept Neha company, and Neha seemed to be enjoying an animated conversation with the big man. Sophie was talking to Martin and his wife and children. TJ wasn't sure if Sophie had met Martin when she stayed at that bungalow, but they certainly looked like they knew each other.

TJ and Tehani toasted everyone who had joined them as they sat down to eat the main meal.

"To all of you, to my beautiful wife Tehani, to my new family and to my new friends and to Neha Ganesh, Sophie Kiebler and Kate Ambrose, who traveled a long way to make this an even more unforgettable event, I offer you a toast to your health, happiness and good fortune. Coming to this island saved my life and changed everything I thought I knew about the world. I will now and forever consider this a home and all of you my family. Love to each and every one of you." TJ held up his glass, and all others followed suit.

TJ and Tehani stayed on the beach until the very last people left for the evening. It was down to them and Afa, Fara and Kate.

"Kate will be staying at our place tonight," said a smiling Fara.

"I have a fan," said Kate, smiling.

"Obviously," said TJ. "Adorable."

The final bonus of the wedding of TJ and Tehani was to be revealed back at the Rey home. All of Tehani's things had been moved in to TJ's room. They were finally allowed to openly sleep together in the house. Not that they hadn't broken that rule many times. They all headed back to the house.

TJ and Tehani laid in the bed facing each other. "I'm so happy," said Tehani.

"So am I," said TJ.

"We videotaped the whole thing for your US family," said Tehani. "Well, all but what's about to happen," she smiled.

TJ laughed. "I don't think they'd want to see this."

TJ and Tehani made love and then fell asleep in each other's arms.

TJ began finalizing plans to return to the USA with Tehani.

"Son, all I ask is that you bring her back here every couple of years. I need to see her and my future grandchildren." Afa was having a heart to heart with TJ, knowing full well that he was planning on taking Tehani to the US.

"I will, sir. I wouldn't pass up the opportunity to return here. I wasn't kidding.... this is just as much a home to me as the USA is."

"Good. And always, take care of her and treat her well. She loves you with all her heart."

"I feel the same. She's my everything." TJ reached his hand out, and tried to match the ferocity of Afa's handshake.

"That was better," said Afa. "Work on it."

"Is it really you, Mr. Carlson?" Rose Carter was shocked to hear from TJ. "Every so often, I thought about you and wondered what had happened. I became kind of invested in your story."

"Rose, it's time. Papeete to Fayetteville, North Carolina."

"You never left Tahiti, huh? TJ, one day I would love to meet you and hear your story. You could probably write a book about it."

"I would also love to meet you, Rose. I will tell you that I met and married an amazing woman here. So, make that two tickets."

"Oh, my heavens!" exclaimed Rose. "Congratulations to you! I love stories with happy endings."

"Thank you, Rose. And thank you for thinking about me and showing concern when it was obvious I was going through some hard times."

"Of course, sweetie. I can sense when I'm talking to a good person. I'm glad things worked out for you. Just give me her information and I will take care of you both. I would love to meet her as well. If you are ever in Atlanta, please let me know. I'll send you my contact information in a separate email. Congratulations again, TJ." Rose Carter hung up the phone.

TJ's thoughts now began to turn to going home. The end of his journey, this time, was finally here. He was going home on his terms and could focus on rebuilding his life in the USA with the love and support of Tehani. And his children would finally have their father back. With a bonus Mommy, as he had decided to introduce Tehani to them.

"Tehani, we are all set."

"Okay, TJ. I'm so nervous. I'm excited but scared to meet your kids. And your ex-wife."

"Everything will be just fine, my love." TJ gave her a hug. They looked around their room.

"Time to start packing what I want to bring," said Tehani. "I'll have my brother ship the rest."

TJ watched her as she started to actively collect the things she wanted. TJ was finally at peace with the world around him. He was finally ready to go home.

Chapter 34

Leaving Bora Bora was going to be difficult. TJ Carlson knew that.
He owed this island his life that it saved. His last night was spent
celebrating at Bloody Mary's with Tehani, her family, their friends
and all the lucky patrons who showed up there that night. A
fitting goodbye to a place that will forever live in TJ's heart.

He and Tehani boarded the plane at the airport in Bora Bora that
was going to take them to Papeete, Tahiti. The first leg of a
marathon that was going to go to Los Angeles, Charlotte and
finally Fayetteville. TJ would have plenty of time to think and
reflect about this journey, and prepare to see the family he left
behind 8 months ago.

The short flight to Papeete was very quiet. Tehani was sleepy and
rested her head on TJ's shoulder. Every so often, TJ would glance
over at her to make sure this really wasn't a dream. That the
woman sitting next to him was now his wife and coming home
with him. What did I do to deserve this beautiful woman, he
wondered?

They boarded the Air Tahiti Nui flight to Los Angeles. Tehani
revealed to TJ that the flight they just took was the first time
she'd ever been on a plane, and she was nervous and scared to
get on this giant airplane to fly across the ocean. TJ comforted
her as best as he could.

"Don't worry…. we'll get you liquored up and off to sleep. Thank
God we have business class seats." TJ's last request to Rose
Carter – business class seats! Seemed like a smart move now.

Their flight touched down in Los Angeles 8 hours later. After 8 months, TJ was back in the United States. The immigration officer thumbed through his passport. "Quite a trip you've been on, sir. Eight months, is it? Why so long?"

"I've been just traveling the world. A lifelong dream," said TJ, hoping the guy would buy it. He did. TJ and Tehani had a long layover and found a lounge to rest in.

"Are you getting nervous?" asked Tehani.

"Yes. Are you?"

"What are you most nervous about?" she asked curiously.

"Honestly, I don't know. Maybe facing Paige. We haven't talked in months. I asked my mother to let her know about us."

"I understand. She's not going to get violent with me, is she?" Tehani asked it jokingly but waited for a response from TJ.

"Of course not. She should be happy for me and for us."

Taking advantage of the free wine in the lounge was having an effect on the two of them, as they were slightly buzzed as they boarded to flight from Los Angeles to Charlotte. They slept through the flight and before they realized it were landing in Charlotte. They had a short layover here before their puddle jumper to Fayetteville.

They boarded the last flight, which was over in a heartbeat. TJ Carlson had returned to Fayetteville, 8 months after the fateful night he got in the car and drove away. The feeling was indescribable to him. He was close to seeing his kids again. He was looking forward to that bearhug from Elizabeth. He couldn't wait to introduce Tehani to everyone.

It was nearly midnight when they arrived, so they rented a car and booked a hotel room for a few nights. Early the next morning, they would head to the house of Ann and Harold Carlson.

They arrived at the hotel, only 2 miles from the Carlson house. "Are you tired?" asked Tehani.

"No, not really," TJ replied. I think I had a full night of sleep on all those flights."

"I'm not either. Let's make love." Tehani smiled at TJ. "And make it a memorable one for my first time here in the USA."

TJ obliged, and they wore each other out, finally dozing off at 4:00am.

TJ and Tehani made the short drive to the Carlson house the next morning. As they made the turn into the street, TJ saw something that both shocked and unnerved him. He thought he would be seeing just his parents and brother on this morning, and then have time to prepare for the kids, and for Paige. But Paige's car was there already. TJ had to brace himself and get himself prepared quickly. A confrontation with Paige, a reunion with his kids and his family, and an introduction to Tehani.

"Are you okay? That look on your face….," said Tehani.

"They are already there. Everyone is there. Get ready."

"Oh my," replied Tehani. "Don't worry TJ, everything will be fine. I look forward to meeting this woman. I'm curious as to what her problem is and why she treated you so badly."

They pulled in to the driveway. TJ could see Elizabeth's face looking out the window, and saw it turn into a big smile when she saw who it was in the car. Elizabeth came charging out the door.

"It's bearhug time," said Tehani.

TJ got out of the car and Elizabeth jumped towards him. TJ caught her in midair and the bearhug commenced. Tehani put her hand over her mouth concealing a big smile.

"Daddy, daddy, daddy!!" shouted Elizabeth. "You're home!"

"Yes, sweetie. I was really looking forward to this hug." TJ held her in the air for as long as he could and then set her down. "I think you've grown and gotten heavier," laughed TJ.

"Daddy, who is she?" Elizabeth could no longer ignore Tehani and was very curious.

"Sweetie, go get Steven and I'll introduce you both," TJ replied.

"Okay!" Elizabeth skipped and jumped her way back to the house and in a few minutes emerged with Steven.

Steven walked up to TJ. TJ stuck out his hand for a handshake. Steven went to grab it, and TJ pulled him in for a hug.

"Hey dad," said Steven, after pulling away from the hug. "Glad you're back."

"Kids, I would like you to meet Tehani Rey Carlson. This is daddy's new wife. Your mother and I are no longer married. You can think of Tehani as your bonus mommy. The two of you are so lucky that you will now have three parents who will love and support you." TJ studied his kids' reactions. He didn't think he would end up being so blunt, but was also proud of himself for just saying it and getting it out there.

"Hi Steven and Elizabeth. I'm very, very happy to meet you." Tehani smiled at both kids and also waited for a reaction.

Both kids looked at Tehani. Steven was expressionless. Elizabeth was mimicking Steven, but was concealing a smile, which she finally gave in to.

"Hi," said Elizabeth. "Where did you meet my daddy?"

"On a beautiful island. Your father is a wonderful man. I'm very lucky," replied Tehani.

"Nice to meet you," said Steven, awkwardly.

"Have you met our mommy yet?" asked Elizabeth, causing TJ to shudder a bit.

"No, not yet," said Tehani, "but I'm sure I will soon."

No sooner had that been said, TJ noticed Paige leaning on the doorframe, still inside the house, but watching what was unfolding out in the driveway. TJ was now preoccupied with Paige, and what she would do next. He didn't have to wait long. Tehani made the first move.

"Excuse me kids. I will go meet your mommy." Tehani shot TJ a look of confidence and walked towards the door. TJ also couldn't help but notice another audience watching what was happening. His mother and father were parked at a window looking out. TJ finally caught their eye. He saw his father chuckling, and his mother looking nervously.

Tehani approached Paige. Paige did not make a move.

"Hello, Paige. How are you?" asked Tehani.

"Hello, Tehani. I'm doing fine. It's nice to finally meet you." Paige stared a hole through Tehani.

"Listen, I just wanted to break the ice here. I know this is going to be awkward."

"Not necessarily," said Paige. "I'm happy for the two of you." Her demeanor then changed to a friendlier one. "I want him to be happy. I think you probably saved him from something really bad."

"He was not in good shape when I met him," replied Tehani. "He tells me all the time that I saved him. He's a wonderful man. As happy as he was to meet me, I was twice as happy to meet him."

"Listen, I won't promise to be the best of friends, but if you ever need anything, just let me know. Let me go talk to him for a minute, then I'll leave and let everyone get reacquainted." Paige walked past Tehani and headed towards TJ.

TJ stood at attention, clueless as to what just happened. Until he saw Tehani flash a thumbs up sign. God love her, thought TJ.

"Welcome back," said Paige, who gave TJ a hug. "She's wonderful, TJ. And I'm jealous of how gorgeous she is. I'm very happy for you. Don't worry, you won't get any drama from me."

"Thank you…. for all of that. I'm sorry I was gone for so long, especially for the kids."

"It was rough for them, but that's past. You can make it up to them. I'm just glad this didn't end differently. That was what I was most worried about."

"You had every reason to be," said TJ. "a lot of it wasn't pretty. But it was all part of the journey."

"I'll head home now. The kids can stay here as long as you want." Paige headed to her car.

"Thanks again Paige," said TJ. Paige waived to TJ and Tehani, who had just rejoined him, as well as the kids who had watched all of that quietly.

"Daddy, where will you and Miss Tehani be staying?" asked Elizabeth. "Can you stay at our house?"

"I'm not sure that's a good idea to stay at the house, sweetie," replied TJ, hoping his daughter would not be disappointed. "But we will be close by, so I can see you every day."

"Okay, good. What about reading me bed time stories?"

"We'll figure that out," said TJ.

"Miss Tehani………. will you read me bedtime stories too?"

"Oh, of course," said Tehani. "And I'll be a better actor than your daddy."

Elizabeth smiled and moved closer to Tehani. "How did you meet my daddy?"

"On the beach. He was getting sunburned. I had to make sure he didn't turn bright red, like a lobster." TJ laughed at how cute that story sounded.

"I love the beach. Can we go sometime?" asked Elizabeth.

"Absolutely. We can go whenever you want."

Elizabeth hugged Tehani. Steven laughed as he stood there watching quietly. "I'm going to go play now, daddy. Tell me when it is time for lunch." Elizabeth and Steven left the dining room, where this conversation had taken place. As soon as the kids left, Ann and Harold Carlson walked in to the room.

"Everything go okay?" asked Ann Carlson.

"Better than I could have ever hoped," said TJ. "Mom and dad, this is my wife, Tehani."

"Pleasure to meet you, my dear," said Ann.

"Watch out for my dad," said TJ. "He loves Polynesian women."

"And so do you, apparently, son," laughed Harold. "I think you made the finest choice on Bora Bora."

"Don't you mean, all of French Polynesia, Mr. Carlson?" laughed Tehani.

"I like her, son. Yes, my mistake Tehani. And please, call me Dad." Harold Carlson had rarely been so kind and charming. TJ was caught off-guard. He really was going to need to keep an eye on his father around Tehani.

"TJ, we're going to plan a big family get together to celebrate your return home. We'll invite your cousins and whatever friends you want. Should we invite Paige?" asked Ann.

"Actually mom, I think she would decline anyway, but go ahead. As a courtesy."

"She was actually very nice to me," said Tehani. "She said if I ever needed anything, to let her know."

"She surprised me a bit," said TJ. "But then again, she'd been over me for a long time, so she's probably relieved."

"She had the same concerns we did while you were gone," said Ann. "So, she cared. As the father of your kids."

"I know," said TJ. "I'm not sure I can ever make up for that."

"You already have," said Ann. "By being here now."

Ann Carlson looked like she was about to get emotional. "Tehani, can I talk to you in the kitchen about something?"

Ann and Harold both walked into the kitchen with Tehani.

"Dear, we both just wanted to say Thank You for saving our son. I don't know what would have happened to him without you. In our eyes, you are an angel."

"Mom and Dad, TJ was just going through a rough time. Deep down, I knew what kind of a man he was. I love him more than anything. And look at it this way, if he hadn't gone through what he did, I never would have met him. It was all part of that "journey" he was on, as he likes to call it."

"Well, we are thankful you were there at the beach that day. And thrilled that we have our son back, with an amazing new part of our family in you, and that the kids have their father back home." Ann gave Tehani a big hug. "Thank you," said Ann.

All three returned to the dining room. Another quick thumbs up from Tehani.

They headed back to their hotel room to call it a night.

"Are you coming to bed, baby?" asked Tehani. "You have to be tired after that."

"Amazingly, I'm not tired," said TJ. "But looks like I wore you out."

TJ walked over and kissed Tehani. "You know, I can't stop thinking about what an amazing journey I took and story I have to tell. I keep re-living it in my head."

"You should write a book about it," said Tehani, right before a big yawn.

"I know…. I really should," said TJ, laughing. "For adults only."

"Good night," said Tehani. "Don't stay up too late."

"So, you met the other woman. How did you stop yourself from tearing into her?" asked Kylie, as she sipped her wine sitting at a bar with Paige.

"Honestly, Kylie, I'm over it. If this is the life TJ has decided he wants, I won't stop him. I fleeced him in the divorce, so I've got no further interest." Paige tried to hide her sadness from Kylie, but Kylie wasn't buying it.

"Bullshit, Paige. I know you better than that."

Paige was getting annoyed. "What do you want from me? To say that I hate him and want to make his marriage fail. I'm not going there."

"It's okay, Paige. We can stop talking about this." No sooner had the words come out of Kylie's mouth, then a handsome, well-dressed gentleman in his early 30's walked up to where they were sitting.

"Can I buy either of you ladies a drink?" said the man.

"My friend here would love one," said Kylie. "Perfect timing, I need to get home to the hubby. Good thing you aren't married, Paige." Kylie said that last line before she gave Paige a quick hug. "You're welcome," whispered Kylie. Paige watched Kylie walk out the door, then turned around to see the man heading back to the table with two beers.

"I'm David," said the man.

"Hi David. I'm Paige. Nice to meet you and sorry if that was awkward. I can't believe she just up and left"

David stared at Paige for a few seconds and then broke into a smile. "Paige, I'll let you in on a secret," he started. "Kylie's a good friend of mine. She told me what you are going through.

She arranged all of this. I hope you'll at least join me for this drink."

"Dammit, Kylie," said Paige, laughing. "Well, at least she has good taste." Paige smiled at David, and raised her glass. "Cheers, David."

They clinked glasses and Paige started talking. They spent two hours at that bar, with David listening to every word intently.

"Paige….," said David, looking serious. "Would you like to go out this Saturday night? There's a ballet in town that I hear is wonderful."

Paige smiled at David. For the first time, in a long time, Paige felt butterflies in her stomach. "That sounds wonderful."

TJ sat at the desk in the hotel room. Again, re-living bit and parts of the adventure in his mind. The thoughts overwhelmed him. At first, he felt like he was simply reflecting on all of the things that happened, but these were firmly stuck in his brain and not going anywhere.

Tehani's comment about writing a book was starting to mushroom in his head. Maybe that was the catharsis that he needed……to tell his story and get it out there. He thought about it seriously. How can I write a book, he wondered? I've never even attempted something like that.

TJ grabbed his laptop computer and set it up. Somebody had referred to his journey as a "Vacation". A hell of a vacation, he thought. Is that what people thought he was doing? But he liked that word. I am indeed a "Vacationer", he laughed. And he instantly knew that that should be the title of the book, to describe and tell his story.

He opened up a Microsoft Word document and at the top of the page, typed "THE VACATIONER" and below that, "Chapter 1". He was going to do this. It made so much sense. He had an insane and entertaining story to tell, with humor, tragedy, excitement, heartbreak, adventure, love and best of all, a happy ending.

TJ thought about where to start his story, and thought about the time when he was at the Cliffs of Moher with Jim Keller. That seemed to be a logical starting point as it was the first time he acknowledged issues with Paige to Jim.

He began writing:

There was no fog or haze to be seen at the Cliffs of Moher. One of the most gorgeous scenes in the west coast of Ireland..........

"TJ," said Tehani, seductively. TJ turned away from his computer to see Tehani naked, lying in bed. "Can that wait?"

"Oh yeah, it can," said TJ, as he walked over to the bed, undressing while he walked.

"I love you, baby," said Tehani, sweetly. She grabbed TJ, twirled him down on to the bed, and kissed him passionately.

....

THE END

About the Author

I had the idea for The Vacationer while sitting on a beach in Motu Mahana, French Polynesia in 2012. The idea hit like a brick while staring out into the water and sipping on coconut water straight from a coconut. It was so vivid, I went and asked for a pen and paper from the bar and began writing down an outline. I wrote the first draft of book while on a three-month sabbatical in Asia and Europe in 2014.

I am the owner of Patrick Adams Books, a company dedicated to publishing and author services. The Vacationer is my first novel and I am excited to bring that idea that came to me while enjoying a sunny day in paradise finally into existence!

www.patrickadamsbooks.com
www.vacationernovel.com